THE INTERVIEW

"Waiting for me?" he asked, joining her. "I'm touched."

"Am I going to be on page one of *New Orleans New Eyes?*"

"Because you stopped pain with your palms and a chant? Sorry to disappoint you, love, but you wouldn't even rank one column on page twelve."

"What?"

"To my readers, hands-on healing is a given, been around since biblical times. Now give me a twist—you're a full-fledged mage out for world domination, you accept vast quantities of grateful donations, you got the gift from an alien abduction, you only perform healings au naturel?" He swept a lingering, appreciative look across her, then raised a hopeful brow.

"Sorry to disappoint. World domination sounds like too much work, E.T. isn't in the picture, and I work fully clothed."

"Pity. Then *NONE* can't use you." With an exaggerated sigh, he straightened. "I, however, am suitably impressed and curious about your talent and more than willing to delve further."

Other books by Kathleen Nance:

PHOENIX UNRISEN
JIGSAW
DAY OF FIRE
WISHES COME TRUE
SPELLBOUND
ENCHANTMENT
THE SEEKER
THE WARRIOR
THE TRICKSTER
MORE THAN MAGIC

DRAGON
UNMASKED

KATHLEEN
NANCE

LOVE SPELL NEW YORK CITY

LOVE SPELL®

March 2010

Published by

Dorchester Publishing Co., Inc.
200 Madison Avenue
New York, NY 10016

ISBN 10: 0-505-52814-2
ISBN 13: 978-0-505-52814-8
E-ISBN: 978-1-4285-0826-2

The name "Love Spell" and its logo are trademarks of Dorchester Publishing Co., Inc.

Printed in the United States of America.

10 9 8 7 6 5 4 3 2 1

Visit us online at www.dorchesterpub.com.

DRAGON
UNMASKED

CHAPTER ONE

Full moon, black ice, and New Year's Eve. Triple whammy night in the U-Mich ER.

Grace Armatrading had barely stepped out of Trauma One—another champagne-and-dancing-induced cardiac arrest successfully revived—before she was waylaid by one of the nurses.

"Dr. Armatrading, more incoming. MVA on I-94. SUV versus compact, and the SUV won."

"Doesn't it always?" Grace cracked the stiff muscles in her back, her scrubs soaked with sweat. God, she was fagged. But now, her vacation beckoned. "I'm supposed to be off duty, Radar."

The nurse—nobody bothered with her given name of Monica—grimaced. "You know our staffing tonight."

One nurse and one intern had called in sick and with the ice, one resident was still creeping her way in.

Dr. Obote, the attending in charge, joined them. "Stats?"

"Four coming here. Two critical. Crush injury pinned beneath, one thrown with possible internal, two bruised and cut. All of them skunk drunk, but at least two were drunks with a seat belt on."

"Smart enough to wear a seat belt, but not smart enough for a designated driver? Where's the rationale in that?"

"Ten years in ER and he still expects rationality?" Grace teased the attending.

"Hope, not expect. Rooms?"

The sound of retching and the aroma of vomit added dissonant notes to their conversation. Grace nodded in the direction she'd just come from. "I finished in Trauma One and the OD is stable. Psych has a bed open."

"Get him out and put the low levels there."

"Trauma Two is open." Tai Nguyen, the other resident, joined them.

Ambulance sirens wailed in the background. Grace tilted her head. "Sounds like another ambulance coming down Geddes, maybe five minutes away."

"You're spooky," Nguyen complained. "No one hears that good."

She lifted one shoulder. "Want to place a wager?"

He snorted. "I've lost too many."

Still, they all knew what the too-familiar sound meant. The ambulance, coming from the wrong direction to be from the car crash, was bringing another crisis to the overwhelmed ER.

Dr. Obote ran a hand along his cropped hair. "Any word on what we're getting?"

Radar called out the triage desk report. "GSW. Female. Twenty-five. Pregnant and gut shot. Medics say it's touchy for both Mom and fetus."

"I'll take that," Nguyen said immediately.

"No," Dr. Obote countered. "Dr. Armatrading takes the GSW. Trauma One. Dr. Nguyen, take the worst of the crash into Two. Interns can stabilize the other. Give the first years the cuts and bruises."

Nguyen's lips tightened in anger. "Dr. Armatrading's shift ended five hours ago, and Dr. Pavel called that she's ten minutes out."

"I'll do it. Last case," she answered. Ten minutes and the GSW could be dead.

"Go," snapped Dr. Obote.

Grace didn't hesitate or let Nguyen's obvious annoyance stop her. Nguyen would make her pay later, but she'd weather his jabs if it meant her patients survived. Racing back to Trauma One with Radar, she issued orders. "Notify OB, and we'll need the fetal monitor."

"Got it," Radar answered, then muttered under her breath, "Thanks for covering this."

Grace only nodded. Nguyen had a year's seniority in the residency program. He should have gotten the more complicated case; his orders shouldn't have been publicly countered. All givens until two lives were at stake. Grace had no false modesty. She knew her reputation, and it was well earned with blood, sweat, and lives. Nguyen was a superb trauma doc; you didn't get to his position without excellence, and if she were in his shoes, she'd be pissed as hell.

But all ERs had unwritten rules and unspoken superstitions. In this one it followed: If anyone could save both mother and baby, Grace Armatrading could.

In Trauma One she gowned up, shoving her thick ponytail into the paper cap, replacing her booties, slipping her arms into the cuffed sleeves of the paper gown. If Nguyen, or anyone, ever found out what her edge was, though, her residency would be hell, her credibility shot. Maybe even her position lost.

Abruptly she stopped, gripping the sink as fatigue crashed onto her, and her hands suddenly shook.

Not again! Those odd, frightening incidents . . .

She brushed off the thoughts, refused to dwell on aberrations. A glance at the clock confirmed the cause of her shakes. Seventeen hours of nonstop crises, already five hours into her much-needed vacation, and when had she last eaten?

Hypoglycemia and dehydration helped no one. She reached into the pocket of her scrubs for a protein bar, lowered her mask, and then chowed down the bar in two bites. At the scrub sink, she cupped her hands for a drink.

Better. Another breath drew up reserves of endurance. One mother, one baby, then she was out.

The doors flew open, and orderlies rolled in the gurney.

A chill skittered down Grace's spine, a scattershot of warning as she caught sight of the crowded, purposeful chaos of the ER. *Someone was studying her like a butterfly on a pin.*

The doors closed, but she couldn't shake the sensation of intense scrutiny.

"Patient's bleeding into her gut, Doc. Fetal sac's intact." The EMT's report broke through the strange sensation.

Snapping on vinyl gloves, Grace scanned the patient, assessing the damage as she listened to the report. Worry knotted in her chest. Not good, not good for either one. She pulled her stethoscope off her neck, then listened. Two heartbeats, but both were too rapid and irregular.

The woman's face was twisted with pain in the agonizing aftermath of a bullet tearing flesh. Endorphin kick was gone, and now that shock was setting in, the patient was losing the survival battle. Grace laid her hands on the woman's belly, establishing two points of contact, and as she felt the stirring of power in her fingers, the patient grabbed her arm in silent supplication, unable to speak for the tubes. *Save my baby*, pleaded the gesture.

"We'll do everything we can." Grace made the only promise she could, as she eased the pain and sent the patient into oblivion. Her fingers burned with her power, the edge that might mean the difference between life and death.

Grace gave another brief glance at the wall clock—another year of stress and insomnia bit the bucket. "Three, two, one. Happy New Year. Cheers all." The team exchanged a chorus of Happy New Year while they attended to the unconscious patient on the table. The pharmacist, exchanging a limp, empty IV Lactated Ringers bag for a fresh liter, hummed "Auld Lang Syne."

"Let's make sure these two live to see the New Year." Grace

clamped the first vessel. Suddenly, a sharp pain lanced behind the bridge of her nose, distorting her vision until the room looked like an Edvard Munch painting.

Not again!

Sight vanished beneath spasms exploding down every nerve and muscle from her head to her toes. The sensation halted in a moment of exquisite pain, then receded in a rush.

Grace blinked and found herself staring down at her gloved hands. Blood was everywhere—her gloves, her gown, a fleck on the protective goggles. Scarlet smears of accusation. Her hands were empty of everything except vinyl and blood. No clamp, no sutures.

No gurney.

Where was the patient? The baby?

Clenching and unclenching her cramped fists, she raised her head, her neck painfully stiff, and caught a glance at the wall clock. Oh blessed Virgin, thirty minutes gone in the space of a blink.

While she'd worked on two patients.

Nausea soured her throat. Damn her arrogance. She should have gotten help. But she'd rationalized that the previous blackouts were isolated, unlucky alignments of fatigue and overwork. They'd lasted mere seconds, and the patients had made remarkable recoveries.

A telltale squeak, the sudden buzz of voices, oriented her— the gurney was exiting. As it vanished, she couldn't see if the sheet was pulled up. She glanced around the room, at the ordinary tasks of cleaning up. Nobody met her eyes.

How did you ask? *Did I just kill my patients?*

Radar pulled off her protective gear. "Are you okay, Dr. Armatrading?"

No. "Just stiff."

"Ready for your vacation?"

"Definitely." Slowly, feeling more ancient than her thirty-one years, she started to peel off her telltale gloves.

Radar nodded to the door. "After that, you'd better get out while the getting's good."

"After that?"

"Bringing those patients back."

"Back?" She sounded like a parrot.

"To the living. When the baby flatlined, I thought we'd lost both fetus and Mom. But, you . . ." Radar bit her lip. "You just kept muttering, 'There's no pain; you won't die.' Your hands moved at a blur, and you were uncanny about predicting the next bleeder, what needed to be fixed. How do you do that?"

"Good reflexes. Instinct."

Radar shook her head, as though not accepting the brief answer, but she said only, "Well, whatever you do, keep on. Those two didn't have a prayer when they were wheeled in here. They're still critical, but at least you gave them a prayer of hope."

No, she couldn't keep doing what she was doing. She stared through the closing doors at the turmoil beyond, her shoulder blades loosening.

Once was a freak occurrence. Twice was coincidence. Three? Her fugue state was a threat to herself and her patients.

The woman, some said, had escaped the first witch trials. Others claimed the ancient one had consorted with the sorcerers of Alexander, Darius, and Ptolemy. This small town, however, perched on the shores of Lake Superior, was bedrock practical and most of the townspeople dismissed the notions with a skeptical snort and muttered: *Doddering hermit.*

Adam Zolton favored none of the theories. One learned more with an open mind. Any tale was suspect until verified, and locating the gold nugget of fact took digging through a bushel of muck. Tonight, likely, he'd end up with only grimy shoes.

But he'd had to come—the irresistible habit of his private insanity. The e-mail had mentioned mages.

Most of his fool's errands weren't so miserable, though. Hunching his shoulders against the skin-biting cold, he reluctantly pulled one bare hand from his jacket pocket to knock at the log cabin door. From his research, he knew the wood was painted blue, but who could bloody tell in this dark?

Wind kidnapped the sound of his knock and flung it to the featureless sky. Adam rapped again, frowning at the dark cabin. He was expected; Madame Grimaldi had set the time. He'd given up his New Year's Eve; she'd bloody well better answer.

Maybe someone else had gotten here first?

Or maybe he was manufacturing lunatic conspiracies. Maybe it was time to say enough. Time to stop chasing a nightmare.

A gust found a path through the boles of the pines and swirled around him like a dervish on speed, sucking out heat and moisture. Shivers ran through Adam's bones, as he knocked a third time. Christ, but he hated the cold. His blood had thinned from the years in New Orleans.

The wind attacked again, penetrating his coat, accompanied by an unnatural howl as piercing as a dragon's call. Adam spun toward the woods, but saw nothing within the black trees. He stilled, listening to the creak of wood. The noise had vanished. Still, he pulled a small digital camera from his inside pocket and recorded the scene. The sudden drops of sweat froze to his forehead as the wretched cold reclaimed him.

One more attempt, then he was through. After stowing the camera, he lifted his hand for another knock, more forceful this time, when a voice from inside interrupted him.

"Who are you?"

"Adam Zolton from *New Orleans New Eyes*." He buried

his fist in a pocket. So, St. Jude, patron saint of impossible causes, teased him on.

The door screeched open. Faith Grimaldi stood in the entrance, barefoot and wearing a shapeless red caftan. Silk, he noted absently; the mage enjoyed her comforts. Her pewter-shaded hair was a trimmed cloud, and her face more wrinkled than the last known photo of her, taken twenty years ago. Then, she'd already looked like a pug, and time had not been kind.

"You're supposed to be a woman." Her strong voice revealed nothing of age, only a hint of accent and accusation.

"Natalie's on another assignment, and you said the matter was urgent. We left messages on your voice and e-mail." He lifted his brows, adding challenge to his smile and shifting the subject away from why he'd taken Natalie's place in this forsaken icebox. "Are you prejudiced against a man simply because of the appendages?"

He took a chance, quoting back her own words with the substitution of man for woman. Despite the precious little he knew about her, one common theme hinted at her disdain for stereotypes.

Faith's eyes narrowed. "You're a cheeky one."

"So I've been told."

"And worse, I reckon. Does your heart match your angel face? Or the blackness of your hair and eyes?"

"Does it matter, so long as *NONE* covers your story?"

"More than you know." Her gaze fixed on him, and Adam felt a prick of pain in his chest, as though he'd been touched by a surgical laser. Bugger it, she actually had some power! Unlike most of his leads, this might not be a fizzle.

As long as she talked, and she wouldn't talk if she didn't trust him.

Let her search. Keeping his gaze latched to hers, he concentrated on who he was today: a curious chronicler of the bizarre, editor and owner of *NONE*, the alternative paper some called tabloid and others called bible.

With luck, that was all Faith would uncover.

A gust of cold wind swirled around them, carrying flakes of snow. Adam hunched deeper into his coat. Faith didn't seem to notice. Even her bare feet and coral-painted toes stayed pink.

The probe in his chest stabbed deep and unexpected. He pressed back a gasp of pain. "Trying to do me in, love?" he murmured.

"You're confusing," she admitted with a frown. "Murky. No, not murky, the parts I see are clear. It's the parts I can't see that worry me."

"No one should be laid bare to a stranger."

"Says the newsman?"

He laughed, genuinely amused. "Except my targets, of course. Am I to be allowed in? It's beastly cold out here."

He couldn't tell what her answer was going to be, a fact that disturbed him for its rarity, when suddenly the strange howl recurred. Fear spasmed the wrinkles in Faith's face, and he spun toward an unseen threat. A finger of red—Fire? Plasma? Aliens?—flared out, then vanished. He'd taken one stride forward, when Faith grabbed his wrist. With unexpected strength, she yanked him backward. "Get in!"

Adam took the invitation. He crossed the threshold, noting the tingle of some unseen barrier. Faith, apparently, had more protection than he'd realized. Curiosity, and, hell, admit it, hope, rose another notch.

As soon as his arse was inside, she slammed shut the door and threw an old-fashioned lock and a shiny new deadbolt. She then chanted under her breath, as her hand pressed against a carving of a rampant lion. When she spun to face him, her face contorted with fear. "Were you followed here?"

"I left the motel without being seen."

"But on the route here? Did you take precautions?"

"Your instructions made no warning, and your address is on the Internet—"

"My address, not my location, you fool. Do you think I'd make it so easy to be found? *Were you followed?*"

"I didn't see any lights after I left the highway." He thought back. "No, I wasn't followed."

"Perhaps we have time, then." She gave a small sigh, revealing the vulnerability of age.

"What's going on, ma'am?"

"Call me Faith."

"Adam."

"Follow me, Adam." She led the way deeper into her cabin.

Adam studied his surroundings. The décor intrigued him. He'd anticipated backwoods cabin—hewn wood and handmade quilts—or mystical new age, but there was nary a patchwork, crystal, copper pot, or vial of fragrant oil. Instead, the room evoked the tropics, with soft fabrics patterned in bright colors and a profusion of plants.

It was also beastly hot and humid. Adam flicked away a bead of sweat, and then stiffened as a flash of black caught the corner of his eye. Involuntarily, his hand shifted to his waist, where a weapon was normally sheathed. Bother, he'd left both gun and knife in the car. He hadn't expected any trouble from a woman who'd asked for a visit, and he'd thought the weapons might disturb her.

Faith gave a high-pitched chuckle. "That's not the danger, at least not to me. My pet smells you. Galanthis, meet our guest." When the animal, whatever it was, refused to show, she shrugged. "She picks her times. Can't cage her, though. Leave her free, and she will always come back. Come, I'll show you why I asked you here."

He followed Faith down a short, unlit hall. She pushed open a steel door, and again, he felt the tingle of a protective barrier, although the source—technical or supernatural—eluded him. Perhaps it was a mix of both.

Faith might be a hermit, but she was not doddering. A fact he'd best keep in mind.

On the other side, he gave a low whistle. "Which electronics store did you plunder?"

"Did you think magick was stuck in the thirteenth century? That the principles couldn't apply to a modern world?"

"If I did, you've shown me different."

From her sharp glance she'd caught the subtle evasion, but she said nothing, allowing him to look his fill. Despite the room's crowded state, it was cooler here, air-conditioned to counter the heat-generating equipment. At the center of the room stood a scarred round table, one carved elegantly enough to have befitted the legendary Arthur. A single office chair pushed up to the table served as seating for the open laptop, which was a top-of-the-line Mac.

Electronics and arcana. The table portioned the room into schizophrenic halves.

A reflection of his hostess?

The smaller piece contained classic magickal paraphernalia—a clutter of oils, books, herbs, quills, crystals. A brazier emitted a thin curl of smoke, scenting the room with the aromas of lavender and sage. His fingers itched to pull out his camera, to record the details, but that faux pas would earn him a quick exit. Instead, he tried to memorize what he could.

The other side of the room was a geek's wet dream. The Mac plus two other computers, a plasma TV—52 inch, he'd wager—a flat-screen monitor on the wall, virtual-reality goggles, all wireless. Mage business must be lucrative.

"Why did you want to see someone from *NONE?*" he asked. Time to get out that shovel and see what, if anything, she knew about the Dragon.

"Sit here," she ordered, rotating the chair to face the wall monitor.

Willing to follow her lead, he sat, and then jerked up as a tube of dark fur leaped into his lap, just missing the family jewels. Ready to swat the threat, his hand paused as he realized the attack came from a miniature sable ferret. Its dark eyes gazed at him curiously, while the beast made itself at home by crawling up his arm.

"The shy Galanthis, I presume?"

"Don't bother our guest." Faith tugged the ferret off him, but as soon as she set Galanthis down, the ferret slid away to crawl inside his pant leg. "She's inquisitive."

"I'd rather have her on my shoulder." He tugged the ferret from his leg and hoisted her up. She promptly stuck her nose into his ear.

Ignoring the tickling sensation, he looked quizzically at the monitor. All he could see was a blur of colors. "What am I supposed to see?"

Faith was studying him, her head tilted, and Adam got the impression he was still being tested, that she hadn't made up her mind about him. Why—and whether he passed— remained unknown. Still, she didn't kick him out.

"Put these on." Faith held out the virtual-reality goggles and a pair of gossamer gloves, which looked as though they'd been woven from a spider's web.

He struggled to don the gloves. Bloody things tangled worse than cheap cling wrap. At last he got them on, donned the goggles, and instantly the light from the monitor screen columned outward, enveloping him in its surreal glow. As he sat in a swirling rainbow, he heard Faith chanting low and keying the Mac laptop behind him. Suddenly, the colors sharpened, and a virtual library popped into focus within the column of light.

He gave a low whistle, covering his rising excitement with an understated, "Impressive." Swiftly, he scanned the titles;

some he was familiar with; others not. Grimoires, ancient herbologies, modern theories of power, neuromancy, applied MEMS tech—the library was as schizo as the room. An eternity wouldn't be long enough to study them all.

"Pull out that brown book, the one on the upper shelf," Faith commanded, her voice faint.

He spied the book she meant. Testing, he reached out. Only his hands entered the cyber library. The sensation was dizzying, crawling around in his stomach like motion sickness, but by focusing, he coordinated physical motion to the disembodied hands and pulled the book off the shelf.

Resisting the urge to place it down and wander farther into the library, he ran a hand across the seemingly solid book. It was old, with vellum pages that had somehow escaped the destruction of time and the Dark Ages. He could feel the brittleness of the pages, smell the distinctive age mold.

"Is it real?" he breathed.

"Do you think I'd allow anyone to touch it in solid space?" she countered.

It existed, and yet it didn't, preserved by some technique he didn't yet understand, a meld of magick and technology. Newsman instincts rose as the twin thrills of discovery and curiosity fired. The Magi lead might be a fizzle, but this library made the trip worthwhile.

"Turn to page sixteen," she ordered.

He turned the pages, occasionally needing to close his eyes when the dizzying nausea threatened. The snuffling of Galanthis on his shoulder, along with the musky ferret smell, helped to ground him.

The book was a collection of predictions, unknown ones, unlike those of Nostradamus. The embers of discovery damped a bit. He was open to a lot of this world's strangeness and believed much that others sniffed at, but divination wasn't something he could accept. The reality of today would have been impossible to predict several centuries ago. Outcomes depended upon too many small choices and chances. He bit back any comments, though; obviously this book meant something to Faith.

Page sixteen was difficult to read, written in Latin and elaborate script, the words fading in and out of focus, but he got the gist. "It predicts that the slaughter of the mages will usher in destruction by . . . is that chaos?"

"Fiery chaos."

"A general prediction of Armageddon?"

"Or a specific kind of chaos, like the eruption of Vesuvius or even the myth of the fire-spewing Chimaera."

"Slaughter of the mages? Old news: fifteenth-century European witch hunts, the Salem witch trials, the Inquisition?"

"Did you read what occurred in Papua, New Guinea a couple of years ago? The women who were burned with metal rods on suspicion of witchcraft?"

"I did. Isolated incident of ignorance and jealousy."

"A symptom of a continuing mind-set. Open the safe on the library wall."

He looked around the virtual library and saw a keypad. That hadn't been there before; somehow Faith's command had made it visible. "What's the code?"

She hesitated, then said, "051480."

When the safe door swung open, the cyber library vanished with a pop, to be replaced by the dark maw of a safe. Inside was a fuzzy stack of colored folders.

"Open the top red one," she ordered.

Inside the folder was an array of newspaper articles. The first one was from *NONE*, an article written a year ago by his best reporter, Natalie DeSalvo, about the chilling magick of her ex-husband, Charles Severin, and her twin brother, Nathaniel. An article Adam suspected had concealed the truly powerful one, Natalie's lover, Ramses Montgomery.

Of the remaining articles, one was from *NONE*, but the others were from regular newspapers scattered across the country. He remembered the subject of the *NONE* article. He'd suspected the chap was careless with gasoline, but they'd found enough discrepancies to run it as a bizarre case of spontaneous combustion.

Swiftly, he thumbed through the remaining seven articles and obituaries. Each detailed the disappearance, or death, of a local citizen. Reading virtually made focusing on the typeface difficult, but he caught the names and realized he recognized each one.

Some were revered, some were feared, some were barely noticed as being gone. Each victim, however, was known for being, as one reporter dubbed the subject, a "colorful character." Each had been a practitioner of magick.

Over the years of his quest, Adam had had occasion to meet each one. He'd found them of varied temperament, varied skill. He hadn't realized they had died, however. Mage deaths. A good story for *NONE*. He could play the random events into a conspiracy.

What was Faith's angle? As he screened the articles for added details, he asked, "You think these deaths are connected?"

"Each victim had a degree of magickal talent."

"Have you told the police?"

"Which department? There are eight different jurisdictions. And the FBI didn't take seriously a conspiracy theory to kill crackpots." The fear in her voice was real.

"But *NONE* will."

"That's what I hoped."

"Even mages die. Why think these are connected?"

"They drowned in the breath of the dragon. And now it wants me."

The dragon. He stilled, the moment becoming a timeless

vacuum, while his stomach muscles clenched at the coincidence. Unbidden, memory played the echo of another woman's last lucid words: *"The dragon burns me."*

Was Faith as deluded as his sister? Was St. Jude offering a bread crumb that led nowhere?

"Put the file back in the safe," Faith commanded.

Perhaps his brain had unthawed, perhaps he'd grown accustomed to the nausea, perhaps Faith had adjusted the resolution or was playing games with him. Whatever the reason, as he replaced the file, the stack below came into sharp relief and atop the folders lay a CD case. The label on the CD was a rainy-day gray, with two words stamped in deep blue: Abby Zolton.

The gold nugget!

Oh, bloody hell. He snatched up the disk, his heart racing against his throat, sweat, cold, and nausea forgotten. Only the snores in his ear from the snoozing Galanthis kept him grounded.

Abruptly, the safe snapped closed, leaving him back in the library, the disk in his glowing hands. Could he get the disk out of this virtual prison? View the photographs? Carefully he tried pulling the disk into reality. "This disk—" he began, his voice rough.

Before he could finish, a high-pitched tone knifed from the impressive tower computer fitted against the wall. "Security breach," shouted a mechanical voice.

With a banshee shriek, Faith spun toward the breached computer. The library—and disk—vanished. She began typing at a speed that seemed impossible for her gnarled fingers. "Viper, you led them into my system."

"No, I didn't!" He flung off the goggles, and peeled off the gloves. Faith ignored him, concentrating on the computer screen.

A red and blue hexahedron burst onto her computer screen, and began rapidly replicating into a caterpillar of sparks. It erased her efforts before erupting from the screen in an electric stench. The twist spiraled toward the Mac laptop connected to the wall monitor, gathering speed.

"What the hell is that?" He leaped to his feet, and Galanthis tumbled off his shoulder. He grabbed the ferret in one hand, then set the beast on the floor.

"A mage-born computer virus. They know about the library."

The head of the virus incarnation bounced off the Mac, unable to penetrate Faith's guards. Instead, it burrowed into the third computer and flashed into the screen, filling the pixels, erasing the merry lines of the screen saver.

The strange virus also deposited a single red-glowing hexahedron in the room, and the remnant began spreading in reality. Adam felt his lungs labor for breath. The growing thing ate up breathable air, replacing it with ozone and burnt electricity.

"You won't take what I know," Faith gasped, her eyes watering as she frantically worked.

"For the love of Jude, woman, I did not lead someone to destroy your library. If I strengthen the firewall, will that help?"

"Not an ordinary one."

"I know unusual code."

She nodded. "Buy me time to activate the library's protections."

Adam wiped his burning eyes and ran over to the library source computer, surprised she wasn't working there to save her data. Rapidly, he keyed in the commands.

Still by the wall, Faith coughed and choked on the thickening poisonous air. "Leave. Take Galanthis. They don't want you."

"Not without you." His lungs spasmed, grabbing the small bits of oxygen left. "Can you erect a shield? Let us breathe?"

"It'll last only minutes."

"Enough."

Faith stopped long enough to lift her arms. Fists clenched, she chanted. Adam didn't pay attention to the words, focusing on erecting his firewall. Wind whistled around her, wrapping her caftan around her legs and flattening her hair. The wind lifted and spread, beating back the virus with a dome of air.

The air sweetened again, although the virus immediately began to eat holes into the barrier. The virtual hexahedron slammed against the edge of the monitor, eager to move into his computer, to the next source of fuel.

"Firewall," he commanded, hitting enter. Electrons, nanoparticles, and talent aligned, slamming up a fresh barrier to the deadly virtual predator. Spinning from computer to computer in a brilliant streak, the firewall closed the cyber paths. Trapped inside its monitor, the attacker darkened to crimson, whirling with hurricane speed and power as it sought a chink to escape.

In the room, the barrier Faith had erected showed pinpricks of instability. Holding his breath against the poison, coughing when he couldn't avoid inhaling, he scooped Galanthis up from beneath the table, where the ferret had gone to ground. Galanthis struggled, the wiry body nearly impossible to hold. Adam grabbed the Mac laptop—the one that held the disk image—then glanced at Faith. She was swaying and paper white. "Get out!"

Faith slumped over her keyboard. He struggled to rouse her, get her upright. Bloody hell, he couldn't carry her, the squirming choking ferret, and the laptop. Sorely tempted to drop the beast, he set down the laptop, then wrapped his arm around Faith's fragile waist and dragged her upright. Her eyelids fluttered as she took in him and the ferret.

"Walk," he commanded.

"Wait, I have to send . . ." She reached out to hit ENTER.

The colors on the tower computer's screen gyrated in a wild stream of data.

With that final act, she allowed him to support her to the door, their progress painfully slow, all three breathing with labored gasps. Rainbow bubbles filled his vision, as his oxygen-starved brain began to shut down.

They almost made it out to the porch. To the snow and the cold and the fresh air and safety.

Suddenly, Faith stiffened. "No!" she shouted, gazing behind him with horror.

The virus shot from the back room in an electric streak and split into a two-headed hydra. One side snapped around Faith; the other side pistoned into him. It rammed against him; every cell screamed as the supernatural punch slammed him backward.

Arse first, he shot out the door, then hit the six-foot snow wall banking the drive. Adam fought for consciousness against the attack of cold and the force of impact. Galanthis shot from his hand. He struggled to his feet, sucking in air, the space behind his eyes spinning, and then stumbled back to the now blue- and red-filled house. Trying to get in, he ran smack into the guardian barrier.

Only this time, Faith couldn't let him through. The twisting hexahedrons filled the room. She stood on the other side of the doorway, frozen, being consumed by the virus. He slapped a hand against the doorjamb. "Faith, open the barrier."

The sound caught her attention. Her muscles strained, then collapsed. "I can't."

"Tell me how." His hands ran across the wood, seeking a way in.

"Prove my trust unwarranted," her voice was a mere croak, "and you'll rue the betrayal." For the briefest moment, he thought he saw a smile, an acceptance of her fate before the attack enveloped her.

At his feet, he heard a tiny mewl; Galanthis perched on the top of his boot. He picked up the now-quiet ferret and deposited her in his pocket. Her head popped up and together they waited at the door, staring at chaos.

An hour passed before the air cleared and the complex barrier failed. With Galanthis in his pocket, he hurried in and found Faith sprawled on a grassy mat. He knelt by her side, but there was no question she was dead.

Without knowledge of the magickal attack, investigators would ascribe the death to natural causes: age and a heart attack.

With a small whimper, Galanthis slid from his pocket and crawled across Faith's face. Offering a short prayer for her soul, he closed the mage's eyes. The world had lost so much tonight, and yet it slumbered on, unknowing. Unknowing of loss and growing danger.

Leaving the ferret, he returned to the rear room. The computers and electronics were humming, as seemingly untouched as Faith. When he opened her files, however, the Mac laptop holding the library portal was empty. So, too, the other computers. The virus had wiped them clean. Then he spied the thumb drive, a tiny knob off the front of the tower. Hadn't that been in the Mac? Oh, St. Jude, had Faith sent the data on?

He looked around at the arcane remnants. They'd have to wait for another day. He retrieved the virtual gloves and goggles. If he could locate that library, he would need them. Back in the front room, he was starting toward the door when a soft mewl halted him.

He turned back. The ferret stared at him. Adam sighed—who knew what would happen to the beast if he left it?—and crouched down. "Come on, Galanthis." He slid the ferret off Faith's body.

The damn thing nipped him. Startled, he dropped the ferret, which promptly aimed for his leg. He waylaid the writhing animal, which twisted, still trying to bite as he held it by the tail. "Come with me or take your chances with animal control."

Galanthis stilled. "Pocket," he offered, holding the beast in his palm.

In answer, the ferret dove into his coat pocket. Not sure what the hell he was going to do with a pet, he picked up the gloves and goggles. "Galanthis is a hell of a mouthful; I'll call you Gala."

Damn ferret nipped his leg.

"Do that again, *Gala*, and I'll dump you into a snowbank."

Gala's answer this time was a plaintive mewl as she rooted deeper into his pocket.

"Trying to make me feel like a heartless bastard? Won't work; I've been dubbed worse. Let's go."

Gala curled into an exhausted ball as they left. He'd started the car, bringing on the blessed heat, when his phone signaled an incoming message. For a moment, he considered ignoring it, but ingrained habits proved too hard to break.

He glanced at the ID. A message from Faith? Had she sent him the library? Seized with a macabre excitement, he opened the message.

Oh, bloody hell. It was a photograph. Of a woman he'd long ago discovered he could never have.

That quick, the tentacles of desire wrapped around him, squeezing his heart with heat, stirring him lower.

Grace Armatrading.

He leaned his head back against the seat rest, drawing in an angry breath. Unable to forget Faith's message below the photo: "You destroyed her once. Now, protect her."

CHAPTER TWO

Shadows filled the outpatient clinic when Grace stepped off the elevator. At this hour the halls were empty, populated only with the sense memories of legions of patients. Fewer than in the hospital behind, but those were kept in check by bustling efficiency and the science of medicine. Here, though, at night, in the abandoned silence, unheeded echoes of pain clung to the brick walls. The memories brushed her skin with breaths of ice.

She ignored them all; they were a legacy of her mutt blood—one-quarter Jamaican, one-quarter New England, one-quarter proper Brit, and one-quarter only God knew. She could sense the pain, but there was nothing to be done about it.

Instead, she fastened up her coat, preparing to face Ann Arbor's latest January freeze. Her crepe-soled boots—practical if not stylish—made no sound as she strode down the hall.

A noise, a whirr of air, broke the silence, the vibrations tickling up her ribs like delicate spider legs. No ghost. Her pager, on vibrate. She'd forgotten to turn the thing off. She fished it out, glancing at the number. ER Triage. Using her cell phone—there would be no interference with the monitors here—she answered the page. "Dr. Armatrading. You paged me?"

"Sorry," said Radar. "One minute into vacation and we're already interrupting."

"I'm not out of the building yet. What's up?"

"Was someone supposed to meet you here?"

"No, why?"

"A case Dr. Nguyen was working; the guy got all hopped up, refusing treatment. He wanted only you. Said the Virgin Mary told him she was waiting for you because you were the best. Guy insisted if you were good enough for the Blessed Mother, you were the one he wanted."

Remembering the sensation of being watched from triage, Grace laughed away the frisson of unease moving along her spine. "My repertoire of friends doesn't include many saints. Do you need me to come see him?"

"Naw, we fed him Nguyen's boast about treating an emperor, and the dude agreed to treatment. We figured he was mental, until the orderly mentioned seeing the case talking to a woman in Waiting. Per the orderly, the lady was pale and blonde. Might be mistaken for an angel. She was gone when we looked for her. Thought maybe you knew her."

She couldn't think of anyone who fit the description. "Maybe I treated her before."

"Probably. Sorry to have bothered you, and enjoy your vacation. When you get back, we'll live vicariously on your tales of sandy beaches and sexy studs."

A twinge of guilt nipped Grace. Somehow the rumor had started that she was heading to a relaxing Caribbean Club Med, and she hadn't bothered to correct the misconception. "Don't expect photos," she said lightly.

"At least you'll be warm. Does sunshine still exist?"

Grace stared ahead at the darkness lurking outside the cold glass, beyond the reach of the pale security lights. Swirls of snow smudged the sky. "Somewhere," she softly answered.

She disconnected and then turned off her pager. By this

time, she'd started down the final yards, a long corridor flanked on the right by the locked glass doors of the clinics and open on her left to a two-story drop to the atrium.

Another sound broke the empty silence, a slithering hiss like an invisible serpent. The hairs at the back of her neck tightened, as reptile-brain instincts gave a reactive warning: not the shadows this time either. She glanced around, seeing no source; yet the sound came again, no louder, but with an edge of menace.

Her throat tightening, she peered forward, behind her, and then leaned over the brick wall to study the atrium below. Empty. There were only two exits from this corridor, the beginning and the end. Like life, once you were here, there was no escape.

Her nose wrinkled on an unpleasant scent, one akin to an unkempt slaughterhouse—moldy straw laced with the aroma of blood. The source, however, remained nonexistent, unless you counted imagination. Still, her pace picked up.

The hiss repeated; the mold scent clogged her nostrils, and suddenly the air temperature shot up. Sweat dampened the back of her shirt with an unpleasant wetness that would freeze as soon as she stepped outside. Instinct warned: *Move. Hurry. Get out.*

"Logic, Grace," she muttered. "Heating vents, contracting pipes, someone walked through with take-out pastrami, you bundled up too soon. Look around; there is no one here."

No one you can see.

Faintly behind her, she heard the ding of the elevator, followed a moment later by running footsteps.

Correction, there *was* no one here. With her heart beating like steel drums on speed, she looked ahead. Still too many yards to go to the end of the corridor; she'd be trapped between glass and empty space when the person behind caught sight of her.

Her lower back, where her right kidney should be, began

to ache, the old scar pulling tight. Clutching the strap of her bag, she sprinted for the glass-fronted lobby and the exit door.

The glass door rattled with the force of her jerk, the vibration running up her arm, but the door didn't budge. Oh, bloody hell! Locked, and not a security guard in sight. Recalculating, her heart drumming against her sternum, she switched directions and scrambled across the lobby to the side exit. The heavy door slammed behind her as she raced up the dingy steps to the parking garage, the reverberation ringing through the stairwell, echoing like a bell chamber. So much for keeping her route a secret.

"Dr. Armatrading!"

A woman called from below as Grace exited the dangerous stairwell into the frigid parking structure.

The solid rough concrete and the whistle of winter wind erased the shadows. Grace's breath fogged in the cold. She pulled on her knit cap, and her boots made thudding sounds as she hustled down the ramp toward the street.

"Dr. Armatrading," called the woman's voice again. "I'm sorry, I didn't mean to frighten you."

Damn, but the woman was persistent. At past midnight, Grace didn't fancy conversation with anyone.

"Adam Zolton sent me."

The name kicked her chest, cutting off air. "Don't know him," she ground out, refusing to slow or turn around.

"He said to tell you, a dragon's awake and breathing fire."

The Dragon's Tale. Grace slammed into the brick wall of memory. Into a private code of warning. She froze, motionless except for clouds of breath, her back tight, then slowly pivoted. "How do you know Adam?"

"He's my boss." The woman stopped some yards away, beneath one of the security lights. "My name's Natalie DeSalvo."

Grace got the impression both the distance and the location were a deliberate choice, designed to ease her fright.

Not necessarily reassured, Grace studied the woman. Attractive. Early thirties, plus or minus a couple of years, shag-cut hair. Maybe that red was natural—the unnatural lighting distorted skin tone—but she doubted it. The tightness in her shoulders eased. Definitely not Virgin Mary material. Whatever had been lurking in the clinic wasn't this woman. "What do you do?"

"I'm a reporter for the newspaper he owns. *NONE. New Orleans New Eyes.* We investigate—"

"The bizarre, the odd, the stories no one else will believe. Mostly it's a pile of tripe."

Natalie smiled. "So you've read us."

"On occasion." Grace pulled on her winter gloves, her hands shriveling from the cold. "Adam should have told you invoking his name might not encourage my cooperation."

"You stopped, and that's all a reporter needs. He did mention to make sure you didn't have anything sharp in your hand. Like scissors."

Grace bit back a twitch of amusement. She'd always wondered if that moment had been a morphine-induced hallucination. "What danger does he think I'm in?"

Natalie flapped her hands against her arms, obviously trying to keep warm. "Do you mind if we move while we talk?"

"I'm headed to the bus stop for the shuttle to my parking lot."

"My rental's on the first level. I can give you a ride to the lot."

Grace hesitated, but caution yielded to the twin prods of curiosity and the unpleasant prospect of waiting in the dark cold. "Thanks."

They settled into a brisk walk down the angled concrete. Natalie began, "I was in town researching an article about Reiki; Adam gave me your name."

"I'm a physician, not a faith healer," Grace snapped.

"He didn't say you were," Natalie returned blandly. "I've been trying to get an appointment with Fudo Umari, but he's not answering me. Adam suggested you might know how to reach him."

Master Umari missing? He was one of the people she'd hoped to see on her time off, although he hadn't answered her calls either. She covered her alarm by asking, "So Adam gave you the dragon code and said to approach me at midnight?"

"Not at first, but he called me tonight—" Natalie broke off.

That smell! In concert with Natalie, Grace, nostrils tightening, spun toward the empty darkness behind them. Her throat clutched on musty air and rotted hay. A ripple of heat beaded sweat on her neck, as the night darkened, swallowing cars and concrete.

Slowly, searching, she backed away from the unseen threat. Natalie, matching her with fists clenched, glanced over. "You . . . feel something?"

"Smell something," she admitted. "Something . . . rotten."

A thread of light wove across the unforgiving structure, breaking the darkness. "You ladies all right?" called the flashlight-carrying security guard. "Bitter night. Not fit for woman or beast."

The scent faded. "We're fine," answered Grace.

Natalie shifted her shoulders, as though sloughing off some weight. "My car's right there."

"You stay warm." The guard continued on his rounds.

"What exactly did Adam tell you?" Grace demanded as they hurried the remaining yards to Natalie's Explorer.

"He called me tonight and ordered me to find you ASAP, not to wait until morning. Told me to tell you, tonight stay anywhere but your home. He'll meet you tomorrow. Any place you like, and he'll explain." They bundled into the car; Natalie fired the ignition and quickly backed out.

Car heater blasting at her, Grace gave directions to the

lot. As they wound through the Ann Arbor streets, she asked incredulously, "That was it?"

"Yes. Are you going home tonight?"

How dare he thrust himself back into her life, issuing orders and expecting she'd listen? Memory, experience, pride, self-preservation all refused to let Adam dictate to her, even for a few hours. Six years ago, they'd been one night away from becoming lovers; she'd thought he loved her as deeply as she loved him. Until she found out he'd been using her for a story, until his story had resulted in the deaths of her dear friends.

All that against one tiny comment, uttered during pain and chaos. *If you ever warn me about a dragon, I promise to listen.*

Words are sacred, child. Her grandmother's caution.

"I'll go to a hotel. What's Adam's number? I'll call to tell him where to meet me." Where he could go, was more like it. Grace programmed her cell with the number Natalie rattled off, then added, "If you give me your number, I'll see what I can do about Master Umari."

"I'd appreciate that."

By the time she'd added the second number to her contacts, they'd reached the lot. She pointed to the hybrid at the far end. "That's my car. Thanks for the ride."

"No problem." Natalie pulled up and Grace got out.

Dead fingers of cold squeezed her chest as she bent against the wind. After glancing uneasily at the other cars in the lot—none were occupied, and all were covered with snow—she hit the auto start, letting the car warm as she dug out her scraper. Natalie angled her Explorer so the headlights illuminated the car as Grace chipped at the icy windshield, then popped from her car, scraper in hand, and started to clear the other side.

Sleet whirled around them, graying out the soccer fields beside the lot, isolating them in a rectangle of yellow light. Other sensations disappeared beneath the single imperative of unrelenting cold. They worked silently until Grace found herself across the trunk from Natalie and was unable to resist asking, "Is Adam still searching for aliens?"

Natalie gave a dramatic sigh. "Has me chasing every farfetched report."

"He came through Katrina okay?"

"He evacuated, took with him two pregnant neighbors and their five children to Lafayette in his precious boat of a Rolls."

Adam trapped with five rug rats? The image was amusing. Not that his charm would have slipped long enough for them to know he didn't mix with tots by choice.

Natalie must have seen her flicker of a grin. "He spent a week detailing the car afterward. Especially since one of the women delivered in the backseat before they reached the hospital."

Grace burst out laughing. Oh, the image.

From the opposite side of the car, Natalie shared her laugh. "But, he ended up with a five-year-old claiming she's going to marry him when she grows up, a boy who's working as an intern at the paper, and one newborn named Adam. He came back to wind damage in his home, but he rebuilt. In his way, behind the scenes, he's helping the city rebuild."

"That's Adam, the devil's charm," Grace added with a catch in her throat at Natalie's obvious admiration.

"Annoyingly so. Fortunately, I'm immune. My heart's given elsewhere."

How could just a conversation about Adam Zolton warm her? Grace cleaned the last bit of glass, adding an extra swipe for the snow accumulating again on her side mirror.

Maybe it was the laughter that covered the awareness of danger. Maybe it was the shrouding storm that blotted out scent. This time, they had no warning.

Two figures, bundled in down, ski masks covering their

faces, burst from the gray. They came from behind Natalie in a silent deadly force.

"Go!" screamed Grace, skidding as she waved Natalie toward the idling Explorer. Before Natalie could spin to see the threat, one attacker caught up to her, while the second slid across the hybrid to Grace. On the farther side, she had a head start of seconds.

She fumbled the car key from her pocket and hit the panic button. Her car erupted in a cacophony of beeps and blinking headlights as she dove for the interior.

The head start wasn't enough to get her door closed. The attacker followed her in, slamming her toward the passenger seat. The gearshift rammed her belly, forcing out a grunt of pain. A second blow across the back of her head crashed her forehead against the glass.

Deafened by surging blood in her ears, she acted on instinct. Opened the passenger door. Tumbled out.

On the closer side now, she saw Natalie struggle in the grip of her attacker. One hand held her immobile, while the other—holding something the color of dull pewter—pressed hard against the side of her face. The reporter went limp.

"No!" Grace had no time for more than that screamed denial before her attacker grabbed her coat lapel. As she scrambled to escape, her boots slipped on the ice; she fell, hard, on her coccyx. Pain jarred up her spine, bringing tears that instantly froze.

At least the fall loosened her attacker's grip. Before he could get a better grasp, she rolled over and jabbed upward with her ice scraper. Frozen plastic drove into the man's nose. Bone gave way in a sickening collapse.

The mask muffled his ugly, dirty curse. A dark stain of blood bloomed on the knit, and he let her go. Grace scrambled to her feet, nausea burning against her throat. Escape or Natalie?

The second attacker joined the first, coming after her.

Her breath rasped harsh against her frozen lips, and her lungs yanked in air as she made a painful split-second decision. Alone, she couldn't physically best the two men, and she couldn't help the reporter if she were caught.

She raced around the rental car, heading for what concealment the weather could offer. But her feet lost traction on an unexpected ice patch, slowing her. The first attacker—now with a shattered nose—reached her. He felled her with a punch to the knees.

Before he could execute a killing blow, however, headlights careened toward the lot, accompanied by a police siren. The attackers spoke for the first time.

"Later," snarled one. Snow and wind hurricaned around them. As silently as they'd come, they disappeared into the now-furious storm.

Pain, so much pain. Grace crawled over to the unconscious Natalie, spread-eagled in the snow, and then yanked off her gloves to check for a pulse. Thready, but regular. *Blessed Mary, still alive.*

Which begged the question—which one of them had the attackers been after?

Why, Grace wondered, were the police acting as though she were the criminal? Dammit, she was the victim!

Pitching the small Band-Aid from her IV site into the red biohazard bag, she stared incredulously at the police officer, a gaunt sandy-haired man who'd introduced himself as Detective Talo. "What do you mean, 'What did Natalie and I argue about?'"

"Just answer the question, Dr. Armatrading."

Thinking, she pulled on her sweater, wishing wool exuded the authority of her white coat and stethoscope.

With the squad car's assistance, she'd gotten Natalie to the ER, where both of them had been examined, her to the accompanying teasing of her colleagues about not being able to stay away. Because of the head trauma, Obote had admitted them for a night's observation. She'd agreed; patients who refused to follow doctor's orders irked her. Besides, she figured the hospital was as safe as a hotel. After she was settled, the police took her statement. They'd been sympathetic. Then.

This morning, while she was waiting for morning rounds and the resident to discharge her, Detective Talo appeared with his decided hostility.

"The answer is we didn't argue," she said at last, seeing no reason to hedge. "I gave my statement last night. Natalie passed on a warning that I was in danger and then offered me a ride to my car, where we were attacked by two men." In bald summary, the facts sounded thin.

The officer jotted down a few words. "A stranger approaches with a warning late on New Year's Eve. That didn't strike you as odd?"

"I was going on vacation. Last night was the only time she could reach me."

"Why does this"—the detective consulted his notes— "Adam Zolton think you're in danger?"

"I don't know; you'll have to ask him. Natalie can confirm my story."

He made a noncommittal sound. "Describe the men again. Did they have any weapons? Attack you with anything?"

"I didn't see any weapons. Only brutality."

"And you bested them with an ice scraper?"

"I broke one's nose; I didn't stop him."

"He bled?"

"Yes." She sat in the plastic- and wood-armed chair, propped her boots onto the bed frame, and then returned the detective's even gaze. Doctors had perfected that same nonjudgmental look, the one that invited confession. Time to confront the elephant in the corner. "What happened?"

"That's what I'm asking you."

"No, I'm asking what happened between last night and now that made you stop believing me."

"Do you have a dislike for reporters, Dr. Armatrading?"

"Why would you think that?"

"You stabbed one once."

Oh, damn, they'd been digging deep.

"That attack was entirely justified," said a masculine voice from behind the drawn curtain that shielded her bed from the hallway.

One of Grace's feet hit the floor, her legs suddenly numb. *Adam?*

He shoved back the curtain, the rings clinking. A few added wrinkles by the eyes, a dash of silver at the temples, but oh, yes, definitely Adam. Suddenly murmured voices, the squeak of a food cart, the beep of monitors, the aroma of antiseptic—familiar-enough-to-be-ignored sounds and scents of the hospital—sharpened. Her head felt light, as though she'd mainlined a dose of Demerol.

"I never pressed charges," he said, but his gaze skimmed over the detective to fasten on her. His expression hardened, and when he spoke, his voice held a rough edge. "Got rather a shiner there, Grace."

"So my mirror says."

"Adam Zolton?" When Adam inclined his head, Detective Talo asked, "You think Dr. Armatrading is in danger?"

"I think she misunderstood my message," he answered, his gaze still caught with hers, his tone altering. This was the voice she knew, low and mesmerizing. "I wanted to see her."

Misunderstood his message? The bastard! Her eyes narrowed. And the detective was swallowing every lying word. That was Adam, too, a strange gift for making the outrageous believable.

I love you, Grace.

The echo of distant lies, ones she'd believed when she was younger and more naive, arrowed heat through her chest.

"Bullshit," she answered. She tore her gaze away from Adam to confront the detective. "You have my statement. I'm about to be discharged. Is there any reason I'm not free to leave?"

"You're free to go, but you might think twice before filing a false report."

"I did not—"

"What do you mean?" interrupted Adam.

He got an answer. Detective Talo consulted his notebook. "Ms. DeSalvo can't remember the attack, denies bringing any warning. Dr. Armatrading said one of her attackers bled, but no blood was found in the lot." He closed the book. "There were no attackers. Only two sets of fresh footprints were found in the snow. Those of Natalie DeSalvo and Dr. Armatrading."

CHAPTER THREE

Adam trailed behind Grace, admiring her confidence as she strode down the hallway. Maturity became her.

Not one of those skin-and-bone model types, Grace had muscles and curves, and he liked that. He liked the auburn sheen of her hair and the raucous curls she still couldn't tame. He liked her flash of anger when she first saw him; he'd take rage over indifference any day.

Six years ago, she'd been a gawky near-woman, filled with raw passion. She'd filled into both the body and the fire.

With luck, her need for answers would keep her from roasting him on a slow spit. Or worse, going off half cocked without knowing the threat.

He followed Grace into the waiting room, where they found Natalie, fully dressed, flipping through a magazine. She looked up. "Dr. Armatrading. Adam?"

Grace sat beside her. "How are you feeling?"

"Sore. Headache, but the other pains are hiding. The nurse gave me a happy pill."

"You're being discharged? Will someone be with you?"

Natalie started to nod, then winced and stopped. "They needed my bed, so they asked me to wait in here. Ram will be here soon."

"Ram?"

"Ramses Montgomery," Adam explained quietly, sitting in a chair facing the two women. "Natalie's friend."

Adam was relieved to hear Natalie's lover, Ramses, would be with her. She had never said, or written, a word about Ram's innate power, but Adam had no doubts the man was more than a mere veterinarian. He fairly crackled with controlled magick.

"You have an odd bruise, like a star," he observed, brushing back the hair over Natalie's temple. "Are those burns?"

Grace tilted for a closer look at the redness surrounding the purple. "Could be. Her attacker had something metal on his hand. Do you remember unusual heat? Cold? Electricity?"

"Nothing from the time you yelled, 'Go,' until I woke up in the ER."

"Any vision changes? Nausea? Loss of feeling in your hands or toes? Strange smells? Odd sensations?"

"No. Should I?"

"Depends on the extent of your *pre*-traumatic amnesia," Grace said briskly. "Either that, or you lied to the police about Zolton's warning." Not a question; the woman never had minced words.

"Warning?"

"The men left no evidence. No footprints. You told the police you never saw them, brought me no warning. The current theory is *I* attacked you."

"That's crazy."

"Why the lie? You can call them back, tell them the truth."

Natalie's gaze flicked toward Adam, and he gave the faintest shake of his head, confirming the quick text message he'd sent her. Normally she had a superb poker face; she must be feeling worse than she was letting on. That, or she liked Grace and didn't fancy the lie.

The lack of footprints was a complication he hadn't anticipated, but that didn't change the fact that the police mucking in affairs they didn't understand would be more danger than use.

At Natalie's silence, Grace let out a small sound. "Ah, I

see. Lies. Deceptions. Go wherever the story leads, no matter who's in the way."

"I'm sorry." Natalie did sound contrite.

"Grace, let me explain," he said. "But not here—"

"Not ever." She shoved to her feet, interrupting him, and then left abruptly.

Not even a second look at him, either. After that "Bullshit," at her bedside, he could have been invisible. Jaw tightening, Adam shoved to his feet to follow the irritating physician.

Natalie's hand around his wrist stopped him. "Her hospital is no place for a confrontation. Eventually, she'll listen. And I need answers, Adam." When he sat, her voice lowered. "What's going down, and don't give me crap; because you asked, I lied to the police about your warning."

"You don't want them mixed up in this either." He also kept his voice low.

"I just hung a nice woman out to dry for you. Give me a reason I should keep lying when it's your ass on the line?"

"Because you appreciate being employed?"

She gave a snort of derision, making Adam smile. Despite their sparring, underneath remained a foundation of respect and loyalty. In a lifetime of other circumstances, he and Natalie might have been more than work chums.

"My ears are not hearing the necessary words," she prompted.

"Try this: A woman died yesterday after telling me a dragon is on the prowl."

"You believed her?"

"She was murdered; she knew something."

"Murdered?" Natalie turned whiter, the bruises standing out in stark relief. "The police *should* be called."

"The police can't do a damn thing. Remember that story about the guy who spontaneously combusted? She blamed the dragon. Something odd is going on here."

"Yeah, we were attacked and my memory was obliterated by men who left no footprints."

"The amnesia is real?"

"Weirdly real, a piece of time short-circuited from my brain."

He lifted his brows. "Magick?"

That gave her pause. "So?"

"Last year, you killed a story about Ram Montgomery."

"I don't know what you're talking about." Her voice was flat.

"Pull the other one." He held up a hand, forestalling further protest. "Newsman here; I can string together facts. I didn't pursue it because you gave me a damn good replacement story. But do you really want the police digging into stories involving you and magick? While you're living with Ram?"

Her lips tightened. "Stay out of my personal life, Adam."

"Stay out of mine."

"So, this is personal?"

"Stop digging." Her loyalty to him, to the paper and her work only went so far. Her deepest loyalty was given elsewhere. That he knew and accepted, and he was drawing his own lines. "This is my story, Natalie."

Her gaze searched his face, and her eyes narrowed. "Why are you after this?"

"That's none of *your* business. Unless . . . could the attackers have been after you?"

"I don't think I was the target. Just in the way."

"Then don't get involved. Take the time you need to heal."

"What about Dr. Armatrading?"

"I'll take care of Grace."

Grace glanced around the parking lot fronting her town house, gathering her courage. No one lurked. No strange smells.

Her leather-clad hands flexed and unflexed around the steering wheel. She was home. All she had to do was open the door and get out. Simple. People did it every day.

Simple didn't matter; post trauma wasn't rational.

The dragon's breathing fire.

Let me explain.

Self pep talks couldn't erase those realities. Or the fact that every inch of her body, including the backs of her eyeballs, ached from the attack.

Still, she looked like an idiot, just sitting here.

As Grace got out, the cold sucked the breath from her lungs. The temperature must have dropped twenty degrees overnight. She slipped on sunglasses as protection against the stabbing sunshine and picked her way across the lot. Sheeted ice crackled beneath her boots.

Engine roar broke through the new morning silence as a black car gunned down the quiet lane leading to her town house, then fishtailed the turn into her parking circle. A shot of fear with a chaser of adrenaline sent her scrambling and slipping across the treacherous lot. She heard the car halt, the door click open. If she could reach her porch, get inside . . .

"Grace!"

At Adam's call, she pivoted, and her heel skidded on the ice. Reflexively, she grabbed the nearest support—a scrawny tree trunk—for balance.

She stopped the fall, but wrenched her left hand. "Damn!"

"Don't go inside. Not alone," Adam called as he closed the gap with two steps, an arm outstretched to steady her.

Pain shooting up her arm, she tore off her gloves. "Zolton, every frigging time you appear, I end up hurt."

He leaned closer to see. "How's your hand?"

She tested it, closing each finger into a fist, then cupped her thumb with her other hand, soothing away the acute pain. She finished by wiggling her fingers and rotating her wrist. "Nothing dislocated or permanent."

But her thumb and wrist would be weak for a few days. Another black mark for Adam. Her hands were her irreplaceable tools.

"Good." Adam picked up her discarded gloves, then held them out to her, waiting, his body radiating an easy calm. So different from the edgy, chain-smoking lad who'd downed gallons of espresso. Who'd broken her heart.

With her good hand, she snatched the gloves, shoving away the temporary accord. She turned her back on him, striding toward her doorstep. "Stop dogging me. Or does this have to do with the mysterious warning you denied sending, making me look like a paranoid liar?"

He hurried to catch up. "It does, but it's too complicated to explain on a frigid sidewalk."

"When I reach my front door, I'm going inside and you're not. You've got three seconds to convince me otherwise."

"Faith Grimaldi—" His sentence broke off into an incoherent shout.

Grace spun around again—at least this time she kept her balance—to see Adam's feet slip out from under him. He landed flat on his ass in the middle of the lot.

"Bloody, sodding ice," he spat, and then glared up at her. "You're a doctor. Shouldn't you be rushing over here? Make sure I'm intact?"

At the sight of the normally collected Adam sprawled in sheer frustration, humor curved her lips. Years ago, during her recovery after surgery, as an antidote to boredom, she'd composed scenarios of their next meeting. At first, she'd met him with blazing, righteous fury. In later ones she'd come back at him with cutting words. Finally, she'd ignored him.

Seeing him flat assed, while she broke out into peals of laughter and smoothed on her gloves, had never been one of the choices. It was better than anything she could have imagined. Around the laughs, she answered, "You're gutter swearing. You're fine."

"I'll probably need a prescription. Something potent."

"Here's one: Get some boots with tread, southern boy."

"I'm a Brit, not a Southerner." By this time, he'd shoved himself back to his feet. Glaring at her, he brushed off the snow with tense swipes. As she continued to giggle, though, his shoulders relaxed. His chuckles joined hers, and he smiled. "Guess that doesn't give me any more expertise with ice, does it?"

She shook her head, momentarily speechless. Not from cold this time, but the sight of his face, softened by rueful laughter at himself.

Blindsided by the undefined emotion, she could only watch him join her, giving silent acceptance. The initial hitch in his gait smoothed out by the time he reached her side. No permanent damage.

"Grace." The humor had also gone as he softly repeated her name. "Let me come in, to make sure everything's safe and to explain. Give me fifteen minutes."

Had she really thought old anger could stand against curiosity, against a promise, against the whirlpool he stirred inside her?

"Fifteen minutes," she agreed.

Cold anger had no chance against cold facts—she'd known she had to hear him out as soon as she'd heard the name Faith Grimaldi.

Grace's attackers hadn't given up. Sure of that fact, Adam edged inside after she unlocked the door. His swift glance around the town house found nothing strange. All appeared in order to his unfamiliar eye and ear. Yet he couldn't shake the specter of danger. The interior was chilly and quiet, like the stillness that hung in the air before the crack of an avalanche.

Grace invited him no farther than the foyer. "Fifteen minutes," she warned.

"Does my time include a glass of water?" he stalled. He couldn't leave without knowing her home was secure. An unexpected yawn punctuated the request, though, as the aftermath of driving most of the night hit. He'd stopped in a local hotel only to set up a secure nest for Gala and shower off the taint of death.

"Looks like you could do with caffeine." She held out her hand. "Give me your coat."

While she hung up his coat, he opened his senses, reaching out for telltale ripples of magick. Nothing. Quieter than Poe's heart.

Didn't mean a mage wasn't concealed or hadn't left a trap; Adam was regretfully aware that his ability to sense magick wasn't infallible. Still alert, he followed Grace as she strode toward the kitchen, with a detour to turn on her PC. When her hand touched the metal, he heard an electric snap.

"Ouch!" She shook her hand. "Static electricity's horrific in winter here."

"I've noticed," he commented, remembering a few jolts. "We don't have that problem in New Orleans; it's too humid."

Two steps away from the computer, however, she jerked to a halt. Tension tightened her jaw as she pivoted to stare at the computer, pinging its way through the diagnostics.

"What is it?" he asked softly.

"The computer's coming on from a cold boot. I left it on hibernate."

"You're sure?"

"I'm sure," she snapped. "I leave it on hibernate because otherwise it takes too long to load." Her jaw set. "Someone's been jacking with my computer."

"Get out—"

Before he finished the thought, she grabbed the nearest heavy object—a pedestal Waterford vase. Throwing the silk bird-of-paradise spray on the floor, she held the vase like a club. "And call the police? About a turned-off computer?

With my cred, they'll be here next year." She stalked out to search her home.

The computer screen opened to her screen saver—some weird pattern of spiraling colored circles. He tensed, but the computer emitted no deadly, magickal viruses. He hesitated briefly, his need to make sure Grace stayed safe warring with the urge to quickly check her computer for a message from Faith. Protecting Grace won.

He caught up with her and nodded at her pricey crystal club. "Gift from your grandfather?"

"On the occasion of my graduation from the university."

Conversation ceased. Together, they passed between the rooms, hunting for some sign of the intruders. Along the way, Adam picked up a fifteen-pound dumbbell lying atop a messy stack of medical journals. Adrenaline coursed through him, as each doorway became a source of potential danger. With senses sharpened, one part of his mind also noted revealing details about Grace.

She wasn't particularly tidy. The functional rooms were scrubbed clean, but littered with odd items she'd failed to put away. In the bathroom, he discovered she used more lotions for foot and hand care than he had owned in his entire life.

She seemed to like water: there was an outdoor view of a frozen pond and a tabletop fountain. Her home smelled like citrus infuser sticks. She'd made haphazard stabs at decoration—like the vase and a framed art deco poster of Bob Marley. He gathered she wasn't here enough to bother with more.

Nowhere did he see the paraphernalia of a mage. Six years ago, she'd been hell-bent on pursuing the inner circles of magick, although as far as he knew, she'd had little talent. At least one blessing had come from that disastrous explosion. She must have given up the art of magick for the science of medicine.

Reaching the kitchen, their final room, was almost an anticlimax. No one lurking, nothing taken, nothing disturbed. "The quixotic vagaries of the human mind," he observed, as they deposited their makeshift weapons onto the table. "A minute ago I was scared spitless that we'd find something monstrous. Now, instead of being relieved, I'm disappointed we didn't get to kick some intruder butt."

Grace laughed. "Yeah, I was ready to inflict damage."

He lifted his brows. "Violence from a doctor? Aren't you supposed to be about healing?"

She obviously heard the touch of sarcasm, for she smiled again. "I'm not noted for my bedside manner. That's why I went into emergency medicine instead of something like pediatrics."

"I would hazard that manners are overrated during crises. Personally, I'd prefer swift competence."

"And direct talk?" She braced her hands on the countertop, her gaze laser-penetrating. "What's on my computer, that someone needed to jack it?"

"Why don't you look?"

"Information first. Outside, you mentioned Faith Grimaldi. Why?"

"You know her?" Adam leaned one hip against the counter and crossed his arms.

"I'm not an interview subject, Adam. Answer my questions. Your fifteen minutes start now."

"I think she sent you information. I'm guessing those men from last night want it."

"Why? What kind of information?"

"A virtual library. Why the men want it depends on their involvement. Why she sent it to you, I have no idea."

"Now you think you can get the information from me?" Her lips curled. "Go back and ask Faith."

He leaned forward, his words clipped. "I can't. She's dead. Murdered."

"*Murdered?*" Her gold-brown skin turned mud pale, and she gripped the counter.

"Killed by magick."

"How? She knew how to protect herself." Blindly, she reached for a chair, and then dropped to the seat.

The glint of her tears before she turned away doused his anger. He sat beside her, laid a hand on her wrist. Heat tingled across his palm. "I'm sorry, Grace. How did you know her?"

"She was my aunt. Great-aunt. Sister of my mum's mum."

A relative? Oh, bloody hell, didn't that complicate matters? Even as he tried to offer comfort, questions clamored. If Faith knew Grace, how much about him had the mage known?

"You were close?" he probed.

"Wouldn't need to use my thumb to count the times we'd met. She didn't have much use for me. Claimed Grandmother and Mum squandered their talents and I hadn't a speck of the gift. But she was family." She swiped her face dry, her jaw firming. "What happened?" Her voice had become clipped and clinical.

"Your aunt was killed by a magick spell conducted to her over her computer's wireless network."

"I didn't know that was possible."

"Neither did I. I've never seen anything like it—deadly to computers and to humans." He paused. Hell, she needed the broad picture. "Although I've heard wisps of rumors about a clandestine movement. Dangerous mages who meld magick and science."

The color just returning to her cheeks fled. "You don't care for the idea?"

"Scares the hell out of me, the power one person could hold."

"Any theories why she was killed?"

"Too many. Had she told you anything?"

"How could she? We haven't spoken in six months."

She had a good poker face, or maybe a good medical face. He might not have felt the lie if he hadn't been keeping a careful eye on Grace. If he weren't talented at reading body tells. If he hadn't missed Grace so deeply the past six years that he'd revisited every memory of her, every move and nuance.

She hadn't known Faith had been killed, but Grace had some angle on the possible reason why it had happened.

Still, he decided to play it straight with her. About Faith's death. If he got into that library again and found the CD . . . well, they'd see. "When the spell attacked, she was showing me a prophecy and data about the death of eight mages. She said they drowned in the breath of the dragon. Do you know what that means?" He stifled a yawn, still watching her above his hand.

That medical-bland face had regained control. "Dragon breath? Not part of an ER doc's business." Briskly, she shoved to her feet. "I promised you caffeine. Red Bull, espresso, or tea?"

"Tea, if you can do a proper brew."

"After living with my grandfather? The proper Lord Smithson? He was a stickler for afternoon tea etiquette. Got my knuckles rapped more than once for holding the cup wrong." She put on the kettle.

"What was Faith like?" he asked.

"Mum said she was eccentric and cantankerous. But, the few times I met her, my one impression was vibrant. She was completely involved in each moment of life. Being with her, I felt as though I'd never really seen colors or tasted food before." Her fingers curled around the tin of tea leaves. "I should be used to death; I see enough of it, but it always makes me angry. Especially for Faith."

"She must have thought more of you than you realize. Her last thoughts were of you."

"Really?" Fussing with the tea, Grace turned her back to him.

Getting the impression he'd hit a nerve, he shrugged. "She asked me to protect you. Did she know about our history?"

"She knew. But obviously she didn't tell you about her being part of the clan." She faced him again. "Why are you involved? And don't tell me you're fulfilling the wish of a dying woman. You went to her."

"A story, of course," he said lightly, knowing Grace would believe that truth. His other reasons had nothing to do with Faith's death.

"Of course." Her mouth twisted in annoyance as she finished assembling the tea, silent until it had brewed to her satisfaction.

Adam didn't mind the break. Sorting through new facts, he found his perceptions of last night twisting. Faith, Grace's aunt, had known more about him than she'd let on last night. She'd contacted his paper, put out hints about mages. Had she deliberately lured him to her? The thought that he might have been played did not sit well.

Had Faith wanted more than a NONE story? If so, what? Too many threads with too little information to connect them: Faith's contact with NONE, the computer-fed virus, the virtual library with the disk he'd hunted, the information on the deaths of eight mages—mages he'd met—a prophecy of Armageddon. All swirling around Faith.

Why had she involved Grace? She was a relative, yes, and people often turned to blood in crisis, but this aunt and niece were hardly more than strangers. Moreover, Grace was a physician; she didn't have magickal talent. So, why pick her? Had Faith sent on information? The library? Or a warning?

Faith had been a pivot point. With the mage's directive to protect Grace, and then the attack last night, he feared the arrow now pointed straight to Grace.

Not that she seemed too perturbed, as she poured cups of Earl Grey and handed him one. "Milk or sugar? Lemon?"

"Black's fine." He took a sip. "Good."

She sat back beside him and eyed him over her cup and saucer. "What are your next steps, Adam?"

He noticed she didn't ask if he was going to continue digging into the story. He nodded toward her computer. "First, I'd like to see if Faith sent you anything."

"I'll look at my e-mail when I'm alone. If she sent anything, she sent it to me, not you. Must have been a reason for that."

"You don't trust me, do you?"

"Let's see. During our last relationship"—she gave two pumps with her forefingers, putting the word relationship in air quotes—"I was crazy over you, while you were bold-faced lying to me, using me to get close to my friends."

"I was already onto the story when we met. Your friends were magick light, playing with notions of power. I was trying to expose deeper, much deadlier forces." Ones who were using her friends without their knowledge.

"Still, my friends were in your photographs, the photographs you published. They were the ones that insane bomber decided to target after seeing those pictures. If you and I hadn't lingered over espresso at The Dragon's Tale pub, I would have been with them, instead of on the fringes when the bomb exploded. I lost a kidney. They lost their lives. You know, while I was recovering, I sometimes wondered if you'd known about the bomb, if that's why you kept me back. An attack of conscience."

He closed his eyes a moment, remembering the two of them escaping through the chaos. Blood, Grace bleeding. Screams, gagging smells of burned flesh and burning metal, choking smoke, inferno heat. Then, later, raw disgust when he learned of his part in the destruction. One moment that had, in so many ways, forever changed him. "I didn't know; I would have tried to stop it."

"Would you have not published those pictures? Or the ones of the blast? They made your reputation. People were clamoring for your work."

He opened his eyes to find her watching him. "To be honest, even if I had known . . . Yes, I would have still published them."

"Dig and report; don't take responsibility."

"Then."

She took a thoughtful sip. "You had the pick of the plum jobs after that, but you didn't take any of them. Why?"

He slid the empty cup across the table. "Look, Grace, we've already established you don't think much of my character, so my reasons for long-past decisions are moot. Just open your e-mail."

"Not until you leave. Your fifteen minutes are up."

What was she expecting to see on that computer? He bit back the question. "Last night I saw Faith killed by something that came through her computer. How do you know that same something isn't going to come through yours?"

"And if it does," she countered, "what are you going to do about it? *You* can't fight magick."

"Better than you."

"You didn't protect Faith. She died!"

That one stung. "So help me, I would at least get you out of this room. No matter what the cost."

She stared at him. "You sound as if you mean that."

"Open your Internet browser. Open your e-mail." He couldn't keep the snarl from his voice. "I won't knock you unconscious with that Waterford just for an uninterrupted peek at your inbox."

"No, but you would take sneaky pictures."

"Camera stays in my pocket."

She gave her head a shake. "I hate when you make sense."

"Especially when you're wrong."

"Reminding me is not a way to ingratiate yourself." She

crossed to her computer, sat, and clicked open her Internet browser. "If nothing happens, you'll leave?"

"Sure," he answered absently as he placed himself a distance away, yet still at an angle to read her screen. As they waited for it to load, he asked, "Is that screen saver a picture of something?"

"An electron microscope picture of the Ebola virus."

"That's morbid."

"Medical people often are."

"Let's hope it's not prophetic." His shoulders tensed as she moved without hesitation into her e-mail. Despite her caution, she still didn't truly believe the danger.

The e-mail gave a merry beep, and that was all. Nada. So far.

While her hand manipulated the mouse and she stared steadily at the screen, she said softly, "And, for the record, Adam, there are pieces of your character I admire. That hasn't changed. You're driven. I can understand that; so am I. You're passionate. You take risks. You can be so incredibly nice."

"But you still don't trust me." He repeated his question from earlier, as he caught a glimpse of her inbox list. Faith had sent her three e-mails.

Grace swiveled, caught his betraying gaze, and scowled. "I don't trust that your interests would lie with mine."

Chapter Four

Grace's footsteps echoed on the slate foyer, across the solitude of her town house. Outside, Adam started his car, and the engine growled a faint counterpoint. She tried to dismiss both the sounds and the accompanying soft chill of emptiness. Loneliness had never bothered her here; after the noise and relentless humanity of the ER, she relished solitude.

Why did Adam's departure dull the sheen of being alone? He'd been here less than an hour. Could the air have been imprinted with his presence, the walls absorbed his aura, in such a short time? Possibly. Adam had that same vibrancy Faith had had, that same awareness of each moment of living.

He hadn't been pleased about his eviction; he'd made no secret of that fact. But she couldn't risk his reading her e-mails.

To confirm that no ugly virus was attached, she'd opened everything in her inbox—immediately minimizing the ones from Faith, deleting or storing the others. Only then had Adam left.

Crossing to her computer, she rubbed her hands across her arms. The cold hadn't seemed so penetrating five minutes ago. Now it snuck in, swelling into the vacuum left by losses. The loss of Adam. The loss of Faith.

Faith couldn't be gone; she couldn't be, yet she was. "She's dead," Grace spat, but even saying the words aloud couldn't release the grief calcified in her heart. For to mourn meant accepting the finality of wasted time, and that she couldn't do. Not now. Maybe not ever.

She couldn't accept they would never get the chance to heal the rift. A newborn chance, carved of nothing more than raw hope and pixels. She hadn't lied to Adam, not if you used politician-style definitions. She *hadn't* spoken to Faith in months. E-mail didn't count as speaking.

She'd contacted her aunt about her fugue state, suspecting what she wouldn't consciously admit: that the brief blackouts had no basis in science, but in magick. To a mix of dismay and anticipation, Faith's answering e-mail had been brief: Come as soon as you can. So, Grace had made arrangements for a vacation.

Now, that chance to find out what was happening to her had been snuffed out. Worse, she'd lost the possibility that she might reach, if not a friendship, then an understanding with her mysterious and tantalizing aunt.

Worst of all, Faith was gone.

Grace bit back the thought. Faith wasn't gone, not yet. *Not until I read those e-mails. Not until I learn who killed her and why.*

She clicked on the first, sent yesterday morning. The message was brief: *Review this on your way north.* No sentimentality or indication that Faith had suffered any pangs of regret or desire for familial reconnection. Grace swallowed back the disappointment and shifted into diagnosis mode. Get the data first.

The attachment contained Faith's files on the mage deaths Adam had mentioned. Grace leaned forward, squinting to read the type in the few clippings. Her casual interest deepened as terrifying details formed an undeniable pattern. Whoa, Hannah, she'd unearthed the opal mine—valuable and cursed.

Quinine-bitter fear puckered her throat. She couldn't stop staring at the last photo: a heap of ashes unrecognizable as human except for a macabre flag, the bone of a finger. Her mind replayed the description of his last moment. "He shouted as he doused himself with kerosene and threw the match. But those last desperate last words made no more sense than the preceding sudden madness. 'The breath of the dragon came upon me, but I return destruction in kind.'"

Madness. Death. All laced up in dark magick. Blackouts and amnesia. *Fugue states.*

Was she in the first stages of the assault that had taken these victims? Faith must have thought so. Grace's hand shook as she printed the attachment. Madness, the loss of sanity and intellect, terrified her.

Her fate? Not if she could bloody well stop it!

With a jerk of her finger, she brought up the second e-mail, sent late last night. Dear Lord, Faith must have sent this just before her death. The finger of the Grim Reaper tickled Grace's spine, shivering through her nerves. This message also was brief. "The unknown betrayer attacks. You're the only one I can trust. Pray my collection gives you answers; I fear you're next."

For a warning, pretty damn effective. For being practical . . . not so much. Maybe the two attachments would give more.

"Circle of the damned beware. Where the dragon enters, madness will reign. The flames of its breath ignite a conflagration none of mind can escape. For the dragon hoards all treasure. From the saga of Cadwaladar 1490."

"Guardian of the fountain, both beneficent and terrible to behold. Legends, Y Ddraig Goch."

She read aloud the two quotes in the first attachment. "Well, that's helpful. Not."

The second was about as useless. Details of a magick ritual, a simple one designed to neutralize locks. "Thanks, Faith, I'll remember that next time I forget my keys," she muttered. "Not that most rituals help those of us with a narrow talent." She scrolled to the bottom, seeing nothing more. She had just moved the cursor to close the attachment when a flash caught her eye. She blinked away eyestrain and caught, in barely discernable yellow, the words *pineapple ink*.

The words faded, vanished, and then sparked back on, only to repeat the fading cycle. She waited, but they didn't appear again.

Pineapple ink. Pineapple ink. It rang a chime of memory. Where had she heard . . . oh, bloody hell, she'd pushed that day from memory. She couldn't have been more than eight, the first time she'd met Faith. With the clearer insight of age, she recognized that Faith had picked a time when Lord Smithson had been out of the country to come test her niece for magickal talent, and that Grace had failed miserably. At the time, all she'd known was that she dearly wanted to impress her flamboyant aunt and that she somehow wasn't.

So, she'd tried a trick she'd read about, one with disappearing ink. Except the cook wouldn't let her use the lemons, as they were needed for tea, and she'd pinched the pineapple instead. With predictable results. She was no more a stage magician than she was a mage.

Maybe Faith's pineapple ink was more effective. With the mouse, Grace highlighted the neighboring blank space.

A grimoire icon. And one phrase. *The Lady of the Lake*. A clue to the library Adam had mentioned? "You could have given me a bit more to go on," she grumbled, opening the third e-mail.

This one blindsided her. A personal note from Faith.

"Use Adam's help; you need him. He's proven a better man than we credited. I regret that I didn't keep you closer, my shining Grace, though you resided in my heart."

Grace covered her mouth, pressing back the sorrow that

washed up in those few words. Grief scalded her throat. "Dammit, Faith," she whispered, and let the tears come.

"Treat, Gala. The nice lady at the emergency vet shelter gave us some ferret chow," Adam called as he entered his motel room. Quickly he shut the door. Likely the tricky ferret had gotten out of the cardboard box he'd turned into a makeshift nest. "Hope you like it better than the canned chicken."

Because it was New Year's Day, his option for ferret supplies had been limited. The open party store he'd found supplied kitty litter, a plastic bowl for water, and the box, but ferret chow was beyond the merchandise mix of Dandy Don's.

He took a single step forward, and the hairs on his nape tightened. A charge prickled across his skin, as though he stood in the eye of summer heat lightning. Not much of a possibility, considering the temperature outside was a not-balmy twenty degrees Fahrenheit.

Which meant one other option. Magick. The remains of energy from a recently cast spell hung in the motel room air, an unnatural gauze atop bland Americana. One step deeper, and the sensation vanished.

So, he'd had a visitor. And not long ago. Had he been ten minutes later, he wouldn't have detected the intrusion.

He scanned the room, but whoever had been here was gone. No place to hide—the bed box came to the floor, and the empty bathroom was reflected by the sink mirror. Still, some unpleasant surprise could have been set. The smart thing would be to back up and leave.

Except, he had a pet to rescue.

The room remained too silent. No sound, even from Gala, when he expected to hear her nails against the cardboard cage. He peered into the darkest corner, and his throat went dry. The top flaps on her box lay open.

Adam set down his and Faith's laptops and the virtual

gear. At least he hadn't left them here. Alert to any small sign that he'd activated a spell, he circled the room. His hands lifted in the defensive posture he'd learned after many hard years, and harder lessons.

"Gala?" he called in a low tone. No ferret.

The specter of a repeat failure—*You didn't protect Faith. She died*—soured his throat. Gala had to be hiding. What would anyone want with a musky ferret?

He sprang no traps, found nothing amiss. No ferret either. Slowly he sank to sit on the bed and took in slow, oxygen-filled breaths.

"Gala," he called again. "It's safe."

The cloud around his heart lifted as the little ferret crept out from a tiny hole formed where the dresser met the wall. With a faint chitter, she wriggled toward her food bowl, then looked back expectantly.

"So, you heard me," he said, laughing a little.

She kept up the conversation while he handled the care basics he'd gotten from ferrets-dot-com. Food out, water changed, litter scooped, hands washed.

While Gala set to noshing on the chow, he propped up a pillow against the headboard. Stretching his legs the length of the bed, he frowned as he toed off his shoes. Salt and snow damage. Damn, those had been expensive shoes. Grace was right; he'd have to get boots.

"Don't suppose you can tell me who was inside this room," he told Gala. Gala didn't seem to have the answer. Or rather, her food kept her plenty occupied.

Who? The same ones who'd attacked Grace? Stealth didn't appear to be their modus operandi. The person or persons who'd been on her computer?

What was the intent of the spell? What had the intruder been after? Information? Capture? Spying? Death or destruction? The familiar frustration at not being able to tell bit him. Under the right circumstances, he could detect powerful magick, that unique energy wielded at the hands and will and mind of a mage.

"Yeah, I'm fabulous," Adam told Gala with wry humor. "I can tell *when* a spell hath wrought. Just can't tell a damn thing about what the spell could do."

Whoever had been here was good. The residual was focused and nearly undetectable.

One possible answer to his visitor's identity struck him. He'd told Natalie where he was staying. Had she told her lover, Ramses Montgomery?

Didn't that possibility put a new clam into the chowder?

Although he'd guessed Ram was a powerful mage, he hadn't pursued the lead, for a number of reasons. Ram had always left the impression he was a decent enough chap, not part of either the Custos Magi or their shadowmates. And, after eight years, Adam had found the passion for his fool's quest waning. He'd almost concluded the man he sought was dead.

Mostly, he hadn't dug further because he valued Natalie as a colleague and a friend. Both were precious in his world. He wouldn't risk those gifts without a strong reason.

Adam filed the possibility. "What do you think, Gala? Wait until we have more proof, and a workable tactic, before we go to Ram?" Finished with her brunch, Gala scrambled onto the bed and began to play "burrow" within the pillows. "I'll take that as a yes. So let's focus on the current problems. There are certainly enough of them."

He wadded up a piece of paper and tossed it to the end of the bed for Gala to chase and roll back, playing ferret fetch while he outlined. "Find out who attacked Grace and why. Find that library and the CD. And maybe, in the process, score a story on the mage deaths. You know who we need to see? Raj Kasin. If he didn't develop that magick virus, he damn well knows who did."

Gala seemed to think that was a stellar idea, as she crawled up his leg. Adam scratched her neck. "My stories have been fluff of late, Gala. I've gotten careless, forgotten the precautions when you chase evil. That won't happen again. Right after this call, we move."

Which meant he had to make the phone call he'd been delaying, because he wouldn't be able to call again for a while. He dialed, chest as heavy as if a troll crouched on his sternum.

"Hello, Tracey," he greeted the girl who answered. "Happy New Year."

"Hey, Mr. Adam. Happy New Year to you."

"Did you and Jerome get the tickets?"

"To the Rockin' New Year? We sure did, and the party was awesome. Thanks for putting the word in to the host."

"My pleasure. You take good care of my mother. How is she today?"

The brief hesitation answered his question. "She's mourning a mite. I'm making black-eyed peas for New Year's luck. Thought she might eat a bit."

"Will she talk to me?"

"Oh, I reckon she'll be eager to. Let me get her."

The troll settled firmly on his chest while he waited through the brief silence.

"Adam!" His mother's voice, still strong, still all Brit, came on eagerly.

"Hello, Mum. Happy New Year."

"You found him? Is he dead? You avenged our Abby?"

Why did he still hope for some different greeting? When he'd been getting the same one for eight years?

"No, Mum." He refused to even talk about the slim lead, a CD that didn't even exist in reality.

In the silence, her bone-deep disappointment wound across the airwaves. Then she sighed. "You will, I know. You promised."

"I haven't forgotten."

"You're vigilant? I couldn't survive losing you, too. The mages are evil seducers."

He bit back a protest that would do no good. He'd been caught in that same hatred, too. Until he'd met Grace. Met, and betrayed, her friends.

"You won't lose me, Mum."

"Then I have faith." Her voice brightened a bit. "Where are you?"

"In Michigan."

"Oh, you poor lad. Must be cold."

"Beastly so." They chatted a few minutes more, like any normal son and mother, until his mother exclaimed, "Well, we'd better hang up. Keep the line free. In case Abby calls."

"Of course, Mum. I love you."

"I love you, too, dear." As he hung up, the troll added a few stones.

Abby, his sister, wouldn't be making any calls, not unless he found the reversal. She'd been catatonic for eight years. Driven mad by the one Adam sought. The man known not by name, but by his mage symbol. The Dragon.

Grace's phone chimed. She sat up, wiping away the tears. They did Faith no good. Finding the killer would.

The text message from Master Umari was brief: Please come, Dr. Grace.

Swiftly, she printed out the information, saved Faith's e-mails to two flash drives, and then deleted the evidence from her hard drive. Likely a useless gesture, since someone had already been into her computer, but just in case. She stuffed the drives and the folded printout into her bag, grabbed a health cookie from the kitchen—she was starving—threw on her coat, and was on her way in a matter of moments.

A slither of concern wound around her, as she backed out

of the lot. On the surface nothing was amiss about the message. Master Umari called her Dr. Grace, and he preferred text to phone calls.

The demand for an immediate meeting was unusual, but she had left him a message earlier, thinking his healing techniques might yield information on her fugue. She'd even considered asking Kea to run an MRI and EEG on her, but she was reluctant to let anyone connected to her work know about her problem, even someone she trusted as much as Kea.

As she drove, she texted the answer that she'd be there in fifteen, then called Natalie and got voice mail. "I'm on my way to Master Umari's. Something urgent. If he's willing to meet, are you available?" By the time Grace reached her destination, Natalie still hadn't answered. Well, she'd mention the reporter to Master Umari and let the two of them take it from there.

Master Umari's home was a two-story model on Main Street, within a hefty walk to the University of Michigan campus. No one had any trouble identifying which building belonged to the Reiki master. Only took one word—turquoise.

"Grace!"

Bloody hell. Adam. She was still debating whether she should follow Faith's advice and work with Adam on the mage deaths, but one thing was certain. She did not want him plastering her on the front page of *NONE*, complete with photos of her catatonia. Or finding out about her work with Kea. Not with his attitude toward mixing magick and tech.

She scowled as Adam slipped up the street to her side. "Told you, you need boots."

"No place is open on New Year's Day." He nodded to the house. "You're going to see Master Umari?"

"How did you know?" Then shook her head as she answered her own question. "Natalie told you."

"She's still too punked to come, but said she would like to meet with Master Umari in a day or so, if he agrees."

"I'll see what I can do." When he accompanied her to the door, she added, "We can meet afterward. I'm perfectly capable of seeing friends without you, Zolton."

"I'm not leaving you on this bloody doorstep," he said, frowning.

He wasn't swearing. The red paint on the door had concealed the smear of blood. Only the drops that spilled onto the turquoise frame stood out in alarming relief.

"A Reiki decorating technique?" he asked.

"Of course not." She touched the blood. "It's dry." Swallowing around a drier lump of fear, she rapped on the door.

Adam didn't bother with niceties. He reached around her and twisted the handle. The door opened, silent as a wraith.

Inside, pulled shades kept darkness enclosed. After the bright sun outside, she couldn't see a damn thing.

"Master Umari?" Her call echoed into the blackness. No answer.

"Layout?" Adam asked, his voice low.

"A welcome area with feng shui crystals on a glass baker's rack. Don't trip on the ceramic umbrella stand beside it. Door to the work area at the left. Private quarters in back."

Crossing the threshold into silence was like entering a mausoleum.

Except heat poured from the interior. Adam joined her inside. "The thermostat must be set over ninety."

"He keeps his rooms warm, but not this warm," she whispered back.

Silently, Adam closed the door, rendering the darkness deep and smothering. Even taking her sunglasses off didn't help. It was as though something unnatural had swallowed every scrap of light.

A thin beam of light sliced in front of her, startling her until she realized Adam had a small electric flashlight.

"Master Umari?" she called again, taking off her gloves and unbuttoning her coat. "It's Dr. Grace."

Profound silence hung in the air; even the plants dared not breathe. Atop the usual green scent of the rooms lurked a hint of mildew. Her heart sped up, making her even hotter.

"Get out!" Adam's warning broke the hush a second before two shadows burst from the back. One of them struck at Adam, and the light flew from his hand, landing with a clatter atop the baker's rack.

"Adam!"

"Go!"

The command broke her freeze-frame. Wrapped in clammy sweat, Grace yanked the door handle. Before she got out, a vicious jerk pulled her back into the chaos. An unseen force smashed the door shut. Two thick hands closed on her throat, squeezing out air. Colored spots gyrated across her vision. Only seconds to loss of consciousness.

"For the nose, bitch," growled a nasal voice.

Her ER training kicked in. Use the adrenaline; don't let panic win. She grabbed her attacker's forefinger. Jerked it to near snapping and max pain. Her other hand drove backward, her thumb aiming for his eye. The pain and the unexpected resistance loosened his grip enough that she could twist away.

With the front door blocked, she scrambled toward the workroom. Fighting back dark panic, she tried to find Adam and his attacker.

Their strobe-lit fight played out in isolated detail as an arm or a knit-masked face crossed the flashlight beam, their grunts and curses the only sounds in the eerie silence. The attacker lunged forward, his fist hammering into Adam's ribs. Instead of hearing the crack of bone, though, she saw Adam execute a fluid twist, and the blow grazed across his chest. The attacker's momentum carried him forward; Adam's twist ended with his foot connecting to the attacker's knee. With a guttural "oof," the man dropped.

Broken Nose caught up to her. Heart caught in her throat,

she grabbed an umbrella from the stand. Jabbed it toward the man's nose. Missed as he avoided the blow. Her insides retreated, anticipating the pain of his retaliation.

Adam's leg swept around, catching Broken Nose at the ankles. The man stumbled, missed Grace. She grabbed Adam's hand and pulled him the final steps into the workroom. They slammed shut the door, and Grace threw the lock. Gasping, they leaned against the door, against each other, listening, bracing for another attack. Her muscles spasmed with a need for oxygen and calcium. The fight had lasted mere seconds; she felt as if she'd run a marathon. Twice.

"They're leaving," Adam whispered, his breath tickling her ear.

Grace nodded, even though he couldn't see her in the impenetrable darkness. She didn't trust her voice or her aching throat to work.

They stood for a moment longer, side by side, as their breathing steadied.

"I don't think they'll come back," Adam said. "Not now. They'll figure we've called nine-one-one by now."

Which they should be doing. Except neither one of them could seem to break away from the other, until Grace whispered, "We have to find Master Umari."

Without waiting for Adam's response, she flicked on the light switch.

Usually, even on the cloudiest, grayest day, the room glowed with an ambient light. With the bright sunshine outside, this room should burst with energy and cheer. Today it seemed dark and musty. Sweat stinging her eyes, her sweater sticking to her chest, she searched the room. Nothing.

They returned to the hall, but the lights there didn't work. While Adam retrieved his flashlight, Grace called, "Master Umari?"

Adam made a shushing noise. "Did you hear that?"

The sound came again. "A moan. From the back."

They raced down the short hall, Adam's light flickering over the route, and into the kitchen. At first, she barely recognized the crumpled mound of cotton bent over the sink.

"Master Umari!" Heat from the ovenlike room plastered against her, as Grace crossed to the too-still body. Automatically, she tested his carotid for a pulse; the flesh seared her fingertips. "He's alive. Fevered. Run the light over him." She pulled her stethoscope from her bag and listened.

A macabre tableaux, straight from Poe's hallucinations, took shape beneath the narrow beam. The ligaments of his neck stood out in tense ropes, while Master Umari's normally serene face grimaced beneath ear-to-ear bruises.

The beam reached where his hands should be. Grace gagged on the horror of nothing. Had those gifted hands been chopped away? With surgical precision, leaving not a sinew or a drop of blood?

No, thank God, a trick of the dark; a towel covered the sink. She wiped sweat from her eyes, and then folded back the cloth. Her breath hissed in, hurting inside her chest. Gratitude was premature.

Master Umari's hands were buried to the wrist in the water-filled sink. Tendrils of steam rose where water touched his shriveled flesh. Around the edges of the water bobbed a few ice cubes. As she watched, one moved close to his wrist and melted. Dear God, the intense heat came from him, consuming flesh and life as fuel!

She tried to lift one of his palms, and he moaned, his body twitching. Carefully, she let his hand drift back into the tepid water.

Adam swore as he took in the scene. "How is he?"

"Vitals are erratic; you see his hands. I'm calling nine-one-one." She pulled out her phone, dialed, and then gave necessary details to the paramedics.

"Nine-one-one won't know what to do about those hands."

"His innate skills will start his healing."

"Not with these." In a gentle move, Adam pushed back the unconscious man's jacket. The flashlight glinted off clear bands bound high on each forearm. Multicolored pricks of light blinked and danced in the depths.

"That looks like a fiber optic cable." Grace reached out a tentative finger.

"Don't—"

"Ouch!" She jerked back from the shock jolting her nerves. "What is it?"

"Dangerous."

"Bloody, yes, it zapped me."

Dangerous and creepy. The colors twisted and blinked in a clear flexible cage that shimmered and shifted in concert. Almost alive, it reminded her of a rainbow snake. A feeding serpent.

"If I have to hazard a guess, I'd say they amplify the life-force energy flow. Hold this." Adam handed her the flashlight. "I'll see what's holding them."

Grace watched him work, his large hands as deft as a surgeon's, and the hairs at her nape tightened. Although he looked down at the band, he never touched it as his hands traced the space above the eerie device. His information came from what? Sight, sounds? From the currents of air and heat across her skin?

"There's a manipulation lock."

Damn, too bad she couldn't do, or remember, Faith's lock spell. "About the zappy thing . . ."

"Removing them may be extremely painful." He looked up, his dark eyes meeting hers. "I know you do pain research. Do we have anything to buffer the pain?"

The suffocating darkness pressed into her small oval of light, gnawing at the insubstantial torchlight. Adam didn't know what she could do, that her talent had bloomed during the explosion. Would his aversion to magick turn him against her?

To hell with it. There was no time for hedging. "I can."

"How?" Then he sucked in a breath. "Not so talentless, then."

"I'll need to touch you."

He flashed a grin, part sexy, part regretful. "Much as I have desired to hear those words, I meant Master Umari."

"You're delusional. I need you to be my second anchor point. Give me a moment."

Her mind's eye pulled up the memory of a bio-electro graph—the chaotic physiology of pain. She knew if she could alter that pattern, she could alter the pain.

She drew in a breath, stretched out the kinks in her fingers, grimacing at the twinge in her thumb, and then intoned one of the two chants she'd learned in her single summer with her Jamaican grandmother. One for blood. One for pain. She placed a hand beneath Master Umari's palms. They carried no weight, no substance. The flesh was just a wrinkly shimmer, revealing tendon, vein, and bone.

"Master Umari, it's Grace. I'll lower the pain; then we'll release your energy. You'll need to regather your power. I can't do that for you." As she spoke, she sought beneath the scorching pain for the pattern tingling her fingertips.

There it was! With the focused talent she had inherited from her unusual family, she concentrated on the energy. Placing one of her hands at Master Umari's neck, near the pain channels, and her other hand on Adam's shoulder, she used her chant to form the pattern.

Something was getting in the way, keeping her from seeing the usually clear energies. Maybe the bands? She shifted her hands to Master Umari's arms. Good, clearer. Gradually, an electron and nanoparticle at a time, she reconfigured the energy, stretching it out to the second anchor until she could recreate the soothing patterns generated by beta waves. Master Umari relaxed as his pain eased.

Already sweaty in the sauna-hot room, Grace struggled

for breath. Adam seemed to be struggling as well, and sweat dotted his forehead.

Then, suddenly . . . She uttered a single profanity as the cascade of pain exploded beneath her skin.

"Grace? What are you doing?"

The temperature plummeted, tumbling shivers down her spine. Grace jerked, and then blinked. Shit, another fugue! "The lights came on."

"A moment ago, when I got the bands off." Adam's fingers dug into her wrist. "What's wrong?"

"Nothing. I was concentrating."

Her whole body ached, and her hands—Oh, God. Stinging worse than if she'd stuck them in a wasp's nest, her flushed hands circled Master Umari's neck, ready to squeeze.

The temperature swung back to normal, but the contrast chilled her sweat-soaked clothes and wracked her arms with tremors. She yanked her hands back, shaking off Adam's grip and gathering herself.

She couldn't have been out that long. She hadn't hurt Master Umari; she'd taken his pain. She . . .

She could have killed him and never realized.

Adam didn't pursue his questions. Instead, he was examining the now-lifeless bands.

Be a physician. Drawing refuge in her work, she tested Master Umari's vitals again. More stable, but still too thready for ease. She examined the master's hands. They were warm, not burning. Sweat beaded along the master's upper lip. Master Umari's hand spasmed, squeezing her fingers in a death grip. Her knuckles were crushed together.

"Master Umari. Let go."

Instead, he laced their fingers together. As he pulled her down, closer, the flesh of her palm began to burn. Suddenly, he collapsed back and his hand let hers go.

"How is he?" asked Adam.

"Bad. Where is that ambulance?"

Abruptly, Adam gripped her wrist, turning her hand. Grace stared at her palm, at the strange symbol emblazoned in burned red.

"Do you know what that is?" Adam's jaw tightened.

"You do?"

"It's a mage symbol. One of the twelve magickal beasts. The dragon."

CHAPTER FIVE

"The bastard ran out from behind the stump, slapping at fire ants. Except he was still wired up. Damned if those wires didn't jerk him backward, on his buck-naked arse, right at Detective Boudine's feet."

Hearing muffled laughter in the police station, Grace twisted on her hard chair to see Adam chatting up the officer who'd taken his statement. Even the detectives at the nearby desks hid smiles.

"She said it was the easiest collar she'd ever made, bastard practically begged to be taken in. *NONE* ran it with the headline: Divinity exposed!" Adam held up his hands, his fingers giving a mock quote.

Biting her lip against a smile, Grace turned away and finishing reading the last paragraph of her statement. How he did it, she couldn't fathom, but Adam could be at a Baptist meeting or a Comic Con and still put everyone at ease.

She signed her statement, and then handed it to her solemn-faced officer. "May I go?" At the policeman's nod, she gathered her things and put on her coat.

"We'll be in touch if we have more questions, Dr. Armatrading."

I'm sure you will. "You have my cell. I'm on vacation."

He was probably biting back the TV standard warning not to leave town. She wasn't a suspect he could shackle, thanks to Master Umari, who'd regained consciousness and exonerated them.

Outside, she found a nearby bus bench and waited. Took only five minutes before Adam strode out. A brief smile lit his face when he spied her.

"Waiting for me?" he asked, joining her. "I'm touched."

"Am I going to be on page one of *NONE*?"

"Because you stopped pain with your palms and a chant?" He braced one foot on the bench beside her, and then bent closer, elbow on knee.

"Yes." Grace leaned toward him, challenging. At least he hadn't brought up her segue into oblivion.

"Sorry, love, you wouldn't even rank one column on page twelve."

"*What?*"

"You're just not sufficiently lurid."

"You're not interested?" she huffed. Shouldn't she be relieved instead of vaguely insulted?

"To my readers, hands-on healing is a given, been around since biblical times. Now give me a twist—you're a full-fledged mage out for world domination, you accept vast quantities of grateful donations, you got the gift from an alien abduction, you only perform healings au naturel?" He swept a lingering, appreciative look across her, then raised a hopeful brow.

"Sorry to disappoint. World domination sounds like too much work, E.T. isn't in the picture, and I work fully clothed."

"Pity. Then *NONE* can't use you." With an exaggerated sigh, he straightened. "I, however, am suitably impressed and curious about your talent and more than willing to delve further."

"No delving, unless it's into Faith's death." She waited, expecting comments about her blithe walk into a nasty trap or further questions about her analgesic ability.

Instead he said, abruptly, "Okay. Show me where you were attacked."

Women joked that men were simple? Well, they'd never tried to figure out the mind of Adam Zolton.

Grace stood in the twilight-shrouded parking lot and watched Adam fist his hands against his hips.

"This is where you were attacked last night?" He didn't bother to look at her. Instead he surveyed the snow-covered soccer fields, turned gray by the coming night.

"No, I brought you to some random lot because I like standing in the cold."

He turned, then, and it wasn't so dark that she couldn't see his grin. "Rather a boneheaded question, wasn't it?"

"Rather." She crunched through the snow, pointing to each location.

"My car was there. Natalie drove up to here. We cleaned the ice from the car, and then the attackers came from that direction. I think Natalie was laid out about here."

"Where'd you break the bruiser's nose?"

"Here. Maybe. Things got intense; I wasn't watching the landscape."

"Mmm," he said absently, withdrawing again as he crouched down at the place where Natalie had been attacked and examined the snow.

"What are you looking for?" she asked.

He wasn't paying her any attention. Instead, he pulled a camera from his pocket and aimed a shot with one hand while the other hand, bare, ran over the snow. She edged closer, trying to see what had caught his interest. "None of those footprints are the attackers'."

"I know." He looked up. "Would you stand over there? And be quiet? I'll be done in about ten minutes." He went back to his don't-tell-a-damn-thing examination.

Like she'd said, women who thought men were simple hadn't tangled with Adam. Still, since men were lousy multi-taskers, she went where he directed and waited. After all his help at Master Umari's, she owed him the courtesy of another ten minutes.

Just ten minutes. After that, it was answers. Or frostbite.

While she waited, she checked her voice mail. One message. Kea wanted her to come by before she left for vacation. He sounded tired; maybe his neuropathy was acting up. She called him back, played voice mail tag, and then logged onto the Web, skimming through the latest news headlines. One caught her interest—Vitae, the giant gaming company, planned to unveil *SciMage VI* this summer. Official details about the update were nonexistent, but blog speculations filled the gap and had gamers salivating. Rumors hinted the game introduced a whole new level of technology, one that would blow competitors out of the field. Everything from immersion virtual reality to 3-D holographic imaging to tactile nanotech controllers had been suggested.

Interesting. She flagged the article to alert her for updates, then pulled up the latest *JEM—Journal of Emergency Medicine*—and started reading. She was wrapped in a study of artificial blood when, nine minutes, thirty-four seconds later, her phone vibrated. She glanced at the caller ID. Unknown.

"Grace, look at this," Adam called, standing about ten feet from the lot.

Caller unknown could leave a voice mail. She bookmarked the article, logged off, pocketed the phone, and then joined Adam. "Tire treads. This could be where the attackers parked."

"They'd have been hidden by that copse." He waved a hand at a stand of hardwoods. "You didn't fabricate them."

"Thanks, I'm aware of that," she said sarcastically. "At this juncture, the police don't care if my story is true. I've got too many other suspicious strikes against me."

"I'm not looking for jury evidence. Whatever's going on is beyond the grasp of the police."

"You're looking for . . . ?"

"Evidence of magick."

"Like bergamot oil? Brazier ashes? A singed feather and wax droplets? Tools for casting a spell?"

"Perhaps they used something more modern." He crouched low and ran his hands across the snow again.

She glanced around. "Even if something was left, seems unlikely you'd find it."

"Unless some residue of energy clung to it."

"How would you detect the energy?"

He shrugged, putting on his gloves. "Sometimes I feel the ripples. Moot point, there's nothing here that I can detect."

He could feel the energy of magick? Apparently he'd hidden some talents as well.

"Do you see anything besides the tire tracks?" he asked.

She tried, but daylight ended early in January and it was now too dark to see much. "No. Do you?"

"No." He muttered under his breath, a curse, perhaps, from the tone, but not in a language she recognized.

They were crouching down, shoulders nearly touching. She felt the heat of him as though wrapped in his embrace. Light flakes of snow drifting between them melted in the narrow gap separating their down and wool jackets.

"Freezing my arse out here and not a smudge of a lead." Frustration etched the curve of his mouth, his narrowed eyes.

He turned slightly, tucking his chin against the cold, his lips now level with hers. Their gazes snagged, and the moment stretched. Even in the windswept cold, the blaze in him heated her.

"Damn," he muttered and lifted one leather-gloved hand to tunnel beneath her hair.

Cold on her nape, down her back, no longer mattered, not when she was now burning. "You expected more?" she asked.

"Hoped for more."

Hoped for more. Three small words that curled like a dark cat with a promise. The urge to shatter the tension between them, to ignore the past and her doubts, was too strong to be ignored.

Her fingers squeezed around the snow, grabbing the chill to prevent herself from touching him. Her body matched his, leaning forward. The buttons on his coat bunched, and his scarf slipped, exposing his shirt. She could kiss him, there, with only the thinnest of cotton between her lips and warm skin.

Self-defense kicked in. She tossed her handful of snow at his chest, landing a direct hit on that small patch not covered by wool. A shocking impact of cold on near-naked skin that widened his eyes. She heard his gasp.

"Bloody hell," he spat.

She scrambled to her feet and danced a distance away. "What? Never been in a snowball fight?" Packing another ball, she aimed for his chest again. Hit where she aimed, too. "Three hits wins, and I'm up one."

His eyes narrowed, and then his lips lifted in a smile of challenge. In a spurt, he surged upward, but not fast enough to dodge her second missile. *Got him on the back.* "Two."

"Good aim."

"Thanks to last summer's slow-pitch league."

Up two zip, she gave him a break, let him get his feet beneath him. Southern boy with no boots? Like shooting ducks in a barrel.

Big mistake. She should have remembered he was as competitive as she. Adam never went down without a fight. He nailed her a solid one while he dodged her third.

The snow melted beneath her jacket. "That's cold! How did you—?"

"Cricket pace bowler," he said, laughing when she swore. He pulled his hidden hand out from behind his back. When had he packed that one? Didn't matter. He got her.

With the score two all, they added defense and respect for skill. Adam laughed as he slipped around the lot, but his innate grace and athleticism kept him challenging her. As the twilight deepened, curveballs, speeders, surprise attacks kept her breathless and smiling.

At last, Grace stopped, her latest snowball clutched in her palm, looking around and listening. Where was he? Night had come in earnest, and she couldn't see past a few feet. Snow began to fall again, blotting out the landscape.

Just like last night.

The thrill of the chase morphed into something darker, into the heart fluttering of the prey. What if Broken Nose returned? Attacked Adam in silence?

"Adam?" she whispered, turning full circle, her eyes hurting from cold and strain.

Someone popped out from the dark. She screamed at the same moment an arm slapped the back of her hand. Her snowball flipped up smack into her face.

"Gotcha!" The figure coalesced into Adam.

"My own snowball doesn't count." She chased away fear with anger.

"Sure it does. You're just mad you lost."

"I'm mad because you cheated."

"No, cheating would be if I kissed you." He moved closer, his body a bulwark against fear and attackers. As he watched her bring her breathing under control, the laughter faded. "You really are mad. Why?"

"Nothing." She plastered on a smile. "You're right, you won. I didn't expect you would be that good."

"Surprise." His victory was halfhearted as he glanced into the night, then turned back to her. His leather-clad fingers caressed her cheek. "They came out of the dark, didn't they? Darkness like this."

Desire, not cold, ran her spine at the tender touch. The muscles in her belly tightened with need. Mouth dry, she slid her hand to cup his jaw. The bristle of afternoon shadow snagged her gloves. He was so warm. The fires of a dark need were etched across his face.

No answer was necessary because some things didn't need saying.

Some things were also inevitable. They couldn't be stopped with time or distance or anger or betrayal or snow. He'd fought for her today, then left himself vulnerable with the admission that he could sense magick. Faith was right: *He's proven a better man than we credited.* And, in many ways, more dangerous.

She leaned forward and kissed him.

"Grace," he murmured, and wrapped his arms around her.

His lips tasted good. Wanting to feel him, she took off her gloves. She tunneled her hands through the long hair at his nape, reveling in the thick silk of it. Craving the pressure of muscle and bone, she shifted closer. His body, tight against hers, melted all frost.

Twin beams of yellow light cut through the snowflakes, slicing across their faces and through the kiss. Breathing hard, she lifted. "The commuter bus to the lot."

"Let the blighters look." He reached for her.

She held him off with her hands. "Not here. Not later."

"Then why did you kiss me?"

"Because I had to know what we'd missed. I had to know—" She swallowed hard. "If we're working together to find out who sent those men, who killed Faith—"

"This morning," he interrupted, "you said you didn't trust me. When do you figure we started working together?"

"When I brought you here." In truth, the choice had been made when he'd shown such tenderness in freeing Master Umari. Or maybe when he'd walked into her hospital room. "We need the answers to the mage deaths and I can't find them alone."

"In other words, I'm a useful tool."

"Yes. No." She couldn't stop herself from touching his cheek. "You are so much more, but this is too distracting."

"I want you, Grace," he said bluntly as he gripped her wrist, stopping her caress with a near-painful touch. "And from that kiss, I'm judging you want me, too. All your talk about *distractions* doesn't negate something that basic."

His hand wrapped around hers, surrounding her sensitive palm with strength and slick leather. The flare that sparked between them, the quickening of her breath, answered him without any words. He tugged her hand to his lips, bestowing a tiny kiss on her nail, and then released her, so they stood separate and cold. "I'll honor your no, but don't misread the fact that I want you eager and sure as lack of interest. And try to avoid sending mixed messages; don't give me credit for more self-control than I have."

She stiffened her spine. She'd deserved that; she had been sending mixed messages. "Understood. Don't hope for more."

"Can't help it, love. I always hope for more."

God help her, so did she. Except hope wouldn't find out who'd killed Faith. She held out the flash drive. "I copied Faith's e-mails for you."

He didn't take it right away. Instead, he stepped away, and his gaze locked with hers. The muscles of his face hardened, no teasing or desire left, only the determination of a clear-eyed, steel-tough male. "How far are you willing to go, Grace?"

She swallowed. "What do you mean?"

"This search will be neither easy, nor pleasant."

"I've faced hard and unpleasant."

"Not like this. Whatever our quarry is after, he's willing to inflict madness and pain, even death, to get it. You're a doctor, Grace, you swore the Hippocratic oath. Where's the line you won't cross? Will you stop me from crossing it? At what point am I on my own?"

Frightening questions that demanded honesty. "I hate death. I fight it every day without judgment. To kill, even if it meant protecting someone . . . I don't know. Would I stop you? I might if I thought there was another answer, a way not to destroy your soul. Until that moment comes, though, I will do whatever is necessary."

"Do you want retribution?"

"For Faith's murder?" She hesitated again, as something dark rose inside her. Something that demanded punishment for evil. Old Testament punishment of an eye for an eye. A strange desire for one who had cultivated neutrality and dispassion. At last she settled for, "I want justice."

He took the drive and pocketed it. "That I can live with."

As they headed toward their parked cars, though, she couldn't silence the sharp voice that questioned: Would the line she couldn't cross be something Adam could die with?

CHAPTER SIX

The motel was utilitarian—Adam never sprang for luxury on his employees' expense accounts—but it held the two items Natalie most wanted after leaving the hospital: a bed and Ram. She woke up a couple hours later, though, to find one missing. No light was on in the bathroom and the room was too small to be hiding a six-foot, dominating male.

Sitting up in bed, she shoved her hair back and rubbed her temple. The bruise itched. Even more annoying was that she didn't know what had caused it. However, the immediate question was, where was Ram?

He'd made a habit of disappearing recently. For a vet, he took a lot of business trips. Oh, he'd put out a smoke-and-mirrors story about a save-some-animal project, but after a year of living together, and a lot more years as a reporter, she recognized bullshit.

The faint sound of a voice drew her attention toward the window. Wide awake and reporter curious, she slipped out of the bed. Her toes curled from the cold seeping through the thin carpet. Cautious from her lingering memory of the attack, she peered out the tiny gap in the stiff curtain. Ram leaned against the motel wall, hunched against the ungodly cold, talking on his cell phone.

What call was that important? She dropped the curtain. None of her business. He was probably being considerate and trying not to wake her. Ram was her lover, not someone who needed her to watch over him. If she'd had some affair she preferred to keep private, she wouldn't appreciate him prying. She turned away.

"Of course I didn't tell her, Khalil. She's too close to Adam." Ram's voice rose in irritation, so that his murmured half conversation carried through the thin walls.

A "her" close to Adam? Ram wasn't telling something of concern to yours truly. More secrets, but this one circled her, so she was damn well gonna pry.

Natalie strained to hear more, but Ram's voice lowered to an indistinct murmur. She laid her ear against the hard glass, but the only thing that seeped in was the cold.

From the corner of his eye, Ram caught a movement behind the curtain. Natalie. She must have heard him. Damn. He turned away and lowered his voice into the phone. "Did you find the library?"

"No. It wasn't on Grace's computer." Frustration clipped the voice of Khalil, Weaver for the Custos Magi. "Faith must have hidden it elsewhere."

"How about Adam's PC?"

"Not in his room. Besides, why would Faith send it to him?"

"Because she didn't trust us."

"She didn't trust him, either. Putting such dangerous knowledge in the hands of our enemy? Not even she was so eccentric and lost to reason."

"You don't know that Adam is your enemy."

"Eight—no, now it's nine—mage deaths say he is, Tracker," Khalil returned, his voice as chilly as this bare-assed porch. "Adam Zolton is no ordinary journalist."

Ram shivered, stomping his feet to rid himself of the penetrating cold. Normally, he and Khalil worked harmoniously, but they diverged on the subject of Adam Zolton. Not that Zolton was one of Ram's favorite people—a few unreasonable jealousy issues over Natalie's close friendship with her boss prevented that—but Ram didn't think he was a cold-blooded murderer. "Keep your mind open to other possibilities. Natalie and Grace were attacked last night."

"*Attacked?* How are they?"

"Okay, although Natalie has amnesia from some kind of neuroscrambler. Adam would have no reason to go after her."

Khalil was silent a moment. "Was there evidence of magick?"

"The attackers left no footprints. Natalie's amnesia, though, could be tech-induced; she has a bruise."

"And each mage death could be explained by science, too."

"What about tech mixed with magick? Like Constantine?" He reminded Khalil of the dangerous mage they had battled six years ago.

"The Triad he hoped to resurrect is no more. You were there when I killed him."

Ram shifted, the scars on his back tightening in memory. "Maybe a renegade mage is using their theories?"

"Who would have the power, skill, resources to reach that level?"

"You."

Khalil laughed. "Then I shall hunt for one with the genius to cloak magick with science, someone who has a grudge against the mages."

"Just because we don't know of such a strong talent doesn't mean he doesn't exist. Even you have been surprised on occasion."

"True." Khalil paused. "I value your insight, Ramses. I shall consider your arguments."

"That's all I ask." Ram got the impression Khalil knew a lot more than he'd shared. Even when they'd been in the field together, the Weaver had been secretive. "I found Adam for you. Do you need anything else?"

"No, return to your animals. Take care of Natalie. And remember—"

"I won't mention this to her." Ram gave a rueful glance at the phone as they disconnected. Khalil had never understood or accepted Ram's decision to limit his activities with the Custos Magi because he didn't want to lie to Natalie. The Weaver also drew Ram back in at every opportunity.

And I've been letting him. Fact was, he found satisfaction in the work of the Magi, the guardian mages. Their purpose was necessary and vital, and he missed that. But the Magi demanded secrecy, and he couldn't keep straddling the two worlds. As Ram tucked the phone back into his pocket, his fingers brushed against the ring box. Not yet. He wouldn't ask her yet. Not until he'd been released from his vow to the Magi, or cut forever the final tie to them, would he be free to make a binding commitment to Natalie.

Frustrated she'd heard no more, Natalie plunked onto the bed, folding her legs beneath her as Ram came back in on a whoosh of cold.

Even after these months together, when she saw him anew, her breath and her heart squeezed with love. Snowflakes glinted on his dark hair, and the parking lights haloed his strong shoulders.

Then the door closed behind him, throwing him and the room back into shadow, for the blackout curtains were drawn. In the darkness, his voice, melodic and compelling, crossed the room to her.

"Is your head hurting?"

The bed sank beneath his weight as he sat beside her. He'd examined the wound earlier, while she stared at it in the mirror, trying uselessly to figure out what could have caused it. Now, his fingers brushed lightly against her temple, tingling across the edges of her skin. The healing touch of the mage.

The faint scent of vanilla tickled her nose. He'd used her soap, rather than the generic Ivory sliver provided by the motel. Somehow that made her smile, eased some of her tension, as she answered, "No headache. Just itchiness."

"Memory still gone?"

"For those moments. Not for other things." She took a breath, and asked bluntly, "Who's Khalil?"

Her eyes had readjusted to the dark, and she saw him frown.

"You were eavesdropping." Not a question in his harsh voice.

His hand, though, continued brushing against her temple, her neck, the soft touch both comforting and arousing. Dispersing her anger, she thought wryly. He had that gift.

"You were manipulating," she said, and his hand dropped, leaving a wake of cold. "I don't like hearing you talk about me like I'm a pawn in some game."

"A pawn? Never." His fingers laced through hers, and his thumb began to slowly rub across her knuckles. The tiny gesture spawned more prickles of desire, a heat neither denied.

"Then tell me who he is."

"He's a colleague and a friend. One day, you'll meet him. Why do you ask?" Loosening their hands, he took off his coat, toed off his shoes.

She braced her elbows on her knees, staring at the faded rug instead of him. "Remember three months ago? You told me you were going to a Wildlife Rescue seminar in London. Well, I called you there."

"Checking up on me?" he asked tightly.

"No. I just wanted to talk; I missed you. I called the hotel and they said you'd checked out. Fine, I thought, he's left early. But you didn't come home for another week, and you didn't mention leaving either. I told myself, 'He doesn't owe you an explanation of his whereabouts; don't be nosy.'"

Ram gave a bark of laughter. "The day you're not curious, my love, is the day your coffin is lowered."

"The point is, I didn't act on those questions. But I heard

the name Khalil about a week later when one of the conference organizers called and mentioned you'd left with Khalil."

"Khalil asked for my help on a project he's involved in. I stayed with him. I didn't say anything, because Khalil's business is his, Natalie, not yours." He pulled off his socks and shirt.

"Then, maybe, but not now. Not when I have this." She swept her hair back to reveal her bruise. Finally she looked at him. "There's a lot I still don't know about you, Ram; I've accepted that. But this is different. It's about Adam's message and the attack last night. I have a right to know; I'm involved."

"You're not involved. Adam dragged you into something that he knew was dangerous. You're just a messenger who got nailed."

She sucked in a breath. "Gee, thanks."

His hand squeezed hers. "I'm sorry; I didn't mean to be so harsh." He stood and shucked off his jeans and underwear, throwing them over the coat he'd draped over a chair.

"That doesn't change the fact that Adam's been a good friend to me. If he's in trouble, I have to help. What shouldn't I know about him? What are you keeping from me?"

"Can we talk about this later?"

"No," she answered, breathless.

"Answer me this, first. When you called the hotel, did you think I was having an affair?"

"No!" Of that she was sure; Ram was not a cheating man.

"Because," he continued, his voice like a curl of dark chocolate around her throat, "if you have any doubt, if you think I'm not making love to you enough"—Naked, he leaned one knee beside her on the bed, then began to run his lips across her neck, raising delicious shivers—"then I'll be glad to fix my behavior."

"No fixing necessary." She leaned back onto the bed, pulling him with her. "That behavior is quite satisfactory."

Then, since honesty seemed to be the policy for her tonight, she added, "Except—"

"What?" Definitely a touch of annoyance there now.

"I trust you, Ram; I just wish you'd trust me, too. Why won't you tell me what's going on?"

He sprawled the length of her, then braced his head with a propped elbow.

"We aren't going to make love until you get some answers, are we?" he asked, his voice resigned.

"What makes you say that?"

"Because you just shifted to lying there with your arms crossed, shutting me out."

"Geez, Ram, you're a man. You're not supposed to read body language."

"I'm a vet. Animals don't talk."

"Comparing me to a dog?"

"No. Dogs don't ask questions." He let out a slow breath. "I can't tell you what I know, Natalie, for a lot of reasons. I've made promises . . ."

She caressed his cheek. "That you would not break a promise, or a vow, is one of the things I love about you."

He turned his head to kiss her palm. "I could tell you to keep away from Adam, to forget everything."

"When pigs fly."

"That's what I thought. Do you think he wants you mucking in his affairs?"

She knew for a fact he didn't. "Doesn't always stop me."

He sighed. "That mage he went to see. She was murdered."

"Adam didn't kill her."

"No. But Adam Zolton is a dangerous man. There are sides of him you've never seen. If you really want to help, then when we get back to New Orleans, start searching for what—and who—caused this." He brushed her temple.

"Any ideas where to begin?"

"No. That's what makes it a challenge." He leaned over,

kissing her jaw, and she felt him smile against her skin. "Now, can we make love?"

"I'm not going anywhere." With that, she laughed and kissed him back.

Adam thanked Grace's GPS as he drove her car through the Ann Arbor streets. A haze of snow shrouded every landmark and smudged the edges of the road. Even the streetlights hid, their yellow light a diffuse glow in the mist. Only the flick-flick of the center line, a ghastly luminescent white, gave direction.

He glanced toward the passenger seat, where Grace stared intently at the window and chanted beneath her breath. What the hell was she doing?

They'd returned his rental, picked up some of Grace's things, then proceeded toward his motel to get his clothes and Gala. At least she'd agreed her condo was no longer safe. Neither was his motel.

To his surprise, Grace had asked him to drive, only to spend the time in muttering contemplation of the door. As she rubbed a hand across the frosted window and scowled, he asked, "What are you doing?"

She waved a hand, silencing him until her chant was finished. "Trying to unlock the car door."

"There's a button—"

"*I know.*" She shook her head in frustration. "Faith sent me an unlocking spell."

"To unlock what?"

"I don't know, but it seemed prudent to try it. You said you could feel the energies of magick; did you feel anything then?"

"Nothing to blip the radar." He lifted one shoulder. "I'm not infallible. It's like hearing. You shout in my ear; I take notice. A whisper across the room? Only with good acoustics. Something powerful, directed at me, I sense. Subtle spells or magick directed elsewhere may not cause a stir."

"Obviously mine wasn't either—directed at you or powerful."

"Once you have the ritual and the necessary focus, then the spell is driven by the will of the mage. Maybe unlocking the car's a nonevent."

"You mean I didn't want to unlock the door enough?"

"Or need to." He fell silent, watching the road, unable to quell an uneasy crawl in his stomach. That mist was getting thicker than a ghost tail. Not only were the roads treacherous, but he couldn't tell if the headlights that hit his rearview mirror on occasion were from one car following them or several different ones. He took an abrupt left, a maneuver to lose their tail if his suspicions weren't sheer paranoia.

When he detoured around the back of a strip mall, Grace asked, "Are we being followed?"

"Probably not."

"But no sense in taking chances." She twisted to watch as they pulled back onto the road. "I don't see anyone."

"Neither do I anymore."

"Can I examine those bands from Master Umari?"

He fished them from his pocket and tossed them to her.

She leaned forward to use the streetlight. The motion brought her close enough that the halo of her curls brushed against his cheek. His hands tightened around the wheel, squeezing out the urge to caress that sweet-smelling hair. The darkness, the close confines of the car, were too intimate.

"What are you looking for?" he asked, trying to distract himself.

"I'm not sure; something about them nags at me," she said absently, apparently oblivious to his undercurrent of keen awareness. She turned the bands around in her hands. "Did you feel any magick from them?" she asked.

"No, but once started, they could have been powered by electric impulses."

"Or maybe they aren't fueled by magick at all."

"I noticed you failed to mention them to the police."

"So did you. So did Master Umari." She prodded the flexible cable with a fingernail.

"Find anything?"

A grunt for an answer meant she was concentrating, so he focused on the light traffic and on her subtle scents of soap and hand cream.

A faint buzz broke the quiet of the car, startling him until Grace pulled out her phone. Instead of answering, she started a rapid-click text conversation.

Judging by her smile, she liked the person on the other end. At her soft laugh, Adam's foot tightened against the accelerator. Who brought that glow to her face?

The car strained around a curve, and Adam relaxed his foot, slowing. A jealousy-fueled wreck, they didn't need. He had no claims on her. Undoubtedly in six years she hadn't taken any vows of celibacy; he'd lived like no saint, either. Still, rational or not, now that Grace was back in his life, he wanted to keep her there.

Which meant knowing his rivals.

"Are you involved with someone?" he asked, as she pocketed the phone.

"I wouldn't have kissed you, if I were. Are you?"

The dark tension in his gut eased. "No." He wanted no doubts on that.

"How long since your last committed relationship?"

He thought back, and realized he'd committed to none of his relationships since Grace. He'd been faithful, attentive, but in the back of his mind, he'd always known they'd end. "Two years ago," he said, figuring that six months of dating qualified. "She took a job in Houston, and neither of us wanted the effort of a long-distance relationship. How about you?"

"Med school. We were serious until I got the residency he wanted. Then I learned some less attractive aspects of his character." She lifted one shoulder. "Since then, I've been too busy to expend the energy for anything more than casual."

Good. No romantic rivals. Only her work, but that he accepted.

"I'll wait in the car," she offered as they pulled into the motel lot.

"Come in and meet my pet, Gala." He didn't want Grace sitting alone in the car, although the headlights he'd noticed didn't seem to have followed him in.

"You have a pet?" she questioned as they got out of the car and trudged through the swirls of wind and snow to his door.

"Don't sound so incredulous." He went inside first, eschewing chivalry for safety.

No magickal intruders. All secure except for Gala's box. The wily ferret had gotten out again. Gathering his few items, he called for the ferret.

Gala poked a black nose out from behind the bureau, and then wriggled to Grace.

"You travel with a ferret?"

"She was Faith's."

"And you couldn't leave her?" Grace's face softened, and for the first time in years he thought he saw a glint of admiration.

"The cabin was cold; she could have frozen." He shrugged and packed up Gala's supplies—the ferret had accumulated more luggage than he.

Grace crouched down and held out her hand. "Hello, Gala."

The ferret sniffed Grace's shoes and hand, then pointedly turned her back and scampered back to him.

Grace laughed. "It appears she's chosen her favorite."

"At least she didn't bite you." He tilted the box. "Okay, Gala, into your travel cage."

Gala looked from him to the box, strolled over . . . and peed on the cardboard.

Grace laughed again. "Guess what she thinks of that idea."

Can't cage her, though. Leave her free, and she will always come back. Remembering what Faith had told him, he shoved his gloves into one pocket, then knelt and opened his other pocket in invitation. Gala scrambled up his leg and into the cocoon.

"Feel like a damn kangaroo," he muttered.

Abandoning the smelly box, they left.

A few moments to stow the gear in the car, and then they were off, Grace driving, Gala scooting out of Adam's pocket to curl up in the backseat. He pulled out his computer and inserted the flash drive Grace had given him.

"I think Faith left us clues to where she hid the library," Grace commented, "but damned if I can figure them out. Maybe you'll have more luck."

He'd better, because he was not losing that library.

"You can look through it while I stop at the lab. That call I got—The project leader for my research needs to see me."

"Kea Lin?"

"You've heard of him?"

"I've read his papers. His theories of pain management are revolutionary. What's up?"

"Work," she said vaguely, "but since the project is military funded, you're not cleared to come with me past the offices."

"It's New Year's Day. No one will be about. You could sneak me in."

"No, I couldn't."

He wasn't sure if her refusal meant the security was too

tight or she simply wouldn't flaunt the rules. He suspected the latter. Much as he didn't like her going in alone, not a damn thing he could do about it, short of caveman tactics. There were disadvantages to being a semicivilized male with an independent woman.

Tabling the fruitless protest, he pulled up the data and ran a quick overview. Not much to go on. "The third e-mail—"

Her jaw set. "Was personal." She tapped out a rhythm on the car wheel. "On the second e-mail, highlight the empty space at the bottom. Faith embedded some information there."

"Right. Lady of the Lake? Still not much to go on. I know this woman, owns an antique bookstore. She might give us a lead on the references." He glanced at his watch. Wouldn't be too late for Glinda. He dialed her up. "Hi, Glinda, love. Adam Zolton."

"As if I wouldn't recognize that accent."

"Putting you on speakerphone so my friend Grace can hear."

She chuckled. "Guess that means I hafta behave. What can I do you for?"

"I'm trying to find two books. *Saga of Cadwaladar, 1490,* and *Legends, Y Ddraig Goch.*"

"Last one you won't find. It's referred to in a few fragments—a tale about an encounter with a dragon—but no copy's ever surfaced. Cadwaladar, though, is available in translation. I have one here in the store. I can put it aside if you want to pick it up."

"I'm in Michigan. Ann Arbor. Can you FedEx it? Fastest possible?"

"I can't send it out until tomorrow, so day after's the soonest you'll have it," she said. "It's not long. Want me to scan it, send you an electronic copy, too?"

"Please."

"You take care now, sugar."

"You, too."

By the time he'd disconnected, they'd reached the lab and Grace turned off the engine. He looked up to see the mist of snow had not subsided. Instead, the minute crystals swirled on a sullen wind, concealing all but a smear of yellow light. In the silence, the eerie whistle sent a chill down his spine. The night looked too much like the netherworld of purgatory for ease.

"I'll be about an hour." Grace wrapped her scarf around her neck.

"I'll wait inside." Adam opened his pocket. "Gala, too cold to stay here."

He was pleased, though no longer surprised, when she seemed to understand. A few curious snuffles around his jacket, then she popped into the pocket. Uneasy with this sudden call, with the limited visibility in the snow, Adam stayed near Grace. He rested a hand at her waist, keeping them close.

Now, there was heat.

Inside the lobby, Grace turned to him. "Would you like to meet Kea?"

"Definitely." Wet diamonds glittered atop her hair. He brushed the back of his hand against the soft curls, wiping away the snow. "Your secrets won't change what's between us. I'll be here when you're finished."

She laid a palm against his shoulder, and he thought she meant to push him away. Instead, she matched his action, wiping away the damp. "I'm counting on that. Afterward, we'll find a couple of hotel rooms—"

He cut her off with a shake of his head. "Not separate. A suite, from here on out, Grace. We can't risk being alone."

He felt a flood of heat at her nod, disappointment at the idea of a suite. What he wanted was one bedroom, one bed.

Good thing magick talents didn't run to mind reading.

"C'mon, Kea will be in his office."

The research grant dollars, Adam decided as he accompanied Grace, had all gone for equipment. The standard-issue rectangles were crammed with gleaming chromatographs, hoods, and computers. Right-brain whimsies, however, were in short supply. No art in the halls. No green plants. Not even a newspaper cartoon taped to a shelf.

A faint tap carried down the hall, followed by a cultured voice calling, "Grace."

Adam turned with Grace to see the man he assumed was Kea Lin coming toward them. Immediate impressions held two surprises—the scientist was younger than he'd expected and the tapping sound came from Lin's cane.

As they waited for Lin to join them, Adam surveyed the man who could beckon at seven on New Year's night and expect Grace to answer. Couldn't be more than late thirties, which put him into genius category, given his numerous papers and accolades. Good-looking in a mussy-brilliant-scientist sort of way. Maybe the need for the cane was why he never presented at symposia.

Lin greeted Grace, and then shook hands with Adam. "Grace never mentioned you."

"Old friend," he answered. "We're looking forward to renewing our acquaintance."

"Then my apologies for intruding." Polite words that meant just the opposite.

All civilized, but here was his rival. Adam's casual nod hid the rush of challenge. As they headed down the hall, Lin rested his free hand on Grace's arm with a familiarity that masqueraded as a need for support. From the subtle body language, Lin was possessive of Grace. Maybe their relationship was not sexual, but the man didn't want Grace distracted.

Not that Grace would appreciate their masculine posturing. Tough. Adam narrowed the space between them.

Lin paused at a door with a card access. "Security only allows authorized personnel past here."

Grace would be safe inside, among the security cameras and the locked doors. No need for a pissing contest; soon, he'd have Grace to himself. "Where shall I wait?"

"The herb garden," Grace suggested.

Adam lifted his brows. "Herb gardens in this stainless setting?"

"One of our researchers is analyzing micronutrients for synthetic-based nanonutrition."

"Nanonutrition. Now's there's a buzz word."

"Dr. Mubarak would be more than eager to share his theories," Lin said. "You could spend three hours talking about calcium—"

"—then segue into another four on free radicals," Grace finished.

"If we meet, I'll make a note of that." Adam would assign the topic to one of his reporters. Nanonutrition. Engineered food. Lot of ways to go. The end of pesticides or of natural growth? An end to world hunger or to biodiversity? Shadows of food wafers or Soylent Green?

"Seems a far cry from battlefield analgesia," he said as they changed directions to the garden. At Lin's surprised look he added, "I read the abstract of her last presentation at the Emergency Medicine conference."

He'd read about the soldier-administered analgesic— an attempt to reduce post-traumatic pain complications— because he'd set up his net explorer to send him any mentions of Grace Armatrading, but he didn't figure he should share that fact. Instead he said, "Medical research is a deep well for my readers, alert as they are for the next Frankenstein or Ebola."

Lin's snort of irritation surprised him not one iota.

Grace stepped between them. "Nano applications are diverse."

They passed through a locked door, into the open air. Beyond the plants, he could see swirling snow—and not much else—but the immediate area was snow free and surprisingly warm.

"You should be comfortable enough," Grace said. "Dr. M keeps the site heated."

"There's also an electronic fence that's alarmed, so don't go past the perimeter," Lin added.

"Thanks." He kept from looking down as he felt the drowsing Gala stir, then wriggle out and into the jungle. When Grace and Dr. Lin left him, Adam called softly, "Roam if you want, but not past the perimeter."

He paced through the herbs, snapping a few photos. Gardening had never interested him, but at least the heaters kept away the snow and cold. For the first time in three days his feet were warm. No friendly little signs identified the plants, but he must have learned something over the years, because he recognized a few of the leaves.

A chill slid across his face, icy and fetid. Nostrils tight, spine tense, he spun, searching for a threat, but saw nothing, felt nothing more. A quick repeat survey through the jungle yielded no intruder. Maybe the ventilation?

Still, he felt center stage in a lush cage. Lions at the zoo had a spacious enclosure without visible bars; didn't mean they weren't trapped.

The perimeter might be alarmed, but the door wasn't. A fact he verified. Peering into the empty corridor, he considered exploring the labs.

Except he'd be abandoning Gala.

Bloody, troublesome pet. Well, he could catch up on work, return some voice mails, keep his mind off his Tarzan-décor cell. He leaned one shoulder against the wall. Too bad he hadn't brought his computer in—

His computer! He straightened, his breath catching. *Oh, my God.* That was it. Faith's Lady of the Lake clue.

He pulled out his phone and sent Grace a text: *Hurry. Know answer to hidden ink. Virus still possible. Where can we be away from others?* When they opened the library, he wanted to be sure they wouldn't endanger anyone else.

He had to get the computer from the car. "Gala," he called, and stuck the phone in his pocket.

His empty pocket. No flash drive. Hell! He searched both jacket pockets, pants pockets. No way had he accidentally dropped it, which meant—

"Gala," he snarled. "Bring it back."

The ferret popped out from beneath a leaf, and sure enough the imp had his flash drive in her mouth. He knelt down and held out his hand. "Give it here."

Instead of surrendering her toy, she turned tail and scurried beneath the plants. Irritated, Adam hurried after, following her rustling. She emerged from the underbrush, heading straight toward the perimeter. The damn ferret, with his data in her mouth, was going to set off the alarms.

"No, Gala!" He dove for her.

A sharp whine over his head set his fillings bursting with metallic pain. The second blast of whatever-the-hell-whine-it-was seared his cheek. Riveting pain nailed him to the ground.

He rolled away from the third attack, seeing Gala scramble across the perimeter. No blaring. Someone had left it unalarmed.

Beneath the cover of leaves, he scrambled to his feet and immediately sidled out of sight. Touching the burning nerves on his face, he was surprised to find no blood. A weapon that attacked from the inside? Handy for making murder look like an untimely heart attack.

The whines had stopped, as the attacker sought his prey, but Adam decided he didn't fancy the prey label.

He had no distance weapon on him, so it was flight or close combat. Prudence called for flight, though primitive man bellowed for retribution.

A thin, cut-off scream—*Gala?*—decided him. He pulled his knife from his leg sheath and stole into the swirls of snow.

The chalky night erased all but basic sensations: white, cold, the muffled whirr of wind. Then, to his left, he smelled body odor. Somebody was sweating. He slid toward the telltale scent. Ah, gotcha, in that patch of dark.

If these were Grace's attackers, there should be a second about. Where? No sign or scent of him. Take out the first and even the odds. He circled behind, struck and ruthlessly pinned the fighter face-first onto the snow. "What are you after?" he snarled, his arm lifting for the final blow.

"You, dead." The answer came flat and chillingly assured.

And in that brief second between the last word and seeing the shadow of the second attacker from the corner of his eye, he realized his mistake.

Should have run. The killing pain slashed across his throat, and Adam tumbled to the ground.

•

CHAPTER SEVEN

"I assume you know who he is?" Kea rubbed a finger along the crease of his lips, a sure sign of irritation. "The editor of *NONE*."

"Of course. I'm surprised you do, though."

"The way his rag exposes power? Puts us in danger?"

"I'm on vacation, and he's . . . It's complicated."

"What about your talent?"

"He knows, and he's not interested."

Kea gave a snort of disbelief. "What about our research? *NONE* wouldn't bury that exclusive."

"He wouldn't—" Grace cut off the protest; Kea's scalpel-sharp accusation highlighted her own doubts. Adam had been very clear he didn't approve of mixing science and magick. "I know, but I have to go with him."

"You won't tell him about us, about the work we do. About me. I want your promise, Grace."

"You don't trust my judgment?" she snapped back.

"Not right now. This is too important for some lurid headline plastered by a reporter who wouldn't know truth if it bit him on the ass."

She swallowed the retort that his judgment of Adam was off base. "Trust me to protect our work."

"I do, but—" He stared at her as if he were really seeing her for the first time tonight. "Grace, what happened? Your face looks like you went ten rounds."

"I was mugged in the parking lot after work."

"Oh, my dear. Was the mugger caught?"

She shook her head, wincing a bit as the bruise throbbed. "And . . . my aunt was murdered, Kea."

"I am so sorry. All that, yet you came for me tonight. And here all I've done is harangue you."

They were sitting in Kea's office, a small windowless square off the primary lab. "That's okay; I know the pain's talking, too."

"That obvious?" He braced both hands on the head of the cane.

"Only to me. Glaze in your eyes, slower gait, and your limp got more pronounced with each step."

"Can't fool a pain expert." His eyes narrowed. "Why are you with Adam?"

For the first time, Grace hesitated. She trusted Kea. More than she trusted Adam, she admitted. Or at least, more than she had forty-eight hours ago.

If she'd faced this question then, no doubt she'd have hashed everything over with Kea. But tonight, too much of her life had skewed into strange.

Faith had warned her to put her trust only in Adam.

She hated to confess weakness. To anyone, even a friend.

In the end, she settled for part of the truth. "Adam can help me get to the bottom of my aunt's death. The police can't."

He shook his head. "Damn, but you are stubborn."

"Says the man in agony." Another reason she couldn't burden Kea. "Let me help you."

"Wait a moment." Kea left and when he returned, he carried a small box. He sank down onto a specially designed chair. The padding offered comfort, but the wood frame gave the support he needed.

"The pain's been worse," Grace observed, pulling a three-legged stool beside him. "And not just tonight."

"Unfortunately," he admitted with a sigh.

Kea's neuropathy was intermittent rather than continuous, a strange mix of pain and vigor. Yet she saw the toll of disease and work stress in his eyes and in the lines at his mouth. Even with the graying of fatigue, though, he was still a handsome man, one who'd cut a swath through the women of the lab.

Why had she never accepted his subtle offer—the one that was out there, but never intrusive or demanding? Maybe because they'd always been coworkers and she didn't believe in mixing work and play.

Or maybe because he had short, wiry hair instead of dark silk long enough to be tied back, or because his conversation was engineer blunt, instead of laced with tales of fallen deities.

She shoved those thoughts aside, to touch Kea's wrists. "Let's get started."

He grabbed her hands in a clasp uncomfortably intimate. "Not the way you think."

For a moment, the hinted suggestiveness of his words startled her; then she caught the gleam of excitement. Her breath sucked in. "The sensors are functional?"

He retrieved the box he'd brought in and handed it to her with a smile. "We'll only know when you test them."

From inside the box, she pulled out a visor—a strip the width of her eyes that looked like a flexible prism—and a pair of ivory gloves, so thin and slick she had difficulty holding on to them. When she got them on, though, they felt as natural as skin. She moved her hands. "The fabric shimmers like ground opals."

"Those are the monitors and haptic transmitters. The visor gives you another visual."

The powerful analgesic they'd developed targeted mu and kappa pain receptors and was absorbed through the skin. Their revolutionary approach came with delivering that analgesic to the proper sites. Kea had attached the drug to functional nanobots, smart bots that would provide rapid and precise pain relief. So far, though, one major sticking point for all biobot research was a source of energy to get the little miracles moving and working in the body.

Kea's very private theory? Her magick talent could activate the bots and direct them toward the pain. These sensors were the first step—to measure and characterize the energy as she worked. If they could scientifically duplicate that spell, they'd have a field analgesic that would precisely locate and stop pain.

"Let me cleanse the area, set up our circle first, Grace."

She watched while he set a smudge pot of sage burning, and then chanted a small circle around their work area, a barrier to unwanted powers and spirits.

"Ready." Kea sat back in the chair.

"Where's the pain the worst?"

"My head."

"No," she cautioned. "I won't go into your brain."

"My left leg, then." He shoved off his pants, leaving himself dressed in a pair of silk boxers.

Paying no attention to his near nudity—at this moment he was her patient—she laid her left hand atop the bare flesh of his thigh. The firing neurons had forced the hard muscle into tight knots.

"Geez, Kea, how do you stand it?"

"The headache is worse."

"One day, if this works, you'll be able to control that, too."

"I'm counting on it," he grunted.

She put on the visor and found it was like peering through prismatic glasses. Everything she looked at was haloed in color. She laid her other hand at the base of his spine, beneath his shirt. Here, too, the muscles twitched and knotted. A faint tingling, like a low-level electric charge, coursed across her palms, begging her to add the song of her own magick to the mix. After one steadying breath, she began the chant she'd learned so many years ago, the minimal magick she'd mastered. To relieve suffering, her primary skill and purpose.

Normally she had to rely on a mental visualization of her kinetic sensitivity to find the pattern of those energies and capture the essence of pain. Once she had that, she'd shift her chant from discovery to healing and pour her power into altering the nerve firings.

Using the visor, though, she saw the gloves glow in an ever undulating, shimmering pattern, like moonlight playing across mother of pearl—the patterns of suffering nerves. The visor picked up the patterns, translated them to a crosshatch of colored, firing lines. She trickled the first bit of her healing energy into Kea. On the visor, a single red line stopped its mad sparking and settled into a soothing flow.

She didn't have to rely on imagination; she could actually see as she worked!

Not only did she see those patterns, she felt them. Not as pain, but as tingling waves on her fingertips. Her body vibrated in resonance with the energy and her hands burned with the fiery power.

"Too hot?" she asked.

"Keep going."

Even with the sensors, though, she couldn't weave a healing pattern amid so much pain. "I can't get a lock on the energy; it keeps sliding away."

Kea reached into his pocket and held up a vial. "One drop left over from the last experiment." The droplet clung to the glass rod on the inside. A nanobot of analgesia.

"No!" The brilliant fool was testing on himself! The magick swirled around her in a maelstrom of power, ricocheting off the circle he'd erected. If she stopped, what damage would she do? Unable to break away from the healing, she watched through the field of crisscrossing lines as he broke open the vial, tilted his head back, and placed the precious drop inside his nasal cavity.

"I've tagged the bot, Grace. Find it. Send it."

The faint opalescent glow on the gloves deepened into a rainbow, so rich that her eyes hurt. Improbably lovely for a mirror of pain. Within the beautiful hurt she caught the pinpoints of the elegant spell Kea had used to mark the bots for her. Shoving back her horror, focusing on her patient, she found the dots of soothing analgesic and scooped them slowly, carefully, into the pain, like water in the fire of blood.

The nanoparticles of analgesic, carried by bots, were activated. By her will, her energy, her magick. As the analgesic worked, she added her skill.

The knots of muscles relaxed. Healing fanned along highways of nerves. Kea gave a peaceful sigh and through the haze she saw his eyes clear.

Suddenly pain needled into her temples from the visor. The glistening colors slithered off the gloves, snaking deep beneath his skin.

Colors that blinked and coiled like the bands around Master Umari's wrists. Kea's sigh turned to a groan, a guttural sound of agony.

She tried to lift her hands, to stop whatever she'd done, but the gloves fused to Kea's flesh with infinitely thin threads of nanocolor.

"Don't stop," he snarled, grabbing her. His fingertips ground into her wrists, digging into the radial artery. Blood seeped down her fingers, adding dark crimson to the jeweled colors.

The pain boomeranged and whacked into her. Her vision tilted, the room and Kea forming into jagged bolts.

Shit, shit, shit! No!

Blackness descended on her.

"You failed to apprehend Dr. Armatrading?"

Lonnie suppressed the involuntary shudder at the pleasantly

voiced question. He knew what happened to failures; he'd seen the experiments, even participated in some.

They'd seemed fun, then.

He swallowed, tasting a trickle of blood from his broken nose, and ignored Ed trudging beside him, as they used the cover of snow to circle the lab. At least he'd been wise enough to phone in, rather than appear in person. "We found her."

"Does that mean you had lost her?" Even through the phone line, the unforgiving voice dripped slivers of warning.

"She had help," Lonnie protested, pressing a hand against his cheek. Fuck, but that nose burned like the devil. "Never saw this guy before." He thought, desperate for some scrap of redemption. "She called him Adam."

"Adam." The venomous tone burned the air. Lonnie couldn't tell if the other knew Adam had been at Umari's or was surprised, but either way, this Adam was no stranger.

"We can finish the job." Lonnie had seen what happened when recruits were no longer needed. That was why he'd always made sure he was both useful and successful.

"That won't be necessary."

"This Adam's taken care of; now we'll finish going after the doc."

"Taken care of? You killed him?" demanded the caller.

"Yeah."

"Got it." Ed picked the lock on the door, heard it click open.

Lonnie's orders were to not kill the doctor, but he didn't have to make the capture pleasant. A faint sound came from the lab building. An alarm? "Doc'll be yours tomorrow." He disconnected and reached for his trusty AK. Those fancy electronic weapons were sweet, but an old-fashioned bullet had its uses. Any other pain-in-the-ass defenders were expendable and to hell with the noise. Maybe offing one would erase some of the pain of his nose.

His phone buzzed. Lonnie stared at the screen, then decided he didn't want the consequences of not answering. "I want to get this right—"

"No." The voice sent that single word across his heating phone and into his brain. "Your rashness is a danger."

His hands spasmed around the receiver, forcing him to hold the connection. He couldn't escape. Not the high-pitched whine that followed, not the energy blast that came through the phone. All choice burned away in white-filled agony. He heard his own voice scream, shrill and harsh. Lonnie whimpered under the Dragon's breath and descended into hell.

The phone dropped.

"Ed." With the persistence of death, the voice sounded over the phone.

Gingerly, Ed picked it up with two fingers, holding it well away from his ear. "Yes?"

"When he recovers, Lonnie will remember the importance of discretion and obedience. Keep him with you, but your orders have changed. Don't go after the doctor. Not yet."

"Do you want me to follow her?"

A pause, as the voice considered. "Not at the moment."

Call finished, Ed gave the phone one last look before he hid it in his pocket. Their gear was the latest tech, but he'd never seen tech act like that. Lucky he didn't have to understand it, just follow orders.

Like his grandpa had learned in Japan, like his daddy had learned in 'Nam, like he'd learned in Iraq—think only how to get the necessary jobs done. He was protecting his people, the life of his kids—that was what he needed to know.

Still, never hurt to keep your eyes and ears alert. Make sure you weren't being fooled about the objective.

As he blended back into the snow, leading a weeping Lonnie and holding his breath against the smell of his partner's involuntary bowel and bladder release, the pocketed phone seemed alive and ominous as an albatross.

She wasn't in Kea's office.

Realizing she was lying down instead of sitting, Grace pushed herself upright. She glanced around, fighting bone-deep aches. How the hell had she gotten onto the lab's crash cot?

She swung her feet to the floor, and then moaned at the wash of nausea and headache. As she braced her head, waiting for the swimming to stop, she noted that her hands and wrists showed no damage. No burns, no trickling blood or nail gouges.

"You're awake!" Carrying a mug, Kea hurried into the room. When she attempted to stand, he commanded. "No, sit. Have some of my coffee."

She took a sip from the mug, which stated: NANO ENGINEERS: CHANGING THE WORLD ONE SUBMOLECULE AT A TIME, then wrinkled her nose. "Blech. Cold and it's got Cremora."

"Evaporated milk. At least you're getting back to normal."

"That was a damn fool stunt." She shoved her hair from her face. "But the bots worked. You're walking without your cane."

He frowned. "What are you talking about, Grace? I haven't had any recent pain, and the bots are still experimental."

"No, you were in pain, using the cane; the headache was new, though. We used the gloves, and . . ." She tried to remember. "Something went wrong."

He gave her a glance she could only deem pitying, damn him. "I don't know what you're talking about."

"You asked me to come here—"

He shook his head, cutting her off. "You called me. New Year's Eve."

"No, I met Natalie—"

"You didn't mention a Natalie. Right after you got off work, you came to the lab." His hard voice was inexorable, interrupting her confusion with cold facts. "You asked me not to tell anyone, asked me to run an EEG. I ran the tests, you said you felt strange and wanted to sleep, so you crashed here."

She raked back her hair. A dream? "What about Faith? Adam!"

"Who are they?"

"Dammit, Kea, this isn't funny. Where's Adam?" She shoved to her feet, strode into the garden, and felt as though she'd slammed into an iron wall.

The sun was poking up above the horizon, bringing streaks of yellow into the gray day. Wasn't it nighttime? But the light let her easily see the garden was empty of anything resembling six-foot-plus of dark-haired, charismatic male.

"Adam," she whispered, swallowing hard. *We stay together.* He wouldn't have left her.

Unless she had dreamt him.

"I'm sorry, Grace." This time, Kea's voice was infinitely sad and soothing. "No Adam came with you. You've been at the lab for the past thirty hours, ever since you got off shift."

CHAPTER EIGHT

Grace fought back a wave of panic. *Use the adrenaline kick. Think.* Either she'd imagined Adam, imagined a kiss both sweet and passionate, or this was the illusion and her closest friend was gaslighting her. They were equally unpleasant scenarios. Either one made her profoundly delusional.

She dug her nails into her palms, bringing pain, and shoved her fists into her pockets. There should have been a thumb drive there, the one she'd created from Faith's files and replicated for Adam.

Nothing but lint and a quarter.

"No," she whispered, starting to shake, her throat raw with nausea. "I'm not catatonic or delusional."

Yet this felt so real. The dry, cold winter air raised goose bumps on her arms. Static snapped when she touched the metal doors.

Kea held out her jacket. "It's too cold to stand out here bare armed. Come with me, Grace. Remember? We're going to find the library. You wanted the Torch of I'celus."

"I did? Yes . . ." Her feet dragged forward, propelled not by her will, but by surrender. The garden blurred to a mass of green, the color of nausea. If only she could find some anomaly that would prove this was a nightmare.

"It's midnight. I came with Adam," she repeated, though the words sounded more and more false. She jammed her hands against the door frame, relishing the cold metal burning them.

She had to believe in herself. In her mind. Wanted to believe her memories were real and *this* was . . . something else. If that belief meant Kea was a lying bastard or that she needed megadoses of Haldol, then so be it. She tilted her head, staring at Kea. "Why are you lying?"

"I'm not." He sounded weary as he rubbed a hand across his eyes. "I'm telling you what I know."

She refused to accept the lie. Her lips curled in tight anger. "Dammit—"

The words broke off. Was Kea as unknowing as she in this alternate world? Was he a mere figment?

What was this? All wrong, all right, or a mix of real and unreal? Brain tumor? Drugs? Delusions? Virtual reality? Created by what monstrous, awesome mind or machine? A dream or a trip to an alternate reality? A slip in the space-time continuum?

Questions spun for later, adding a jumble of possibilities on top of confusion and doubt. Too damn much to think about.

Don't think. At the whispering command, her mind let go of details. What had she been doing?

"Come inside," Kea said gently.

Why was she braced against the door, like a small child refusing to go inside after a day of play? She lifted one hand.

Her hand and arm prickled, as if spiders with claws were running up the bare flesh. She shook it hard, throwing off the invisible pest. A faint, different scent came to her. Not mold. Not Kea's light aftershave. Not greenery.

Musky. Like a ferret.

"This is not real," she whispered, holding that one truth. How to break the gruesome grip of insanity?

She turned her back on the lab and drew on a mantle of

icy logic. She needed something important to grasp. Adam. If she was standing in the garden, and he wasn't here, then something had happened to him.

Adam. Her anchor. Not her job, not a return to the bustling ER, not any of the docs or her softball teammates. Maybe because he was wrapped up with Faith, and with magick.

Because he was the part of her where id overruled ego and rationality.

Grabbing her coat, shoving her arms into the sleeves, she stormed out of the garden and over the lawn, calling his name. "Adam!"

"What are you doing?" Kea hissed. "People are watching."

"Let them. Adam!"

"You're putting on a display. Losing their respect."

She faltered as she looked around and saw puzzlement and wariness on the faces dotting the research campus. Reputation was such a fragile asset.

She drew in a breath. She was not crazy.

A whiff of musk led her forward. Beside her, Kea vanished. Her surroundings blurred, like a painting smudged by water. Reformed into a jungle obscured by fog, a place both eerily familiar and utterly wrong. Where was she? Sweat collected at her nape, her brow.

"Lead me," she whispered.

Grace.

A call that could not be heard, was not a part of this world. Yet somehow the deep voice with its faint accent rolled inside her, wrapping around her heart.

He wasn't here.

She ran forward, eyes closed, blotting out the world painted before her. Instead, on the canvas of imagination and sanity, she pictured the world she wanted. Night. The gray behind her eyes darkened to charcoal. Cold. Her skin tightened, her nostrils pinched against crisp air. She stuck out her tongue. The taste of swirling snow. Her mind's eye traveled forward, into the reality that might be true madness.

Her feet slammed into something hard, and she tripped. Flailing the air uselessly for balance, she tumbled to the ground, slamming her hip against frozen ground, burying her face in snow.

A fist of pain punched agony across every nerve and tissue. She seemed to burst out of her skin, exploding with pain and release.

The pain vanished.

The sun behind fog vanished.

The dark that now covered her was night, not fugue illusion.

She was spread-eagled in a foot of snow, aware of new sources of pain. The wet cold sent numb aches up her knees. Her whole body shook as though she'd been given a local nerve block. A migraine stood on the bridge of her nose and stomped down with both feet.

Vomit rose in her throat. She turned her head to the side, pressing her lips together hard until the urge faded. And at that moment, she realized she wasn't alone.

She'd tripped over Adam where he sprawled in the snow. Her legs were draped across his cold chest. Gala, an inch from her face and chittering madly, dropped a flash drive into her palm and then nipped her finger. Frantically spitting snow from her mouth, Grace righted herself and crawled to Adam.

"Grace, what the—" Kea hurried up and swore as he caught sight of Adam. "Is he dead?" Yanking his cell from his pocket, he called for an ambulance.

The question galvanized her. Rapidly, she sought a pulse and found one, very faint, and fading. "I'm losing him!"

Kea crouched beside her and turned his cell so the screen cast its pale blue light over Adam.

"His throat's bruised." Her fingers touched the mottled,

cold flesh, and her mouth filled with the taste of iron. "He's still bleeding."

Internally suffocating on his own blood.

She had to stop the hemorrhage. She couldn't. What if drawing on her magick made her vanish back into that netherworld? What if she killed Adam?

"You have to stop the bleeding, Grace. If you don't, he'll die." Kea's faint voice vocalized her thoughts.

If her last sane action was saving Adam, the price was worth paying. Grabbing air, Grace laid her hands on him, digging deep inside herself.

Power flowed through her, stronger than she'd ever felt, a deeper well than she'd ever drawn on. At first something inside him fought against her.

"Adam, it's me. Grace. Let me help."

At the sound of her voice, his defenses relaxed. Flesh knit beneath her fingers, and Adam's throbbing pulse steadied and strengthened. At last, as the red circle of an ambulance cut through the night, Adam opened his eyes. He tried to speak, but apparently his throat was too raw, for the sound was less than Gala's squeak.

"The ambulance is here," she gently told him. "I'll be right behind." At the assurance, he closed his eyes again.

She wasn't allowed to ride in the ambulance. After scooping Gala into her pocket—to her surprise, the ferret hadn't gone running off—she turned to Kea. She had to know what had gone on tonight. Which story he would proffer.

"You ran up here, but earlier tonight you were in pain."

"Worse than it's been for quite a long time. The bots worked!"

For a moment, she couldn't resist the thrill of discovery, knowing they stood on the cusp of something awesome; then she scowled at him. "That was dangerous. Crazy science, Kea. We don't experiment on ourselves."

"I was desperate."

"And you brought me into your desperation without any options."

He snorted. "You put on the gloves; you were eager to test our theories."

She bit back her retort, knowing one part of her, the one that had always driven her into her worst troubles, had been excited to take the next step. Otherwise, she would have found a way to stop it. Not the issue right now. "Then you had the gall to deny everything. Adam, the pain, the bots."

"*What?* When you healed me, something . . . boomeranged. Maybe your power tried to link with mine? I don't know. All I know is, whatever happened, it knocked me senseless."

"Did you have hallucinations?"

He shook his head. "I was out for a few seconds, that's all. When I woke up, you were gone and I heard Mubarak yelling someone had set off his garden alarm, so I ran out."

"Why were you so anxious for me to heal Adam?" she asked with suspicion.

He reared back as though struck. "What kind of a monster do you suddenly think I am? He's a human being and your friend. What more reason do I need?"

Kea was a man with blinders when it came to his research, but he was a good man and a good friend. She shook her head. "I'm sorry. Whatever happened affected me differently."

"How?"

Not now. She wasn't ready to share every detail with Kea; she had to get to the hospital. Striding to the cars, she said, "We can talk about it later."

"Are you okay now?"

"I'm fine." A thought occurred to her. For, if she believed in her own sanity, then tonight had been a very clever, very dangerous attack. "The circle you established, what spell or entity could have penetrated it?"

To her relief, he didn't take affront at the question. "None that I know. My shields are adept, and I've always been well protected."

"How about something nonmagick?"

He sucked in a breath. "Like a bullet or a tranq dart?"

She shrugged one shoulder, leaving the question open-ended.

"I protect against magick," he said at last. "Not technology."

Grace leaned against the brick wall outside the ER, bouncing a small rubber ball. Toss, catch, toss, catch. Rhythmic action had always helped her focus, gave her chaotic thoughts or emotions structure.

Tonight, however, the ritual didn't work.

Beyond trying to make sense of what had happened to her, she was beset by anxiety. Adam was being examined, tested, probably admitted, and because she wasn't a relative, she was banished to the fringes. Just one lonely stranger in a familiar crowd. She had empathy, now, for the families who waited for word of their loved ones, sitting on hard chairs, wrapped in their individual circles of pain.

Red light circled across her eyes. Another ambulance, another crisis. As the paramedics wheeled in the victim, they barked out their report. "BP's 70 over 40. Hand's crushed." If she were inside, she'd be issuing orders: Pressors and D5 Lactated for the hypotension, splint the broken bones. Triage came as naturally as breathing.

So, how could she name the damaged bones, calculate the dose of dopamine and yet not trust this was real?

Because her gut confirmed what her mind experienced. If she couldn't trust mind or memory, then she'd have to trust instinct and intuition. Relying on intangibles unsettled her, though.

Get over it, Grace. She stiffened her shoulders and caught the ball, then shoved it in her pocket. Her fugues had a cause, and she'd find it.

The two paramedics who'd brought Adam in came out of the ER, having dropped off a fresh case. One of them came over to her.

"How's your friend, Dr. Armatrading?"

"I don't know. He's being seen."

"You aren't waiting with him?"

"You know the HIPAA privacy rules. I'm not family."

The paramedic grimaced in sympathy. "He was stable with all vitals when we got him here." His phone crackled at his waist. "Sorry, gotta run." Picking it up, he turned on his heel, headed back to his wheels.

"Wait, LaVon." Maybe Adam had woken up while they were in transit, said something.

The air around LaVon shimmered, like heat off an oasis if it weren't so damn cold. He turned, peering right at her with a puzzled look, but not answering.

"Did Adam wake up on the way here?" she asked.

He scratched his jaw and glanced around as if looking for something, then, to her surprise, turned away without a word.

"Your words sound like buzzing to him," said a smooth voice beside her.

Grace spun to find a man standing too close, within her two-foot personal radius. She took a step back. Another bloody hallucination?

He put a single finger to her wrist. "Don't move away."

She froze. Her heart beat against her ribs, but that was the only muscle making contractions. *Wake up, wake up.* God, she hadn't even had a warning this time. "Are you real?"

He chuckled, a pleasant, melodious sound. "Very."

That she could believe. The man radiated masculine vitality. Handsome, too, if you favored your men with smooth dark hair, desert gold skin, and a face from the Greek gods—cheekbones, nose, and all.

This felt different from her fugue. Weird, but real.

"Why can't he hear me?"

"I've thrown a glamour around us. We're invisible and silent." He gave an impatient glance toward the ER entrance. "We haven't much time, Grace."

"How do you know me?"

"I'm Khalil, Weaver for the Magi. I was a friend of Faith Grimaldi."

"She never mentioned you."

"She never mentioned you, either. Or the power that swirls inside you."

"Power?" Grace gave a snort. "I can stitch a wound without a suture kit and kick in a few endorphins."

"Those are not such common gifts." He glanced at the swirl of chaotic efficiency. "No magick? Bah! As a doctor, you allowed your science to get in the way of your soul."

"You're saying I have no soul?"

"*No*. I'm saying magick needs four things—the will of the mage, the words of the formation, the way of the focus, and the wings of the energy."

"What does that mean?"

"That you do not know means you need training." He smiled and even though she didn't trust him, didn't want to know him, had no room in her heart, she felt a flutter of interest. "You know only a few words, Grace Armatrading, but we can teach you the rest."

"We?"

He hesitated. "The Custos Magi. Your aunt was one of us. There is a war going on, one you know nothing about, for the battle wages not between nations but between good and evil. Unfortunately, Faith catapulted you into our realm. With your undisciplined power, you are both vulnerable and dangerous."

Grace reared back, realizing his hand now manacled her wrist. Around her, passengers left cars, orderlies caught a smoke, EMTs shepherded their charges, all oblivious to her and Khalil. She twisted her arm. "Let go!"

Fleetingly, his fingers tightened before he released her. "Don't be a fool. We can teach you how to access your power. How to defend yourself."

She wanted to dismiss this very dangerous man, but she couldn't. Couldn't walk away from the possibility of answers.

"Come with me now."

The invitation curled around her in siren sweetness. Beckoned her.

"Grace?" Adam's voice came to her, rougher, huskier than normal, but distinct amid the glamour-muted noise. She glanced over her shoulder to see him striding out from the ER. His gaze met hers, then flicked over to Khalil. His face hardened.

He could see them!

He started running, dodging through the crowd toward her. She dug in her heels, grabbed onto a bush branch for an anchor. "No."

Khalil's face twisted. "Adam Zolton is no friend of magick, Grace. He killed your aunt."

"You're wrong."

"He has not been truthful with you. He has dangerous secrets."

So did she.

He touched the phone at her waist, and she heard a spark of static electricity. "You have my number. Call and we will meet at the time and the place of your choosing. But do not tell Adam. Do not trust him."

Three things happened simultaneously. Adam joined her, Khalil vanished into the crowd, and a passerby bumped into her, giving her a surprised look and an apology before hurrying away.

Apparently the glamour was gone.

"Did he hurt you?" Adam asked fiercely.

"I'm fine. You, on the other hand, should have been admitted."

He waved a dismissive hand. "My butt was already shot full of antibiotics. I'm not spending the night getting CAT scans and donating tubes of blood because they think I took some drug not on their tox screen and knocked my head."

Radar hurried from the ER, clipboard in hand. "Mr. Zolton, the doctor recommended you be admitted for observation."

"Not a chance."

"Since you're leaving against medical advice, sign this." She thrust out the clipboard with a form attached.

Adam scrawled his signature, then turned to Grace. "Can we get going?"

Grace nodded as she reassured Radar, "I'll keep an eye on him."

"Now there's a pleasant job." Radar leaned closer, whispering, "Dr. Nguyen's theory of drug use is bullshit, isn't it?"

"A pile of crap."

"Am I ever going to know the true story?"

"Probably not."

"Then I'm free to make up my own. Trust me, it will be steamy."

Grace laughed as the triage nurse left.

"She's blunt," Adam observed, threading his arm through hers, as they headed toward her car.

"She's a nurse."

"Who was that with you? He was working some powerful magick."

"He said his name was Khalil, and he was a Weaver for the Custos Magi. He thinks you killed Faith."

Adam's face hardened. "Did you believe him?"

"No. You heard of them?"

"Rumors, hints." His jaw worked. "They're dangerous."

A dangerous man, Khalil's accusation whispered back.

Apparently, there was a war on. Which side would she take?

Inside her car, Grace turned the key in the ignition, and Adam leaned his head against the headrest. Gala crawled out of Grace's pocket to snuggle atop his chest, her nose burrowed against his ear.

"Turn the heater on full blast," he said. "I'm still chilled from that damn snowbank."

"What happened?"

"Two chaps attacked; I wasn't smart enough."

Her throat tightened as the implications of his terse statement struck. He had shivered in the snow, but she was the one trembling now. Awkwardly avoiding the steering wheel, she leaned over and wrapped her arms around him. His cheeks were cold to her touch. Yet his body was strong, his mind active, his essence so vitally alive.

His hand brushed against her hair, a light caress that sent shivers, not of cold but of need, across her shoulders, deep into her spine.

"Not sure what brought this on, but I won't complain." She felt his smile.

"You almost died tonight, Adam. If I hadn't healed you, that ambulance would have been a hearse."

His hand stilled. "Your magick healed me?"

"Does that bother you?"

"Does it bother me to be alive?" he asked with a chuckle. "No, but it surprises me." Then, he tilted his head, just a tiny move, and his lips kissed the sensitive skin beneath her ear. "This is more effective than any car heater."

More shivers, more need.

More people passing by, watching. Reluctantly she lifted herself, and Adam made no move to stop her. Instead, he touched the sore spot around her black eye. "Aren't we a fine pair? You battered and bruised. Me with a throat that can barely speak."

"Then let's get some rest. Tomorrow, we can try to open the library."

"We need—"

"—someplace private," she agreed. They were taking a risk with the virus, and they couldn't endanger anyone else. "All taken care of. While I was waiting for you, I rented a cabin in a recreation area."

"Sounds good," he said, his voice drowsy.

"Where is the library?"

He patted his computer. "Right here."

CHAPTER NINE

Incredulous, Adam finished his hasty examination of the rustic cabin. Hasty because the amenities were nonexistent. Four bloody *bunk beds*. With no linens, and mattresses the thickness of credit cards.

He dropped his bag onto the rough-hewn table. "There's no loo."

"It's called a vault toilet." Grace paused in unwrapping her scarf. "It's outside."

"*Outside.*" Horrified, he opened the back door. The stiff wind drove against him. With that cold, the wind would be the only thing stiff. His balls would freeze out there.

Swiftly shutting the door—one minute and he'd lowered the room temperature by five degrees—he asked, "Heat?"

Her lips twitching with mischief, Grace gestured to the iron stove and the pile of wood. "I was a Girl Guide; I can start a fire."

"So can I. Doesn't mean I want to revert to Neanderthal."

"Quit whining. You'll survive one night."

"I happen to enjoy comfort."

"You agreed we need someplace isolated to open the library. It's either this or drive hours north. We were lucky it was open." She took a deep breath, her face still dancing with mischief. "Smell that pine. C'mon, you have to admit the snow is pretty on the trees."

Look too long and he might agree the white-topped trees held appeal. He took a sniff. "Do I smell horse?"

"This is the cabin by the horse trail," she admitted.

Beyond the ball-freezing loo and the equine aroma, its primary fault lay in the fact he'd been imagining sharing a timber-post lodge and down-thick beds with Grace. "Do we have electricity for the computers?"

Grace paused in her unloading. "Electricity is also on the list of missing amenities."

"Computer. Electricity. Can't use one without the other."

"Battery power," she returned. "You charged up in the car."

"We don't know how long this will take." Adam sat on a stick chair, tapping two fingers against his mouth in thought.

Grace took the wicker rocker. "All we need is to make sure there's no lurking virus. That shouldn't take long. Once we know everything's copacetic, we can go anywhere to finish looking for Faith's clues."

"Well, sooner we start, sooner we can get back to linen sheets." He set his computer on the table and powered on. "We might never know how Faith created the library or where it exists, but I think we can access it."

"How?" Eagerly, Grace pulled her rocker nearer to the laptop.

"The grimoire icon." He quarter-turned his computer, showing her his wallpaper: a satellite photo of Lake Huron.

"I don't see the icon."

"Do you know the myth of the Lady of the Lake?"

She gave a snort. "Duh, Brit here. She gave King Arthur his sword, Excalibur."

"Well, that dot"—he shifted his cursor to the center of the screen—"is an island named Excalibur." He clicked the pinpoint image of the island.

Nothing. His jaw clenched in frustration; he'd been so sure. Had Faith sent the portal to the actual island? Unlikely.

"Maybe the cursor wasn't centered," Grace suggested, laying her hand on his shoulder.

His thumb rubbed against her knuckles as he savored their momentary connection. She squeezed his shoulder, a brief response she quickly erased by withdrawing her hand. "Concentrate, Zolton. Island. Click."

Still, as she leaned sideways to catch a better look at the photo, her shoulder connected with his. Learning from his mistakes, he didn't acknowledge the contact, just enjoyed it.

Carefully positioning the cursor above the island, he focused a moment, making sure the instinctive barriers he normally raised against magick were dormant. He clicked, double clicked. At first, nothing, then . . .

He felt it! Power swelled from deep inside his computer, like a sleeping dragon coming awake. Electric and fiery, it raced through silicon and copper, spread through the screen diodes, and then hologrammed out into a mass of swirling, restless colors. The hairs on his arm stood up.

"Holy Hannah," Grace breathed. "Is that it?"

"Yes." He dug out the gloves and visor. "Can't see it properly without these."

He donned the accessories, and the mass came into focus as a thick door with metal bands, like the gateway to a medieval dungeon. Breath clutching in anticipation, he gave a virtual tug on the iron handle, but the door didn't budge. Looking around for a key, he saw only the smudge of his computer screen, so small it seemed a kilometer away.

"The unlocking spell," he said impatiently. "Say it, Grace."

"It didn't work in the car."

"Try!" She did, but her hesitant chant wouldn't open an eyelid. Useless. "Say the words as if you mean them."

"I am," she snapped. Her second attempt was snarled with anger, but no more successful. Neither was her third effort.

"Again."

"This isn't working. I'm not repeating the bloody spell."

He started to rip off the gear, until he smelled a foul odor attached to a foreign energy. The sensation rippled across him, as dark and dangerous as the snout of a gator in black water.

Magick, and in here he had no protections. Alert for attack, he took a virtual walk over to the computer screen. A gold-colored key hung above the hippie-blend of colors on the screen. "Speak the spell once more."

"I told you—"

"I know; this is an experiment."

As she chanted the words, the key shimmered, seemed to lift off the screen, but fell back, as though attached with elastic. In the brief seconds it lifted from his screen, he peered into the depths, looking deep inside his computer.

Something lurked there. He sensed rather than saw—tasted the mouth-puckering evil, smelled the odor of raw mold.

"Do you want me to repeat the spell?" Grace asked.

"No." He peeled off the gloves and visor, then handed them to Grace. "Use these. Tell me what you see, but don't try the spell."

She did as he asked, then instantly groaned and doubled over. "You could have warned me."

"About what?"

"About this being a manic carousel." She grabbed his arm. "Damn spinning door."

"That didn't happen with me."

"Well, it's whacking my middle ear; oh, Jesus, I'm going to throw up."

"Close your eyes."

Her hand dug into his forearm as she drew openmouthed breaths. Her breathing stabilized. "I'm going to try opening my eyes—" She clamped her lips shut. Her skin turned the color of opals, ivory white tinged with green.

"Look toward three o'clock. Away from the door."

"That's better. The periphery's churning, but I'm managing."

"See the smudge of my computer screen? Do you see anything inside it?"

"I—" She swore again and tore off the visor, then tilted her head between her knees. "Zofran, please," she muttered, as she peeled off the gloves.

"Fresh out." He handed her a bottle of water.

"That"—Grace gulped the water, then raised her head—"was both fiendish and paranoid."

"She must have set her protections so only I can get into the library, but what good does that do if I can't open it?"

"That's my part in the puzzle. Except Faith miscalculated. I can't."

"She must have believed you could." Something crossed her face, a fleeting expression he couldn't read, but he hazarded a guess. "Bothers you?"

She shrugged one shoulder. "I accept what I can, and can't, do."

"Bollocks, you've never accepted anything half-arse."

"I've *tried*."

"Then try something different!"

"Why are you so hellfire determined to get into that library?"

"Faith sent it to *us*; we need to know its secrets." He raked a hand through his hair. "But for some known-only-to-her-and-God reason, she made accomplishing that contingent on us working together."

"So why are we fighting?"

Her question undercut his frustration, restored his humor. "Because you're stubborn?"

"And you're not?"

"I'm male. We're Mars. Logical, not stubborn."

She laughed. "What did logical Mars expect seasick Venus

to see inside a computerized virtual library protected by magick?"

"Whether a nasty spell had tagged along with the library."

"Right. That's logical."

His lips twitched at her dry humor; then he grew serious. "Did you see anything? Sense anything?"

She shook her head. "Nothing, but if you say something's there, I'll trust you."

"We need to get it off before we open the library."

"A moot point, if I can't work the lock."

"You will," he said confidently.

A small smile touched her. "No one ever saw a smidge of talent beyond my healing. Not even Kea—"

"Kea knows about your ability?"

Her lips pressed together at his sharp question, as though she were trying to recapture that slip. She nodded in answer.

"Because you've relieved his neuropathy?"

"Yes. About the library—" She cut off further questions. "How do we get rid of the trap you're seeing?"

He tapped his fingers against his lips, thinking. "Raj Kasin. He's a magick hacker."

"I didn't know that was possible."

"Magick draws on the energies of nature. Electricity and silicon are newly tapped forms of that energy. If anyone could defuse a computer-borne spell, it's Raj. Hell, he's top on my list for creating it."

Grace's face hardened. "And the virus that killed Faith?"

"List topper there, too."

Her hands clenched. "Then we nail that bastard, and we turn him in."

"To whom? The magick police?"

"If he created that virus, then he has to be stopped."

"He isn't our target. Raj is the ivory tower, or, rather, in his case, steel tower. Doesn't give a damn about the application."

"And you'd trust him?"

"If I pay him enough. And then only until someone pays him more." He tapped out a text message on his cell. "Let's see if he'll meet us."

"You can pay him?"

"I'll think of something he wants." Adam closed the phone, praying they weren't too late. "If Raj created that virus, he's in as much danger as we are. Whoever *used* that virus is a killer."

"And killers don't like loose ends."

Wary—a visit from the Magi's pet hit man was never good news—Kea Lin watched Khalil run a hand over the stainless-steel table.

The Weaver Magi's lips curled. "Blending magick and science, Kea?"

"It's the way of the future. The council would see that if they stopped debating the merits of focusing through amber or whether the last word in the Vortex ritual is inspired or inhaled."

"The discussions can get detailed." He smiled. "One of the advantages to being a Weaver of spells; they believe I'm working, when I'm merely bored to sleep."

Kea returned the smile. They'd never been friends, but he did appreciate Khalil's humor. Even if the Weaver was a boneheaded traditionalist.

"Our enemies don't hesitate to use the power of technology."

"Which is why we are changing."

"At the pace of a glacier."

"Because we need to remember, ultimately, our power must come from here." He laid a fist over his heart.

"Will, shaped by the wisdom of ancient scrolls, fueled by the power of the ages and the connections, focused by the raw elements. I haven't forgotten. I just use new words, fresh powers and elements." Kea shook his head. "A useless argument. What has the council in a twist?"

"New technology shaped against us. Our enemies grow cleverer and bolder. Bold enough to murder." Khalil tossed the mage rings of the eight victims on the table, their metal clattering against steel in a hollow knell. "We know they have developed the power to scramble the mind. These mages all died in madness."

"A tech mimic of the Spell of I'celus?" Kea failed to keep the horror from his voice. "Do you know who?"

"We found a trail to the underside of Vitae. But some new elements have raised questions."

"What questions?"

"What are you working on now?" Khalil picked up the opalescent gloves.

Damn, he hadn't put those back. Knowing better than to evade, Kea answered, "Nanolevel analgesia."

"Ever solve the problem of the nanobot propulsion?"

"Not yet." The scientific world wouldn't learn of his progress until he and Grace had replicated the magick through other sources, and he was not yet ready for the Mage Council to know, either. Casually, he took the gloves and stowed them away, then perched on a stool. It felt so good to at last be free of pain.

"That's the science piece. What's the magick piece? For I know, even if the scientific world does not, that your research always has a side interest."

"Very little at this point. By adding a tracer spell to the analgesic, we're characterizing the energies generated."

"What role does Dr. Armatrading play?"

"She's a research assistant. Damn good one, too. Why?"

"Don't play games," Khalil spat. "You don't move with agony anymore. We know that she has a gift for healing, relieving pain."

"She's a doctor."

"And she is melding her science with her magick." Khalil's voice turned low with menace. "Your strengths lie elsewhere; she's the one who hones her talent for healing with this research, not you."

"Yes," he admitted. "But she has no other talents."

"Bah, none that are unlocked. She's doing complex spells with no training, no preparation, no circle of protection, in the middle of a bloody, chaotic emergency room. You haven't been so long apart not to realize that means she has a wealth of potential, untapped and unformatted. That makes her very dangerous."

"Grace would do no harm."

"We need to make sure of that." Khalil held out a pack of well-worn Tarot cards. His finger rubbed with an easy familiarity across the symbols of the top card: The High Priestess. "This tells me she's a pivot point."

He'd be the fool of the deck if he discounted Khalil's divination. "Why not bring her in? You have that power."

Khalil turned the deck over to the Temperance card. "This tells me we need her cooperation or we will lose her." He held out his hand, the one bearing his mage ring. The topaz glowed warm in the cool gray of the lab. Carved into the depths of the stone was Khalil's own symbol, the spider. "You took the oath of a mage."

Kea jerked back his sleeve, revealing the steel cuff on his forearm. Made of thin twisted metal strands, the pattern hid the symbol. At the center nestled a scarlet emerald, the rare gem gleaming like a red eye. "What do you ask of me?"

"Convince her I'm not the enemy."

"You're a Weaver, adept at blending spells, building cooperation. Why not approach her yourself?"

For the first time, he saw discomfort in the Weaver. "Our first meeting didn't go well."

"You tried to coerce her?" Kea gave a bark of laughter. "Get with the twenty-first century. That never works with a woman like Grace."

"We need her brought to us."

"I won't betray her."

"Not betrayal. You're saving her." Khalil leaned forward. "Those eight mages died because of Adam Zolton."

"He's part of Vitae?" Cold determination settled deep inside Kea.

"We don't know his exact role, but he is buried deeply with them."

"I'll get her away." He touched cuff to ring, stone to stone. Power arced between the two mages.

Khalil kissed his cheek, the Middle Eastern version of a handshake. The kiss of vows cemented the promise. "Let it be done."

After Khalil left, Kea sat a moment more in the lab, relishing the scents and sounds that surrounded him. This was his element, the future of magick, and eventually the Mage Council would understand that.

At last he pushed off the stool, stretching. He pulled down the sleeve of his lab coat, covering the steel and gem cuff, hiding once more the eye of the dragon.

Grace had to admit, she liked Adam's choice of sleeping accommodations better than hers. This chair she sprawled in was big enough and soft enough to double as a bed. Her foot moved up and down to Nightwish—CD and player provided by the hotel—as she read through the scanned pages Glinda had sent. The empty plates of their lunch had been wheeled out to the hall for pick up. A glass of white burgundy waited near her elbow.

They'd left the cabin as fast as Adam could power off his computer and pack up. Then he'd booked a suite at one of the area's most exclusive hotels, explaining his choice as better security. Anyone could break into a rustic cabin, but try getting past a luxury hotel's watchful concierge. Whatever the reason, she wasn't arguing.

She could get used to room service.

While she finished the last page, Adam set his copy aside and logged into his computer. The legend proclaimed Cadwaladar the first of the great mages—originator of the Custos Magi—and the epic poem detailed his various exploits.

"Learn anything?" Adam asked when she looked up.

"More than I ever wanted to know about Cadwaladar and deciphering old English, but not so much about this mysterious Dragon. What was Faith's quote?"

"'Circle of the damned beware. For where the dragon enters, madness will reign. The flames of its breath ignite a conflagration none of mind can escape. For the dragon hoards all treasure.'"

She riffled through the pages until she found the quote. In these stanzas, Cadwaladar—hunting the Triad, for Cycil had warned of their power—had just entered the misty cave of the second member, the dragon who had destroyed his circle of the damned to rise above them. To confirm his purpose, Cadwaladar had quoted from Cycil, a powerful oracle who had seen the evils of the Triad power.

"This prophecy of Cycil," Adam said. "I found the entire quote online."

She left her comfy chair to sit beside him on the couch and read over his shoulder.

Oh circle of the damned, listen. The Triad shall rise above all. Unstoppable, the hands of power create the infernal almighty. Body unceasing, mind all knowing, spirit unfettered, by these shall ye be bound in miserable servitude. Be aware for ye shall know the rise by these three prophets:

the burning of the knowledge, the destruction of the
mages, and the fusion of the elements.

She let out a breath. "Infernal almighty and miserable servitude are pretty dire warnings. Do you believe in prophecies, Adam?"

He shook his head. "The future's too mutable. But someone could be using this as a blueprint. See the first elements? Body unceasing and the burning of the knowledge? Natalie's ex-husband was a mage who melded science with magick to recreate the power of the Phoenix. He had a library that burned."

"In the lines Faith sent, Cadwaladr's after the dragon. So is the one we're after that dragon? The mind all-knowing—whatever that means—causing the destruction of the mages?"

"Nine mages *have* died."

Adam's quiet reminder shivered down her spine. She got up and retrieved her glass of wine and Faith's data on the eight mages. "If they're in a damned circle, maybe we can find some commonality. Like age?"

Adam scanned the information, but he didn't see anything startling. "All older than thirty. Career? Everything from unemployed to professor."

"Lifestyle choices?"

"Level of magick talent."

"Pets."

"Hobbies." At each suggestion, Adam tried to find some point of intersection.

"Vegan, vegetarian, or omnivore."

Their suggestions grew silly as no commonalities emerged.

"Favorite breakfast cereal," Grace suggested, stretching her arms overhead. "Maybe Pop's got a grudge against Snap and Crackle."

Adam bit back a smile. "Innie or outie?"

"Briefs, boxers, or commando?"

Joining her laughter, Adam set his computer on the floor. "I can't read one more line from these faded newspaper articles." Lacing his fingers together, he stretched his arms over his head. "God, I'm fagged."

Grace yawned and leaned against him. "If I back-check one more dead-end possible link, I think my eyes'll burn."

It had taken all his willpower to stay focused on the data, to keep his mind on anything but wanting her sprawled on top of him, touching, kissing.

He closed his eyes and pinched the bridge of his nose. *Task at hand, Zolton.*

"I know this chap, Brando—"

"You seem to know a lot of chaps."

He shrugged. "I've met a lot of people over the years, kept in touch. Brando's good at digging. I'll send him the data, and he can cross-check for us." There had to be something that connected the mages.

Oh, God, there was. As he looked at the dates on the articles, the connection finally smacked him.

"Maybe the only connection is that they were mages," Grace suggested. "Driven mad by someone who hates magick." She nestled closer.

Reluctant to share his realization, Adam shifted his hips, allowed her better access to the cushions, and laid his arm across her shoulders. Their bodies snuggled, and the honeyed warmth of her eased his sudden headache.

"How would our unknown assailant target them all as mages? Some were flamboyant about their talents, but others were low-key. Lincoln Landry was paranoid about anyone knowing his talents. He'd let a kitten die before performing any ritual beyond the privacy of his protected sanctum. And Lizzie the Hermit, she was sharp as a saw blade once you got past the smell, but most everyone thought she was schizoid."

Her toenails were colored with pink polish. He dragged

his eyes away from the subtly sexy feminine touch to find Grace studying him.

"How did you know that Lincoln performed rituals only in his sanctum? Or that Lizzie had body odor?" she asked. "Neither factoid was in the data."

"Because I met them."

"Did you know the others?"

"Yes. Went to see each one."

"How much time between your visit and their deaths?"

He stilled. "Hours. A day at most." And he had no alibis, having driven alone to meet them. Couldn't even produce a return airline reservation.

"There's our connection. You." She stood. "No wonder everyone keeps warning me about you."

His gut clenched. "You think I killed these people?"

To his dismay, she actually paused to consider. He had hoped for some measure of trust.

He could see the deliberations going on in her mind, by the way her pink-tipped feet waggled to an interior rhythm. Unfortunately, he couldn't see the path those evaluations were taking. When she still didn't answer, he shoved to his feet. "While you decide whether I'm a serial killer or not, I'm going for a swim."

He went into his bedroom for a quick change. Laps, pushed as hard and fast as he could go, might take the edge off.

It should only take a thousand or so.

He tossed a towel around his neck, and when he came out, Grace was waiting. He strode toward the door. Only when his hand was on the knob did she say, "You're not a killer, Adam. At least, not of those mages."

He pivoted. "You took a long time to realize that."

"I knew that before you asked the question. I don't doubt you could kill. To protect someone. Maybe even to avenge someone. Or in the heat of a battle. But these deaths were vicious and calculated."

The knot in his back loosened. "Why'd you take so damn long to tell me?"

"I was trying to figure out why you didn't tell me you'd met them."

"I've met a lot of odd characters who *didn't* die."

"Don't insult me, Adam. Why didn't you tell me?"

"I knew I'd met them, but it wasn't until we started going through our list that I realized how close my visit was to their deaths. I was looking for some other connection," he admitted. "And I was afraid of your reaction."

"You want to tell me why you went to them?"

"No." His jaw tightened. "But I will." He rubbed a hand through his hair. "I'm going swimming now; we can talk over dinner."

Searching for connections and patterns, the right-brain leaps beyond logic, he always found water helped. Swimming, showering, standing in the rain.

And he had a lot to think about.

Whether he had led a killer to eight mages.

What pattern fit Faith's cryptic clues.

How the hell he was going to carry on when this was over and Grace left.

As Adam left the room, Grace let out a slow breath. For swimming, he followed the European custom of small and tight. And damn, but she was grateful, for the man looked fine. Flat belly, dusting of hair on the chest, muscular legs. What had caused that intriguing, serpentine white scar right above his heart?

Not just a pretty face, though. A quick mind and sly humor were attached to that body.

Although a swim sounded appealing, Grace decided to

leave Adam to his solitude and take advantage of the decadent hot tub in their suite. As she slid into the heated water and the lilac-scented bubbles frothed around her, she played over again the few words that Faith had left them regarding the reason behind the murders.

The message made no more sense than it had yesterday or two hours ago.

Instead, she tried other paths, letting her mind drift until it settled. The wristbands! Something about them had nagged her, but with so much going on, she'd forgotten.

Eager to follow up, she toweled off, threw on sweats, and pulled one of the bands from Adam's pocket. She opened her phone, noting she'd missed two calls. One from Kea, one blocked ID. She'd call Kea after she finished looking at those bands. Maybe he had some new data about the oddness yesterday.

Borrowing Adam's computer, she pulled up the MMORPG *SciMage*. The multiplayer game was simple on the surface, but complex the deeper you delved. The purpose—destroying a cadre of evil warlocks—was basic enough, but instead of fighting magick with magick, warlock with guardian, the gamer became a tech warrior, using the energy of technology, sometimes blended with magick, to defeat the evil. The game had been around awhile, but increasingly advanced upgrades kept it cutting edge.

While the game loaded, she checked on Gala and found the ferret snoring in a mound of their socks. Well, Adam's socks. The beast had squirmed away from all of Grace's socks, which were tossed far across the floor.

"Be that way," Grace muttered, and retrieved a pair for her chilled feet. She settled into the couch, and then began to work her way up through the levels. There it was, level ten: Rialta captured the Dark Dragon Hedda with the cable snakes. Thin threads of iridescent fiber, glittering with fiber optics, wound across the dragon's chest.

That was what she'd remembered. Her hands shook as she set the computer aside. Someone had taken that concept of the game and made it real.

She picked up the single band, a sliver of fear winding her gut. Thin, supple, the quiet serpent hid the fangs of its death dealing.

Was it magick? Or technology? Prying at the end of the band, she worked a nail beneath its cap. A residual charge tingled against her fingers, like the last spark of an eel.

She flicked at the end, and suddenly the cap popped off. Out fell a camera-sized battery. If it were magick, then it was magick fueled by a battery.

A small V stamped on the inside caught her eye.

Vitae. The company that had developed *SciMage*. But it was more than just a software company. Its technology was cutting edge—hardware for the company's software and electronics was so unique, it almost seemed like magick.

She remembered the news article. Apparently Vitae was poised for another breakthrough.

Drumming her fingers against the sofa, she tried to catch a wisp of a memory. Something she'd been told . . . no, something she'd recently overheard about Vitae. One of her teenage patients talking to his buddy. "Play *SciMage*," he'd said. "See what tech warriors can do."

"It's a game," his chum protested.

"No. Vitae supports us. Our fight needs you."

She'd remembered the odd comment because of the reference to *SciMage*, but had dismissed it since the boy was on heavy-duty PCP and narcs.

Now, she pulled the company up on the Internet. Jonas Washington, the founder, lived not too far from here, with homes in Ann Arbor and on an island in Lake Huron.

Good luck getting an invitation to visit the island. Jonas wasn't a hermit by any means, but his social life was always in Ann Arbor. Few were ever invited to his island. No one talked about the experience.

She dug deeper, but found only useless facts about Vitae. Glancing at her watch, she yawned. God, she was tired. And hungry. Follow this thread, then she was done. Retrieve Adam and find a restaurant.

Her phone rang, and she glanced at the caller ID. Blocked number. Again? Picking up the phone—damn static electricity—she answered with a snapped "Hello."

No answer. Shaking her hand—that static electricity had packed a punch—Grace went back to the Internet and opened the last page on her search into Vitae. Her fingers went as limp as discarded latex gloves.

The picture was grainy, obscure. One of the few images available of the founding of Vitae, when it had been a simple game with intensely realistic graphics. A picture with the prediction that the two young founders would one day rival Gates in money and influence.

Two founders, not the single one everyone talked about today. Jonas Washington had provided the business acumen that had propelled the company to major New York Stock Exchange salivation.

But that first game, the one with the imaginative format and the intriguing graphics, had been the brainchild of the cofounder.

Adam Zolton.

CHAPTER TEN

The water worked its own brand of magick. Adam churned down and back through the pool, his mind freed to explore, as he worked off energy. He'd assumed the eight mages had been killed because of what they knew about the Dragon. What if they'd been killed simply because his visits had identified them as mages?

No, magick had definitely killed Faith. Magick lurked behind the library. Magick and a renegade mage—maybe following the prophecy—were at the heart of this, had to be.

Except during the attacks on Grace and himself, he hadn't detected so much as a whiff of magick. Were there two factions of mages? One tech oriented, one traditional? At war over what? Why was Grace caught in the middle?

Difficult as it would be, he had to tell Grace about Abby, about what had driven him to take those photos and still colored his decisions. A shiver ran down his spine, and he realized his arms and legs were getting heavy. Rolling to his back, he paddled until his breathing returned to normal, as fresh, ugly thoughts intruded.

What was the relationship between Kea and Grace? He'd caught no hint of a secret affair, but their bond went beyond colleagues and the possibilities tangled his insides. His fist clenched against his dislike of the scientist.

Grace did not belong with Kea; she belonged with him, Adam.

If not an affair, then . . . their nano-analgesia pain research?

He got out of the pool, noticed that Raj had left him a text message: nine pm. He glanced at his watch. Not much time to get there.

He toweled off, returning to the questions of Grace's research. *Oh, bloody hell.* He braced himself against one of the chairs, as his breath caught on a possibility. Their analgesic was fused to nanobots, but biobots weren't workable yet because of power issues. What about bots fueled by magick?

What immense power a mage could control with the combination.

Acid rose in his throat. Grace knew too little about magick, was too close to the thrills of discovery, was too much a bloody find-the-answers researcher to see the implications. Was Kea a mage? Or a dupe? Had someone else made that same leap of logic and attempted to kidnap Grace? To use her or to stop her?

He threw on his sweats, shrugged on a T-shirt, and strode from the room. *You're reaching, Zolton.* Yet that was what he did, how his best articles took shape. Fashion a story from isolated oddities.

When his phone rang, he was glad of the distraction, until he glanced at the image ID of the posh woman. Regan Hollister.

Some distractions brought fresh complications. "Hullo, Regan."

"Hello, Adam." Her sultry voice held a touch of warm pleasure. "I spoke with your mother, heard you were up our way."

"Ann Arbor." He dried his hair.

"What a smashing coincidence. I'd love to meet. For a drink?"

For a moment, he was tempted. When she elected to be, Regan was charming and amusing.

Temptation passed. "I can't tonight. Other plans."

"Later then?" At his hesitation, she gave a throaty *tsk*. "All this way and you weren't going to stop by? Jonas would be disappointed."

"I want to see you both. How about tomorrow?"

"Excellent. Lunch at the office? I'll send you the directions."

"I remember how to get there. I'll have a guest with me."

She gave a knowing laugh. "Ah, Adam, I should have known a lady was involved. What's her name?"

"Grace Armatrading. She's a physician at the U."

"We'll be delighted to meet her." Her next words held no polite societal amusement. "I saw Abby last week."

Guilt awoke with a fresh roar at the mention of his sister. "Mum said she was no different."

"Mary doesn't want to see the changes. Involuntary spasms are not smiles. Abby's deteriorating, Adam. There's no longer even a flicker of her in the madness. When you go back home, you should go see her."

"I can't, Regan." His avoidance was neither admirable nor honorable, but he simply couldn't force himself to see his sister. Even his visits to his mother had grown deplorably sparse.

At least Regan didn't ask for a nonprogress report on his search for Abby's tormentor. She knew he'd made none; Regan was the first person he consulted regarding any viable leads.

Before this week, that was. As they said their good-byes, doubt washed across him, doubt about his oldest, and most loyal, friends. He stood in the glass elevator, bracing his hands against the rail, and stared at the lobby guests growing smaller as he rode upward, solitary and exposed.

Had he been so focused on his own biases that he'd been blinded? Because of Abby, Regan Hollister and Jonas Washington both had a wide knowledge—and a deep dislike—of mages and magick.

Had they stepped beyond emotion into action? Used him to identify eight targets? Head down, he drew a long breath against a tide of loneliness.

Grace paced the room, brooding at the burned-in memory of that photo. She had been well duped. As Adam strode into the room, fresh from his swim, her anger-sharpened senses kicked up, flooding her with heated details. He smelled of chlorinated water, and she resisted the urge to brush off the droplets that clung to his chin. He needed a shave, one of those men whose five-o'clock shadow would roughen a lover's cheek if he weren't considerate.

Somehow she knew Adam would be very careful of the woman in his arms.

She set her jaw against this fresh tide of awareness, and her fingers curled around the heinous bands. "We need to talk."

"Later. We have an appointment with Raj. Get ready." He headed into his bedroom, tugging his T-shirt hem over his head. With his face covered, his voice muffled, he added, "We've been invited to lunch at Vitae tomorrow; Jonas Washington is a friend."

She froze at his words. Was he delivering her to the Vitae lair?

She followed him into the bedroom and threw the bands on the bed. "Tell me about these. And Vitae."

"We can talk in the car. Otherwise we'll be late." He paused before shoving down his swimsuit, his thumbs hooked into the Lycra. "I'm changing here."

"I'll close my eyes. I want answers before we run off to Raj or anywhere."

"What the hell is going on here, Grace?" He looked innocently puzzled.

"Those bands were made by Vitae, and they're modeled in the game *SciMage*." She tapped him on the chest, feeling a spark of static electricity, then stepped back. "Vitae and *SciMage* are your brainchildren. Why did you visit those mages?"

He absorbed her words, her implications, quickly, and his face turned hard. Keeping his gaze locked on her defiant one, he shoved down his swimsuit.

Blessed be, he was one fine man. Unyielding muscle, scars on his thighs that matched the corkscrew on his chest. Sweat beaded on her forehead. Every day she saw the male body inside and out, and never paid attention to beauty or wrinkles, only to the details that answered one question: What's wrong?

Nothing dispassionate or clinical in her response to Adam, though. These details were unadulterated feminine appreciation and lust. He turned and the muscles in his buttocks bunched as he yanked on silk boxers. Damn fine ass.

Grabbing a pair of jeans, he stalked over to her, invading her space, and glared at her. "If you think I'm the killer mastermind of an antimage underground, then why the hell are you still standing here?"

Good question, one that had occurred to her, as well. Grace didn't retreat. "Because I want answers. Did you know those bands were made by Vitae?"

"No." He threw on the jeans.

"Did you suspect?"

"Yes."

"And you didn't say anything?"

"We've been busy."

"You recognized them from *SciMage*?"

He gave her a slow smile, one that held only cold mockery. "Love, I designed the game."

"You dreamed up those bands?" The thought tightened her throat.

"Along with a neuroscrambler that erases powers by amnesia. You'll find that in level twenty-three in the Drakken lab."

"The star-shaped bruise on Natalie's temple?"

"I created weapons for a bloody video game, Grace, not for reality. I didn't use them."

"Do you still own Vitae stock?"

"Forty-five percent." His face vanished as he put on a T-shirt.

She sucked in a breath; everything she thought she knew about Adam Zolton twisted to a new shape from the torque of that one small tidbit. Wall Street had been salivating over that stock for years, but Vitae had remained a privately held company, owned by Jonas Washington. So much for Wall Street assumptions. "Hell, you must be as rich as the queen."

"She has the palace and the crown jewels." He sat on the bed to put on socks and boots. "That's eight questions. We're not playing to twenty. Ask what you really want because as soon as I'm dressed, I'm leaving to meet with Raj." He raked a scathing look across her. "Come if you trust I'm not going to throw you out of the speeding car."

He was royally pissed. Well, so was she! Anger crashed against her, unstoppable as a tsunami.

"You won't leave without me." Furious, she strode to the other bedroom and exchanged her loose sweats for a pair of jeans, as Adam, fully dressed, charged after her.

"Then get your coat on," he snarled. "I leave when I want."

"Not until I say so." She snatched up the car keys and dangled them from her fingers. "My car, my keys."

She might as well have dangled meat before a lion.

"Don't press me." He grabbed at the keys.

Recklessly—too recklessly—she shoved them into her front pocket. His hand followed, plowing deep into the denim. She grabbed his wrist with both hands. Twisting, he fought her to extract his hand, but she had the leverage and a grip honed from restraining combative patients.

And maybe he didn't give the attempt his full effort.

Her fingers dug in. "Question nine. How deep is your involvement with Vitae?"

"I'm on trial, right? Paying again for the heedless act of a brash youth."

"You betrayed me!" she shouted. "Used me. How can I trust you?"

"You betrayed *us*. Never gave me a single moment to explain. I have paid for six bloody years, and I'm getting damned fagged of battling your doubts every time I turn around. What's the price of atonement, St. Grace who's never made a mistake or kept a difficult secret?"

Ignoring the voice of fair play that accused her of hiding dangerous facts, she replied, "Why did you go see those mages?"

"What the hell do I have to do?" His free hand shot toward her face.

The swift violence of the motion shocked her. "Hit me and we're through."

He stepped back. "Don't be brambled; I've never hit a woman. Mum taught me that fundamental when she left my sot of a dad. She never said anything about this, though." His hand caressed her jaw, a brushing touch in stark contrast to the stone of his face and the glitter of violence in his eyes.

Grace's nipples tightened at the touch, initiating tremors that reached lower. The body had few responses—heart pulsing, nerves firing, breath changing. Only the mind distinguished between love and hate, fury and desire.

"I have wanted you for so long." His hand trailed downward, the tips of his fingers barely grazing the soft flesh of her neck. Her pulse pounded, filling her with a heated mix of lust and anger.

"I didn't ask for this." The words scratched her dry throat.

"No? You're holding me." His voice was as husky as hers, a rasp of need.

She was. His hand in her pocket had let go of the keys. It flattened against her hip, cupping the bone with care, his thumb lying in the hollow crease of her thigh. The tip of his thumb stroked across against her femoral artery. His other hand rested against the neck band of her shirt, the thumb against her carotid artery. In both places, she gripped his sleeves at the wrist.

Pushing him away or holding him close?

He leaned forward, his warm breath minty, his skin radiating heat. His lips didn't touch her, leaving a scant barrier of air between them. "I want you. Badly. I'll have you, too. Now. If you don't let go," he demanded.

Both his thumbs rested against life-flowing arteries. He pressed in, a tiny pressure, not enough to harm, only enough to warn.

One imperative slashed through her. *Fight. Don't back down.*

His body forced her back three steps, until she met the unyielding wall. He pinned her there, with full-body length and thick arousal. She might hold his hands, but he imprisoned her body. Pressure everywhere stole blood and breath, leaving her dizzy. One wanton part of her, one she'd never encountered, gloried in the violence. The other part demanded retribution.

Primitive urges mixed with primal fears. His lips lowered to hers. For one moment, the kiss was a brutal punishment. For one moment she defended herself.

This was not Adam. As soon as flesh met flesh, that realization sliced through the blue haze. Abandoning her grip, she lifted her hands in surrender. "This is wrong."

He jerked off her, as though shoved by a giant hand. "Magick," he gasped, his hands braced against his knees. He stayed still, his eyes closed, as he gathered back the mantle of control, then shoved his hands in his pockets. "A bleeding spell. Powerful and so subtle I didn't protect against it, didn't feel it until we kissed."

His voice was full of disgust, and when he opened his eyes, she saw a fresh wariness and a cool distance there. "I'm sorry, Grace."

She took the steps to close the abyss between them and touched his wrist with her forefinger. He yanked away, as though burned.

"I bruised you," she said, nodding toward the mottling skin. "I'm sorry."

"You have nothing to apologize for. I wanted you so badly, if you hadn't, I would have torn your clothes off with my teeth."

"In a perverse way, that's rather flattering." She added a small smile, knowing they were both too raw to risk another touch. "Is the spell gone?"

He tilted his head, as though testing some unspoken code. "As far as I can tell. I saw this used before; it dies once you sever its grip. Once logic returns."

"What was it?"

"A spell directed against the superego. Takes off the civilized controls."

"And the reptile brain takes over." She thought about that. "That's why the spell is so strong, so subtle. It's not about lies and deception. Instead it intensifies truths and emotions already there."

If she needed added proof of the divide between her and Adam, then some unknown had just provided it. Glancing at him, at the way he donned his coat, taking care not to touch her, she saw he was steps ahead of her. He'd already reached the same conclusions: Beyond the exposed mutual desire, part of her still hurt, still didn't trust him; part of him hated that she hadn't let him explain.

Maybe he had a measure of right on his side. She was

judging him by years-old criteria, afraid to see him with fresh eyes. Afraid that she would care too much about what she saw. Last time, she'd physically lost a kidney. The real organ she always risked, though, was her heart.

The bombing had irrevocably changed her; she wasn't the same person she had been, for the aftermath had uncovered her healing powers.

She also understood how fears and loyalties could seal the lips. Out of loyalty, she hadn't told him about the research she did with Kea, and every time she thought about confessing her fugues, her throat closed.

Why assume Adam was unchanged? Had had no good reasons for his actions?

Grace reached out, brushing off the ashes of the past to start fresh, and laid a hand on his shoulder. "Someone wants us at odds. We won't let them win."

He took her hand, lifted it to his lips, and gave her knuckles a kiss. "That person also knows where we are. We should pack up, stay somewhere else after we find out what Raj can tell us."

"Agreed."

Swiftly they packed their few belongings, the biggest obstacle to leaving being finding Gala. When at last they discovered her cowering behind the microwave, and persuaded her into Adam's pocket, they were off.

Outside, Grace took in a deep breath. The damp cold washed away the last traces of lingering anger and desire, leaving her with only an amused competitiveness when they both headed toward the driver's side. Adam held up the keys. "I ended up with these."

She made a face. "I know the roads."

"But there's something I want to show you while we drive."

Once on the road, he began, "You asked about my involvement with Vitae. I own forty-five percent. So does Jonas Washington. Regan Hollister owns the remaining ten percent, so if Jonas and I disagree, she holds the power. We've had our differences, and Regan's always sided with Jonas." He gave a small shrug. "Gradually, I left the running of the company to them."

"How'd you end up editor of *NONE*? You could live off your profits, I assume."

"One of the useless, tabloid-feeding rich?" His scorn was evident. "After the bombing, my stepdad, who started *NONE* offered me work. I wanted out of Britain so I took the offer. I traveled, picked up a few odd skills, learned some things. Then he wanted out, so I bought the paper, shortly before he died. Discovered I had a knack for nosing out oddities. We're free to explore any story we want, take any angle we want, and I like that."

"Among the fluff and spin, you've exposed some dangerous frauds and evil abuse of powers."

"I like that, too," he said softly.

And that, she knew, was his true calling. "But you're still connected to Vitae?"

"I do beta testing for new releases, work on some concepts, that's all. I asked Jonas and Regan once if they wanted to buy me out, but they refused." He paused, then added, "None of us wants that final break."

"Could they be behind the attacks on the mages? On us?"

"Maybe," he answered promptly, indicating he'd considered the idea. "But I doubt it. They'd never use magick. Magick killed Faith; magick tried to set us against each other."

She had also suspected that her fugue was magick-based. Nothing she could pinpoint—either she'd subconsciously picked up a clue or she had a desperate need for an explanation beyond a career-ending health issue.

"And I think magick is behind the deaths of those mages. I've heard rumors, collected data on the Custos Magi. Supposedly they're guardian mages, dedicated to fighting evil. But I think some are more interested in power than protection.

I've been hunting for one, someone I know only as the Dragon, and, unfortunately, that's not an uncommon mage symbol among the Magi."

"Why are you hunting him?"

"He drove my sister, Abby, mad." He thrust out his phone. "This is what I wanted you to see. She was so pretty and vibrant, the most important person in my life."

He'd called up two video snippets. In the first, Abby was opening a present, and it was her birthday, judging from the paper crown on her head. Adam's gift, a crystal pendant on a silver chain, must have pleased her, for she jumped up and hugged him. The love between the siblings was obvious.

"Vitae had started to grow," he said, his voice husky. "She'd craved that crystal, but it was quite dear. Finally I could afford to give her something splashy. She wore it constantly."

The second video flashed on, showing an unfurnished room, stark and gray. In one corner huddled a gaunt and disheveled Abby. She was screaming at some terror only she could see, endlessly screaming.

"After a few months, her voice gave out," Adam said flatly.

"Was there any warning?"

"None." He shook his head, as though wiping away the memory. "She follows directions—eats, uses the loo, walks—but always locked in that terror."

Horror burned in Grace's throat as the video went blank. Was her fugue a prelude to this? "There was a burn mark on her forehead."

"The shape of the crystal. She wore it constantly, imbued it with her energy. The Dragon might have used it as the link to her mind."

Adam had lived with this guilt for far longer than she'd known him. She sucked in a breath. "That's who you were after when you infiltrated our coven."

He nodded. "There was true power there."

"Didn't the bombing kill the Dragon?"

"Sometimes I've wanted to believe that, but I need proof."
He rubbed his face. "Those eight mages had connections to
the Dragon. The ones who were still sane when I visited
claimed the Dragon was dead and they didn't know his identity. But they were still scared."

She took a breath. "It's a long shot, but I may be proof
your Dragon is alive."

He gave her a sharp look. "How?"

Her throat and her will closed on the admission. Another
deep breath. If they were to get anywhere with this investi-
gation, both of them needed all the facts. Adam's confession
had not been easy, either.

He might plaster her story across the front page of *NONE*.

She glanced at his phone. Unless she found a way to stop
the attacks, was that madness her fate? Still, she owed him
the truth.

"Because maybe I'm this Dragon's next victim."

With a curse, Adam pulled across three lanes of speeding
I-96 traffic, ignoring honks and flipped fingers, to pull off on
the graveled side. Undoing his seat belt, he turned. "What
happened?"

She explained briefly about the fugues. "I only have impressions, not facts. I have no memory of most of them. But
that last fugue, when you were attacked, I had some bizarre
hallucinations. I thought I was going crazy."

His fingers bracketed her face, drawing her glance into
his. "You are not insane," he said fiercely. "You are grounded
and intelligent and caring."

"The blackouts have only happened when I'm healing, as
if whoever's behind this needs that particular link."

His face tightened. "Magick."

"You think there's a mage with the capability of mind
linking?" She hated saying the words, giving the chilling
prospect such power.

"I don't know what happened with Abby." Adam let out a long breath. "What brought you out of the fugues?"

"The first times? I don't know." She gave another shrug, hating that she knew so little. "Maybe the link wasn't strong, or needs X number of connections or some third factor for permanence. The starts and stops are quite painful. The night you were attacked, though, I got free when I stumbled over you."

"Any idea why you?"

She shrugged one shoulder, not liking to admit her conclusion. "Because I have power, but not many protections."

"Maybe you were chosen not because you're weak, but because you can heal. Or simple proximity; because you're convenient."

"Someone I know?"

"Or treated."

"That could be anybody." She shook her head. "I'd hoped Faith might have some answers, but all she sent were those three e-mails."

"And we'll figure them out. Together." He leaned forward and kissed her. His lips were gentle, but the torrent of need rising inside her was a force of nature.

Gala wriggled out of Adam's pocket, scampering up his arm to where Grace's hands clung to his solid shoulders. The ferret nosed at Grace's hands, trying to shove them off, adding a nip as incentive.

With an unsteady laugh, Grace let go, spreading her hands wide in surrender. Gala perched upright, as though saying, "This is *my* shoulder."

Grace laughed harder, feeling her tension loosen. Sharing hadn't stopped the fear, but it had eased the burden.

Adam gave the ferret a disgusted look. "Jealousy does not become you, Gala. Get used to her; trust me, you don't want to make me choose."

Gala gave a small click and darted back into the pocket.

Adam took Grace's hand. "We'll stop those fugues. Whatever it takes." His fingers tightened. "Is there anything else you want to tell me?"

Tell him about Kea. About your fusion of nanobots with magick.

Hands-on healing might not rank a column in *NONE*, but this sure as hell would. How far did she trust him?

Not with all her secrets. This wasn't just about her. Kea had asked for her silence. She still owed him, and the project, loyalty.

"No." She leaned her head back against the headrest, feeling ten kinds of small. "Nothing."

Chapter Eleven

"You have arrived," announced the smooth male voice of Grace's GPS, and Adam pulled the car over.

"That building is prime real estate." Grace stared up at the glass-fronted apartments. "Deadly virus creation must be lucrative." Her voice turned as gray and hard as the ice-edged concrete.

"Raj Kasin is both unique and very good at what he does. That's reflected in his price. And his paranoia." With a hand to her arm, Adam stopped her from getting out while she was thinking of Faith. "We're here to get that Trojan horse off my computer and find out who paid for the virus. Not revenge."

"No justice?" she asked bitterly.

"Not here. Not now. Not us. If you can't put aside your anger, then we leave right now. Anything else is too dangerous."

He waited for her decision, relieved when her face steeled into a mask of detachment. "Like treating an obnoxious drunk with a dump in his pants."

Adam got out of the car, with Grace exiting from the other side. He hoisted his laptop strap onto his shoulder, checked that Gala was snuggled into his pocket, and then tightened his muffler. Good thing he'd taken the time to purchase warmer outerwear, including a hat and boots. The day had deepened into pitch night, with the frigid breath of winter gusting off the St. Clair River.

Raj had texted instructions half an hour ago. Adam and Grace were to stand visibly alone, call, and Raj would buzz them in. Following the directions, Adam called up.

"Come to the warehouse behind," clipped Raj. "When I ring you, you'll have five minutes."

"Got his edge on," Grace murmured.

"A paranoid antisocial genius."

"Hate to think how he'd be if we weren't invited."

"You know the cliché."

"Even paranoids have enemies."

They reached the appointed warehouse, which was surrounded by a chain-link fence and rolls of prison-grade barbwire. Boards covered most of the windows like wooden eyelids, and the few with glass reflected back only leaden air.

"Urban renewal extends only a block deep." Grace glanced around. "I'd say this was abandoned except for the satellite dish."

They made it past the initial fence in the allotted five minutes, and then wound through a twisted maze of barbwire. As they neared the final steps, Adam moved closer to Grace, the hairs on his neck rising.

Strange touches of magick seeped out of the concrete building. More energy brushed against his ankles. From buried wires? Raj had taken his meld of magick and tech deep.

They reached the institutional concrete walls and were buzzed through. Blinded by darkness, Adam moved immediately to Grace's side. By mutual accord, they waited in silence until their eyes adjusted.

The warehouse was echoingly empty, one vast space of dust and mold.

Grace pointed to winding stairs, the only exit other than the closed door at their backs. "Shades of *SciMage*—I think we're supposed to go up those."

"In the game, the steps lead to a deadly trap of sharp knives and scorpions."

"Well aware of that. Is Gala okay?" Grace nodded toward his inside jacket pocket.

"Snoozing. That ferret sleeps more than Rip Van Winkle."

"At least she's not shitting on your socks."

Adam bit back a snicker at the acidic edge in her voice. Grace had not been happy with Gala's small gift. Then, humor dying, he glanced at the stairs. "Maybe we should turn back."

"Or maybe we should find out what the hell Raj Kasin knows." Grace vanished around the first curve.

At the upper level, a climate-controlled, dust-free room stretched the entire top of the warehouse. Faith's jumbled mix of arcane and tech was a nursery compared to this. Serious banks of computers, an electronic workbench, industrial diamonds and crystals, a full-size mannequin of a tusked warrior, a powerful circle for incantations. Bits and pieces of computers were cobbled together with fiber optics and gemstones.

Only two computers were on—one with a spiraling screen saver, one playing an RPG sequence that mashed together several commercial products, judging from the snippets he recognized. Adam assumed there was an organization to the overstuffed mix—Raj was, at heart, a linear-minded programmer—but he couldn't decipher the scheme.

Throughout and beneath thrummed the energies of magick.

"No scorpions?" Grace observed under her breath.

"Or skulls with bladed teeth?" added Adam. With a touch to her wrist—*cover me*—he began a subtle prowl, checking the underlying magick.

"You would recognize my nods to *SciMage*, Adam." Wearing skintight black denim and a sleeveless black T-shirt, Raj materialized out of a dark shadow.

To date, all their contact had been electronic. This first look at the man who billed himself as a creative hacker intrigued Adam. Late twenties, maybe. He took in the tats on Raj's arms, running from shoulder to wrist, the steel ball at the center of his lower lip, the shaved head, the caramel skin that hinted at mixed ancestry—Indian and African, he'd hazard.

"Hard to miss the entrance to the Tenth Level of Death." Grace drew Raj's attention.

Bad actor. Raj pretended he'd only just noticed her. "Only if you've reached that level."

"Was your avatar Azrael?"

"How'd you know?"

She nodded to his arms. "Tat pattern's the same."

"Observant. Who was your avatar?"

"Ariel."

Having ID'd at least two defensive systems, Adam rejoined them. "I was Drakken Laird." He'd been so full of himself then.

"Legends in the early game," Raj noted, with a measure of respect that had been missing. He nodded to Adam's laptop. "You said you had an interesting problem."

Adam fired up his computer and handed it over. "Open one program. Delete another."

Raj's lip curled. "Standard fare that's a bullshit waste of my time. And worse, boring."

"Not this. Besides, we agreed on a price." Adam leaned one hip on the back of the sofa, then abruptly stood. At the tenth level of *SciMage*, ensorcelled furniture would, if touched, eat flesh with acid. He held up a USB drive. "*SciMage VI*. Due out this summer."

Raj's nonchalant shrug didn't hide his eager reach for the drive.

Adam pulled it back. "After my computer's clean."

"If you wanna pay for scut work . . ."

"Use these." Adam dug out the visor and gloves, and saw the twin gleams of avarice and interest light inside Raj.

The programmer donned the visor and gloves and a grin broke through the layers of nerd-cool. "Frakken!" At first, his only motion was a slow turn; then his hands moved, a pantomime of door opening. Moments later, all color left his face, and he clamped his lips together. He tore off the visor and bent over. "You could have warned me."

"Nausea a bitch?" Adam asked.

"Level twenty-grade." Raj sucked in air, then raised his head. "That door's DNA coded for one person. If you want me to break that code, then leave the computer, along with the gloves and visor, give me a month, and triple my fee."

Adam glanced at Grace. She might not believe in her talent, but Faith had, and so did he. "We'll take a pass. Did you see the spell program?"

"No." Raj sank into an armchair, stretched out his feet, and put the visor back on. Adam saw him turn in another direction. "That gold sparkle?"

"That's what I want you to take off. Can you?"

"Of course." His hands starting typing on the keyboard in a blur of strokes.

Grace leaned in to whisper, "See that computer in the far corner, at the periphery of the circle?" At Adam's nod, she continued, "It's running a continual virus checker."

He looked closer. "And those door locks are new."

"From the fading on the chair fabric, those shuttered windows are usually open. He's also got a lot of computers that are off." She exchanged a glance with Adam. "He's scared."

Raj peeled off the visor. "The program's off." He handed the computer back to Adam.

As soon as Adam touched the case, his fingers tingled with vestiges of power running through the wires. The bastard had removed the computerized piece of the program, but he'd left the magick tracer.

Raj folded the gloves into a tidy stack. "I'll keep these and the visor."

Adam's hand shot out and clamped his wrist. "Those are mine."

"Do you think I'm defenseless here? Go now or suffer the consequences. Your choice." He smiled as his outstretched foot pressed onto a small rug.

The light collapsed into black, accompanied by a mind-spearing electronic screech. In the immediate disorientation, Adam felt Raj wrench from his grip.

A single beam of light stabbed through the cave, high-lighting the steps they'd come up. The path out. Grace stood in the beam, looking furious as she searched the impenetrable darkness for a vanished Raj. "He isn't keeping Faith's equipment," she spat, her anger more lip-read than heard.

"No." But Adam guessed they didn't have much time, and he had to make sure Grace was protected. He shoved the laptop into Grace's arms, then pulled two obsidian knives from an ankle holster. Holding the hilts in one hand, he slashed his palm across the points, piercing the skin. Blood dripped down the blades. He focused on the energies within his own blood, the strange ones with the power to reflect magick. Red and black melded.

Swiftly he pressed against her—if only he could stay here, kissing the sweet skin beneath her ear—and circled his hands, each holding a knife, around her. The droplets fell as dark crimson in the white-hot light. With his blood, he guarded her. Grabbing Gala by the scruff, he deposited the ferret on her shoulder. "Do not move," he warned them both, mouth directly against Grace's ear so he could be heard above the headache-producing whine. "The magick will reflect off you until the blood dries. When that happens, get the hell out!"

When a mulish look narrowed her eyes, he swore, "Dammit, Grace, keep Gala and that laptop secure!" He stepped back, closed the blood circle, and then sped after Raj.

"Your mistake, Drakken Laird," Raj said with a laugh, his disembodied voice above the noise giving no hint of his locale.

But Raj was the one making a mistake, thinking this was

a game. Adam had never confused game codes for life. Reality was complex and painful. Death was messy and harsh and tragic. There was no reset code for Faith.

Not bothering to answer the taunting programmer, Adam focused his senses on locating the defense systems Raj had set up. His knives slashing through the magick-enhanced blackness, Adam took two leaps toward the first. His foot smashed through a pile of ebony. Abruptly the darkness receded to the edges of the room, carrying with it the noise, as he turned back the darkness spell.

Blinking, ears ringing, he spun around to look for Raj and spied him speeding for a door in the wall, one that had been hidden until now.

Startled at the light, Raj glanced over his shoulder. He dropped the visor and gloves as the heel of his hand stretched toward the second defense Adam had found, a gas duct. Adam threw one of the knives. The obsidian blade spun hilt over point and embedded itself in a crack below the hinge, sealing the door.

Raj scowled. If he let out the gas now, he'd be a victim, too. He grabbed at the knife, then let it go, howling. Cradling his burned hand, he glared at Adam.

"The hilt rejects any traces of magick," Adam said, picking up the visor and gloves. "Take the tracer off my computer, answer one question, and we'll go."

"Advance!" spat Raj.

The walls dissolved into a streaming mass of scorpions. Claws snapping, stingers waving in search of victims, they covered the floor in a wave of death.

"Their poison is quite real," Raj said gleefully, "although I'm immune."

Hadn't seen that one. Heart filled with fear, Adam spun toward Grace. The circle still held; the scorpions parted around her. So they were at least part magick. Part mechanical, judging from the clicking bodies, probably part organic, judging from the smell.

Raj really was brilliant, if a bit theatrical.

Too bad he stopped to gloat.

Adam moved in a blur, grabbing Raj and twisting his arm up his back in a grip he knew was painful, but not harmful. Yet. "Stop them."

"Holding me won't shield you."

"Grace, what's the quickest way to exsanguination?"

"Cut the carotid artery," she answered promptly and pointed to her neck. "Here."

Adam pressed his knife against Raj's neck, just at the spot she'd indicated.

"What the hell?" Raj's skin turned muddy.

"Cut lengthwise, so it doesn't clot," Grace called. "The heart will keep pumping out the blood."

Adam pressed hard enough to break the skin.

"The scorpion poison isn't really deadly, it just knocks you out!" Raj shouted. "Same with the gas."

"Not betting my life on your say-so."

"I can stop them!" Raj struggled, but couldn't escape Adam's grip.

"Do it!" Adam snapped, feeling the circling brush of death. He couldn't keep them all at bay forever. "Otherwise I've got two options. Kill the magick in them or use your blood as a shield. Either one starts with killing you."

Panting, Raj spat out the words of reversal. The scorpions stopped at Adam's shoe. Adam lifted the knife away and lowered Raj's arm to relieve the pressure. "Back into the walls."

With Raj's chant, the scorpions slowly receded, disappearing into the darkness. Still holding Raj, Adam sidled over and retrieved his other knife, while Grace collected the visor and gloves.

"We had a bargain," Adam said evenly. "I paid you to take

off the program. You did it only halfway. Take off the magick-formed piece as well." He lifted the knives, but kept them close as he handed over the notebook.

Sullenly, Raj took the computer inside a circle of highly polished brown, red, and black stones. Kneeling on the wood floor, he tapped a blur of strokes onto the keyboard and pulled up a swirling mass of puce and lime green onto the screen. "The program could be used to trace your whereabouts," he said, his back to them. "The spell anchors it while tendrils reach toward that door, like an octopus searching for succulent mussels."

"Or a cancer?" Grace muttered.

"The magick is dangerous, but I can get it out." Raj put on a great show: chants, a column of swirling colors, a stink of burned wire, a high-pitched whine, ending with an explosive clap. He leaned back, smiling at last. "Done."

Adam took back his computer, checking it thoroughly, including a pass-through from virtual reality. Clean.

Raj held out his hand. "*SciMage VI.*"

Adam hesitated, then tossed him the drive. He kept his bargains.

"What can you tell us about a magick-blended computer virus? One that smokes along the Internet, bursts between computers, if they're networked or in physical proximity. Eats air."

"Can't be done." Raj stacked his hands behind his head as he lolled in his computer chair and stretched out his feet. He tried to look innocent. Instead he looked like a skinny cat with canary feathers.

Adam lifted his brows. "Who's smarter than you?"

Raj scowled. "No one."

"Somebody must be. You say can't do, but the virus exists."

A black-painted nail picked at a thread. "You saw the virus in action? What happened?"

"If you didn't make it, why do you care?" Hand at her back, Adam ushered Grace toward the door.

"Wait!" Raj called again. "I made it." The arrogance returned, and he resumed his relaxed pose. "Let's talk bargain."

Enough of this. Pivoting, Adam pressed the full length of the knife against Raj's cheek, and cut. Not deep, but he drew blood. Over Raj's howl he said, "You just tried to kill us, the bargain is we don't return the favor."

"Not for real. I was gaming you, man."

Adam didn't lift the knife. "Who bought the virus?"

Panting, Raj shook his head. "Can't tell you that. One reason I can command my price. My services come with an absolute guarantee of privacy."

Adam gave him a long look. "You're afraid of what you might have created, and now I've shown you that your defenses are vulnerable."

"How long," Grace added, "will they let you survive?"

His jaw worked convulsively. "I was given parameters, spells to include. I only built it. I didn't set it out."

"How can I find who did?" Adam hammered.

"I don't know who it was. A man, I think, but even that's not sure."

"How did he contact you?"

"E-mail, phone."

Adam pressed a fraction deeper. "You know more."

"One call." The words tumbled out. "The number wasn't blocked, so I traced it. Came from a downtown nightclub—the Spider Net. The voice that answered was different. Evil."

"Yet you finished the virus," Adam said flatly, then pulled away the knife.

"The challenge." Raj smiled. "Irresistible."

"They also paid well."

"That too. I swear, that's all I know." As they readied to go, Raj grabbed Adam's arm. "What should I do now?"

"Don't turn on your computers."

Rubbing the cut on his cheek, Raj watched the car pull away. Fucking arrogance, to think they could stand against Azrael and the Dragon. Carefully, he reset all his defenses, then, on second thought, added a few stronger spells. Only when he was secure did he pick up his BlackBerry and call.

"I know where the library is." He laughed at the answer and fingered the USB drive. "You'll have to figure out another way to find it. I took off the tracer. Why? Because you only paid me to put it on, not keep it on." He inserted the drive into the game console. *And Adam Zolton had the coin.* "But I can tell you who's got the library. For a price."

He named a figure, made sure the money had been transferred to his account, before he said, "Adam Zolton. The library's on his computer."

When he hung up, he double-checked the balance, and gave a satisfied sigh. He finally had enough; all the plans had been made, his new identity set up. He was getting out of here—in two days Raj Kasin would vanish and a very wealthy Tamor Balin would take his place among the elite of Mumbai.

His phone rang, and he glanced at the ID. Number blocked. He didn't bother to answer.

Unfortunately for Raj, the breath of the Dragon did not require his cooperation.

Adam and Grace were two blocks away when a blast pierced the leaden air.

"Raj!" they shouted in unison, and Grace spun the car around.

From the street, they watched as sparks flew from the windows, flames crackling madly. Adam grabbed her arm when she would have dashed upstairs. "No! You'll only get yourself killed."

"We have to help!"

"There's nothing we can do."

He was right, and she watched helplessly as the warehouse became an inferno.

CHAPTER TWELVE

Despite the late hour, the Spider Net was wide awake. As they paid the cover to enter the neon and steel nightclub, Grace wished she'd had the time to change. The crowd was urban sophisticated, mixed race, young.

Despite the bandage she'd put on his hand, Adam seemed totally at ease. His leather coat and sharp-fitting jeans blended in. Her casual sweatshirt did not. Add to that her black eye, runaway hair, and the clinging aroma of smoke, and she felt like the grubby party crasher. Quickly, she tamed her hair back with a pair of clips and put on lipstick. Better.

After all, they weren't here for a good time.

Adam held out his hand. "Let's dance, love."

The endearment was casual, natural; Grace's breath hitched. She wanted to hear that familiar heated accent when they were together, naked, holding each other in tight tenderness.

If they got free of this web of magick and deceit, did they have a chance?

When you're powering nanobots and he's exposing the dangers of combining magick and technology?

They moved to the dance floor. Here the city pulsed in an urban sensory assault. Her ears took the first punch from blaring techno. Her nose took the second as she pressed back a cough from the smoke of tobacco and marijuana.

Adam stood intoxicatingly near, his hands at her waist, while they swayed to the beat. He leaned forward, speaking close to her ear, the only way to be heard. "We need a game plan."

She nodded, but neither one offered a suggestion. Instead, he seemed as unwilling as she to shatter this moment together. Their gazes melded, and the pressure of his hard body communicated every move, sliding them as one through the dancers. Adam pulled her gyrating hips closer and pulsed against her.

If only they were just out on the town together. Dinner, dancing, then back to their hotel to accept the invitation in those hips.

Instead tonight was deadly explosions and a nightclub that suddenly seemed too raucous and harsh, while tomorrow was lunch at Vitae, not for a pleasant get-together with friends, but for discovering secrets.

She stopped dancing. Sinking into the natural curve of his arm, she looked up at him and saw the same regrets reflected in his face. "We should circulate."

"If we go to the balcony, we'll have a bird's-eye view."

They found a free table away from the noise of the dance floor, and Adam procured them a pair of rum-free colas.

"What were you working on while I drove?" she asked, drawing a finger through the sweat on her glass, letting the ice cool her.

"Looking for who owned this, but the records are buried. So, I asked Brando to check on that when I sent him Faith's data on the mages." He pointed to the Spider Net logo on their napkins. "Odd sort of corporate symbol. Looks like a fuzzy centipede."

"Odd? Try creepy. Reminds me of cranial nerves formed by snakes. Who builds a logo of neurons and serpents?"

"In myth, the dragon is often portrayed as a serpentine figure."

"I always preferred the Chinese version. Fierce when angered, but also a protector and bringer of rains." She bunched up the napkin and shifted her shoulders to dislodge the fear slithering down her back. Something about this place irritated worse than an eyelash on an eyeball.

She leaned closer to Adam. "Do you feel any magick?"

"No. Let's wander, see if we can find the heart of the Spider."

In the darkest corner of the main floor, they found two service doors labeled "Employees Only." Behind one were the lockers, break room, and bathroom for the employees. Behind the other was a stock room and an ordinary office. Nothing else.

They were about to leave when Adam pointed out a third door, one she'd missed. The nearly invisible door, sunk into an unlit alcove and labeled "No Admittance," proved to be locked.

Adam put his hand on the door. "There's a trickle of energy. Maybe a spell to discourage entry?"

"I think the keypad—the one we don't have the code to—does that."

"Double protection, must be something important behind there. Let's check the alley."

After the heated club, the raw night buried her in cold. Deep in the alley, shadows cut off the few streetlights. A sound spiked her adrenaline.

"A cat," murmured Adam, pointing to the calico tail disappearing behind a Dumpster.

Espionage, she decided, wouldn't have been a good career choice for her. She'd have had ulcers within a year.

"That's the service door. I'd say this unmarked one is what we want." Adam handed her a flashlight. "Hold this."

Grace hunched her chin deeper into her scarf as she trained the light onto the lock. Adam bent down to see if he could undo it.

Mastering that unlock spell would have come in handy.

While he worked, Grace glanced around, her spine tightening with the sensation of being watched. At least four cameras dotted the alley. So why wasn't security after them?

The door clicked open. Apparently Adam had picked up a few handy, if larcenous, skills. He stood and brushed the snow off his jeans. "Ready?"

The door swung ajar. Darkness filled the small gap, giving not a hint of what waited beyond the threshold. A whiff of incense and mold stung her eyes.

"That was too easy," she told him.

"We need answers." He started to go in.

Around them, brick and concrete whispered, *bad idea*. She grabbed his arm, stopping him. "Don't go in, Adam."

He toed open the door. Two openings led off the anteroom, each entry highlighted by a pale light from a steel fixture, illuminating only a few inches.

"Mmmmrowww."

Grace jumped back as the calico cat darted past, chasing a rat inside. Light swelled along the beasts' path, revealing what had been hidden.

Monitors covered every centimeter of the walls. Scene after scene flickered on, showing rooms and streets, all vulnerable to a spying mage. From the unlit depths, the rat's squeal broke off. The cat froze, hair bristling, back arching. A foul stench rose from the darkness.

"Get out of here," she snapped to Adam, taking off at a run. "Now!"

He didn't argue, following at her heels as they dashed out of the alley and around the corner. Grace thought she heard shouts, but maybe she only heard the roar from her own ears. They cut across the street and into the rubble of an abandoned building. Grace plastered herself against the crumbling Sheetrock, angling so she could see out of the window. Adam stood behind her, looking over her shoulder, shielding her from anyone following.

This close, she caught the fresh-washed scent of his after-shave. His slowing breath brushed across her hair. Despite tension, despite the possibility of a pursuer, she allowed herself to enjoy this stolen moment.

"What did you see?" he asked, keeping his voice low.

She told him about the four alley cameras. "If we're dealing with the Dragon or Vitae, we're talking major tech savvy. Much as I respect your skills, Adam, do you think their version of a secure door could be opened by an amateur lock pick? My condo has better security."

"Much as it bruises my lock-picking ego, I agree. Someone wanted us in."

"A contingency plan laid when the Dragon let Raj see that phone number."

They waited a few more minutes, saw no pursuit, then agreed all they were accomplishing was freezing their buns. Circling the long way around the block back to their car, they passed the farther end of the alley.

All was quiet and empty except for the calico cat. It huddled against the brick wall, shivering.

"Adam, we can't just leave it." She bent down, holding her hand out to the frightened cat. With a snarl, the cat raked her hand with its claws, and then disappeared into the night.

CHAPTER THIRTEEN

Vitae was unlike any office Grace had ever seen. The colors were rainbow hued. The artwork was holographic scenes from Vitae's stable of games. The arm-tattooed and brow-ringed receptionist was young enough that the ink on her college diploma might still be wet, but she took seriously her role as gatekeeper.

They weren't on her list of scheduled visitors; they couldn't go in until she confirmed their appointment.

Adam could have pitched a fit, pulled rank—he was a major stockholder, the originator of that full-size figure of Drakken Laird brandishing a crystal laser in the corner. Hell, the thing even bore a resemblance to him. Instead, he charmed the receptionist, seeming perfectly relaxed, while Grace edgily fingered the bands in her pocket.

Their conversation ended when an enthusiastic female voice called out, "Adam!"

Adam smiled at the woman coming from the inner door. "Hullo, Regan."

Regan Hollister was an elegant blonde, whose casual dress of jeans, Uggs, and sweater had nothing casual about the price tag. Her face, a perfect, smooth oval, with makeup applied so tastefully it seemed invisible, could have served as model for the old masters' paintings of the Madonna.

But as marketing director for a multimillion-dollar company, she had to have some steel beneath that angelic appearance.

Pale and blonde. Might be mistaken for an angel. The snippet of conversation with Radar three days ago about a woman asking for Grace in the ER came to mind. Could that have been Regan?

Regan and Adam greeted each other with affectionate hugs and cheek kisses; then he introduced Grace. As they shook hands, Grace asked, "Have we met before? You seem familiar. Ever been in the U-Mich ER?"

Regan shook her head. "Fortunately I've never needed emergency care. If we've met, I don't remember." The warm smile eased what could have been a subtle dig.

"You didn't need to go through the receptionist," Regan scolded, as they made their way deeper into the offices. "You could have come right in."

"Just following protocol," Adam answered. "I'm an unfamiliar face."

"Since when did you care about protocol?"

Grace listened to their catching-up conversation with half an ear, as she took in the inner details of Vitae. News crews had never been allowed inside, and she was intrigued by the atmosphere of work hard, play hard. Although most everyone was at work singly or in groups around a computer, she saw evidence of unconventionality. Grace, Adam, and Regan dodged two people acting out a sword fight while a third made a digital record of their motions. Two employees hit a ball and ideas back and forth over a foosball table.

Nowhere, however, was a hint these people were anything but what they claimed to be—developers of some of the most sought-after games and innovative hardware in the industry.

"Adam!" From another door, Jonas Washington joined them, wearing jeans and a Block M T-shirt, and carrying a tray of crudités. He was about the same age as Adam, with spiky black hair and a watch the size of New Jersey. She noticed another similarity to Adam—when they were in the room, they commanded attention, even without saying a word.

Jonas set down the tray, and then took off his glasses and wiped steam off them before he greeted her and exchanged manly hugs and back slaps with Adam. "Adam, when are you going to add HD content to the *NONE* Web page?"

"I'm saving that for the first irrefutable photos of a UFO."

"Still hunting for life beyond earth?"

"Others are out there. I'm going to be the first to prove it."

"So when E.T. shows his face, we'll get the exclusive rights to the game?"

"*Certainement.*"

Jonas retrieved the appetizer tray. "I've made lunch for us. Try a gingered pineapple cracker." After Grace took a few bites, he asked, "What do you think of the balance of alkali and citric acid?"

"Ah, fine?" The cracker was good, that was all she knew.

"Try a tenth of a gram less baking powder next time," Adam suggested.

"Good thought." Jonas pulled out a PDA and made a note.

"Jonas is an engineer to his core," Adam explained. "When he cooks, he weighs each ingredient, and the granite countertops are covered with every gadget known to God and chef."

"Whereas Adam throws random bits and pieces, along with jalapenos, into a pot and creates a meal."

"So what's today's whiz-bang?"

"A dry ice freezer for blueberry ice cream. Lunch is ready." Jonas glanced at the pair of foosballers, who had been joined by two others in their rapid-fire brainstorming. "We're eating in my private quarters. It's quieter."

The relaxed atmosphere did not extend to security, Grace noticed, which was subtle, but pervasive. Every bit of flooring under mike and camera surveillance. Key card and thumb print scanning to pass through doors. Probably some she was missing.

Adam took photos, as he had on the way in. When Regan noticed, she put a playful hand over the lens. "Remember the 'no photo' policy?"

"Standing rule," Jonas added. "Even for Regan and me. Only preapproved publicity shots. Security and all."

"Sorry. Habit. Can I get one of you and Regan?" He turned them slightly, took the shot, and then stowed the camera. "I'll delete the others."

Along the way, they were stopped twice by employees with questions and suggestions. Apparently Regan and Jonas weren't ivory-tower executives. Their employees knew, and liked, them. At last, though, they reached the well-appointed rooms where Jonas's buffet of smoked salmon, homemade kettle chips, and Michigan salad awaited.

As they hung up their coats, Regan asked with a laugh, "Adam, what beast have you got in your pocket? Or are you that glad to see us?"

Grace and Adam both looked where she pointed. Gala's head and front claws poked above the hem of his pocket. Her back feet scrabbled against the inside, making the fabric vibrate in small points. She had a grin on her face, as she eagerly tried to escape.

Adam made a scolding noise, and then held his hand for her to jump on. "This is Gala."

"What is it?" Jonas was definitely skeptical.

"She's a naughty ferret who was not supposed to stow away in my pocket."

Keeping her gaze locked onto the black-eyed ferret, Regan held out her hand. "Welcome to Vitae, Gala."

Gala sniffed at the outstretched hand, put one paw against the French-manicured nail. For a moment, Grace thought Regan would join her in the pee-on-your-clothes corner, but Gala, after a few more sniffs, took the proffered perch.

Regan lifted the beast to her shoulder. "I seem to have found a new friend."

Damn ferret. The only time Gala sat that quietly was when she was sleeping, but there she was, sniffing away and still.

Jonas scratched behind Gala's ear. "What does this little lady eat?"

"We have chow back at the hotel. Maybe a dish of water?" But when Adam tried to lift her off Regan's shoulder, the ferret jumped and ran away.

"Gala!" Adam chased after her.

Grace followed, along with Regan and Jonas, but the wily ferret had found a hiding spot somewhere in Jonas's inner office.

"Never play hide-and-seek with a ferret," Jonas said, after none of them could locate her.

"Jonas, I'm sorry—"

"Don't be; I'm sure she'll come back in time." He clapped Adam on the shoulder, and Grace saw the charm partially responsible for his phenomenal success. "Maybe the aroma of my salmon will draw her back."

The charm continued through the lunch with wide-ranging conversations on the economy and medicine and film. Much as she wanted to find a villain, Grace found it difficult to see either one as a killer. Yet, fingers pointed toward Vitae.

As conversation died, Jonas and Regan eyed first her, then Adam, obviously sensing undercurrents to the visit. Adam had fallen silent, fingering his water goblet, likely reluctant to spoil these last moments of peace.

They had come here with a purpose. Up to her, then, to raise the stink.

Jonas spoke first. "You work with Kea Lin, Grace? He's done extraordinary research with nanobots. We've used some of the principles here."

"You're working with nanobots?" She hadn't read anything

about that. Adam stopped vacillating over the water glass to give his friend his attention.

"All quite hush-hush. Be a decade before the competition catches up with our technology."

"What use?" Adam asked.

"We've embedded them within a *SciMage* prototype for more organic options in the game," Regan replied. "The game learns and grows with the player, adding complexity or hints as needed, depending upon the skill level. Each player's experience is subtly different; the possibilities are nearly infinite."

"The bots are functional?" Grace asked, her spine tightening. Powered bots were almost unknown; only a few high-level research centers had them, and their use was strictly regulated. "How do you power them?"

"Body electromagnetic forces."

What kinds of fringe science did Vitae employ in these never-seen labs? "Those bots aren't workable outside the body; the force range is too small."

"Oh, but these are," he said softly.

"You need FDA approval."

"Only if we were injecting into the human body. We aren't. Because the game controller is in human hands, we can take advantage of a very clean power source." He sat back. "I admit, there are still kinks before we can take them to market."

"We can only program a single action; then the bot dies," Regan explained.

"You still need safeguards against independent action by the bots and against cross-contamination," Adam observed.

Jonas gave a small laugh. "Thus speaks the traditionalist."

"Thus speaks the journalist who's read every science-gone-wrong story," Adam said with a hint of irritation. The first sign of tension between the men?

Yet Adam still didn't mention the bands, as they'd planned.

Time to shake things up and see what fell out. She pulled the bands from her purse and laid them on the table. "Do these contain your nanobots?"

"What are they?" Jonas seemed genuinely perplexed as he picked up one band while Regan examined the other. The band wound around his wrist in sinuous welcome.

"It appears to know you."

Jonas held up his arm. "*SciMage*. Level ten: Rialta captures the Dark Dragon Hedda with the cable snakes. Adam's conception."

"Not my execution, though," Adam said tartly. "Someone's making our imagined weapons."

"If we figure out who, I'll sue them for copyright infringement." Jonas touched the winking colors. "Or hire them. These could be popular as an action figure add-on."

Grace slapped a hand against the table edge. "This isn't about bloody copyrights. Those abominations aren't toys. They were used against a dear friend of mine. Nearly killed him."

"They work?" Jonas examined the bands with greater interest.

"An energy feedback loop," Adam explained.

"Your friend had magickal talents?" Regan asked.

"He's a Reiki healer. A gentle soul."

"If he's using magick, then he's dangerous."

Grace stared at her, aghast. "You don't even know him."

"I know what magick can do. Ask Adam. You can't ask his sister; magick made her a vegetable." Regan laid the band back on the table, her voice cracking with emotion. "To my mind, anyone with such power is the abomination."

"Adam told me about Abby." Underneath the table, Grace reached for his hand. "One man did that. Not everyone who wields magick is the same."

Adam gave their laced fingers a squeeze, and then let her go. He leaned forward in his chair. "The markings say Vitae made these, Jonas. You know every detail about this company. Are you telling me these are a surprise?"

"Yes. It must be a counterfeit TM. Regan, do you recognize these?"

When she shook her head, Adam asked, "Are you sure?"

Jonas gave him a hard look. "You're doubting our word?"

Adam's moment of hesitation wreaked the damage, unspoken words that could never be taken back. "I know you both hate magick and mages."

"So do you," retorted Jonas.

Adam shook his head. "Not like before. What I hate is abused power."

"You can't deny nonmages should have protection," Jonas said evenly.

Grace's gaze flicked from one to the other. "Those bands aren't protection. They're killers."

"Sometimes protecting yourself means going on the offensive," Regan said.

"Like killing Faith Grimaldi and making it look like magick?"

"What are you accusing us of?" Jonas sounded genuinely astonished. And angry.

"If she was a mage, then she deserved her fate," Regan answered.

"Regan!" Jonas looked between the two. "You can't mean that."

"She was my aunt! What did you use against her? Against Lincoln Landry and Lizzie the Hermit?"

"Grace," Adam warned. "Slow down."

"I'm just putting together the facts." She turned back to Regan. "What else have you adapted from *SciMage*? The silvery light? The sonic disrupter?" She flicked a glance toward Jonas. "Nanobots that destroy the mind's reality?"

"Like magick did against Abby?" Regan said coldly. "If you're one of them, then you're no longer welcome at my table."

"Fine." Grace shoved to her feet.

"Regan, she's with Adam," Jonas said conciliatorily. "She's a guest."

"You'd share your table with a mage?"

Again that moment's hesitation and indecision, which revealed the heart. "You don't know that," Jonas replied.

"Then let me clarify." Grace surprised even herself as she stepped firmly onto her chosen side. "I'm a mage." Glaring at Regan, she saw a flicker of something in that social-cool face. Satisfaction? Recognition?

Grace sucked in a breath. "You knew. You *were* there. In the ER. Three nights ago."

"Confirming what one of our work-study interns told me."

Grace remembered the boy who'd talked about Vitae. He'd been combative when she'd stopped his bleeding; she'd attributed it to the PCP, but maybe he was fighting the magick. "He said he was a Vitae tech warrior."

"There is no such thing," Regan retorted. "He's an odd one. Lives for the game. Probably hallucinated a connection between his work here and his immersion in the game."

Not believing a word of the denial, Grace braced her hands on the table. *"What are you using against me?"*

Regan's smile was sweetly malicious. "If I knew what you were talking about, I'd be sure to make it Vitae's next project."

Jonas's face drained of color, and he lifted his arm with the band. "Regan, do you know where these came from?"

"No," she stated emphatically. "My theory? Tech-savvy mages. They've found a weapon they can blame on us."

"I'll look into how someone obtained our stamped alloys," Jonas offered.

One of them had to be lying. Grace turned a glance to Adam, whose attention was fixed not on her, but on his two friends. Suddenly the fight left her, replaced with a deep sadness. The violence of hate and prejudice was so *useless*.

Staying here served no purpose; she wasn't going to learn

anything more. Without another word, she turned her back on them. In the outer office, she found her coat on the floor, Gala curled on top, snoozing. Damn ferret must have pulled it down. She yanked the coat out, sending Gala scrambling. Throwing it on, she strode outside.

Afternoon had brought snow-swollen clouds that grayed the air. Crap, she'd forgotten her boots. Snow fell into her Top-Siders, soaking her socks and freezing her toes. She glanced around. On days like this, no one came outside. She was alone.

If Regan had sent those attackers . . . A knot of fear wound in her chest.

"Grace!" Adam caught up, carrying her boots.

"Got your ferret, too?" she asked.

"Pocket."

"You were no help, and don't tell me nothing's wrong. You know we—"

He kissed her. Abruptly and hard, silencing her. She started to protest, until she realized he was saying something against her lips.

"Don't say anything. Security."

The everywhere cameras. He'd angled, she realized, so his face was above hers, hiding his mouth.

"Mmmm," she murmured, an acknowledgment that could be taken as passion. For show—and then for herself— she sank deep into the sweet, firm kiss. Her body held his in tight heat, steaming away the flakes of snow, as she wrapped her arms around his shoulders. His fingers tunneled through her hair, cupping her head, knocking off her hat. She didn't care about the cold or the cameras. In this moment, only sensation mattered. The taste of him. The muscular press of his thighs. The chill roughness of his cheek.

Slowly, they parted, lips clinging for a final savoring nip. As she put on her boots, her toes curling against the cold, he added, "This lead's a dead end."

She nodded, not trusting her voice to agree to the for-security lie. Only when they were in the car and well away from the eyes and ears of Vitae did she say, "*You* were supposed to show them the bands."

"Last-minute decision. I thought I could learn more if they didn't know our suspicions. Now we'll have to go in to-night."

"Could you have clued me in on the change in plan?"

"I thought you'd realize, when I didn't follow the script, that I had something else in mind," he said, a touch tartly.

"Calling me impulsive?" She took her eyes off the road to glance at him.

The moment of tension passed, as his lips curved in a smile. "Decisive. You never let a decision get stale." He rummaged in his pocket for his camera.

"What are you looking for?" she asked, as he paged through photos.

"I'm not sure. Sometimes I notice details that don't consciously register until I look at the pictures. I got that edgy feeling today. Don't you have a small flashlight?"

"For examining pupils. In my pocket."

When she retrieved the light, along with it came a knot of paper clips, shiny buttons, and a glittery pebble.

"Good Lord, woman, why do you carry all that?"

"I don't." She glared at the beast peering over his pocket. "Your ferret seems to be using my coat to stash her pret-ties."

"Naughty, Gala." His scold was more afterthought, as he tossed aside the mass and aimed the light at the screen.

Had to be hard to see. Grace pulled into a tree-rimmed lot and stopped beneath a sulfur-shaded light. While she waited for Adam, she pulled out her phone. Navigating onto the Net, she surfed for something—the game, tech warriors, amnesic technology, mind-meld theorists—anything to connect her fugue states to Vitae.

For she refused to believe her mind had betrayed her. There had to be an external cause. *Had to*.

Except that, too, came with chilling implications: Someone or something could get into her mind? Control her thoughts and consciousness?

Mind control. The two simple words sucked all the moisture from her mouth.

How? Magick? Technology—like nanobots? A combination of the two?

Either was an invasion. Transformation from the inside out. She rubbed her temple, as though that simple action erased what could be deep inside her. "When you get into their systems, I'd like to see how deep they are into the nanobots," she told Adam.

He nodded; then his shoulders stiffened. He shoved the camera to her. "Upper right. Look at the truck." Abruptly he opened the door and strode out into the cold darkness, slamming the door behind him.

It took a moment to focus on the picture. When she did, though, her heart went tachy.

Adam had taken this picture on their way into Vitae. A man was caught in profile, outlined by the F-150 window frame in a brief second of passage. Even the sun glinting off the glass, though, couldn't hide the thick bandage across his broken nose.

Chapter Fourteen

Adam spun out of the car, hoping the cold would knock sense into him and freeze out the sour taste of idiocy and betrayal. Had he been played for a fool by his oldest friends? He plunged into the uncut woods, plowing through shin-high drifts. Grace followed. Less of the shrouded sun penetrated here, leaving them in twilit gloom.

When he reached the riverbank, panting and sweating despite the cold, he stopped. He braced one gloved hand against the rough pine bark, and tapped the other against his mouth, not looking at Grace. The held-back pain of being a trusting fool rushed back, nearly buckling his knees.

He dug his fingers in hard. This close to the tree, he caught a faint whiff of woody sap. Before him, the river churned past. How could there be a hint of life amid the sterile whiteout of the moaning, whirling storm?

"I'm sorry."

"I'm sorry."

Their words crossed paths.

"I'm the one who screwed up, Grace. I was so sure they were clean. So sure a rogue mage orchestrated this whole mess."

She laid a hand against his back. "I'm sorry because you're hurting."

"But you were in danger because of my friends. I'll get you out of this, I swear, whatever it takes."

With a pressure to his shoulder, she turned him to face her. "Don't beat yourself up; your only fault is loyalty."

Her face, pale in the cold, showed only sympathy. Beads of tears clung to the tips of her lashes. Crying? From the cold? Or for him?

He didn't want her damn pity, not for a screwup. "Like last time, when you ended up in the hospital?"

"Betrayal hurts like hell; trust me, I know."

God, he finally understood how she'd felt.

But she didn't stop there. "You wanted to give them a chance. You still do, I'd wager."

He nodded, realizing he was still looking at alternatives. "Maybe the attacks on us originated here. But something else is going on. Magick killed Faith. Set that spell against us. Hurt Abby. Vitae wouldn't use magick."

"See? That's more trust than I showed you," she responded.

His fingers splayed across her cheek; his thumb wiped the tears from her lashes. "You had to be hurting this bad. Worse. Your friends died. I should be glad you only had a pair of bandage scissors handy."

"I'm glad, too," she whispered, "because I never want to hurt you." She rose to her boot tips then, and, cradling his face in her hands, kissed him.

Her lips were soft and warm, despite the iron day. From that point of contact, heat flooded through him, until with a groan, he pulled her body flat against his. There was no one watching this time, no security camera filming the show. Just the two of them and their passion.

Bracing against the tree, he kissed her back. Layers of clothes padded him from feeling all of her, so he satisfied himself with her lips, her mouth, her tongue, as they entangled deeper. He rained kisses along her jaw, while she bent her head back, giving him free access. Her hand stroked up and down his neck, even delving beneath his collar. Cold struck his nape, but he didn't give a damn as long as she kept kneading him.

At last the kiss slowed to a sweet lingering caress, then faded to an end. Their breath, quick as marathoners', mingled in white clouds. Adam braced his forehead against hers. "I've heard making love outside in the cold is memorable."

Grace's body, pulsing against his in age-old rhythm, stilled.

"Says the southern boy." She gave a shaky laugh. "Ice pellets up my ass are no aphrodisiac."

Damn, too fast. He was filled with heat, utterly needing her. With reluctance, he laid his cheek against hers and realized he was too numb to appreciate the touch of flesh against flesh. "And if I opened my zipper, my nuts would flee to my tonsils and my rod would probably crack like frozen steel."

She chuckled, a warmer, less wary sound. "Now that would be a real shame."

"Given the circumstances, not a wise option."

She leaned back a little. "When is making love ever about wisdom?"

"I suppose it's not about a public park, either." He settled back into responsible mode. "We need to find out exactly what's in Vitae's underbelly." Reaching into his wallet, he pulled out his Vitae access badge. "Fancy a little snooping?"

Vitae held a different atmosphere at night. Lights at half power, the cheery conversations erased by emptiness. The air still held the faint hum of computers, since most had been left on, and once or twice in the distance, Adam saw a spray of light from the desk of a night-owl programmer.

Grace tapped him on the arm and pointed to a hallway they hadn't gone down earlier today. He nodded and swiped his card.

The door opened on soundless hinges. Fortunately, security hadn't changed enough that his all-access privileges were modified. Grace slipped in ahead of him, nearly invisible in black jeans with her hair bundled into a knit cap. She'd left her bright-colored ski jacket at the hotel room and layered a dark sweater and sweatshirt beneath a windbreaker. He hoped his coat concealed him.

Not that black clothes would fool the security at Vitae, but there was no sense in advertising.

Nothing could conceal the raw ugliness of his actions, though. He was spying on his best friend.

Vitae wasn't an immense complex, and they soon worked their way to its heart. He found his steps slowing, and Grace, waiting in front of a small sign labeled RESEARCH, gave him a puzzled look.

He hesitated—would this be an unforgivable breach?

Even so, he needed answers. If Jonas or Regan had acted alone, the other needed to know. At the very least, he had to know if they'd had anything to do with the deaths of those eight mages.

Clenching his jaw, he swiped his card.

Research was packed with computers, lathes, controllers, and a hell of a lot of equipment Adam had never seen before.

Grace gave a low whistle. "Kea's well funded, but this makes us look like the poor cousins."

"Do you recognize the equipment?"

"Most of it." She nodded toward the bank of computers. "Can you log me in? I might be able to decipher their nanobot research."

He logged in, located the drive, and then moved aside. As Grace paged swiftly through the data, he peered over her shoulder. "How advanced are the bots?"

She frowned. "Very, but not enough for anything dangerous. They still have problems with power and with replication. Their main focus isn't in the game application, though, but applying the bots to immersion virtual reality." She gave a small whistle. "We use VR in medicine, but this is revolutionary—haptic technology for the sense of touch, 3-D imaging. Wow!"

Abruptly, the lights blinked to bright. Adam spun around to find Jonas watching them, his arms crossed. His face held no warmth, no expression whatsoever. Only his eyes revealed his fury. "If you wanted an update on our research projects, Adam, you could have asked."

"You know what we want."

"And you didn't trust me to give it to you. I said I'd investigate." Jonas slapped a sheaf of papers on a table, and then laid a flash drive atop them.

"What did you find?"

"Regan's program was in its infancy, a nugget within a larger, legitimate initiative to develop game tie-ins," he said coldly. "The bands. A neuroscrambler. A few suggestible lads. No *murders*."

"Where's Regan?"

"Left hours ago; she'll be taking a leave of absence until I sort this out." He tapped the data. "That's all of it." With that, he pivoted and walked away, turning his back on them. "I'd hoped your coming to Ann Arbor meant you were taking a renewed interest in Vitae, Adam. Guess you are."

Adam stared after him, then at the empty door frame, unable to blink and erase the final image. A touch on his arm drew him around.

"Go talk to him," Grace said.

"You shouldn't be alone."

"I can wait here, look at Jonas's data." She waved around the secure area. "It's a locked room, with limited access. I'll be fine for a few minutes."

He nodded, then leaned over and kissed her cheek. "Thank you. Don't go anywhere; I'll be back soon."

When he located Jonas, he called, "Wait!"

Jonas spun around. "Why? First Regan, now you. Didn't either of you think to come to me first?"

"Would you have approved what she did?"

"I understand Regan's choice, and so do you, Adam. Hell, yes, part of me sympathizes and agrees. We don't have your innate protection; we need defenses. If she'd talked to me, maybe I could have steered her to a better course. And you? All you ever had to do was ask."

"We did; you denied everything."

"Because I didn't fucking know!" he shouted. "Vitae is yours, too, Adam. It always has been. Anything here is open to you. Instead you're acting like some sneaking cat thief. Neither one of you trusted me." For a moment his face twisted with his pain, and then he charged away.

Regan stood on one side of the divide, while he stood on the other, and the two of them were tearing apart Jonas. Probably the best one of the trio.

He couldn't let so many years of friendship wash down the loo. Adam caught up again and put a hand on Jonas's arm. He found a sliver of hope when Jonas allowed himself to be turned.

"The men who had those bands attacked Grace. Violently." He thrust out the camera, pointed to the truck with the Vitae parking sticker. "At least one's your employee. Do you recognize him?"

"Lonnie Baronski."

"After seeing that, for Grace's safety, I couldn't take the chance on trust."

"Grace," Jonas spat. "Consorting with a mage. Why?" When Adam didn't answer, Jonas searched his face, and then sucked in a breath. "My God, you're in love with her."

"Yes." Adam had long ago admitted that fact to himself.

Jonas recoiled. "Have you forgotten Abby, and what magick did to her?"

"Forget? I've never stopped looking for her tormentor!"

"He was killed in the blast," Jonas said, flatly. "Regan recognized his name—Louis Meltone—and his family identified the body. Others in the group identified that he took the dragon as his symbol, that he and Abby were close. Trust me, I did my research. Abby's Dragon is dead. Good thing, or I would have killed him myself."

Adam stared at his friend, as the facts clicked for him, too. "You were in love with Abby?"

"Am in love," Jonas corrected. "I know where I stand for her. Do you? If you had to choose between freeing Abby and saving Grace, what would you do?"

Adam's heart squeezed at the specter of the impossible choice. "Don't talk like that. I have never stopped looking for a way to help Abby."

"Don't ask me to accept Grace. Or accept that it's okay to tread between two worlds." His hand curled to a fist. "You offered a while back to let me buy back your shares of Vitae. Maybe it's time to hammer out those details and sign the papers."

Adam braced a hand against the wall, suddenly dizzy, as rootless as a dandelion puff. "If that's what you want. Whatever you draw up, I'll sign."

Jonas gave a harsh laugh. "No negotiations, no hardball? Not much of a businessman."

"I'm a rather good businessman; NONE does well. This isn't about business, Jonas."

"No, it's not." Once again, Jonas pivoted sharply and continued his journey down the hall.

Adam tried a final time to reach him. "Those men who attacked Grace, your men—they tried to kill me. I would have been dead if not for her talents."

Jonas hesitated, and for a moment Adam thought he'd

reconsider. But the moment passed. Jonas stiffened his shoulders, turned a corner, and vanished.

Regan's program was in its infancy. Grace put aside the papers. Interestingly, Regan had developed the bands based upon data from Charles Severin—the ex-husband of Adam's reporter, Natalie.

Severin postulated the role genetics played in what he'd called the parallel talents—resonance, reflection, nullification. He'd believed Natalie was a resonant, capable of magnifying the energies of magick. Regan had used his theoretical calculations and replicated DNA patterns with fiber optics in creating her bands.

Did Natalie know of this? Grace debated a moment, and then sent Natalie a quick text. A few moments later she got a text back: *Will visit C. Send copy of info.* Grace took a picture, then streamed the data to Natalie.

She was marveling at Vitae's advances in VR when a faint click from the opening door cut through the night silence. Adam was back. Grace powered down the computer. She started to let him know she was ready, but hesitated.

Adam would have called out when he came in.

A foot scrape came from two aisles over, moving quickly and quietly. The desk lights gave away her position. Get someplace else. Fast. She sped in the opposite direction. Was he chasing her? She couldn't hear over the blood roaring in her ears. *Weave through the equipment. Round a desk. Beeline to the door.* In the hall, she jerked to a stop.

A man loomed just a foot away. Waiting for her. With a gun pointed at her. "Don't move," he commanded.

Grace froze. Damn. The foot scrape had been a ploy.

"Hands up." He motioned with the gun.

Heart beating in her throat, Grace obeyed.

"Intruder in research contained," he said, not taking his

eyes from her. He wore an earpiece, she realized. She was hearing his half of a conversation.

Security. She recognized the uniform, the badge with his picture and his name, Ed, beneath. Ex-military, she guessed from the buzz cut and ramrod spine.

Tension easing—not too much since he still had a gun pointed at her—she said, "I have permission to be here."

"Show me your access card."

Damn. "I came with someone else; he has the card."

Wrong answer; his faced turned steely. "No one's allowed in here without proper access." He tilted the gun, indicating she was to walk down the hall.

Grace took reluctant steps, her captor at her side. He looked too damn ready and capable of shooting. "Check with Jonas Washington. He made an exception."

Her upheld arms started to shake as her boots scraped along the hall. He couldn't just shoot her; this wasn't some street bust. There were cameras recording everything.

He kept his gun trained on her. "Keep walking," he said as he touched his earpiece. From the one-sided conversation, she surmised he was speaking with Jonas. The stern jaw eased, as he concluded, "Understood, Mr. Washington. Describe her for confirmation. Yes, I'll do that. Sorry to disturb you, sir."

"Can I lower my arms?" she asked.

"Yes." He reholstered his gun. "My apologies, if I frightened you, ma'am. With *SciMage VI* set to release this summer, we've tightened security."

"I understand." She shook her arms a little to loosen the stinging muscles.

"Mr. Washington requested I escort you to the VR lab. He said he has something to show you."

Maybe something about the bands. "Which way?" She'd followed the direction he'd pointed for half a hall before she realized he was limping.

As if he'd been kicked in the knee.

At Master Umari's, Adam had hit one of the attackers in the knee. Fear dried her mouth. Oh, God, she'd been an idiot. Her second attacker was a marine clone named Ed.

"Grace," Adam called into the research lab. "Ready to go?" When she didn't answer, one minute's frantic search confirmed she wasn't there. He raced out, punching the autodial for Jonas on his phone. Thank God, he answered. "Grace is gone."

"Maybe she left—"

"Without a keycard, she couldn't have gotten ten feet. I'm going to the back lot. Check with security. Who accessed research after I left?" There was a moment of silence, and Adam clenched his jaw against the ripping inside his chest. He never begged, but he was begging now. "Please, Jonas, whatever you think of Grace, do this for me. Help me find her."

One second, then, "We'll find her," Jonas said briskly and disconnected. As Adam reached the back door, Jonas, running, his cell phone to his ear, joined him. He barked into the phone: "Check every exit. Check the parking lot for her car or for a black F-150. No one leaves without a direct okay from me. *No one*, including Miss Hollister." He disconnected. "Regan came and left research during your absence."

"Regan, or someone using her keycard?"

Jonas lifted one shoulder. "When we find Grace, we'll know. Security's on it, too."

They stepped outside, and got slammed with another wet whiteout. God, he detested snow.

"There are no footprints." Jonas started to go in, but Adam stopped him.

"They can erase them."

Both of them stilled to look and listen; both of them saw the interior light flare as a vehicle door opened. No! Sliding across the icy blacktop, Adam raced toward the light. The truck took shape in the blurring snow.

Engine growl cut the night. The black monster hurtled past, spitting snow and ice. With a futile shout, Adam watched it disappear. His fists clenched in fury as he scrambled toward his car.

"Adam!" A voice brought him around to see Grace sliding toward him.

In a rush, he joined her, held her, kissed her. He lifted from the kiss to bracket her face. "Are you okay?"

"A little scared when I realized the security guard was the other attacker, but unharmed."

"How did you get away?"

"Sheer luck. His bum knee gave way in the snow, and then the alarms started."

"Who was he?" Jonas asked quietly.

"Ed, according to his badge. Do you know him?"

Jonas shook his head. "I recognized the other as one of security. Lonnie Baronski. I'll show you files of our security. See if you can pick him out."

But when she went through the files, twice, she found no trace of him.

For Vitae, Ed did not exist.

Ed cut the remote feed from Vitae security, erasing the fact that he'd ever been inside their system, and closed up his computer. He was good at what he did. That was why he'd always been in charge of security and surveillance on the black-op missions.

Even though he'd failed to complete the job tonight, the evening had had some benefits. He hadn't realized Zolton owned part of Vitae. He'd also thought Jonas Washington supported their plan.

Yes, some new pieces to chew on. None of which would change the fact he always followed thorough on the mission. That doctor was a mage and thus a traitor to her own kind. She had to be stopped.

CHAPTER FIFTEEN

"Mr. Zolton? Dr. Armatrading?" The hotel concierge caught their attention as Grace and Adam got off the elevator. When they stopped, he handed them each a book-sized package. "These arrived today."

Grace took note of the return address on hers. What would Kea be sending her?

"Thank you, Fernando." Adam slipped him a tip, and then they went into their rooms.

"Is yours the Cadwaladar book from Glinda?" Grace pulled back the tab opener on her package.

"Yes. What have you got there?"

"Also a book." A slim volume, old with a dusty red cover, slid into her hands. Faded gold lettering read: *Teachings of Cadwaladar*. "Great, more Cadwaladar. There's a note. 'Forgive me the small deception of using Dr. Lin's name on the return, but I feared you would not open this otherwise. There is no deception here, no hidden power. Simply basics you should know.' It's signed, *Khalil*." She handed it to Adam. "Do you feel any magickal booby traps?"

After a moment, he handed it back to her. "No. Could be dormant."

"Still, I'll take a look through. It seems to be a primer on theory and practice." Despite the book's apparent age, its vellum was supple and the ink bright. Curious, as she headed to her connecting room, she paged through. Deciphering the elaborate script and archaic words would take some effort. What was in here that Khalil wanted her to know?

She laid the book on the bed and sat down to undress.

"What do you know about magick?" Adam gave a perfunctory rap on the connecting door and then strode into her room.

Grace finished taking off her boots, afraid she knew where this conversation was heading. Him insisting she try to open the library, her failing. "Not as much as I should. Mostly what I learned from my English friends and a single visit to my paternal Jamaican grandmother."

"Magick for the masses." He sprawled on her chair, occupying most of the room with his sheer presence, and touched his throat, still slightly mottled with a bruise. "Your healing skills, though, are a cut above. When did they emerge?"

"When I ran in to help the bomb victims, they just sort of . . . came. Afterward—in med school—I didn't have enough skill to do more than tweak in desperate cases, and I was too busy to learn more. Until two years ago."

"What changed?"

Kea's secrets weren't hers to tell, so she offered a partial truth. "Working with Kea. For our research we measured the energy patterns of pain. Electrical, chemical, molecular. With those visuals, I could pinpoint my healing better. That knowledge strengthened my talent. Since, I've studied bits here and there."

"What have you learned?"

"That magick is the will of the mage calling on and shaping power. In a crude analogy, it's turning on a light directly with a spell, not needing the intervention of a switch, wires, and the local power grid. Traditionally, the energies of nature, the spirits, are used or the energies of human interaction—like power circles—but some modern disciplines suggest other energies could be tapped."

"Like nuclear and electrical."

"Or the body." She thought about the conversation at Vitae. "Like Jonas is doing with his nanobots, activating them with the body's electric energy."

"Few can tap those energies and fewer have the will to control and shape that focus. You make the concept of magick sound simple."

She gave a bark of humorless laughter. "Voice of experience. Not. I've tried all the schools of technique—ceremonial high magick rituals, folk magick chants, shamanic traditions with spirit guides, elementals, crystals and candles, Chinese feng shui, covens." She yawned. Now that she'd stopped, fatigue finally caught up to her, and she flopped back on the bed and closed her eyes.

"Yet you have that gift, Grace."

"To a degree. You have something that you think might get me to open that library? Spit it out, and I'll sleep on it."

"Magick requires personal energy, focus, and it needs a way to organize that energy. That's the function of the accoutrements—oils or candles or blades or robes. Something that speaks to the soul."

"Will, words, way, and wings," she said drowsily.

"What?"

"Something I heard, although I didn't understand it."

He said softly, "Magick is the will of the mage, the words of formation, the way of the focus, and the wings of the energy."

"That was it. How did you know?"

"I've picked up bits and pieces. It means the mage decides the purpose, speaks that purpose in a chant or song, follows one of the magick traditions to give shape and guidance to that purpose, and acts from a source of energy."

She braced on her elbows. "Get to the point, please, before I fall asleep."

"Maybe you're thinking too hard, analyzing too much, letting your diagnostic mind override your inner power. Start with belief in your power and what speaks to you."

"And desire." She stripped off her socks, and then pulled her sweatshirt over her head. Her T-shirt rode over her belly. "You told me I needed desire."

He was silent, and when her face was free of the hem, she saw him gripping the doorjamb, his face tight with need.

Nice move. Talking of desire and stripping.

Their gazes met, as they stood on opposite sides of her words. At last Adam drew in a breath. "Yes. Desire. Good night, Grace." He closed the door.

Adam glared at the icon arrow, its unceasing blinking mocking him. The only thing he'd accomplished in the past hour was to finally get rid of the bite of need that had barnstormed him when Grace took off her sweatshirt.

Blast Faith's convoluted schemes. She'd sent him the library files; he had the necessary gloves and visor. Neither did him a lick of good; he couldn't open the file.

For that required magick.

In other words, Grace.

In her death, Faith had thoroughly knotted them. Not that he minded being in a tangle with Grace, but he was beginning to wonder about Faith's motives in showing him that CD in the library.

He shoved away from the desk. "I don't like being manipulated," he told Gala, who was curled around the computer.

She lifted her head long enough to yawn, as if to say, "Get over it," then settled back in a snooze.

Eyes burning from weariness, he shut down. At least Grace was near. He took a deep breath, rewarded by the faint, indefinable scent that reminded him of her. Some essence of her lingered in his hotel room, and his rebellious body reacted. Bloody great. Just what he needed when he was fagged beyond coherence, a hard-on.

With frustrated motions, he stripped and got into bed. Where he lay with his head on the stacked pillows, staring into the night, sleepless.

Last night had been anything but restful. He'd jerked awake over and over, torn from slumber by unremembered terrors.

Tonight as he waited in the darkness for sleep, he heard a brief scrabble of tiny nails, then smelled a faint musk. The computer must have cooled enough that Gala had abandoned her perch for her clothing nest.

In the end, he settled for lying on his side, with one hand outstretched against the wall. With the blessing and curse of imagination, he could have sworn he felt Grace's hand lock with his.

Finally, he descended into sleep. In his last moment of consciousness, he heard a cell phone ring.

Dreams should not smell. Adam's nostrils tightened at the mix of foul rot and electricity. Yet the source remained hidden beneath a kaleidoscope of lightning. His eyes hurt from brilliance that formed into nothing coherent. Just white and gray that remained maddeningly impossible to focus on.

He turned in a circle—at least he thought it was a circle—and his head began to pound, each throb coming a scant second before the elusive flares. Each pulse cut through his brain as easily as lightning cut a cloud. The scent also strengthened, gagging him.

Sharp pain lanced into his rib. He looked down to see a needle attached to a syringe piercing flesh, breaking into the muscles. A colorless liquid dripped from the syringe, and he tasted bitterness.

Drugs.

*Though his mouth opened, he couldn't get a single breath.
Not even to shout.*

Panic set in, the reflex of suffocation.

Grace jerked awake, pain pinballing from her skull down
every vertebrae. She bent over, almost retching, and her
hand spasmed away from the hotel wall. She'd been clutching it as though life itself depended upon that contact.
Gasping, she washed away the sourness in her mouth, grateful for the cold, stale air.

In the dream, she'd felt everything that Adam—

Adam!

Her heart leapfrogging over logic, she raced out of the
bed. Adam was in danger, mortal danger. Dying in his sleep
just a thin wall away.

Damn, how had the bolts gotten thrown? She pounded
on the adjoining door, even as she threw her own bolt.
"Adam. Adam. Wake up. Dammit. Wake up."

No answer. She yanked at the door. Stuck. Locked. Sealed.

She spied her cell phone open on the bed—hadn't she
gotten a call right before sleeping?—and tried to call Adam,
even as she pounded on the door.

No answer.

Security. She'd call hotel security to break down the
door . . .

. . . because she'd had a bad dream?

By the time she found someone, even supposing she con-
vinced them to break down the door to a guest room, Adam
would be dead. For nothing in an EMS bag could save him.

Magick. The unlocking spell she'd been trying to master.
She needed desire? She'd never wanted anything so much as
to get that damn door open.

Take a breath. Panic only meant failure. Working magick required control, stillness around the surging power of the mind.

Fortunately this spell was a simple one. Formative words. Something to channel the focus. What the hell did she have? In desperation she pulled out the small flashlight, her closest approximation to a candle.

While one hand held the on switch, she laid her other against the bolt. One more deep breath cleansed her mind, and then she focused on the beam of powerful light, seeking with her mind's eye the bolt on the other side. Draw on the power of her flesh, the forces between atoms, across nerve synapses.

"Bend this to my purpose." She intoned the final words, eyeing the bolt on her side. Her body tingled, ripples of power shimmering from deep in her flesh into the tip of her finger, just as it did when she banished pain or stopped blood.

Same power.

Different purpose.

All driven by her passion. She *had* to get this door open.

"Move. Unlock. My will commands."

A faint click was her reward. Such a tiny sound for such a profound change in her powerless reality. She'd done it!

No time for celebration. She charged into Adam's room and found him sprawled supine on the bed, mouth open. Not moving.

Except the intercostals. The muscles between the ribs were taut, as though they strained against some invisible force.

His chest was bare, as he wore only boxers, so the first thing she noticed was the fist-sized bruise on his side.

With one knee on the bed, she shook him. "Wake up!"

The dark room suddenly got darker, as though the ambient light had been snuffed. The spell attacking Adam grabbed for more flesh. It swelled from him to her.

Burning threads of pain shot through all ten fingers. Air vanished as though a rag had been thrust down her throat.

She collapsed on top of him, sprawled across his cold

body. Beneath her hands, she felt the muscles of his chest straining. With the last bit of movement possible, she pressed on her flashlight. The pencil-thin beacon cut through the darkness. *Focus on freeing him.* Her lips brushed against the unbound silk of his hair, as the single breath she had left touched his ear in a whisper. "Move. Unlock. My will commands. Adam. Help."

"Adam. Help."

The plea broke the grip of suspended twilight. Adam followed a sharp sliver of light, shoving himself into wakefulness. At the moment of coherence, all his innate gift, all the reflexive defenses he'd learned, snapped into action. Reflect and deflect the magick, his soul a mirror to the toxic energy.

The talons of the spell retracted, scraping in angry denial. His freed lungs expanded, his opened mouth gasped in cool air. Another deep breath cleansed the rotten taste; a third began to oxygenate the remainder of his body.

Grace held him, he suddenly realized, and, like a drowned man revived, just as suddenly his blood responded to the nearness of her curves and her scent, to the corkscrew of her hair that tickled his cheek.

Except his body couldn't move, resulting in an exquisite pain in his groin. No time for that. The spell still bound them, kept his legs and arms from moving. Kept her breath bound.

Concentrating, he found he could lift and tilt his head. He pressed his lips against hers, and then breathed into her lungs, sending tiny slivers of himself to turn away the magick that bound her. He could not open a vein for her, but he could do this.

Would it work? His talent had never been bound so intimately with another. Yet he continued.

At last! He felt the return of her breath on his lips. Then, he began to concentrate on peeling back the spell, sending it down from his shoulders, his chest, like peeling a used condom off his prick. When he could move his arms, he wrapped them around Grace, pulling her as close as he could, freeing her from the confining spell an inch at a time.

Her lungs drew in bigger breaths. Good news, except for the way each inhalation brushed tight nipples against his chest. As blood sped to its tasks, feeling and motion returned with a vengeance. Pain spiked his groin, and his whole body jerked alive. Heat spiraled outward.

Grace's eyes opened, widened. At their proximity or her paralysis?

"In a moment you'll be free," he managed.

She blinked once, indicating she'd heard. With a barely audible sigh, she waited, her head on his chest.

One painstaking cell at a time, he reflected the magick away, ridding the two of them of the last remnants of the spell.

Grace gasped. Her body tightened against him. Death passed, and life returned, demanding its dominion.

His cock responded with a rush, filling and pulsing and demanding release. Her pushing against him wasn't helping, not one bit. Every fiber of flesh and nerve screamed to be close to her, inside her, sharing that newly cleansed body.

Mindless with need, still holding her, he rolled over, sinking with her into the mattress. Without a by-your-leave he settled between her legs, pushing her thighs apart with his knees. His mouth took hers in savage need as knife-edged desire slammed into him.

He needed her. Only her. "Grace," he moaned. "I need you."

If she'd said no, he might have heard it. He might have even heeded it.

But she didn't.

Instead, he surged into her. Oh, blessings! She was sweet and hot and wet. And grabbing him with muscles that pounded in rhythm with his own swelling. Pump once. Pump twice. Reach as deep as possible, hold her as tight as possible, kiss her as hard as possible.

Pump three and he spilled himself inside her, pleasure enveloping and snaring him more thoroughly than any mageborne spell.

He thought she came, too; she shouted, he realized with savage satisfaction. But he was too deep into his release to be sure.

The starving need retreated, leaving him hot, breathless, only partly sated.

He shifted, pulling his weight off hers, and buried his face in the mattress. The breath he drew in this time was all of Grace. For a man who made a living with words, he never had found adequate ones to describe the scent of her. Not flowery, not citrus. Just soul-satisfyingly Grace.

He growled, "I didn't plan that, but I won't apologize."

"Did I ask you to?" Her hand skimmed his shoulder, not pushing him off, but as though she wanted to remember the feel of him. "That was . . . intense."

"Are you hurt?"

"No."

He hesitated a moment, then licked her jaw. "Can we do it again?"

She laughed softly as her hand drifted lower. "This time, more mindful."

He caressed her belly. "Absolutely."

Grace woke to musk and the sting of little ferret claws digging into her shoulder. Irritated, she shoved Gala off and opened her eyes. The room was dark, too early to be getting up, but the bed was empty except for her and the beast.

Apparently she had female competition for the space in Adam's bed.

Gala butted her head against Grace and bared her teeth.

Grace lifted one finger and stared down the ferret. "This space is mine. You have his pocket and dirty socks."

The standoff stretched for two breaths, and then Gala curled away with a lift of her tail, turning her back on Grace before leaping into the small pile of clothes Adam had collected for her nest.

The best she could hope for at the moment, Grace decided. An understanding, if not quite a truce. She sat up in the bed, shoved her unruly hair off her face—Dear Lord, she must look like Cousin Itt. Where was Adam?

A swirl of shadows on the balcony gave her an answer. She threw on her discarded pajamas, found clean socks for her feet, and then joined him.

Damn, it was cold out there. Her breath congealed in a thick cloud, and the frigid air made a mockery of her thin clothes. Adam was staying warm by pacing, short angry steps back and forth across the tiny space.

"I need a bloody cigarette," he muttered.

She wrapped her arms around her waist. Hell, even Gala had sense enough not to be out here. "How long since you quit?"

"Four years, five months, three days, and"—he glanced at his watch—"four hours. But who's counting?"

"Then you can go to five hours," she said unsympathetically. "Cigarettes stink, and this is a nonsmoking room."

He looked at her, and his eyes were dark as old moons. "Thanks for the bleeding obvious."

She lifted her brows. "Haul off the sarcasm, Zolton."

"Then take off the doctor coat."

"Happy to, but it's too damn cold out here. What's gotten into you?"

"Magick." His lips curled around the word as if he sucked lemons, and his fists tightened. "I will be no one's punching bag. Or puppet."

The venom beneath the words stung, but she said only,

"Damn, I'm freezing." She jerked her head toward the bedroom. "Inside. Warm."

At least he followed her inside. She sat cross-legged on one bed; Adam sprawled in a chair halfway across the room. Putting distance between them? Since she didn't believe he was a love 'em and leave 'em guy, something else had gotten his balls in a twist.

She offered an opening sally. "Someone tried to kill you tonight."

"So it appears." Instead of saying what troubled him, he picked up the desk pen and rolled it around his fingers.

"You're awfully sangfroid about attempted murder."

"No. I'm not."

When he didn't say anything more, she gave an exasperated huff. "Stop making me drag it out of you. Why were you snarling and stomping on the itty-bitty balcony?"

"Because the magick shouldn't have touched me." The pen clattered to the table. Apparently the nicotine fit had passed. "Last night should not have happened."

That hurt. "I found it pretty damn wonderful."

Her tight response got his attention. He stood and strode the single step across the gap to her, pulled her up to meet him. His hands cupped her cheeks, chasing away the chill. Callused thumbs caressed the corners of her eyes. "Making love with you was the most necessary, the most inevitable, and definitely the most exquisite part of the whole evening."

"I like an eloquent man." She closed the gap this time, leaning forward with a kiss.

He responded, with passion. Their tongues tangled, breath mingling, until at last he lifted away. His fingers traced the curve of her ear, tunneled beneath the mass of her hair. "And I love a woman with magick in her hands."

She sucked in a breath. Loved her? Accepted her magick? Was she reading too much into one comment? Could she deal with this new tangle? Not until she knew she could go to him without fearing for her sanity.

Instead, she switched direction. "That's twice I almost lost you. Are you getting too close to the Dragon? Is that why they're after you?"

His fingers slipped beneath her top and grazed up and down the bare skin of her back. Arousing her, tightening her, moistening her. "Maybe whoever it is knows that I would give my last breath to protect you."

He didn't give her a chance to process that unmistakable bombshell. Instead, he kissed her, and she kissed him back, pressing as close as she could. His cock was already hard, the thick length straining up for her. But rubbing against him wasn't nearly enough satisfaction.

With undeniable masculine demand, he pressed her down onto the bed. No matter that he didn't bother to ask, her body was doing all the answering for her. *Please don't stop.* She arched into him, fell backward. The pressure of his hard muscles angled her deep into the bed as he followed her down. Unrelenting kisses kept her mindless, a mass of nerves soaking up sensation and pleasure.

His hair was smooth, a thick joy to touch. His three AM beard rasped faintly against her neck as he nuzzled and nipped her jaw.

She wanted to give him as much pleasure as he brought her. "Let me on top," she whispered, knowing he was too strong for her to turn if he didn't want to.

He promptly rolled to his back, casting off the last of his clothes, while she did the same. She went back on him, straddling him. Her hands kneaded up and down his chest. While she watched, his face tightened. She listened to the guideposts of his exhaled pleasure and his fevered *yes*, as she caressed him, cherished him.

When she teased him with her breasts, he reared upward,

taking her into his mouth. His lips sucked hard, pulling her deep, while his tongue gave tiny flicks to her sensitized nipple.

Lightning jolted downward, burning an ecstatic path. Dampness flowed. She returned the favor, licking and sucking her way down to his thick cock.

"Ah," he strangled out.

She smiled and swirled her tongue around the pulsing vein. She did love an eloquent man. Loved to make him speechless.

"I'm going to come, if you don't . . ."

"That's the plan," she whispered, and swallowed around him.

He lay there gasping, but still hard. She slid upward, slid him inside her, both of them wet and needing. Then even syllables were lost—all they could manage were grunts and sighs and moans, and at last, joined shouts of release.

Grace collapsed and Adam reached down and threw the bedspread over them. Entwined, they fell toward sleep.

One thing she had to do first.

Adam murmured a sleepy protest as she got out of bed, but she soothed him with a "shhh," and a kiss to the cheek.

She didn't have all the accoutrements; she'd never done this alone. But she'd be damned if she didn't try to stop another attack.

Awkwardly holding her penlight and a tiny bottle of perfume from her purse, she circled the room, sprinkling the scent. Gazing into the light beam, she chanted under her breath the words of the protection spell Kea had always used.

Underfoot, Gala circled with her. Grace got the impression the ferret wasn't so much trying to trip her as adding her approval. When they completed the circle, physician and ferret stood in the center of the room, satisfied.

"So mote it be," Grace whispered, sealing the spell.

Gala scampered back to her nest, while Grace climbed back into bed.

"Circle of protection?" Adam murmured.

"Yes."

"I like the incense." With that, he drew her close.

She laid her hand across his chest, snuggling close to his hot, hard form. No one would get through to him. Not while she had breath in her body.

CHAPTER SIXTEEN

"One good thing about last night." Grace scraped her spoon around the carton, getting the last of her breakfast yogurt. "The library. I can open it! I had to open a lock to get to you." The fear—and the power—of that moment still lingered with her. "You were right. All it took was desire. I never wanted anything so much as to get that door open."

Adam sat back from his empty plate, his hands curled around his coffee cup. "I still think we should be isolated when we open it, and I know just the place. One that includes indoor plumbing. Excalibur. I'll call Captain Emil, see how soon he can take us there."

"Can you pilot the boat?"

Adam shook his head. "Lake Huron may not be as wild as Superior, but my navigation skills are rusty."

"Can we trust this captain?" She hated that her life had come to doubting everyone but the man sitting across the table.

"I think so. Captain Emil's salt of the earth. You've heard the phrase 'honest as the day is long'? That's him."

When Adam called, however, the yacht was undergoing minor repairs and wouldn't be available until the following morning. They set a sail time for ten.

At the end of the call Adam sat back, clearly frustrated. "A day wasted. I suppose we can—"

Grace laid a hand over his mouth, shushing him. "We can take the day off."

At his mulish look, she sat back and crossed her arms. "Adam, we're battered and stressed. We both have bruises from the attacks by Lonnie and Ed. A day will let our bodies heal and give us a fresh perspective on whatever we find in that library. Maybe Brando will report in. Or Natalie. I found a link from Vitae to Natalie's ex, and she's going to see him. So, today, we play."

"What kind of play did you have in mind?" His look was suggestive.

"To start with, I need a workout."

He grinned, his mind obviously heading straight to their bedroom. "I'm sure I can assist."

She laughed. "You can spot me on the bench press. One of the privileges of staying at an upscale hotel is access to a well-equipped gym. And don't tell me you don't exercise. You don't get a body as fine as yours by sitting on your ass."

"You like my body?"

"Very much. As I intend to show you. Later."

His smile widened. "Anticipation as an aphrodisiac. I can deal with that. After the gym?"

Her answer was interrupted by her phone's ring tone. Kea again. She couldn't keep putting him off. "Hey, Kea."

"Grace, I need to see you. As soon as possible. Alone. Can you meet me at this address?" He gave an Ann Arbor location.

"Are you in pain?" He sounded desperate.

"No. I'll explain when I see you."

"Give me an hour." She disconnected. Not liking the thoughts and conclusions running through her, she told Adam, "I agreed to meet Kea. He wants me to come alone."

"When pigs fly."

"I figured you'd say that. I know meeting him's not wise,

since my last fugue occurred in his lab." She hoped Adam would understand why she needed to do this. "Before, I didn't give you a chance to explain. Kea's been a good friend. I don't want to make that mistake again."

His eyes hardened. "Could Lin be part of this?"

"I don't know. Possibly." She took a deep breath. This secret she couldn't keep any longer. "We powered our analgesic bots with magick."

"Your power or his?"

"Mine." That had been easier than she'd expected. She stared at him, irked that his only response was to calmly finish his coffee. He didn't seem too excited. "You knew?"

"Suspected. That's what I do, reach far-fetched conclusions from odd bits of data."

"And you were just waiting for me to tell you?" She slumped, deflated. "Now that I have, what will you do?"

"I don't know," he admitted. "Normally, I'd be jumping all over this."

"Because magick and science shouldn't mix."

"Because it's an unprecedented power, and that's dangerous. Except there's the factor of you." His lips twitched. "I understand why Natalie refused to include Ram in her story exposing Charles. You and Ram are the optimists, looking for ways to expand knowledge. Natalie and I are the pessimists, pointing out the downsides. I think the world needs both."

"Then I'll have to trust your decision."

After a moment's silence, not looking at her, he asked, "Did you tell Lin where we were staying?"

"No. Why?" Her mind clicked on what he was asking. "You're wondering how the attacker found us last night?"

"There are mage trackers, but I'm normally invisible."

"I haven't called—Omigod, my cell phone! The static electricity." She fumbled for the phone, her hands shaking, and showed him the history screen. "I've been getting number-blocked calls, but when I answer, no one's there. I answered one last night. Could a tracer spell have been put on my GPS?"

"We can't take the chance. We'll ditch these phones. Get new ones."

Grace groaned. "And I can't risk importing my address book."

Adam laughed. "So, we know how we'll spend part of today. Data entry."

Natalie had been to the parish prison before, interviewing contacts, but never had it given her a chill like today. As she waited for her ex-husband to be brought in, she rubbed a hand up and down her arm, claustrophobia itching at her skin. Her nose wrinkled against the scents of urine and mold.

At last, a guard led Charles out. Even wearing an orange jumpsuit, he managed to look confident and charming.

Like the man she had once married.

"You grew a beard," she observed when he picked up the communications phone.

"A new look for a new life." With a faint smile, he leaned back in the chair a little, studying her. Waiting.

He wasn't going to give her an opening, ask why she'd come. Nervous, she started to swallow, then stopped. No sign of fear or weakness for him to exploit.

"Do you know of a company called Vitae?" she asked.

"Who doesn't?"

"Are you acquainted with anyone there?"

"Only what I read in the papers."

"Regan Hollister?"

He lifted a brow. "Should I?"

"She used your research to create a weapon against mages." Natalie held up a copy of the paper Grace had streamed to her.

He read it intently, and then smiled. "Bravo for her. I'll need to inquire about royalties."

This was getting her nowhere. She decided on a different tactic. "Tell me about your research combining science and magick. Has anyone ever developed a neuroscrambler?"

He tilted his head, studying her, and a frisson of warning passed across her. He contemplated her as he might a colorful insect, one he planned to dunk in formaldehyde, and skewer with a pin for his collection. "Who wants to know?"

"Does the answer make a difference as to what you'll tell me?"

"Only if it's your new lover, Ramses Montgomery, and he didn't have the balls to come himself."

Hell, he'd tell her nothing useful. She braced her hands against the table, ready to leave.

"Wait," he called. "Sorry, that was crude, but you can't ask me to aid the man who stripped me of power and put me in this hellhole."

No reason not to tell him, not when the truth might get her some answers. "The information's for Adam. And for me."

He whistled in a breath. "Zolton."

Adam's involvement interested him. But why?

He didn't say, instead answering her first question. "Ms. Hollister did contact me, once, about a side avenue of my research. Believe me or not, you're a resonant, Natalie. Your blood and DNA intensify magickal energies. I theorized molecular bond energy with your DNA pattern, coupled with a resonant power source, could enhance magickal power, even to the point of danger. I laid out a sample of the pattern, but I didn't have the mechanical knowledge to go further. Apparently Ms. Hollister did."

"Magick can act on the cellular level?"

"Theoretically. If you could tap it, there's energy in chemical reactions, molecular bonds, nerve transmissions."

"Your focus was genetics. Do you know anyone who knows how to combine magick and neurology?"

"Like in that neuroscrambler?" He referred back to her earlier comment. "Or perhaps send the mind into virtual reality?"

Did his soft drawl hold a touch of warning? "Can you do that?"

"No," he said flatly.

She eyed him closely, not sure she believed him.

"Are you still with Ramses?" he asked.

"We're not getting into my personal life."

He lifted his hands. "Not prying. I suggest you ask him about the Triad." He laughed softly. "Or hasn't he told you about his work with the Magi? Because if he hasn't, then you two have as big a gap as what developed between us."

The guard indicated their time was up. Natalie pushed to her feet, not sure she'd learned anything useful.

"When you come back," Charles said, "there's something I want you to bring."

"I'm not coming back."

"Yes, you will. And when you do, bring that photograph from my desk. The one we took on our honeymoon. You'll find it in the ruins of my library."

"Why do you want it?"

"Oh, don't be so suspicious. Take it out of its frame if you must; there's nothing hidden behind it." He paused, swallowed. "I simply want a picture of better times. Regardless of what happened later, you were the best part of my life. You won't believe this, but if there is anything I regret, it's hurting you."

"You're right, I don't believe you."

"The picture, Natalie. Have your boyfriend check it out for any spells, but bring the picture."

"Why are you so sure I'll be back?"

"Because you'll want to know about the Triad. Three of us who took magick in new directions. Phoenix, Chimaera, Dragon. Body, soul." His gaze flicked to the bruise at her temple. "And mind."

The utter starkness of the room took on fuzzy unreality, as fear slid into her gut. Charles stood out in brilliant colors against the utilitarian walls. Not a hint of magick about him, but she was slammed with a sharp awareness that once, and maybe again, he was capable of cool-headed evil.

"If you need more incentive"—his voice was serpentine—"then tell Adam Zolton I know about his sister. About the Dragon. Tell him I know a way to heal her."

The grove of trees was stark brown against the white land-scape. Their limbs lifted in gnarled twists toward the gray skies. *Witch's trees,* Grace thought, hunching against the light wind. She glanced back at the car, where Adam waited for her, and smiled. He was on his new phone. The man really didn't understand the concept of idle time. When he saw her looking, he tapped his watch and mouthed, *fifteen minutes.*

She nodded, then went inside the dark-timbered hut where she was to meet Kea. The contrast from the gray light outside to purple shadow blinded her. Allowing her eyes to adjust, she stood quietly, testing for scents and sounds.

Cinnamon, no more sound than a crypt.

Eyes adjusted to the gloom, she looked around. Although the interior was warmer than the wind-driven exterior, a shiver passed over her. She was standing in the center of a circle of power, marked with chalk, candles, and gems. She took a step back, her skin tingling. A sideboard at one wall held more candles and matches and a small pile of colored rocks. A dark blue robe hung from a hook.

This was the altar of a ceremonial mage.

"Kea?" she called. This place bothered her. Not because

of anything overtly evil or smacking of the black arts. Dark magick had heat. This felt cold, clinical, like a lab. As precise and unyielding as stainless steel.

"Grace." A rustle and greeting heralded Kea's entrance. "I'm sorry, I didn't hear you ring."

"I didn't. Is this place yours?"

He nodded. "A small retreat for my ceremonies."

As with Adam, a man she'd also thought she knew, she was discovering new facets and depths in Kea. She'd known he was a strong mage, but this was power beyond what he'd shown her.

Both men made her uneasy, although in different ways. Both made her wonder if she'd lost out on the female intuition portion of the X chromosome.

Kea gestured her into the next room, a cozier sitting area with a small fireplace. The lit gas logs offered no counter to the chill inside her. She sat where he asked and waited.

Pacing, Kea began, "I belong to a group called the Custos Magi. So does Khalil."

"I've heard of them."

"We normally keep our activities secret, but if I don't tell you, you'll have no reason to trust me." He stopped in front of her. "Magick can be used for great evil; it's a strong power that needs equal strength to keep it in check. For over two thousand years, the Magi have fought that eternal war."

"Good versus evil." She lifted her brows.

"They are both very real. For your own benefit, you need to join with us."

"My own benefit? I hate when people tell me something's for my own benefit, because it's usually more for theirs."

"Why haven't you listened to the warnings about Adam Zolton?"

"I did listen. I didn't happen to agree."

Kea's face turned hard. Anger put the tendons of his neck into taut relief. "Your naive disbelief doesn't change the facts about Zolton. You've seen beneath his civilized controls. You know his true feelings."

Seen beneath his civilized controls. She sat back, sucking in a breath. Adam was right about the dangers of undisciplined power. "*You* used that superego spell on us. How could you?"

"*You needed to see his true colors.*"

She shot to her feet and strode to the door. "And when that didn't work, last night you tried to kill him?"

The door slammed shut in her face. Slowly she pivoted, trying to hide her fear. "Let me out, Kea."

"I didn't try to kill Adam."

"I suppose you didn't find me by putting a tracker spell on my GPS, either?"

"I knew where you were because I called every damned hotel in a fifty-mile radius."

"What have you been doing to me? What's causing my blackouts, like the one at your lab?"

"What? I don't know what you're talking about." His face creased in concern. "Blackouts?"

"God, Kea, I thought you were my friend." She glared at him. "Unlock the door."

The latch clicked open. "I am your friend. Give me five more minutes, to explain."

"That's why I came," she said softly. "But I'm not hearing what I need."

He rubbed a hand against the back of his neck. "I'm sorry about the spell; casting it on you was wrong. But I was worried. The work you and I do is revolutionary, and I was afraid I'd turned you into a target for Zolton. He's already killed nine mages."

She crossed her arms. "Adam didn't kill them. He thinks they were killed by one of you, to prevent him from finding the man who raped his sister's mind. Didn't you ever consider that the murderer could be one of the Custos Magi?"

He dropped down onto a chair. "Oh, my God. And you say you're having blackouts?"

"Yes. You know the cause?"

"I've heard whispers, hints of one ritual—the Spell of I'celus. The master of the spell can enter your mind. Erase thoughts. Implant new ones."

All heat left the room, replaced with a cold, primal terror. "Mind control?"

"The ritual is supposed to be impossible. If the rumors are true, only one mage since Cadwaladar has mastered it."

"Who?"

"Khalil." Kea cradled the sides of his head, and his fingers raked his hair until the strands stood straight out. "Grace, you need protection. I'll call the Mage Council—"

"No." She put her hand on the door. "I have all the protection I need."

Natalie stood with her hip against her car hood, appreciating the warmth of the engine as she surveyed the ruins of Charles's library. The Louisiana winter was chilly, with a damp wind that penetrated her woven jacket. When her phone rang with a number she didn't know, she was reluctant to take her hands from her pockets. Still, she answered and was surprised to find Adam on the other end.

"Hey, Adam, you've got a new phone number?"

"Yes. The other phone fell into the river."

"How you surviving the cold?"

"Weather's bloody miserable."

She laughed, feeling warmer. She'd missed that Brit accent. "Although we at NONE enjoy your daily barrage of e-mails, texts, and voice mails detailing assignments and checking progress, when are you coming back?"

"There's still unfinished business."

"Is Grace part of that business?"

"Some of it," he said with a hint of humor. "Has any of your memory returned?"

"Bits and pieces, nothing coherent." She switched the phone to her other ear, so she could put a hand in her pocket. "I went to see Charles."

"That couldn't have been easy."

Though he couldn't see her, she shrugged. "He didn't say a whole lot that was useful. He did admit that Regan asked about his theories on genetic resonance. He suggested using molecular energy to amplify magick power."

Adam gave a low whistle. "That's intense. Did he say anything else?"

"He said there was a Triad. He was Phoenix. The others were called Dragon and Chimaera, and he said he knew about your sister. That he knew how to heal her."

The long silence told her Charles's information had struck a major nerve. How could Charles have known something so intimate about Adam when she'd had no clue he even had a sister? She was amazed anew by the fact that there were layers to Adam Zolton about which she knew nothing.

At last he asked, "Can you find out more about the Dragon? About this cure?"

She stared out over the burned library, her breath cold. "Yes."

"Thanks, Natalie. You'll deserve a raise."

"I just recorded that statement."

When they'd said good-byes and hung up, she shoved the phone in her pocket and tromped over to the library. Despite the months that had passed since the fire, she smelled the acrid remains of smoke. She picked through the rubble of Charles's library, keeping thoughts of the past—both good and bad—at bay. *Find the picture; don't worry about remembering Charles's delight in a new book or the still-terrifying reality that Ram almost died here.*

She brushed aside the invading kudzu at the spot where

Charles's desk had stood, and to her surprise, saw the edge of the photo frame. When she pulled it from the sodden ash and brushed off the soot, the wood fell apart in her hands and the cardboard backing disintegrated. She peeled off the cracked and heat-warped glass.

The photo was intact. An odd survivor of a hellish night. No energy attached to the picture that she could feel, but it wouldn't hurt to be sure. Ram was in London with Khalil, and he hadn't said when he'd be home, but maybe he would point her to someone who could vet the picture for hidden magick. She'd also let him know what Charles had said about the Triad.

Because she didn't believe for one minute he'd abandoned his schemes.

The prison guards allowed Charles to receive the photograph, which a friend of Ram had declared clean. Charles tucked it into his pocket, then smiled at her. "You want to know about the Triad."

Natalie put away the uneasy sensation that she'd given him something quite valuable. "About the Dragon."

He gave a little tilt to his head. "We aimed to expand the boundaries of magick. We were not the only ones, but we were among the best. As oxymoronic as it sounds, we blended scientific discoveries with the energies of magick."

"That worked?"

"There were challenges. And the Custos Magi considered us dangerously unprincipled. They sent their best tracker, Ram, who found Chimaera. Because of him, Chimaera is dead."

For the first time, she saw deep emotion beneath the veneer of casual conversation. Charles was furious at the death of his co-conspirator, felt a deep-seated hatred for Ram. She swallowed against a parched throat as her hands curled into fists. Damn him, but he wouldn't play her to hurt Ram.

"Who was the third member of this Triad?"

"The Dragon, Louis Meltone. Also dead, thanks to Adam Zolton." He settled back into his chair, his face smoothing. "Ironic, that the two other men you're closest to were the ones who destroyed the Triad."

Something about his answer was off. There'd been genuine grief and anger when he talked about the death of Chimaera. Not so with Dragon. Which meant either Charles didn't care about the Dragon's death, or the Dragon wasn't dead.

"You blended genetics and magick. What did Dragon and Chimaera focus on?"

"Neurology and quantum physics."

"How did you plan to use these blends?"

He hesitated, then smiled. "The ring of the Triad. If you can find the lost library of Tayasal and retrieve the codex of Itza, you'll have the piece we could never find. Once all the obstacles were overcome, we still needed that final spell to create the ring of the Triad." He rose to his feet and motioned to the guard, indicating the visit was over.

"Wait. You said you knew how to heal Adam's sister."

"Abby? Well, only death can do that, although tell him there are many kinds of death. Good-bye, Natalie. I expect we won't see each other again. Or least, not until I'm out of here."

One small sentence of innocuous words. Yet the whole of it packed an undeniable threat.

She stared at his retreating back, anger burning away fear. As he vanished into the prison bowels, she said softly, "And we will be ready, you bastard."

As soon as she was free of the prison, she called Adam to tell him what Charles had said about Abby. God, she hated making that call.

The prison had disappeared from her rearview mirror by the time she called Ram. The memory of the threats had not.

The central sanctum of the Custos Magi had always impressed Ram Montgomery with its painted, vaulted ceilings, perfect acoustics, and majestic stained-glass windows. The aura of thousands of years of history had seemed a comforting link to wisdom and purpose.

Today, though, as he sat in one comfortably appointed alcove with Khalil and two of the elders, both powerful masters of magick, those traditions seemed oppressive.

"Grace Armatrading has talent," Khalil reported. "It's blossoming, but she's dangerously untrained, and she's thrown in her lot with Adam Zolton."

"The mage killer?" asked one elder.

"He isn't a killer," Ram said tartly.

"He owns Vitae," Khalil retorted. "They fashion weapons. He's obsessed with chasing a phantom."

"He's not so deluded." Ram leaned forward. "Natalie went to visit her ex, and he's talking about the Triad."

The second elder tapped his fingers together. "Phoenix is in prison. You and Khalil killed Chimaera."

"We cast Constantine into lava. That doesn't mean he died."

"No one could have survived that." Khalil's voice was gentle. "You might not remember that night well."

Ram shifted in his seat, the scars on his back tightening. They hadn't bothered him in a very long time. Until recently. Constantine had burned away Ram's magick that night, with a whip of unnatural power and a stealth Ram had never encountered before or since. Only Natalie had brought him from that powerless, hellish netherworld. "I remember every detail of that night," he retorted. "What about the Dragon?"

"The Dragon was identified in time; Louis Meltone was killed in a bomb blast years ago," answered the second elder.

Khalil frowned. "Meltone's skill level was low. You thought he was the Dragon?" Khalil gave Ram a worried look. "I think we need to look at this further."

"Then you shall," answered the elder. "Ramses, you'll go—"

"No." Ram fingered the ring box in his pocket. This was why he had come here. To make this final break. "I'm out. I won't keep lying to Natalie."

"We've all made such sacrifices," sputtered the elder.

Before Ram could answer, the other elder, who'd been sitting back, listening, his steepled fingertips gently tapping, lifted one hand.

Silence fell across the other three.

"Have you broken your vow of silence about us, Ramses?" he asked gently.

"No."

"He's too valuable to lose, Master," Khalil added. "I keep drawing him back in."

"Times—and partners—are different now," Ram argued. "Secrets can't be held, not forever. Maybe less secrecy would benefit us."

"We must continue to honor our traditions."

"But we also adjust to the times. Don't we communicate with e-mail instead of missals of parchment? Travel by jet instead of mule?" retorted Ram.

"And we must be able to counter the technology of our enemies," added Khalil. He leaned forward. "This gives me an uneasy feeling about the Dragon. Perhaps we were misled."

The first elder sat in contemplation a moment, then nodded, although what he was agreeing with, Ram wasn't sure. "Ramses, we would keep you with us. You are given leave to tell Natalie whatever you desire, in your best judgment. Khalil, handle Grace however you deem best. You must follow the trail of the Dragon." He fingered the cuff of his shirt, a surprisingly nervous gesture. Something about the possibility that this Dragon was still alive scared him.

"By what means?" asked Khalil.

"By whatever means you deem necessary. Both of you, though, remember our activities must not invite public scrutiny."

Khalil sat back with a smile. Apparently he'd gotten exactly what he wanted from this meeting. Ram shifted again, his shoulders burning.

Exactly what plot was Khalil weaving?

Charles Severin stretched out on his bunk. God, how he hated this place. Seeing Natalie, so fresh and feminine, only reinforced the prison's dreariness.

The first days in here had not been easy. Without his magick, he'd relied on the physical skills he'd learned. The others had been surprised to learn the rich, prep-school grad they'd deemed fresh meat knew a wealth of dirty moves and wasn't hesitant to use them.

When the first glimmer of magick had returned, he'd added that to his repertoire of defense, although he'd been increasingly frustrated when the glimmer had refused to get any stronger.

Until Natalie had contacted him.

He pressed a hand against his pocket. If his theories were right, that deficiency was about to end sooner than anyone thought.

He took out the picture, scraped a fingernail across Natalie's image, and then sucked off the small residue. Closing his eyes, he whispered, "Water the powers that reside in me. Feed the powers that reside in me. Grow the powers that reside in me."

Long ago, when he'd realized that Natalie was a resonant, he'd imbedded her blood and DNA, the codes of her power, within this photo.

Now, that ability should work on him.

He only had to wait.

He supposed the Dragon had eliminated all the witnesses and continued to refine the necessary skills for the Triad— God, he pitied anyone unlucky enough to be caught in that enchantment of madness and pain.

But the Dragon would be ready and so would he.

The library would surface somewhere, of that he was certain, and when it did, they would find the spell that had eluded them.

And he would hope that Chimaera had found a way past the ties of death.

Adam was in the gym with Grace, spotting her on the bench press, when Natalie called about her visit with Charles. Grace thunked the bar back, watching as he listened. He managed a polite "Thank you," and an encouraging "Let me know if you hear anything more," before he disconnected.

He stared bleakly out the windows. His chest felt as stripped as the barren cornfield on the other side of the glass.

"What is it?" Grace sat up and wiped her face with a towel.

He summarized the raw facts. "There is no cure except death."

"Maybe we'll find something in the library."

"One more lead," he said bitterly. "Always just out of reach."

After a moment's silence, she said, "You're not pursuing the Dragon for revenge, are you? You're chasing hope."

His fists tightened. "Not everything can be fixed. Maybe I need to accept that."

Grace tilted her hydration bottle and splashed icy water on his head.

"What was that for?" Adam spluttered.

"Because you must be delirious if you accept the word of such a stellar citizen."

She laid a hand on his arm. "Sometimes the only thing we can believe in is hope."

Was Severin lying? Adding six twenty-five-pound plates to the press bar, he took his place on the bench. Grunting, sweating against the strain of the weights, he clung to one elusive, taunting wisp of hope.

Maybe the person who had to die was the Dragon.

CHAPTER SEVENTEEN

With snow and fog mixed to a gray sludge of ice and air, the waters of Lake Huron were stirred to restless, white-topped waves.

A yacht waited for Grace and Adam at the pier. The bearded captain, dressed in serviceable parka, waterproof pants, and flexible tread boots, greeted them with a taciturn nod.

"Storm's coming up; best get on board."

Grace took the captain's proffered hand as she balanced one foot on the dock and one foot inside the boat. With an easy tug, he guided her onto the rocking vessel, and then he reached across the bulwark to greet Adam with a warm handshake. "Been too long, Mr. Zolton."

"*NONE* keeps me busy."

"Busy? Bah, you just don't like the cold," muttered the captain. "Cast off those lines."

"You'd melt in our humidity." Adam began to undo the thick ropes looped around the moorings, tossing each rope end back onto the boat, while the captain started the engines.

"Can I help?" Grace asked.

"Sit over there."

And stay out of the way. She got the message.

"Can't stand the blizzards?" the captain asked Adam.

"Can't stand the hurricanes?"

While the two ribbed each other, Adam jumped into the boat with an easy grace and the captain backed away from the dock.

"Captain Emil, this is Dr. Armatrading," Adam introduced them.

"Doctor." He tipped his cap.

"Call me Grace."

"You prone to seasickness?" he asked her. "We got a weather pattern moving in, and the ride'll be rough."

"Not that I know."

"Hang over the side if you do. Puke's not good for the deck varnish."

"Aye, aye," she answered, resisting the urge for a smartass salute.

Grinning, Adam gestured toward a cushioned seat beneath a canopy. "If you sit there, you can get fresh air and still be protected from the wind."

"How long's the trip to Excalibur?"

"About an hour."

Half an hour later, Grace stood in the prow, letting the freshwater spray wash her face to combat the growing queasiness in her stomach.

Adam joined her, his breath a frosty plume. "It's cold out here."

"The fresh air is nice."

"Knock off that N and I might agree." He gave her a knowing look. "At least out here I don't feel one swell away from parting company with breakfast."

"I feel fine," she replied primly.

He gave a bark of laughter. "And I'm a monk."

She smiled at the notion of Adam as a celibate hermit.

He pulled out his camera and stood with feet apart, braced against the pitching of the boat as he recorded a shot of the island, barely visible in the leaden fog. He turned and took a rapid succession of pictures of her.

"Beautiful," he breathed.

"Oh, please, the mist's washed off all my makeup." Self-consciously, she straightened her skewed ski cap. "At least they're easy to delete."

The boat lurched over a massive wave, sending her stumbling into Adam. His arm wrapped around her, keeping her upright. Pressed together, they rode the final roller-coaster dips together. Their breath mingled in cold clouds.

She lifted her gaze to his. His gray eyes, focused on her, reflected the flat lead of the sky, turning them unfathomable. His arm cushioned her waist; her gloved hands steadied his shoulders.

When the last breaker passed and the yacht leveled, neither one stepped back. Adam's eyes now seemed fired from below, like a kiln fire melting silver.

"Would you like to see what I saw?" Without waiting for her answer, Adam shifted, nestling her into the curve of his arms so she could see the camera's view screen.

The skill of the spontaneous portrait was amazing. He'd caught a wave in action, a contrast to the pale image of the mysterious island. She was barely in the photo, smudged by the weather. He'd caught her before she turned, highlighting a side of herself she rarely saw. She'd always considered herself reasonably attractive, but the pose gave her an ethereal beauty.

"You are good," she said. "You have an eye not only for the detail but for the story behind the picture."

"You seemed like an elf returning home to the misty isles." He traced the air above her virtual cheek, and Grace swore she could feel the gentle brush on her skin. Or maybe she shivered from the touch of his warm breath as he leaned closer to the screen, to her. "On sunless days, skin can look gray, but yours glows." His finger traced the virtual laugh lines radiating from the corners of her eyes. "There's character here. Determination. Mystery. Eyes that see beyond deception."

He touched a button on the camera, and the photo vanished, replaced by one he'd taken of only the island.

"Oh." He'd deleted the picture. As she'd asked, she reminded herself, suppressing the pang of disappointment.

"I didn't delete it," he said, correctly interpreting her reaction. "I sent it to my phone as my new background photo."

He let go of her then, his hands gripping the rail beside hers. "Is Excalibur what you expected?" he asked, pointing to the island.

"I'm not sure what I expected. Some medieval rock-clad fortress maybe."

But Excalibur from the approach side was only cliffs and trees. Bare limbs struggled upward from a morass of thick trunks. The few spots of color came from evergreens, their emerald needles muted to silver in the fog-kissed air.

"Has anyone come out to the island recently?" Adam called to the captain.

"Last trip I made was in November with Mr. Washington."

"Can you circle the island? Make sure no other boats are here?"

Captain Emil shrugged, as though the strange requests of his employers rolled off him as easily as water off a slicker, and turned the boat to the right.

As they cruised without seeing any other boats, Captain Emil cut back the engine. In the ensuing silence, Grace heard the crash of waves against the rocks lining the shore. Otherwise the spot of land was bathed in an ominous silence.

"It's a wilderness. I expected habitation. Are you sure there's electricity?"

Adam's laugh dispelled the pall, like sunshine on fog. "Trust me, you won't be roughing it."

They rounded the end of the island, and Grace drew in a breath. "What a spectacular home."

The builder had taken care to match the natural elements as much as possible in the wood-and-stone home, even matching the upright posts to the forest wood. "What's on the roof?"

"Sod. It's eco-friendly, like the rest of the home."

Despite the rustic exterior, she could see touches of elegance, such as the carvings on the porch. The house was bigger than she'd first thought, she realized. She couldn't imagine the square footage or begin to put a price tag on the charm.

Despite its beauty, Grace tucked her arm through Adam's, unable to shake the feeling that coming to this isolated fortress was a bad idea. "Is there security?"

He chuckled. "With Jonas sometimes working here? The security is the most sophisticated available on—and off—the market. Video monitors, motion sensors. The only way in is by boat or seaplane. So far there's no evidence anyone's here. After we land, I'll check the security systems. Trust me, if anyone's slipped onto the island, I'll know. Once we're sure we're alone, we can set the alarms. No one will get past."

When the boat docked, Adam nimbly jumped onto the wooden pier; Grace followed, less nimbly. At least she hadn't puked on Captain Emil's spotless deck.

They set the moorings and unloaded their bags. Captain Emil nodded, tipped his hat, slung his duffel over his shoulder, and then headed in the opposite direction.

Inside the house, they hung their coats on a tree stand, and Grace surveyed the open floor plan. A two-story riverstone fireplace, etched glass, a wooden spiral staircase—she barely took in the rich details, before Gala climbed out of Adam's pocket to begin exploring.

"You'd better tell her not to go outside," Grace said.

With a swish of her tail, the ferret immediately headed toward the door.

"If she gets outside"—Grace pretended to ignore the ferret

to talk to Adam—"she might have an unpleasant encounter with a fox or a wolverine . . ."

"Gala," he warned.

The ferret slinked away from the door and headed up the stairs.

"Take the groceries to the kitchen while I carry our bags upstairs and check the security." Adam handed her the grocery sacks.

"Sure." Grace easily found the kitchen. She unloaded their produce, although the kitchen was stocked well enough that they wouldn't have needed them. When Adam rejoined her, she asked, "Are we secure?"

"Snug as bugs."

"Then let's see if I can open the library."

Adam's stomach growled. "Let's have lunch first. Eager as I am to get inside that library, we shouldn't try intricate work without fuel."

They worked in companionable silence to assemble their sandwiches and lay out apples.

"Have you ever done magick?" Grace asked, swallowing a bite of turkey.

"Can't even if my life depended on it. I tried twice. Once I nearly killed myself as the unfettered spell ricocheted inside me, seeking a way out, and once I destroyed a room with a careening spell." Neither was an experience he wished to repeat. "Similar things happen when I act on magick not directed at me."

"In that book from Khalil, Cadwaladar talks of resonants, reflectors, and nulls. People with the talents not of magick but of modulation." She thought a minute. "You're a reflector?"

"Not perfect. Surprise or unusual strength can get past my shields."

"That's why your blood stopped Raj. Why, at the lab, I couldn't heal you until you let down your guards."

"Pretty much."

"So what went wrong two nights ago?" she asked.

"I'm vulnerable during sleep. No, not sleep, falling asleep or waking up."

"Between times."

He nodded. "I worked hard to make my talent continual and instinctive, even during sleep. That attack was the first time anything's gotten through in a long while. If you hadn't woken me up, I would have suffocated."

"And looked like you had a heart attack in bed."

"One more white male inexplicably cut down."

The awful possibility stole her breath. She reached over and hugged him. "Let's go find some answers, because I don't want to risk losing you a third time."

"I'm not the primary target."

"Are you sure?" She took their plates to the sink. "Cadwaladar wrote about reflectors. He said a mage should use the resonant to amplify power, but avoid the reflector or the null. I think he said something like, 'For the null shall destroy the power and the reflector must interfere with the proper casting.' Do you think that's why I've had such trouble doing the unlocking spell? You interfered with me?"

"No," he said, flatly.

Okay, apparently that wasn't a subject up for discussion. She remembered something he'd said. "You said dangerous things happen if you go after magick not directed at you. But what about after my last fugue? It was broken when I fell on you. How did that happen?"

He stared at her. "I don't know. That should have been impossible."

They chose a small, enclosed den to work in. Grace set up a protective perimeter, while Adam plugged in his computer. Although he wanted to be able to surround her with protection, he couldn't repel outside magick while walking inside the magick-generated library.

When she finished, he gathered her in his arms. He kissed the wave of her hair, then nuzzled her neck. "You smell delicious, Doctor."

She kissed the sensitive skin behind his ear, sending sweet shivers down his spine before she reminded him with a laugh, "We're on serious business here."

"Then let's get started before my body starts to have other notions."

Her hips shifted a little. "I think it's too late for that. We could open a window for nature's equivalent of a cold shower."

"No thanks, I'll control myself." His hand cupped her cheek. "If you notice anything, any intrusions, any pain or memory loss, you let me know. I'll get out as fast as I can."

"Agreed."

He found a seat in a wingback chair, then donned the clingy gloves and virtual goggles. "Open the file."

Grace started the chant. The words sounded like the ones he remembered Faith using, but the door didn't open.

"What's happening?" Grace paused to take a breath.

"Nothing."

"Damn," she muttered and fell back into the chant. Frustration bit at the words, and her voice grew hard-edged. The door started to fade, blending into the background of pearlescent gray—featureless, formless, but with hints of muted color that spun when he tried to focus on them.

"Stop!" he ordered, and Grace cut off the chant.

Adam lifted the visor from his eyes.

"Why can't I do this?" she snapped.

"You will. You can do magick. You've saved me twice already."

She waved a hand. "That was different."

"How?" He braced his elbows on his knees. "How is this different from when you help someone in the ER? Or saved me?"

"No one's bleeding or dying."

"So the immediacy isn't there, the life and death, the adrenaline."

"Planning on stabbing yourself, then? Give us some blood and danger?"

"Ah, no." He leaned back, steepling his fingers to tap together. What else was different?

Grace picked up the paper with the spell and read it through, muttering under her breath. Her foot tapped in cadence. He remembered how she'd paced when they were trying to figure out connections between the mages.

"When you were in med school, how did you learn all the facts you need to retain? Did you write out notes and read them? Listen to lecture tapes?"

Looking perplexed, she answered, "To be honest, most things didn't click into place until I had a chance to be on the floors and working with actual patients. Before then?" She gave a small laugh, her face lit in a pleasant memory. "My methods drove my study group nuts. They needed silence to process carefully transcribed notes, then Socratic drills to cement the knowledge. I had to pace and mutter. They kept me around because I could always come up with a unique mnemonic to remember things."

"Faith was typing at her computer when she opened the file. Maybe she was the same way and designed the spell to be both verbal and kinetic."

Grace reexamined the chant. "If I change 'know and learn and find' to 'find, learn, know' . . ." She hummed the rhythm. "That's smoother to my ear. Ready, then."

As she poised her fingers expectantly over the keys, Adam settled the visor, swallowing against the instant sense of disorientation. Grace's voice and the click of her keyboard were muted, but the increased confidence in her chant immediately sharpened the image of the elusive door.

"It's working."

"You can enter the library?"

"Not yet." Carefully, he walked his mind forward, heading toward the door. Though the colors behind it stopped swirling, he still felt as if he were on a carnival ride.

Then, with jarring abruptness, a door slammed open as though driven by a gale, and he found himself in the library.

"You did it! I'm here."

"Excellent." Her satisfied pause disrupted the chant, and the library wavered in the silence.

"Keep the spell active," he warned.

"One monotonizing ritual filling your space." Her amusement made him smile.

He found her silky voice and speedy typing reassuring, which gave him pleasure and confidence as he returned to the library.

Thousands of references popped into focus. Not in neat Dewey-decimal order. Random piles of CDs on tables and floating book stacks with no discernable support stretched to an impossibly distant indoor horizon.

How to find what he needed? As he took a step deeper, the scene shivered. Books dropped into new places; walls shifted to a new configuration.

Buzzing black dots swarmed his skull. With a virtual hand, he swatted one, and as he touched it, the dot swelled, becoming a thin flash drive.

He gave a low whistle. "She not only has old manuscripts here. She collected all magick, ancient or cutting edge."

"Bet mages would kill to acquire that knowledge." Grace grunted, the clicking of her keyboard accelerating.

His palms began to sweat beneath the gloves. No wonder Faith had used so many safeguards. Especially if she didn't know which mages she could trust.

Think about those implications later. Right now, he had to find the references Faith had identified. He tried the simplest approach—asking.

"Where's the saga of Cadwaladar?"

At his question, a series of irregularly shaped white dots dropped in front of him, winding toward the stacks. Before disappearing, they paused and lit in succeeding pulses, like a stadium wave, urging him to follow.

As if he needed incentive, a wind shoved at his back, the currents carrying a scent of fresh-baked, yeasty bread. Bread crumbs.

Adam chuckled. "Faith had a sense of humor."

The damn bread crumbs better not be leading him astray. He found he had to concentrate on only the Hansel and Gretel trail, for the surroundings were disorienting. He lost his sense of direction when the trail led him through a gap in the shelves that hadn't been there a second before.

At last he found the book and pulled it from the shelf. It felt oddly heavy.

No time to read it; he felt something strange happening, a pressure against his eardrums.

"Hurry." Grace's voice was strained. "Get what we need."

"Something wrong?"

"Anomalies."

As though the books had been shaken to release spores of mold, the air grew musty. With time running out, he tucked the book under his arm and said, "*Legends Y Ddraig Goch*."

Five thin images danced around his spotty vision.

He needed to narrow his search.

He touched the one that seemed most promising, and then took off after the bread crumbs. At least this one was close. Breathing hard, he nabbed it.

The room began squeezing around him. His chest grabbed for air.

"I'm losing," Grace shouted. "Get out, Adam!"

Not without that CD. "CD," he said. Thousands of dots whirled in a maelstrom.

"Take off your visor before you're trapped."

"Not yet. Abby Zolton." One CD. He snatched it and added it to his stack. "Exit."

Grace screamed.

"Grace!" he shouted.

"The Spell of I'celus requires the torch. Get it," she commanded, her voice hollow.

The room elongated and distorted. Like an elastic band, with him fastened to one end. Too late, he tried to deflect the magick. Instead, he snapped across virtuality into a green-lit corridor. A single book stood out like a shiny toad.

He ignored it. He had to get out. "Exit!" Damn. Nothing.

He tried to move, but a whoosh of heat coated his face in sweat. Grace started choking.

He grabbed the book. *Get out. Don't race blind. Think.* He halted, ignoring his panic. Nothing familiar. Couldn't retrace his steps. What had he seen when he first came into the library?

Like sorting photographs, he riffled through the images in his mind. One stuck, a healing text he'd noticed because of the title. *"Vitae Curatio."*

The bread crumbs appeared. Racing after them, he plunged through the stacks.

Electricity zinged around him, short bursts that singed his breath and cracked across his skin. Walls collapsed toward him. His heart skipped. Turning a corner, he found the title *Vitae Curatio* glowing. He was at the edges of the collection, and there was the exit.

He grabbed the book. Plunging through the exit, he found himself in the featureless transition space. A rush of cold air raised gooseflesh and set his teeth chattering. He felt as if he'd been flung into a snowbank.

Adam focused on his free hand and then snatched off his visor. He flung himself back into the chair, ricocheting out of the magick. Gasping for breath, he became aware of two facts simultaneously.

He had the books and CD.

Grace stood at the circle's center, her arms outstretched, her hair blown back in an invisible wind. At her throat circled a whip-thin line of red.

CHAPTER EIGHTEEN

Adam was free. "Don't!" Grace jerked away when he reached for her; his touch could break their defense. Throat aching, she threw her energy into strengthening their protective circle. The shadow mind retreated, howling its frustration.

Only when she was sure they were alone did she relax. She swallowed; the sore throat was gone.

"Are you okay?" Adam's hand hovered above her cheek.

"Fine." She pulled him to her, holding him close, her head resting against his chest. "I was so afraid you'd be trapped in that damn library. Are you okay? No bits of your psyche left behind?"

"No. You kept the library open long enough for me and all the books to get out."

"Whoever's after Faith's library must have caught the latent energy."

"Did you recognize whom?"

"No." She held him closer, as if his warmth could banish the taint of raw evil. "The seeking was simply energy. Nasty energy."

She could have stayed in his arms all day, holding him, reassuring herself he was safe, but embraces wouldn't bring answers. "I don't want to let you go, but we should look at what you brought back."

They retrieved the references and his computer, then

spread them out on the table. Finding herself starving, Grace rummaged in the kitchen and came back with colas and a bag of Oreos, then pulled her chair next to his.

He hooked his arm around the chair back to face her. "Did you have another fugue?"

She shoved her loosened hair out of her face and bit into a cookie, joining bits of memory. "No. Tonight the energy stayed outside me; I was merely a tool. Something inside the library awoke and called."

"An embedded spell?" He let out a breath.

"I haven't examined anything. Being in that library was a grab-and-go."

Adam picked up the book generating the embedded spell, and discovered it was no book at all.

"It's a box." Adam turned it around. A sheen of reptilian green coated the intricate carvings. As they watched, the emerald veneer began to glow and melt, spreading out from his fingers. Adam quickly returned the box to the table, as they shielded their eyes against the brilliant spot of color and the dissolving box beneath. Within moments and without even a whisper of sound, the glow vanished, leaving behind a metallic double helix. At one end, the intertwined coils met in a sharp point and at the other, they were attached to copper, intricately woven into wings. The metal helix was an unknown alloy—shimmering and refracting like a multifaceted prism.

This had been painstakingly forged; Adam had never seen anything like it. He ran a finger across the coil's tip, drawing a drop of blood. The metal was honed sharp.

"Reminds me of a caduceus," Grace observed. "Two snakes coiled around a staff."

"Those round crystals near the top could be eyes. There's a bloodred halo around them." He touched a finger to one crystal, and his hand snapped back, nerves screaming as if he'd touched a live wire. "This may be DNA coded to one person."

"Do you know who I'celus is?" Grace asked.

"The bringer of nightmares."

"The name is familiar." She thought a minute. "In my fugue at the lab, the vision I saw of Kea told me to find the library and the Torch of I'celus. When I last saw him, he warned me there was a complex ritual, the Spell of I'celus, that could be used for mind control. For wiping out reality."

"And now we've released the Torch of I'celus." He turned it, studying it from a different angle. So this torch came into Faith's possession. Maybe it spurred her to investigate the Dragon and she found the connection to the eight mages. Maybe she was killed because of what she knew about the murders *and* because she'd hidden the torch."

"Wonder how it works." Avoiding the eyes, he lifted the helix, pointing its wings skyward. Every stray beam of light shattered into a dozen rainbows. Slits of color laced the room, while the lights dimmed to an anemic gloom. Grace had always thought rainbows were omens of happiness.

These weren't.

Adam glanced around the room. "Looks like a pack of malevolent eyes."

"So I'm not the only one getting uh-oh vibes?" The pulses of color reminded her too much of the fiber optics in the bands.

"Not at all." He put the torch inside a grocery bag. The rainbows disappeared. The sensation of being watched did not. "Which one of us gets to be Frodo and pitch this thing into Mount Doom? Or, barring a fiery volcano, the watery equivalent, aka Lake Huron."

"My precious," she crooned, her hand hovering above the bag. At his wary look, she laughed and put her hand behind her back. "Gotcha, no spell there. But I don't think we should get rid of it. For one thing, we don't know if we can. For another, you're holding ancient history, Adam. History we might need and could never get back."

"So you're of the group that thinks the CDC is right to keep a strain of smallpox in case we need to study it, when keeping that strain could be the only way to precipitate the epidemic they're trying to prevent?"

"I'm of the group that believes burning books because we're afraid of their contents is wrong. You're not holding the one torch to rule them all, even though someone might use it for evil."

He hesitated, and then set the bag aside. "We can destroy it later. So, Kea told you about I'celus?"

"He said that Khalil was rumored to be the only one who'd mastered the spell." She sighed. "Too much supposition. Let's look at the other references. What's that CD you brought out?"

"I think it might be connected to Abby." As Adam put the CD into his computer, she gave one last glance at the grocery bag. One undeniable, bitter truth had kept her from touching the torch. Any magick in it wouldn't affect Adam; she couldn't say the same thing about herself. Fact was, her mind appeared to be an open text, free for the riffling. She flexed her fingers, squeezing back a remnant of lingering pain and fear.

While Adam opened the file on the CD, Grace picked up the saga of Cadwaladar. She was curious to see if there was anything different in this version from the pages Glinda had given them.

"Sod it, Faith!"

Adam's exclamation cut through Grace's labored translation of Cadwaladar. He shoved to his feet and paced two steps, back and forth, as he raked a hand through his hair. "I was your right gullible git."

"What's wrong?"

He gestured toward the screen. "She got me to come after

the library by giving me a glimpse of that CD. There's nothing there but the bloody photos from Abby's first art fair."

Grace slid over to the computer and arrowed through the photos. As each photo filled the screen, her hope that Adam was overreacting died. The images were all familiar London scenes: Eros at Piccadilly Circus; Adam with a cigarette in his mouth, photographing the fog; Regan and Jonas on a picnic; a musician at a tube station.

Adam wasn't the only Zolton with a photographic eye. Abby was skilled with composition and the juxtaposition of colors and shadows, although she didn't have Adam's flair for meaning, for story. The only picture that hinted at a depth beyond the obvious subject was one of Regan, shading her eyes as she looked into a park. One immediately wondered—what was she looking at? The camera had caught her from behind, catching just the hint of expression that could have been anything from sadness to eagerness to loathing.

The last photo pushed a lump up Grace's throat: a group of friends laughing and posing together in one of the cars of the London Eye.

All of them killed by a bomb.

"What am I missing, Grace? There has to be something."

"Then I'm missing it, too. Why did you think the CD was important?"

"Abby was attacked hours after that art fair opened and her dark room was destroyed. I thought she had other photos, ones the Dragon didn't want seen. Photos on that CD. Hell, everybody's seen those." He pressed his fist against his lips. "Maybe one's a different style or subject than the others."

He sat down with the photos again, while Grace finished the Cadwaladar translation. When he shoved the computer back, she asked, "Find anything?"

"Faith drew me in like a master angler," he said with a touch of bitterness. "Then hid the library on my desktop and designed the library's defenses so both of us had to open it. Why the hell did she bring you into this quagmire?"

Grace flinched at his savagery. After the past few days, she'd hoped his anger was for putting her into danger, not for the fact he'd been forced back into her orbit.

Triage. One problem at a time. Airway before bleeding. They had to stay alive before she could tackle the foolishness of her heart. "I think she didn't know which of the mages she could trust. And I was already drawn in. I'd written her about my fugues."

The look he gave her was hooded, his gray eyes as welcoming as flint. "She counted on me to protect you. At least until you were strong enough to open the library. Like I said, a right gullible git."

"The library's open; I don't need protection. So if you're going to be pissy, feel free to head back to New Orleans."

"Don't be daft."

"Because you still need to find the Dragon, and this is your best shot?"

"Yes."

She had just squelched the pang of disappointment that he wasn't staying for her, when he bent down, one hand on each chair arm, caging her in the seat.

"And this." With that terse declaration, he kissed her. A hard, brook-no-arguments kiss, one that shot heat clear to her toes and left her gripping his arms in an effort to meld body to body.

"I don't like being played for a fool, but I will never regret that she led me back to you." His second kiss was short, but no less powerful.

"We'll find your answers," she whispered against his lips. "So let's get cracking and see what other primrose paths my eccentric aunt is leading us down."

This time they curled together on the sofa, with Grace resting in the crook of his shoulder and the array of books around them. Adam picked up the saga so she started on *Legends, Y Ddraig Goch*. The book spoke of different images of the dragon: the treasure hoarder, the flame breather, the poison-skinned serpent, the benevolent bringer of rains.

Was Faith trying to tell them to look for someone with all these characteristics? Who today breathed flames? A smoker? Were these lines a clue to the Dragon's purpose? She read the last line again, the one that had been in the e-mail. Nope, still nothing.

Except . . . in the e-mail, that had been a clue to something else, something known only to her and Faith. She ran her finger across the blank bottom half of the page and spoke aloud. "Pineapple ink."

Brown lettering written in an old-fashioned hand scrolled down the page. "Brita Jorgensen. The Dragon hunts her." Following this was an address in Marshall, a small town about an hour west of Ann Arbor.

As the letters faded, she found a piece of paper and wrote down the name and address before she forgot them. "Pineapple ink," she repeated, to check her memory.

The page remained blank.

A chill ran through her as she stared at the paper. Faith had taken great pains to keep this as secure as possible. Grace held the paper out to Adam. "Memorize this."

"What?" He looked distracted.

"Memorize this."

He stared at it a moment, then nodded. "Got it."

"I think—"

"Give me a moment, I'm on to something here." He logged onto the Internet.

While he went back to the saga, she burned the paper. When the last ash had fallen, she started reading the *Vitae Curatio*.

At last, Adam sat back. "Dear God, I know what the Dragon wants."

Grace shifted to look at what he had on the computer screen. It looked like a scientific paper.

"Faith pointed us to the prophecy. To the Dragon. Remember what Natalie reported from Charles? Five, six years ago, he and his cronies were re-creating the Triad, using science as an aid to their magick."

"Then Chimaera was killed, and everyone assumed Dragon was, too, in the bombing blast."

"But Dragon is very much alive and behind the destruction of the mages."

"Why?"

"You said Kea suspected the Spell of I'celus was responsible for your blackouts. Remember Lincoln Landry? One of the mages killed? Landry was a professor of psychology, quite the whiz kid. When he was in college, he wrote an obscure article about mind control. His theory was that mind control wasn't possible, except for very brief periods. The human mind is too robust. His article was in the files Faith sent you." He pointed to the computer screen.

She read the article's conclusion. "Mind control requires strenuous ongoing effort and harms the attacker."

"According to the newspaper article about his death, in his final hours his words and phrases made no coherent sense. He kept saying 'Spell of Ice.' What if he meant I'celus? What if it's possible, with the spell of I'celus, for the Dragon to get inside your mind? Long enough to pluck out whatever he wanted? Your talents, every fact you've ever learned, your fears, your secrets."

She shuddered at the primal and intimate violation.

"If Landry's initial conclusion is right, that mind control harms the attacker, maybe the Dragon wants your healing talents, and you haven't developed the protections to stop him?" He opened the book. "Cadwaladar comes across the dragon, holding a flaming torch and surrounded by the slain bodies of his acolytes. He tells Cadwaladar he destroyed his circle of the damned in order to rise above them. His circle is three groups of three."

"Nine mages. Faith was investigating eight murders when she was killed. The Dragon's killing anyone who knew him from before."

"This Brita might be the only survivor." He tilted his head, listening. "The storm is still powerful; we can't leave until morning. Once we hit the mainland, we find out what Brita knows."

"Faith took great care to hide her name. She didn't want the Dragon to find her. We've been traced before. What if we lead the Dragon to his last witness?"

"Knowledge has a way of surfacing, hidden or not. We need to warn her. We need to know what she's hiding before the knowledge is destroyed."

"You're right."

"There has to be more," Adam said, feeling along the spine of the saga. "*The Saga of Cadwaladar* is available from other sources. Why did Faith want us to have this particular book?"

"She hid Brita's address and the torch. Could be something hidden there, too."

"If so, I haven't found—Wait." He poked at the vellum cover, and then jerked his hand back, shaking it. "That stung. There's more magick."

"Residual? After all, it is a book from a virtual library."

"Brilliant!" He leaned over and kissed her.

"Glad to help." But she didn't realize what he meant until he grabbed the gloves and visor, donned them, and opened the book.

At once he slammed the book shut. He pressed his lips together and ripped off the visor. A moment later he dragged in air. "Now I know what you meant about that nausea." He handed her the visor and book. "This one's for you."

With trepidation—the last time had been singularly unpleasant—she put on the visor and gloves and then stepped into a soft, soothing world of blue velvet. No trace of the mind-spinning she'd encountered before.

The saga rested on a stone lectern in front of her. She opened the book in real space, and the virtual book also opened.

Grace gasped as smoke streamed from the pages, then solidified into an image of Faith dressed in jeans, a gold sweater, and layers of bracelets. Older than Grace remembered, but still vibrant. Her heart recalled its grief, as tears sprang to her eyes. She reached out. "How—?"

"No questions, Grace," warned the hologram. "I don't have much time. And you can't touch me; I'm no longer part of this plane of existence. How I wish I could see you, but I must settle for your photo while I record this. If you've gotten this far, then you are stronger in your magick than before. I hope I've made you strong enough to keep the torch from the Dragon. If he does succeed, you might stop him with this." She held up a computer disk. The image of Faith froze a moment, and Grace feared it was going to disappear. Then the image shook the disk and snapped. "Take it!"

Virtual Grace held out her hand, and the disk dropped onto her palm.

"I regret I can't give you more, but I've learned so little. Not even who he is, or whom to trust. Brita was confused when she brought the torch to me for concealment. She only said that, without it, the Dragon could not succeed. If she's still alive, perhaps you can get more from her." The image hesitated a moment, while Faith's hands plucked at her knit sweater. "I assume Adam is with you still. That"—she inclined her head toward the disk—"is complex magick. You'll have to work hard to master its intricacies, and I'm not sure you will be able to, for I fear you will not have much time. Adam's innate reflection could hinder you. You must do this on your own, without him." Faith looked at her then, a single tear at the corner of her eye. "We have to make difficult choices for our magick, Grace, and this will be one for you. I've faced hard options, and I have had regrets. But I've never doubted my magick. I made sure Adam would protect you. But, in time, and soon, to master and command the magick inside you, you must tell Adam good-bye."

Abruptly the image vanished, and the soft blue around Grace changed to hard gray. "Faith!" she shouted, but she was left alone with a disk, a book that had morphed into a laptop, and an impossible choice.

She stared at the disk, her chest a hollow echo. She hadn't found Adam only to lose him again. No, Faith had to be wrong.

Yet they had to find a way to stop the Dragon. He was getting into her mind; he'd even gotten to Adam through dreams. If this spell would keep Adam safe, then she'd do whatever she had to. Setting her jaw, she put the disk into the laptop.

The disk images played out in the featureless space around her. The ritual was a variation on a protection spell and beastly complicated. Strange words—how the hell did you pronounce *xntrophthus*? Five days of fasting from sunrise to sunset—thank God the days were short right now. Maintaining an inner space of nothingness.

She started to absorb the spell, reciting the stanzas, committing the hand motions to muscle memory, yet pressure on her shoulders kept her from concentrating, from moving the way she needed. The words danced before her eyes. She shook her shoulders, trying to relieve the irritating pressure.

It was interfering with her concentration. Her shoulder, her real shoulder, she realized, still rested against Adam, while his arm embraced her on the other side. They were close, physically, emotionally.

In that moment, she believed Faith's warning.

She could never fully master the spell with Adam near.

Adam set aside his phone and computer when Grace finally took off the visor. She'd been in that virtual world, muttering and gesturing for so damn long that he'd proofed the next issue of *NONE*, approved the content for the following one, and assigned enough additional stories to fill two more.

He stretched his arms, working out the kinks. "What kept you in for so long?"

"A hologram from Faith," she said.

"That must have been hard to see." He stroked a hand across the cloud of her hair. "What did she say?"

"That Brita gave her the caduceus for safekeeping."

"That's what started Faith on the hunt for the Dragon?"

Grace nodded. "She gave me a ritual to protect against the Dragon."

"How so?"

She frowned. "I'm not sure; I don't quite understand the nuances, and it's the devil's own son to master."

"Then try something else. Maybe your way's different." He ran a hand up and down her arm in invitation, then bent to nibble her jaw. The heat of her skin filled him with desire. He'd never thought of the scent of soap as an aphrodisiac. "It's late. Let's go to bed."

She worried her lip with her teeth. "I can't yet."

The gnawing need to complete a project—he understood that kind of dedication, even if right now he wasn't appreciating her work ethic. His problem, not hers. He settled back. "I'm nocturnal. I've got some more work—"

"No. I need to be alone." The teeth came back to worrying.

A hard knot lodged in his chest. She was keeping something from him again. "Anything you want to talk about?"

"Later. There are some things I need to work out."

"I'll make sure the house is secure." He got to his feet.

She nodded, but her mind had already gone somewhere else. Into that damn spell Faith had sent, he'd hazard, since she was putting on the visor.

Grace had told him about the fugues; she'd share this in time, too. Yet as he checked the security systems, then headed to bed, he couldn't shake the feeling that again they stood on opposite sides of a magickal rift.

Grace typed the details of the spell into her phone. Letting the words scroll across the screen, she walked in the circle as commanded. Thrice around and . . .

Nothing. The spell hung as useless as a sodden towel.

It hadn't felt right, hadn't sounded right. Not enough motion. She adjusted a few words, got a bowl of water, and then started again. Holding her phone in one hand, the bowl of water in the other, she walked a spiral circle. She focused on the motion of the water and the scrolling words, as she spoke the chant into the night. Gradually she tightened her circle, wrapping herself in the words of protection. When she reached the center, she set down the phone and bowl and smiled.

She hadn't fasted or created nothingness inside herself, but with the adjustments she'd made, the energy flowed around her, smooth and powerful. She'd woven an elegant spell, stronger than anything she'd done before. In her mind's eye, the shield pulsed and glistened.

And collapsed.

Damn.

Try as she might, she couldn't master the charm. Not even the first step that didn't take five damn days of fasting. Every attempt failed. The magick was there; she could feel it, could catch it with the tip of her hands and her mind. So close.

Until the energy slipped away into a heap of nothing.

She had to master this. *Had to*. She had to keep the Dragon out of her mind. She would not surrender control of the very essence of her soul to some megalomaniac.

Frustrated, Grace glared around the room. Maybe this house stopped her. Maybe Adam, sleeping upstairs, unknowingly interfered. She didn't want to believe that, the idea sounded so wrong, but Faith knew a hell of a lot more about this magick than she did.

Try something different. Wasn't that what Adam had told her?

She stormed from the room. Grabbing her coat, she headed outside into the hail and lashing wind.

Adam found sleep impossible, while Grace was still downstairs. He was staring out at a fir tree, its needles shivering in the storm, when a cold gust stormed through the house. The windows rattled and a thick limb blew off the tree. The wind slammed it against the house, and from the library he heard the crash of glass.

"Grace!" He raced down to her. The library was empty. Grace was gone.

She couldn't have gone far; they were on an island. That rush of cold? Sod it, she'd gone outside.

Adam grabbed his coat from the tree stand. Shoving his hands into his sleeves, he sprinted out the gaping front door. The threatened storm had hit, rattling ice through the trees and blinding him. Waves crashed against the rocks with booming echoes. And Grace was out here.

Which way? Bless the thin coat of snow—her footprints left a clear track; she'd headed toward the water. He scrambled after her.

"Grace!" The wind snatched his call, erasing it with a howl. He peered toward the lake, squinted to focus. The bobbing motions were all wave and not human. Dock to the left, sheer rock face to the right. He clambered to the left and when he rounded a boulder, he found her at the farthest edge of the pier.

Her bare hands were raised. In one she held a crystal bowl filling with water and ice. In the other was her purple cell phone. The wind blew back her unfastened coat and whipped her hair into a dark halo. She turned in a slow circle, until she was facing him.

His heart clenched at the sight. She was so beautiful and so strong. Her face was pale from the cold. Her jeans were soaked from the spume of waves splashing onto the dock and freezing around her. Yet, she smiled with such joy.

Her gaze fell in his direction, although he knew she didn't see him. Her attention was directed inward.

Energy scattered around him, like tiny crystals of snow glittering in the sun. Everywhere, his body tingled. Her magick, he realized. She was working a powerful spell. Something inside him swelled outward, wanting to share that exquisite experience, but he forced himself to stillness.

He was a reflector; he would interfere with her mastery.

For the first time, he faced that awful truth. Grace was finally coming into her own with the magick. She was one of them; she belonged with the magi.

Still, despite the freezing storm and the doubt, he would wait here for her, make sure she was safe. A gust of wind, powerful enough to have brought down the pines, swept across Lake Huron. Carrying the moisture and power of miles of water, it slammed into Grace, then him. Adam staggered and fell to his knees on the slick ground.

To his horror, he saw Grace's feet slip from beneath her. Clinging to the bowl and phone, she skidded to the edge of the icy dock. Frigid waves reached hungrily for her, soaking her sweater and jeans. Cold wracked her body with tremors.

If she fell in, with that riptide . . .

He raced to her, nearly losing his footing on the ice-coated dock. Teetering above the churning lake, she dropped the bowl and grabbed for a post, pulled herself back. A wave reached up, swallowing her dangling foot.

Adam lunged forward, grasping for her. His hand caught hers. He'd forgotten his gloves, and in that brief moment of contact, his flesh ached with a cold burn. Ripples of energy flowed across his back, evaporating into the night.

At his touch, Grace scooted backward, away from the deadly water, and then scrambled to her feet. She looked around, wild and confused, a moment before she jerked her thumb toward the house. Together, they retreated from the treacherous dock and back to shore. He didn't pause to question her. Out here, he couldn't do a damn thing. Couldn't even hear what she was shouting. Instead he slung an arm over her shoulders, and they hurried back into the house, the wind slamming the door behind them.

"You need to get these wet clothes off before you catch pneumonia." He helped her strip off her coat.

"Wet clothes don't cause pneumonia; that's an old wives' tale," she said around chattering teeth. "Hypothermia, now, that's a distinct possibility."

"I'll go crank up the heat; then we'll talk."

"Wait." Her call stopped him, and she came to him, hugging him with soggy arms. She laid her cheek against his, and the rush of heat between them had little to do with frostbite recovery. "Thank you."

He gave her a quick kiss. "I put our bags in the first bedroom, top of the stairs, right. Now that heat."

"See if you can find some pain meds. I've got a killer headache."

After a trip to the thermostat, he rounded up a bottle of aspirin in the bathroom, as well as several other medications.

He found Grace in the bedroom. Was it only a few hours since he'd hopefully stuck both overnight bags in the single room?

She'd hefted her bag onto the bed and was fumbling with the zipper. Her lips were still blue.

"You're still dressed," he admonished, as he poured his treasures onto the nightstand.

"So are you." She lifted her knotted shoe with frustration. "My hands are too stiff to undo that tangle and the jeans are too tight to get off with my shoes on. Now I can't even get something dry out of this bag. I hate being so clumsy."

"Let me help."

Not to his surprise—Grace was practical about health issues—she sat down on the floor and held up her foot. In a matter of moments, he had the knots undone and shoes off. While she got up, he undid her bag and got out her sweatpants and a sweater. Briskly, he unsnapped her jeans and waited for her to shimmy out of the wet denim.

Heaven help him remember she was hurt. Because that little red triangle of underwear was an invitation to bloodpooling-low amnesia.

When he knelt beside her to pull on her sweatpants, he lost the fight against desire. Not that he'd been trying too hard.

Letting the cloth pool at her feet, he leaned forward and kissed her belly button. She wasn't model flat, but he liked that little curve. His tongue circled the ring she had there; then he delved lowered, pushing aside that damp red silk.

"Dangerous territory there," she murmured.

"Do you mind?"

"Not as long as you let me return the favor."

Let her? In a moment he'd probably beg her. After another intimate kiss, he stood and undid the zipper on his jeans.

There was nothing clumsy about the kiss she gave him, her lips teasing the root of his shaft. He yanked up the hem of his shirt, pulled off the wet wool, and tossed it aside.

"I need help with my sweater, too," she said.

Her top joined his, and then he leaned back to admire her breasts cupped in red lace.

"Do all doctors wear such fancies beneath their staid corduroy and lab coats?" He laid a kiss atop each curve spilling from the lace.

"I can speak only for one, and she waits for special occasions."

"What's the occasion?"

"You."

An unfortunate shiver marred the moment between them. From her slight grimace, he guessed desire wasn't the source.

"You're still ailing." He stepped back.

"The headache," she admitted, and searched through the medicines he'd found. She swallowed two aspirin, and then held up an amber prescription bottle.

"I found something useful?" he asked.

"Imitrex. Regan must suffer from migraines. I don't know if the drug will work when a fugue strikes, but I'm willing to try anything."

He gathered her into his arms, desire banking to a simmer. He could feel her now, which meant his skin had warmed. For the moment, he was content to hold her and know that she was near. He could have lost her tonight, and that terrified him more than any renegade mage.

"So, we table the sex?" he said.

She looked up and grinned. "Table the sex? Definite possibilities there."

He swatted her butt. "Behave. I want a bed."

She chucked his chin. "And a few hours. If you're *up* to it."

He laughed and reached down for their sweaters. She stopped him. "The headache's gone."

"Aspirin doesn't work that fast."

"But the fact that I want you does." She grabbed his shoulders and pulled him flush against her. "Kiss me, Adam."

"I thought you'd never ask." He was happy to oblige. Only

when they were both breathless with need, did he pull up. "Here or the bed?"

"The bed. Tonight we're going slow and long." She moved toward the bed. "I'm using you, Adam."

He didn't know what the hell she was talking about, but he bloody well didn't care. Not when she was holding his hand and those sexy red triangles were leading him to the bed.

"Mind if I'm on top?" Grace asked.

"No arguments here." Red lace and silk boxers slid to the floor. Kissing her, stroking her, he fell backward onto the mattress.

She straddled him, slid onto his ready cock. Hot, wet, she was so ready. No condom—they'd already established that she was on the pill, and they'd both tested clean. The long-missed touch of flesh to flesh nearly undid him.

"Hold on," he gasped, gripping her hips to stop her motion, his control on a thread. He gathered himself, wanting this to last for her. *Think of something to distract from the exquisite pleasure, something for more stamina than a ten-second wonder. One hundred, ninety-three, eighty . . . eighty-fricking what?*

She leaned forward, her breast grazing against his lips, as she braced herself on the pillows. Back under control, he took the breast in his mouth, drawing in as far as he could, filling his mouth with her, flicking at her nipple with his tongue. Stroking her with his thumb. The other breast received the same attention until she shouted, "Now!"

"Let yourself go, love." He sat up, gathered her close, holding that feminine strength, kissing her, until she exploded in his arms. She arched against him, holding nothing back. Her agile hands gripped his shoulders, caressed his back, as her mouth returned the touch of his tongue and the heat of his mouth, and the orgasm shook her and receded.

Rolling her over, he moved lower and strung kisses along her breastbone and her belly. He feasted on her, on the sounds of her returning pleasure and the rising heat of her skin. The strong muscles in her thighs tightened as she spread wide for him and his mouth brought her another release.

"Let me," she gasped, pushing on his shoulders.

He returned to his back and she straddled him, sliding his cock inside her. His hips rode up and down. Slick pulsing grabbed him. She dropped atop him, her arms holding him as tight as he needed to be held.

He clung to her. "Yes!" Balls and bum tightened as he exploded inside her. The heat of unstoppable pleasure raced from groin to toe and head.

Grace gripped him everywhere—shaft, arms and legs, chest and back—and she shouted her own release. Fire melted against him.

Slowly their breathing returned to normal. A thin sheet of sweat dried atop their skin. Cold no longer afflicted a single molecule of their bodies.

He kissed her temple. "Use me anytime."

She rolled off him, only her hand lingering on his chest, her fingers winding through the small hairs. "You weren't just a convenient body. If anyone else were here, this wouldn't have happened. Only you touch me so deep."

"Did something else happen here besides incredible sex?" He stroked his hand across her bare bum. For once he wanted to hear the words from her, hear that she loved him, too.

She let out a long breath, then sucked in as he dipped his finger between her legs, stroking her. "That feels good," she purred.

He rubbed against her. "You got something to tell me?"

"Talk can wait." She slid down him and touched her tongue to his shaft.

"Right," he agreed.

CHAPTER NINETEEN

Brita Jorgensen—the woman who had brought the I'celus torch to Faith—lived in Marshall, a small town noted for its Victorian homes and its Magic Museum, a tribute to escape artists and stage magicians.

Brita's quarried stone home blended into the gray morning with a seamlessness bordering on fluidity. Grace squinted, trying to bring the Victorian fussiness into sharper focus. Those were gargoyles perched on the four corners of the roof, ugly bastards that sneered at the witlessness of any who would enter.

Mismatched paint and oddball stained-glass windows added to the off-center aura.

"Magick," she noted around the edge of a headache. "Keeps her secluded in plain sight."

"Damn fool way to hide from a mage," he retorted.

"What gives? You've been snappish all morning."

"Morning? This barely qualifies."

"After two shots of espresso and Tabasco sauce garnished with eggs??"

"Says the woman who's been chewing coffee beans."

"I'm fasting for Faith's damn spell," she snapped back.

"No wonder you've been a bear the whole trip from the island." His shoulders relaxed on a laugh.

"What's your excuse?" She poked his chest.

He lifted her hand off of him. "Something's been eating at you since you got out of that hologram, and I'm wondering when you're going to tell me."

Why was he always so damn observant?

"Let's see if our resident witch will open her door." Not waiting for Grace's answer, he rapped on the door, and then nodded toward the life-sized ceramic wolverine guarding the porch. "She has a unique decorating sensibility."

"Be glad her magick hasn't extended to making that thing real. Wolverines are vicious." Grace turned away from what she swore was a sudden light in the beast's eyes. Adam was right; she had been a bitch all morning, and she knew why. Normally she had no trouble being straight with someone.

Normally, though, her heart wasn't involved.

Get it out.

"Last night," she said, "in the hologram, Faith said I could never come into my full powers as long as I'm with you. Being a reflector, you'd interfere."

He spun around. "Faith's wrong," he said flatly.

A knot in the wood swiveled, as though an eye were checking them out. "Who knocks?" boomed a disembodied voice.

As Adam mouthed, *Later, Grace,* she answered, "I'm Grace Armatrading. My aunt, Faith Grimaldi, sent us."

"Never heard of her." The eye winked shut.

Okay, they hadn't expected that. Maybe the lady was one gene short of a chromosome. Grace shared a glance with Adam. "What next?"

The knothole opened. "Who's the tall, dark, and handsome?"

"Adam Zolton," he answered.

The air around them grew still, and then the door opened. They went inside. Grace jumped as two figures loomed from the mist-blurred entryway.

"A mirror." Adam moved closer, his breath a small fog over her shoulder.

She saw that now, as the mist eddied away, revealing the man-sized gilt-edge mirror opposite the door. "Chilly in here."

The last home she'd entered ungreeted had been steaming hot.

Had had two attackers.

Had brought pain to someone she admired.

Adam laid a hand at her back. "This house is deceptive."

Grateful for the closeness, for the heat of his hand, she took in the cluttered foyer. It held everything from a tree stump table to a brilliant red fire hydrant to Canadian souvenir plates. Then, beneath and between the clutter, she saw what Adam must have seen. Eyes, hundreds of them, very faint. In the peacock tails and dolls' heads, in the wallpaper pattern, in the swirls of mist.

Eyes that should not move, but did.

"Brita?" Adam called. He tried to see some movement, some hint of where she might appear, but the disorganization deceived his eyes.

"Why do you come?" A disembodied whisper condensed along the walls.

"To warn you. Do you know these mages?" He listed the eight. "They're all dead."

"Pity. Lizzie was real nice." The figure swelling from the recesses of the room was no mere reflection. Brita Jorgensen was vividly real—six-foot tall, arms with more tattoos than flesh, and capable hands toting squat, lethal guns.

With a shot of adrenaline, Adam jumped in front of Grace.

"Move, I shoot. Be a hero, I shoot. If you're lying, I shoot." Brita's eyes flicked in anticipation. She began to hum. "If you are another one, I shoot. But how can I know? Reality frosts two layers, slipping across the truth. Naught but a sheet hides me."

Sod it, the woman was a raving nutter. He tensed, weighing options. Was the best course to inch out or try to stop the clearly deluded Brita?

Grace touched his elbow, urging him backward.

Brita's gaze sharpened, stopping their shuffle. "I need proof who you are. If you're Adam Zolton, you'll know the Kenilworth theory of alien abduction."

"The bright lights are the inter-dimensional path. Aliens are alien to this time continuum, not to this galaxy."

"And the major obstacle to time travel as espoused by Rodriguez?"

"Belief in reality."

"How many issues of *NONE* have you put out?"

"I've been editor of three hundred sixty-two."

"Wrong answer." She lifted the shotgun.

"Did you forget the extra on Roswell and the one on magickal beasts?"

Her eyes clouded and her voice turned singsong. "Pegasus, Centaur, Jaguar, Spider, Thunderbird, Unicorn, Phoenix." Her tone grew harsh. "Chimaera." Her throat spasmed in terror. "Dragon."

Her gaze flicked back to Grace, lucid again. "Prove who you are."

"I could show you my driver's license."

Brita lifted her chin. "Slide the purse over."

Grace bent and placed her purse on the floor, then slid it closer to Brita. Still keeping her gaze, and her gun's aim, on them, Brita bent over and riffled through Grace's purse.

"You a doctor?" she asked, tossing the stethoscope aside. "Specialty?"

"Emergency medicine."

Brita grunted an acknowledgment, and then found the wallet. She studied Grace's photograph from the license, shifting rapidly between picture and face.

At last, she gave another grunt and toed the purse, with wallet and stethoscope returned, over to Grace. She gestured them inside. "We can talk."

"Mind putting those guns away first?" Adam said, not moving.

"I'm alive because I suspect everything." She stroked the barrel across her jaw. "And I'm ready." Then she gave a cackle and lowered the weapons. "Welcome."

Adam and Grace stepped farther inside, and the door slammed shut behind them. The crack of wood on wood reverberated through the dark house. Adam shoved his hands in his pockets.

"Your warning comes with questions. Ask."

"What do you know about the Dragon?" Grace asked.

"Dragons are part of all mythologies. Chinese dragons can be benevolent powers, but fierce when crossed. Kinda like the Greeks. Zeus, you know. Water, not fire. Then there's old George and the fire-breathing kind. Serpentine monsters, hoarders."

"What kind of a dragon can alter reality?" Grace interrupted the rambling.

"Ah, I feared that. You've come for nothing."

"You don't know?"

"Won't tell. Value this wrinkled brow too much. Although—" She glanced over her shoulder, frowning. "Maybe it's time for the glorious pyre. We shall have a barbeque of dragon."

"I'd rather not." Adam glanced at Grace. *Think we'll get anything lucid from her?*

Grace examined Brita through narrowed eyes. She gave a subtle nod of her head, as she said, "You're scared, Brita. I understand. He's gotten inside me, too."

"*He* has?" Brita scratched at one of her tattoos—Cerberus, the dog of three heads and six eyes. "What's real can get confusing?"

"Sometimes," Grace admitted.

A shudder ran through Brita, and her fingers tightened on the guns as she led them deeper into the gloom, until they entered a formal parlor, complete with stiff, unused wingbacks and a dusty carpet. Brita sank into one of the chairs and laid the guns on the floor. "Don't suppose those would stop the Dragon, anyway. Talk fast. We don't have much time."

"What can you tell us about him?" Adam asked. "What's his name?"

Brita rubbed her head. "Got a migraine. Dragon's coming close. Not sure. Not sure. Never tell." She started to chant.

"It's a protection spell," Grace whispered.

Obviously the idea of revealing the Dragon's name sent her into a barmy spin.

He tried another tack. "How did you know Lizzie?"

Brita smiled. "We planned to upend the magick world, be a part of the new glory. Until I realized exactly what that meant. There were problems, you see, and we were expendable."

"What kind of problems?" Adam leaned forward, bracing his hands on his knees. If they skirted the Dragon, maybe they'd get more answers.

"Pain. Excruciating, unbearable pain. Combining two minds is not natural."

"And only one mind can be in control," Grace added softly.

Brita shuddered, and her eyes glazed over. Before she could slip into another tangent, Adam asked, "Were there other problems?"

"Millions of synapses." She jerked forward, stopping within an inch of Adam's nose, and laughed at his involuntary flinch. Her hands spread wide. "How do you control them all? Find what you want?" She sat back, looking smug. "Fix that with science, eh?"

"What stopped you?" Grace asked.

Brita plucked at a dream catcher woven into her hair. "We

wanted fun, not pain and madness. So we hid. Mostly. When the Dragon came to power, the lowly, the witnesses, would not be forgotten. Or saved." She leaned forward with a hint of malevolence. "I was the last to go. I recognized the danger, but hungered for the taste of power. I stopped the spell. Only I know where the torch is." She began to hum, her eyes closing. "Hide this, Faith. Keep it safe."

In one fraction of a second, the change slipped onto Brita. "Faith!" she shrieked.

One moment, Adam was attempting a rational conversation, in the next he saw the same panic he'd witnessed right before a mage set himself ablaze.

And he smelled the rank mustiness of a body too old.

Her wild gaze fixed on Grace. "Faith sent you. Has he found the torch?"

"No, we have it," Grace answered before Adam could put forward a lie.

"You fools!" Brita reached up and grabbed Grace's hair. Before Adam could act, Grace grabbed Brita's wrists. He wasn't sure if Grace twisted or hit a nerve point, but with a screech Brita let go. Grace scrambled to her feet with only a few strands of hair pulled loose.

"Get out!" Brita shouted. She grabbed the guns, pointed them. "Get out. The Dragon comes." The cocked hammers added impetus.

"We're going." Adam stood and started backing out with Grace.

"Faster. Run."

They sped out of the house, hearing the front-door lock snap behind them. When they reached the opposite side of the street, they stopped and looked back.

"Did you feel any magick?" Grace asked.

"No. She's gone balmy, like the others."

"There was real fear there."

"Real fear, yes, but that doesn't mean there's a real source."

Suddenly an agonizing scream rent the morning, coming from the second floor of Brita's house. The upstairs window was flung open, and Brita, wearing no coat despite the cold, stretched forward. Only the pressure of the sill on her hips kept her inside. Her hands clutched at her face, her fingers digging into the flesh.

"Get out. Get out. Aaaaahhhhh. Don't."

Grace ran back across the street. "I can help with the pain, get you to a hospital. Let me help you."

"No," shouted Brita again, her fingers raking down her face. Blood welled in crimson furrows and dripped off her nails.

"I'm coming in," shouted Grace.

Adam sprinted with her to the door. Grace would always go to the blood and the pain. If he couldn't stop her, then he'd damn well watch her back.

But the door wouldn't open. Grace tried the unlocking spell Faith had taught her, to no avail. Adam found a rock and started hammering at the lock. While he worked, Grace stepped out so she could see Brita at the window.

"My God, no!" she shouted. "Adam, she's climbing out the window. There's no ledge, nowhere to stand. She's going to jump."

He ran to Grace and looked up. Brita was straining out, holding on with one hand and one foot. Her other foot reached to empty space, as though she tried to stand on invisibility. Her free hand reached up, and her face contorted.

"Don't, Brita!" he shouted. "Let us in. Let Grace help you. We'll find another way."

And for one brief moment, her face, her eyes, her body, were filled with utter sanity. For one brief moment, he knew they'd gotten through.

For one brief moment, she smiled. "No, there isn't," she said, and jumped.

They ran over and Grace immediately began checking Brita's vitals as he called 911.

Adam knelt beside the seizure-wracked body and took her hand.

She opened her eyelids, but her eyes were rolled back in her face.

Suddenly, her hand tightened on his in a spasm so tight his breath caught.

She began to speak. Mere breaths, as though each word had to be forced out. He leaned over, trying to catch the final gasp.

As the last word left her mouth, Adam felt the blood rush from his head. He braced his hand against the cold ground.

Brita's eyes rolled forward, returning her face to its normal character, and she smiled.

"Free at last," she whispered, and died.

Grace went into a flurry of CPR, but even after the EMS arrived, their joint efforts could not resuscitate a spark of life. At last, defeated, Grace sat back on her heels and declared the time of death as 11:15 AM.

He wrapped his arm around her, while they watched the body of Brita Jorgensen being carried off. Inside he was cold, filled with the icy threat. Grace was shivering.

"What did she say?" Grace asked, her teeth chattering together.

He snuggled his coat tighter, the day's bright sunshine bringing no heat. "If I can't have Abby, I'll have Grace."

CHAPTER TWENTY

The police wrote off the death as suicide, a tidy summary of a messy end. A neighbor confirmed that Grace and Adam had been outside, trying to stop Brita's plunge, and that Brita was "an odd duck. But quiet, real quiet," and apparently that counted for a lot.

Freed by the police—who held no more than a passing interest in the cover story Adam wove about a *NONE* article—Adam and Grace drove off. They stopped in a small municipal park abutting Brita's backyard, however, and went back to the house.

The lock gave up easily now to Adam's pick, and they slipped inside, hidden from the neighbor, to search for any clue to the Dragon's identity.

"This place is still creepy," Adam observed, as his flashlight played across a stuffed cat.

"Morbid, too." Grace's light fell on a replica of the human brain. "We should separate; we may not have much time."

Adam nodded. "I'll take the upstairs."

He'd gotten partway through Brita's bedroom—the only occupied room on the second floor—when his phone rang. Grace.

"You finding anything helpful?" she asked.

"No."

"Then come back to the parlor."

He took the stairs two at a time, and was surprised to see

a door open in the parlor's paneled wall. When he walked through it, he gave a whistle. The room was thick with incense and littered with papers and candle stubs. A pink bathrobe hung in one corner.

He picked up a book of matches and tossed it in his hand, the smell of old smoke tickling a nicotine craving. The room was smaller than it first appeared, since the walls, ceiling, and floor were mirrored. From the open door he could see the walls were as thick as a bomb bunker. "So this is where she practiced her magick. How'd you find it?"

"Years of reading Gothics, and noticing there was another six feet of house beyond the front window." She held up a sheaf of papers. "She seems to have created a lot of her own chants and words of shaping."

"We can gather up the lot, look through them later."

She shook her head. "I don't want to have them with us. Brita was more of a disturbed bird than we realized. Some of these are . . . malevolent. Curses. They're simplistic, but downright creepy."

"Then let's get through this pronto." Adam rubbed a hand across his neck. "Something's stirring."

The next few moments were silent as they skimmed through the papers. Grace had been right in her estimation. Although he recognized a lot of the spells as simple magick for well-being and balance, Brita had apparently had trouble achieving that peace. Some were definitely twisted.

"Adam." Grace held up a thick hand-bound book, her face pale in the crazy reflections. "Look at this. Brita also stole the Dragon's grimoire."

He took the book, handling it gingerly, for the first page was brittle. The words from the ancient spell were hard to read, a smudged mimeograph grown faded. After taking photos of each page, he started reading. "Torch of I'celus, light the gateway of realms. Sacrifice of Prometheus, fuse will and thought. Grant no secret shall prevail against the dreams of the joined." He looked at Grace. "This must be the Dragon's spell."

"The one he can't complete until he gets back the stolen torch."

Relieved to be on familiar ground analyzing, Grace pointed to the margins. "There are penciled comments."

They fell silent, reading the entirety of the complex spell together, but not willing to give power to the horrifying words.

The Dragon wasn't interested in creating a horde of shuffling zombies. Instead, he craved knowledge. This spell gave him the ability to enter any mind at will, to pluck any knowledge or skill or power. Reading the cold words on a shabby paper in a crazy woman's box, Grace was vividly conscious of the *violation* of it. She pressed a fist against her mouth in a rush of fury. "This isn't mind control, Adam. This is mind rape."

She flinched when Adam ran his hands down her arms, but when he backed off, she demanded, "Don't stop. You're the only person I'd trust to touch me right now."

His gentle massage eased her over the hump of pain. He could reflect away magick, and somehow that touch felt as though he severed the unnatural bonds that connected her to her tormentor. Everyone had dark impulses—she channeled hers into fighting death—but right now, if the person who'd done this to her were here, Hades help them if she had a blade in her hand.

"This bastard isn't going to win," she said flatly.

Adam kissed her forehead. "We'll find a way to stop him."

Touched anew by his understanding, Grace caressed his jaw. "You really are a beautiful man."

He turned his head a little, placing a warm kiss on her palm. "Men like to be called handsome. Or better, yet, stud."

"I meant beautiful inside," she said with a laugh, then tacked on, "stud."

"She called me stud; I can die happy."

All humor left her. She caught his hands. "Don't. Death isn't a joke."

"Don't doctors have a graveyard humor?"

"This doctor doesn't when it comes to you." She leaned forward to kiss him with passion, with love, and then sat back, loosening his hands. "Damn, I wish we were someplace else."

He stiffened, his head tilting. "Grace, we need to get out of here."

"What is it?" She stuffed the book into her handbag—they could finish reading the additional notes later—not waiting for the answer before heading to the door.

"The house is stirring around us, little ripples of magick. Someone's traced us here."

"Or maybe the Dragon finally found Brita." Had the touch of mind against mind driven her to suicide?

Whispers, dry as old lumber, brushed across her hearing. "The house says barricade. We can survive days in the magick room. Brita did."

She and Adam exchanged a glance, and he said bluntly, "No bloody way am I turning into Brita."

"Good, because you'd be in there by yourself." The whispers breathed again, repeating the urge to go to the safe room. "I saw a side door, off the kitchen. Maybe we'll have a better chance of getting out that way."

They sped through the gloomy house, which had grown so dark that she hit her shins against furniture. Damn, she could have sworn that table had moved a foot, just in time for her to bang into it. An incredible sadness rooted in her chest, a grief that brought tears. "The house is sinking into mourning for Brita."

"It doesn't want us to leave. How can a house be as bloody nutters as its owner?"

A cookbook flying across the kitchen was his answer. He ducked just in time to avoid it.

Of course, the door was locked. "Can you twist the magick away?" she asked.

He shook his head. "The magick's acting on the house, not on me. Things go haywire when I reflect that kind of magick. Looks like you're on board."

She placed one hand on the deadbolt, the other on the handle, and began the words of shaping. The energy shoved through a mud of insanity, struggling to reach the lock workings. Sweat dampened her collar as she forced it forward. When it met the energy radiating from Adam, the spell spun like a crazy top, careening toward the shuttered window before she brought it back. Shaking with the effort of control, she held it steady until at last the bolt clicked. A twist of the handle, and they were out into the fresh, cold air. With Adam at her side, she sprinted for their car.

Half an hour down I-94, they pulled into a rest area. Grace sat on a picnic bench and leaned against its wood topback while Adam let Gala out of his pocket for a litter break.

"Fifteen minutes," Adam warned Gala as she scampered off.

"You think she'll listen?" Grace turned her face toward the sunshine. Although the temperature had dropped after the storm passed, the high-pressure system also brought a beautiful clarity to the air. Hadn't taken but one winter here before she learned to savor each brilliant beam that cut through the usual gray of January.

"She'll come back." Adam sat beside Grace, turning up his collar and burying his hands in his pockets.

"Hopefully before tomorrow morning." Grace opened the notebook and thumbed through the unread pages, squinting to decipher the faint writing and the precise notes—observations of effects when the spell was attempted, problems and possible solutions.

Adam read the pages from his camera photos. "The spell

can be used to steal the knowledge of the mages. Using patterns of magick energy, the caster can join minds with the target and take his thoughts."

"With brief contact, the . . . host continues normally, fully capable, but the memories of those moments are imprinted on the mind of the invader. When the Dragon withdraws, he takes the memory, and the host is left with a brief spot of amnesia."

"Your fugue state," Adam said softly.

"This says lock equals madness," she read. "The Dragon discovered if he stayed too long or tried to become a permanent invader, the other went mad."

Adam didn't answer right away, and she looked up to see his face carved into a murderous look. His fists clenched and unclenched.

Abby. The Dragon had learned that particular limitation from Abby.

At last Adam regained control and said tightly, "Acquire knowledge and to hell with who gets hurt. When the bastard was hunting for Brita and the torch, he deliberately drove those mages into madness. He knew what he was doing."

Grace leaned against him, offering what comfort she could while she turned to another page. "The Dragon outlines what he thinks are the limitations of the spell here: Identity—how do you find and join one mind in billions? And passivity—the caster can only learn what is engaging the host at the moment."

"The spell is also dangerous for the mage casting it." Adam read from another section of notes: " 'Imposition of will requires absolute control of one's own mind, lest the self bleed. Sacrifice of Prometheus—the mage must be willing to endure excruciating pain.' "

Grace shuddered. "Each time I went in and out of a fugue, the transition was highly painful. I can't imagine having to endure that for any length of time."

"Our Dragon has a useful tool—he can connect to the mind of another." Adam stretched his legs out, thinking. "But he has to find a way to be sure he's entering the right mind and can take what he desires to know. And the strike must be swift and short because it hurts like hell. He doesn't like those odds."

"So, he applies science to circumvent the limitations," Grace said softly. "Like DNA modeling to pinpoint one in billions."

Adam gave a slow whistle. "Turn to the next-to-last page. He was planning to modify aura-identification software and GPS, like on our cell phones. Brita's been in hiding with this book for years. The Dragon must have come light-years since then."

"Look at this penciled note: 'Passivity/Virtual Reality?' The night you were attacked, Adam, the virtual Kea brought up the subject of a library. My God, the Dragon planned to link to a mind, implant a virtual scenario that forces a particular reaction, and boom, he gets what he wants."

"A virtual Tesla of magick."

"And the pain? He's using me. Connecting with me to learn how I control pain." Grace wrinkled her brow. She was missing a piece here. "Why does he need the torch? He's already connected with the mages, with me. Even used virtual reality at least once without it."

"He hasn't conquered all the bugs." Adam, looking at the pages on his camera, started to curse. He shot to his feet, shoving the book in his pocket. "Gala!" he shouted. "Now!"

The ferret rocketed from the underbrush, her little feet scurrying faster than Grace had ever seen. Adam scooped her up and started back to the car in one move. "C'mon, Grace."

"What is it?" She hurried beside him.

"We need to destroy that damn torch."

"We decided—"

"Look at the last page." He opened the car door for her,

and then sprinted around to the driver's side. Gala was in the backseat and the car was started before Grace had even gotten her seat belt on. As Adam merged back onto the highway, she turned to the final page of the notebook.

Her blood ran cold.

The Dragon's solution to his *problems?* A permanent link to one mage. One mage to act as an anchor, to absorb and negate his pain, while the Dragon connected and played out his virtual scenarios as long as he needed. One link to limitless power for the Dragon, to pain and madness for the anchor. One link forged when the Torch of I'celus welded two minds, and fused the link between reality and nightmare.

All the Dragon needed was one mage—with a talent for healing, but few defenses.

All the Dragon needed was the torch. And Grace.

CHAPTER TWENTY-ONE

From the corner of his eye, Adam saw the book drop from Grace's hands. Her face turned pale, and her palms braced against the seat, keeping her back stiff. She drew in a slow breath, then a second, which brought back her color. And her determination. "I will die before I let that bastard do that to me."

"Death's not a joke, Doc," he reminded her, her words scouring out a piece of his heart.

"No. It's not." She turned in her seat. "Any ideas how to destroy that torch?"

"Do you see any weaknesses?" He pulled the torch from his suitcase and held it out to her. She hesitated a moment, then grabbed it.

"The copper handle is cold. Like frost." She rapped it against the dash, putting a dent in the car.

"Hey, watch it," he joked. "Rental car. Damages."

To his relief, she laughed. "You can afford it. Apparently I need something harder to test whether or not it would shatter." Playfully, she tapped the coil against his head. "Nope, didn't think destruction would be that straightforward."

He rolled his eyes. "Are there any fault lines?"

"None visible. No rivets." Rainbows sliced the car as she took her penlight and examined the metal.

"Time to take a cue from Tolkien. I know a chap, jewelry

maker, lives in Canada. He has a forge." He dialed up the number.

Grace frowned. "I'm not sure we can destroy this by natural means."

"It's worth a try." He got voice mail, left a message. "Take the bridge across, and we can be there by dinner."

"Maybe we should ask a mage with a higher level of skill than mine."

"You got someone in mind?"

She licked her lips. "Kea. He's a powerful mage."

Adam's hands tightened on the wheel as white-hot anger raced over him. "And you never thought to tell me this!"

"Kea's secrets were his to keep."

"My God, woman, didn't you ever wonder why he never bothered to teach you anything?"

"Because I never asked? Because I didn't have the talent?"

"Didn't have the talent? You can stitch an artery with your mind in the middle of a chaotic ER and you think you don't have talent. He wanted to keep you untrained and beneath the radar of the Custos Magi." His eyes narrowed. "You said the fugues only came when you were doing magick. What were you doing the night Lonnie and Ed attacked me?"

"I was relieving—"

He saw the moment she realized she'd been betrayed; her breath left in a whoosh. God knew, he'd had the same experience when he'd discovered Regan's betrayal.

"Kea," she spat. "I was helping Kea deal with his neuropathy. *I was helping him.*" She shoved her hair back. "That was the first night we tagged the analgesic with magick and I used the virtual reality gloves and visor. No wonder the fugue that night was different. VR tagged with magick. He can control everything. Our Dragon has to be Kea. No one else is doing this kind of research."

"Vitae is also working with bots and VR."

"But they don't put magick into the mix." She stared at

him. "He knows about the spell of I'celus and who knows better what I can do than Kea?"

He pulled out his phone. "Let me put Brando on locating where he might have go to ground." While he was talking to Brando, he heard Grace on her phone. "Hi, Lakisha, this is Dr. Armatrading. Can you put me through to Dr. Lin? What? Signed out? Is his car in the lot? No? No, don't page him; I have his number. Thanks."

When they'd both finished, Grace said, "As far as I can tell, Kea's gone for the day. This will be our best chance to search his office, and we can get the VR gloves I used."

His phone chimed with an incoming call. He glanced at the ID and had to answer. "Hi, Mum."

"She's gone." Without a greeting, his mother wailed into the phone. "Nobody will tell me anything, but she's gone."

"Who's gone?" he asked, terrified of the answer.

"Abby."

The car swerved, nearly sideswiping his neighbor in the right lane, as heart pain doubled him over. Choking, he pulled off the road. Grace laid a sympathetic hand on his shoulder.

"When, Mum? How?" He could barely force the words past his grief.

"This morning. I went to visit her, same as I always do, after lighting a candle and praying the novena for her recovery, and she was gone."

"What did the doctors say happened?"

"They're a group of fools. Nurses, too. No one saw her leave." She gasped, and the tears cleared from her voice. "Adam, this is it, I know it. Blessed Mary, I didn't see the truth. This is my miracle."

"Mum, what are you talking about?"

"No one saw her leave. She walked out on her own. Now, you need to find her. Before she comes to harm."

His mother's words tilted his world back. "Abby's not . . . dead?"

"What? No, she's missing."

He let out a breath, his hands dangling over the steering wheel. Abby was still alive. There was still hope.

"How soon can you get here, Adam? You have to find her for me."

"I'll be there—" The automatic promise stopped in his throat. "One moment, Mum." He put the phone on mute and looked at Grace. "You heard?"

She squeezed his hand in understanding. "That's where you should be; I'll drive you to the airport."

"But you. The torch."

"I'll take it to your friend."

The plan sounded reasonable, the best solution for their dilemma, yet he couldn't shake the gut feeling that reasonable was the wrong choice.

How could it be wrong? Abby was his sister; he had to protect her. He thumbed the volume on. Looked at Grace.

The Dragon wanted Grace and wanted him out of the way. Adam's doubts vanished. He knew what he had to do.

"Mum, you still there? I'm sorry, I can't get back right away."

"What's more important than finding your sister?" The hurt in his mother's voice could have wrung tears from a stone.

His hand clenched around the phone, and his stomach churned, knowing he had to make this impossible choice. "I have to. Someone else is in danger."

"You have to protect her?"

"Yeah, Mum, I do."

He heard his mother's shuddering breath. "What should I do?" she asked.

"I have friends on the police force, and I know a chap, a top-notch detective. I'll get them right on looking for Abby."

"You'll come as soon as you can?"

"Yes."

"All right. You're a good son, Adam. I love you." She disconnected.

For a moment, he couldn't bear to let go of the phone. Then, his jaw set, he dialed up the police and the detective, gave them the necessary information.

"Adam—" When he finished, Grace laid a hand on his sleeve.

"I don't want to talk about it." He tossed the phone onto the console, shoved the car into gear, and then slammed into traffic.

"She's your sister."

"I damn well know that. And you're my lover."

"I can take care of myself. We had a workable plan."

He glowered at her. "Workable in Fantasyland, and we both know it. I know you're capable, Grace, but . . . I can't leave you. I don't know what's happened to Abby. She could be wandering a block down the road, she could have woken up with a craving for beignets, she could have been taken by the Dragon. But I don't believe in coincidences. My being in New Orleans won't make a damn difference to what happens there. Being up here could; my gut says stopping the Dragon will take us both. Whatever happens . . . I won't leave you."

They were on the outskirts of Ann Arbor when the explosion rocked the car. Cars around them skidded across black ice until movement stopped in a mash of crushed metal and broken glass.

Grace gripped her seat belt, bracing herself as Adam skillfully brought the car out of the spin. When they were straight, she twisted to look over her shoulder at the wreckage. "People are hurt. Adam, pull over!"

As soon as the car stopped, she was out, coat flapping, stethoscope in her pocket.

Adam joined her, talking on his phone. "Multicar pileup on I-94 going east. Near exit—?" He looked quizzically at her.

"Zeeb Road."

He finished giving the details—for 911, she assumed—as she reached the first car. Broken arm, bleeding scalp. She folded the man's mitten and pressed it to the wound. "Put pressure there. Keep that other arm braced until an EMT can splint it." When the man put his palm on the makeshift bandage, she left. Triage for life-threatening injury first.

"Conventional healing only, Doc," Adam warned.

She nodded, then wiped the moisture from her stinging eyes. A pile of tires had caught fire, sending thick black smoke into the melee of screams and shouts. She went from car to car, following the trail of destruction. More bleeding, more shock, more lacerations and breaks.

Through each step, Adam was at her side, ready to put pressure where she asked or hold a pair of thrashing shoulders. He had a gift, she discovered, for keeping her patients calm, for bringing a reluctant smile amid the tears. But always he watched the crowds, on the alert for their Dragon.

The first serious injury was a piece of tailpipe protruding from a spleen. "Don't take it out," she warned, as she packed gauze from a vehicle first-aid kit around the wound. The patient would bleed out if the metal plug were removed.

"It hurts," groaned the young man. "Can't you do nothing?"

Grace clenched her fist, aching with the need to help. The boy was in pain.

Despite that, he would heal. Instead of giving relief, all she could do was tuck a blanket from his car around him. He kept moaning, moving.

"What's your name?" she asked.

"Darwin."

"Darwin, you need to lie still," she cautioned, keeping her voice low and soothing. "Breathe slow and steady." Dammit.

Last week she would have relieved this agony, kept the boy quiet. Adrenaline-fed anger washed through her. The Dragon had hurt so many people in so many ways.

"But it hurts." As the boy writhed, blood seeped into her makeshift bandage.

She had to blunt the edge of the pain, a brief touch of calm. Otherwise she'd lose him. Her hands pressed lightly onto the wound.

Adam grabbed her wrist, stopping her, glaring.

"If he keeps moving, that pipe will gouge out his insides," she told him in a low tone.

Adam laid a hand on the young man's shoulder, catching his gaze. "You think algae are the next biofuel?"

Okay, that was a random question.

Darwin's eyes lit with an enthusiasm that defied pain. "At thirty times the yield per acre? Halophytes are the answer."

Apparently not as random as it seemed. As she moved Adam's hand to put pressure on the bandage, she noticed the lettering beneath the blood on Darwin's shirt: DTE ENERGY— UM CLEAN ENERGY CONTEST. And the bumper sticker: BLUE ALGAE=GREEN WORLD. Details Adam must have seen.

She heard a groan. Somebody nearby was injured, but with all the smoke she couldn't see whom. She tapped Adam on the shoulder.

"I'll be right over there," she told him, shouting to be heard over the flame's roar. "Hold that pressure until the paramedic gets here. When he does, tell him Darwin's lost a lot of blood, and he's getting shocky. He needs a liter of D5 Lactated, but don't take out that tailpipe until a surgeon's near to tie off the bleeders."

"Don't get out of sight."

"I won't." The first ambulance had reached the scene. She waved over the paramedic, and then ran toward the thick smoke. An eddy of wind parted the oily blackness, revealing a crumpled body curled in the weeds. She hesitated, glanced over at Adam. One paramedic was hunting a vein as another took over applying a pressure bandage.

Adam would rejoin her in seconds.

Seconds counted in trauma.

She jerked her thumb. "Just to the weeds," she shouted, and plunged into the smoke.

Thick clouds blinded her, covered her in impenetrable darkness. The burning chemicals brought tears to her eyes. She couldn't see worth a shilling.

What the hell? This area had been clear a second ago. Wrapping her muffler over her nose and mouth, she held her breath and turned back. She had to get out. If she collapsed from smoke inhalation or seared her lungs with chemical burns, she'd help no one.

Her route vanished beneath the toxic smoke.

It only took ten seconds in the smoke to realize her mistake.

"I knew you would stop to help," gloated a familiar—and unexpected—voice. "Sigils can be answered in strange ways."

The precise blow to her temple came at the eleventh second.

"Grace!" Adam plunged forward as Grace vanished behind a curtain of smoke. He was only steps behind, but when he crossed to where she'd disappeared, he was seized by choking and coughing. His eyes swelled shut from the chemical vapors. Salty, stinging tears tried to wash away the assault. Bent over in another coughing jag, he tried to peer through the haze. "Grace!"

Firemen in full regalia and air masks had followed him. One grabbed his arm and shoved him back. "Get away from the tires."

Adam resisted. "Dr. Armatrading's in there."

"We'll find her. Go, sir. Now."

Go before we carry you. Adam was willing to take on the

lot of them if he thought that would save Grace. But he couldn't see. Or breathe.

Then, suddenly, he knew Grace was no longer inside the concealing smoke.

The Dragon had her.

He wove through the crowds, looking for some glimpse of her. Or of Kea Lin. Described them to rescue workers, anyone who would listen and might have seen her, until his voice gave out.

Shit, she'd vanished. Where—?

The torch! He'd left it in the car with Gala. *Please, please, please* . . .

His prayers weren't being heard today. The driver's side was unlocked. Gala was hiding in the backseat.

The torch and the Dragon's notebook were was gone.

"Hey, you the guy looking for that woman?" a passing fireman called.

"You saw her?" His heart double-timed.

"Back by that building." He pointed toward the thickest smoke.

"Thanks." Scooping up Gala and a flashlight, he wound his scarf around his face and scrambled toward the trees. The smoke hung in a heavy pall among the trees and coated the brush like a foul wraith. He snapped on his flashlight, and the light gleamed a sickly yellow.

The woods were empty of everything but trees and snow turning gray from ash. He played the light across the surface, and thought he saw a smudge of footprints. He raced after them, his light beam jerking across the snow and the deceptive twilight terrain. Grace would have fought. They couldn't have gone far; even powerful mages couldn't transport through time and space. Damn, if only he knew what kind of car Kea drove.

His beam scanned ahead, through the trees, passing over a dark lump, glinting off—

He shot the beam back to the lump, his heart jumping to his throat. A body. Dear God, no. Let her be only unconscious.

The body wasn't Grace's. He could tell that as he ate up the final meters. Too bulky.

He knelt in the snow, and with a shaking hand, turned it over.

Kea Lin. Dark, sticky blood matted his chest, and his lips were drawn back in a rictus of pain and horror. With numb hands, Adam felt for a pulse. Thin. The scientist was alive. Barely.

Where was Grace? Adam pulled his knife and held it as he shone his light on the snow beyond. A farm road, with a fresh set of tire tracks.

Suddenly a fanglike prick pierced his neck. Adam stiffened. He reached up and yanked out the small dart, all he could do before his body went numb and the knife and flashlight rolled from his grip. His assailant strode from the wood.

Khalil! The single thought registered as Adam pitched forward.

When Adam awoke, he was immediately conscious of two things: Grace was missing, and he wasn't face-first in the snow. Where the hell was he? The darkness was a black so intense that it had no depth.

He stepped out, only to be brought up with a cruel jerk on his wrist. His arm was chained. He yanked, and the chain, pulling taut against its rock anchor, bit into his wrist. No magick, only unbreakable metal.

The air was chilly and damp, like the January winds off Lake Huron. Dampness dug beneath the layers of his clothes, flaying his flesh.

As his eyes adjusted to the gloom, he made out the rocks around him. Gleams of light pricked the otherwise unlit space, iridescent as the fish found in the dark ocean depths.

Fish? Oh, bloody hell.

He turned to find Khalil standing a short distance away, watching him closely. "We're at the bottom of a lake? Lake Huron?"

"Nothing so grand. A rock quarry. But only scuba divers would find this, and not at twilight, in January."

"Rather melodramatic."

Khalil shrugged, unfazed by the sarcasm. "Privacy's hard to come by."

"Why the chains?" The manacle was seamless; there was no lock to pick.

"You have the talent to bend or alter our magick, if rumors are true. Welded to rock, with only my magick keeping this bubble of air, you'll think twice before doing so. I do not underestimate you, Adam Zolton."

"No, you judge, and misjudge, me."

Khalil leaned forward. "I want the library Faith sent to you."

The answer "Go to hell" and a few less mild responses came to mind. But, at that moment, Adam felt the press of tiny feet up his side, then along his arm. Gala. From the corner of his eye, he saw her scamper to the end of the chain. Her paws scrabbled at the crumbling granite. She was loosening the rock around the anchor.

Adam shifted to hide her, and turned back to Khalil. Talk. Distract Khalil, until he had his freedom. Before Grace ran out of time.

"Library? Don't have it."

"Don't waste our limited time. The library needs to be protected."

"If Faith thought you could do it, she would have sent it to you."

A slight flare to Khalil's nostrils said that his jab had hit home. "Faith was confused. The dangerous secrets within that library need to be protected."

"Secrets like the Torch of I'celus?"

Khalil took a step backward, his smooth expression startled.

"You're after something else?" Adam asked.

"What I'm after is none of your concern."

"You're right, I don't give a damn about you, Khalil, except for the fact that you've put Grace in danger. Let me go," he warned, tight-lipped, barely holding fury in check. "Because if something happens to Grace, there will be no place you and the Magi can hide from me."

"You killed Kea and those mages. How did you drive them mad? *What have you done with Grace?*"

Adam lunged forward, yanking the wrist chain. Was there some give? "The Dragon has her. And don't give me that crap about Meltone being the one who destroyed my sister. He's dead; the Dragon isn't."

"There are many who use the symbol of dragon. Your scattershot justice has claimed more than I can allow."

"They were killed by the Spell of I'celus."

"Bah," Khalil scoffed. "This is the Spell of I'celus." He sat on a shelf of rock just out of reach, humming, arms outstretched, fingers splayed. In each palm, he held a rock—glittering mica and light-absorbing obsidian.

Energy eddied across Adam's skin, like the first whisper of death. The wavelets came from all sides, passing over him on their path to Khalil's hands. Adam couldn't see the energy, yet he sensed it braiding into a strand as powerful as any surgical laser.

Khalil was a Weaver! When spoken of at all, their name appeared only in the oldest fragments. Able to weave the entire power of the mages into a single strand so powerful and so thin as to touch a single neuron. Or into a veil as vast as the night.

Reaching out, the strand touched Adam's forehead, like

the touch of the frost king's nail, then melted beneath the skin, each touch deeper and colder. His thoughts spasmed against the unseen, intolerable invasion.

He pressed his lips tight and sought the inner strength to repel the probe. He had been taught how with pain and with exhaustion, but never against such skill. After each of his counter moves, the probe reformed from sand, from water, from air and thought.

"Now you see," said Khalil with the quiet hiss of a serpent.

"I see power unchecked by morality," he ground out.

"I do what is necessary."

"Then what makes you different from the one who killed those mages?"

The answer came not as pain, but as a delicate caress. Had Adam not been who he was, able to feel the touch of magick, he never would have known Khalil was inside his mind. But delicacy was not weakness. Adam couldn't stop the seeking. Couldn't repel the power that teased out his memories, his feelings.

This was the power the Dragon sought, except he thought to wield it without cost or effort.

Was there any way to repel it? Remembering the Tai Chi master who had once told him that he held too much of the ox, Adam stopped resisting, stopped being a hard reflection. Instead, his energy bent with the press of power. Dark blood, like the surface of obsidian, drew in the magick. Tiny shards of energy, like the fleck of mica, glittered between the magick. Negative wove with positive. His mind freed itself.

The pressure vanished, the invasion pulled back. "So, the rumors are true. You have a remarkable gift, Adam Zolton. The first I've met who could counter I'celus."

"Did you scrounge all the details you needed with your dirty little spell?"

"I wasn't interested in carving out facts." Khalil's nostrils flared. "Your secrets are secure. The Spell of I'celus is about knowing the truth of a man's heart."

"Tell that to the Dragon. He wields that spell like a sledgehammer, not a scalpel. He's after mind control, starting with my sister."

"He would not suffer the limitations."

"What limitations? The fact that the melding of two minds drives his victims crazy means nothing to him. Not when he can use VR-tagged nanobots to maintain contact over distance and has Grace to relieve his pain. A powerful mage, who knows Grace and is skilled with computers and nanotech. Sound like anyone you know?"

As Adam waited for Khalil to respond, the cold from the quarry water pressed hard against his chest, grabbing his breath. An icy droplet splashed against his forehead. Then another.

"Shit, Khalil," he shouted. "Someone's breaking through!"

Too late! A fiery bolt shot through the water.

"Gala, pocket!" Maybe she'd find a bubble of air. The ferret leaped back to him.

Sizzling, roiling through the water, the bolt pierced Khalil's protective shield and grazed the mage's forehead. Khalil jerked backward, unconscious. Adam only had time for one huge breath before the air bubble collapsed.

His heart sputtered at the shock of cold, and only by the merest second of sanity did he keep himself from gasping in the water. He yanked at his chained arm.

It moved out an inch.

His chest burned, screaming for more air.

Yanked again. One inch. Yank.

Freed, he tumbled backward, tripping over Khalil's body. Scooping up the unconscious mage, he shoved upward.

His vision darkened. Just go up. Damn, he hoped he was going up. Darkness confused his suffocating brain. He swam with one clumsy arm, two legs that flailed a plea for oxygen, and two dead-numb feet.

Grace. Couldn't die here when Grace needed him.

A pale shard of light split the darkness. He followed the beacon.

One more kick, he commanded. His head broke through the quarry surface. He gasped, dragging in air, hoisted Khalil up the rocky edge, and then levered himself upward.

Cold met wet. Coughing and retching, his body was wracked with shivers, his clothes crusted with frost. Gala, sneezing, skittered up his arm and onto his shoulder, and then dove beneath his jacket, seeking body heat. He had to find heat, get to Grace. Had Khalil even survived the magick-sped bullet?

The light that had led him to the surface came closer. "See, I told you I saw divers."

"You dumbdog, where's the wet suits? And the tanks?"

"Ever heard of mini breathers? Special suits?"

Adam focused behind the light to see two boys, about thirteen.

"Call nine-one-one," he said. "He needs an ambulance."

To his relief, the boys had cell phones. As they dialed, he took in the surroundings. Not far from the fire. He staggered to his feet.

"We got a blanket we were sitting on," one offered.

"Give you twenty bucks for it?" With the blanket around him, cradling his chained arm, Adam forced one foot toward his car.

"Where you going, Mister?"

"Get that guy to the hos-ital," was all he could force out from between lips that couldn't form the P in hospital.

He stumbled his way to the car, astonished to find it still there. Inside, he started the engine and blasted out heat. Warmth crept past his frozen flesh and dried out his clothes. His hand slapped the steering wheel. *Come on, come on,* he urged himself, trying to beat back the panic, the despair. Neither would help her.

Yet he didn't move the car. Other than finding someone to saw the manacle off his wrist, he didn't know where to go next.

The damnable fact was, with Kea and Khalil crossed off the list, he was out of suspects.

CHAPTER TWENTY-TWO

Crypt-thick darkness cloaked the room around Grace. For a moment she thought she'd been double blindfolded, until she located the thin beams from her captors' penlights and recognized their faces. She worked her mouth around the gag, trying to catch more breath. Clammy sweat soaked the rag, making it stick to her skin, but at last she got it to her chin. "Damn, it's dark. What is this? A vampire lair?"

"Shut your trap," commanded Lonnie.

"Like you and Ed here shut yours?"

His answer was to jerk on her binding, making sure the cord bit into her wrists. Her hands were encased in the analgesic gloves from Kea's lab.

"You allowed to tell me where I am, Ed?" she demanded of the man who had fastened the manacle around her ankle. Ed seemed the saner of the two.

Sane, but still dangerous—he'd been the one who'd known the pressure point to knock her out long enough for him to get her bound, gagged, and hustled here. Wherever here was.

"Not part of mission parameters," he said shortly.

"Last I looked, words make a rotten lock pick." Still lying on the rock floor where they'd dumped her, she waggled her bound foot.

"Too bad," sneered Lonnie. "You won't get anything out of us."

He was the one who made her shiver. He was the one who'd shot Kea.

Ed finished trussing her, then stood back to check his handiwork. "She won't get free. Time to go."

Refusing to lie there helplessly, she sat up.

Lonnie was busy staring at her boobs, rubbing the bruise on his cheek where she'd hit him. Ed got between him and Grace. "We're going now."

"Go on. Think I might stay a few minutes," Lonnie said.

"No."

At the suffer-no-nonsense tone, Lonnie cast him a belligerent look, but the thug must have seen something he didn't want to challenge. "Yeah, the tits aren't that great," he muttered, and shuffled out the door.

"Ed." She caught his attention before he left. "When did the military code start including kidnapping innocent medics?"

"War is hell," he answered, his back stiff.

"Regan's nuts."

"I always complete my assignment."

"Admirable. If you're on the correct side."

"Save your energy." He paused, then added, "You're underground near the river." With that, he vanished out the exit.

"Which river?" she shouted after him, but got no answer.

He'd taken the penlight, leaving her blinded by darkness. A wash of panic rose from the coward within. Frantically, she struggled to get free, but the effort failed. Her arms remained locked, and her feet chained to the hard floor.

All she accomplished was to soak her clothes with sweat. She laid her head on her knees, unable to stop the flood of tears. She freed the emotions that would overwhelm her if she kept them bottled. Cleansed out negativity, doubt and fear.

At last, with a hiccup, she whispered, "Adam."

Please, God, she didn't want to lose him because of Regan's paranoia.

And here all she'd thought she had to worry about was the Dragon.

"Adam," she said again, stronger. The warnings about his stunting her magick didn't matter. They'd figure that out. Together.

She wanted to hold him and care for him. To laugh with him and fight with him and make love with him. She wanted to buy him a case of hot sauce to drown his eggs and help him fight the nicotine cravings. She wanted to talk about alien abductions and magick spells and the possibilities of VR. She wanted to tell him that being with him filled her with mystery and joy. Mostly, she wanted to tell him she loved him, beyond any logic, to the end of days.

"Be safe, Adam." She prayed he hadn't been caught. Or killed.

Like Kea. That rock of regret sat hard on her chest, squeezing her breath.

Her thoughts about Kea had been massively uncharitable, when in truth he'd been a friend. When he'd discovered her with Lonnie and Ed, he'd tried to rescue her, and that had gotten him shot. His final words had been an apology, for not seeing her talents beyond his need for her pain skills, for not getting her the necessary training. Memory punched her with grief.

Unless everything was a VR-manufactured reality—Adam's absence, Kea's death, this prison. Maybe this was like in the movies, and all she had to do was stop believing. Kea would not be dead; Adam would not be missing.

She tried to see some pentimento of reality behind the nightmare, but the air stayed dark and cold, and her hands still tingled from pooling blood.

Think, Grace. You can go batty later. She could almost hear Adam's clipped voice. That kind of mantra had gotten her through many an ER crisis.

Think. When she'd looked at Ed, she'd seen a strap. *Her purse.* Maneuvering, with her hands bound and her ankles manacled, wasn't easy, but she finally got her fingers on the strap. She dragged it into her lap.

Her eyes had adjusted; there was light here, she realized. A hint of a glow, like phosphorescent lichen, lined the cave-born darkness. The gleaming pricks of red could be electronic power buttons or monster eyes.

She was rooting for the buttons option.

Whatever, the light was enough for her to find her phone. Eagerly she thumbed it on, dialed Adam. Nothing. Damn, of course it couldn't be that easy. No bars.

Where was she? She pulled out her penlight and shone it around, but the light didn't reach deep enough into the dark to see much. So, what *did* she know?

She was inside a building, for the air tasted of stale wood. The one piece of wall she could see was concrete, but the floor was polished stone. Cool, no wind—a basement? Surprisingly low humidity, since Ed had said she was near the river. Must be climate controlled.

She became aware of a rhythmic thudding above her head. Grace tilted her head, listening, and then she realized what it was. Music.

No! Hand shaking, she shone her light across the floor until it revealed markings—a large circle of burned soot surrounded white crisscrossed lines.

She recognized the pattern. There were hundreds of nightclubs she could be beneath, but only one had nerves and serpents as a logo.

The Spider Net.

Light-headed, she grabbed her thighs, forcing herself to stay upright. Because Ed and Lonnie had brought her here, she'd thought Regan was behind her abduction, planning revenge.

Instead, she'd been brought to the lair of the Dragon.

The torch! Galvanized, she grabbed up her purse and dumped everything in a frantic search for something she was now sure was gone.

"Looking for the torch?" The voice came out of the darkness.

"No, a protein bar." Five days of fasting be damned. She opened one and starting munching. "My last, but I wouldn't ask you to share anyway, Regan. Or should I say, Dragon."

"You recognized my voice." Laughing softly, the polished blonde stepped into the ambient glow. She wore a cocktail dress—short, tight, elegant. One hand with polished red nails carried the Torch of I'celus.

Grace squeezed her fingers into a fist. "Had you pegged."

Regan chuckled again. "No, you didn't; I made sure too many threads led to Adam, then Kea. He drew his final breath inhaling your mistrust."

Grace refused to answer, afraid of breaking down. Regan's games would not defeat her. "You think you've been in my mind so now you know everything about me?"

"Not everything, yet, but that will change tonight. Your mind, every bit of your skill, will be mine. Whether I need a massive chunk or a delicate morsel."

Though her gut clenched, Grace made a show of yawning. "Talk, talk, talk."

"You prefer action?" Regan slapped her hands together and the lights in the room flared on.

"Clap on, clap off," Grace muttered, even as she took in the vast space that was revealed. Computers, VR equipment, altar.

"Perhaps this will convince you." Regan sounded irritated at the irreverence. She thrust out her hand. The logo on the floor vibrated and hissed. Heat poured from it until Grace was coated with sweat. From the writhing mass, a serpent—pure white, with a red eye—rose out of the stone. Its forked tongue flicked out, seeking a prey's heat, finding her. The snake slithered across Grace's feet. Another one soon joined it, then more, until the floor undulated with their slithers and hisses. Their stone-cold bodies wound and tightened around her, squeezing her legs, her feet, moving higher to her chest and throat, surrounding her with liquid stone and the aroma of mold.

"Not exactly subtle," she gasped, starting the chant of protection she'd practiced on the island.

"Lessons never are." Regan smiled and clapped her hands together. "You have to learn not to resist." One snake struck, its fangs sinking deep into Grace's shoulder. Fiery venom coursed through her, eating at her skin, and she screamed. Another struck her wrist. A third rose upward, near her face, poising itself above her eye. A drop of black venom dripped from the fang's point and burned across her brow.

"You could scoop out the venom," suggested Regan.

Grace resisted, concentrating on establishing her unperfected shield. The rising shield rammed against the snakes, sending them hissing to the floor, returning them to stone. Through glazed eyes, she saw Regan jerk up.

Regan's eyes narrowed. She rubbed a finger up the bridge of her nose—as if she were situating a pair of glasses—then straightened and smoothed her hands down her skirt. "You don't have enough training to stand against me. Do that again, and the venom will be quite real."

Had her resistance surprised Regan? The mage hadn't been as in control as she professed.

Regan pivoted on her high heels.

"Wait," Grace called.

Regan turned. Her plucked brows lifted. "You want to know about Adam?" A flicker of genuine regret passed across her face. "I tried to save him. I stopped my swords when they attacked him. I tried to get him to leave, to stop meddling. I called him home, but the damn fool wouldn't listen." She looked at Grace. "He's dead. There will be no help from that quarter."

Grace shook her head. "I'm not asking about Adam." *Because I won't believe a damn word you say about him.* She lifted her gloved hands. "You know about our analgesic. How?"

Regan smiled. "Dear, treacherous Kea. When he found out about the work I've been doing for years, he wanted to share my power. He thought we were collaborating. Tonight, he learned the truth. The Dragon doesn't share her treasure."

So, if Regan were to be believed, Grace's doubts about Kea had some substance, after all. "That night, how did you change my perception of reality?"

"Nanobots. Programmed by science. Powered by magick. You were our first test subject. After tonight, I'll be able to control whomever I want."

"No mind can stand against the might of Regan?"

"Not just minds. Magick. Even the power of the first master of the Custos Magi." With that, carrying the torch, she disappeared into smoke.

"Stage trick," Grace muttered, refusing to believe that Regan had the power of transportation. She looked at her wrist. The fang mark had disappeared.

She leaned her head back, taking in a deep breath to clear Regan's rich perfume out of her mind. If those snakes had attacked Abby, no wonder she'd gone mad.

"I am damn well not going to end up like that," she said flatly. "ABC—airway, breathing, circulation. Open the airway. Breathe. Circulate the blood."

Always start with the basic and most vital. She had to find a way to keep Regan from completing that spell.

Somehow, she would find a way to slay the Dragon.

Adam drummed his fingers against the wheel, beating away the powerlessness of not knowing where to hunt. God, he wished he had a cigarette.

"Which way, Gala?" he asked the ferret, who'd darted from his pocket to her lair in the backseat as soon as they'd gotten back to the car. But she was too busy munching chow to answer.

He pulled out his computer to review the pieces for anything he'd missed. A blinking icon notified him of unread e-mail, and he logged in. Work, work, nothing he wanted to deal with now, nothing as important as Grace.

Except two from Brando. He clicked open the first. This one was a detailed chart of commonalities among the eight mages, along with a comment that Brando hadn't found any lead on Kea.

"Hey, man," began the second note, about the provenance of the Spider Net.

> *I thought you were giving me a Jell-O job—one easy swallow and it's done. Should have known better. She knew what she was doing, hiding in rings and layers. But yours truly finally tugged the last thread and here's your list of the original consortium, along with everything else I could find about the place. Dug a little deeper, though, and found out they've gradually been bought out by the lady.*

Adam swallowed hard against the cold knot in his throat. He knew the name even before he got to the end of the e-mail.

Regan Hollister.

She had double fooled him. Pieces clicked into place— the migraine medicine they'd found, the weapons that could be used by a mage as well as a nonmage. All those caring visits to Abby—Regan had been freshening her hold. Abby's photos *had* shown the Dragon; he just hadn't seen her.

Regan had planned this night for a very long time.

Tossing his computer onto the seat next to him, he put the car into gear and floored the accelerator. Fortunately, Michigan drivers viewed their highways as a racetrack, and he hadn't seen a cop car since Marshall.

Hold on, love.

He pulled up two blocks from the Spider Net and turned the car off. What if he'd guessed wrong? If Regan had gone to ground somewhere else? No, she'd spent too much time establishing the Spider Net. In the silence, he whispered, "I'm coming, Grace."

The need for action shoved at him, urging him out, but he forced himself to ignore the compulsion. *Don't go unprepared.*

He reached into his gear bag for a gun and a knife. Once the spell was underway, he couldn't kill Regan or disable her, or even interfere with her. If he did, the results would ricochet onto Grace.

He pulled out his camera and ran through the photos he'd taken when he and Grace had come here the last time, studying the camera angles for a route in. Even though Jonas was the hardware expert, he expected Regan had enough resources for sophisticated security; she'd know someone was coming. But, every second he gained was one less second she'd have to prepare.

If they'd brought Grace here, though, there had to be another way in besides the obvious. Two blocks over, lights flashed on a cop car. Her captors wouldn't have risked alerting the Detroit police.

Maybe the attachments from Brando would have something helpful. He was skimming the building history when one fact caught his attention. The Spider Net building had been a stop on the Underground Railroad.

So where was the smuggling entrance? Quickly he opened the rest of the attachments. Bless Brando's obsessive-compulsive heart, he'd included schematics and maps, both modern and historical. Adam studied the details. There! A tunnel led from the Spider Net to . . . He scanned the buildings around him, compared the landscape to the grids, and located where the tunnel originated.

As a last measure, he read through the copy of the Spell of I'celus. Regan would use Grace's raw power and ability to control her pain. So, where was the chink in the plan?

He looked up to see that Gala had come out of her backseat nest and was staring at him. Maybe he was becoming one of those nutters who thought their pets were people, but he could have sworn her dark eyes held no mischief, only solemn purpose.

"Are you coming?"

With a flick of her tail, she scampered into his pocket; then man and ferret went out together into the dark, urban night.

When he got to the Spider Net, he still didn't have an answer on how to defeat Regan. A line outside waited for admittance. Of course, he had no intention of using the front door. Instead, he slipped around the corner, past the alley's far end, to an empty building a block away. Snow and rain had come in the broken windows, leaving behind sodden wood and black mold. He swung his light through the empty room, and then headed down a rickety circular staircase. Sloshing in a quarter inch of slush, he shone his light on a grilled opening.

A shadow disengaged from the murky edges and jammed a gun against his ribs. "Mr. Zolton."

Adam lifted his hands and tensed, waiting for an opening. "Ed?"

"I wouldn't try anything," said Ed. "You've gotten lucky a couple of times, but I reckon I have a lot more experience at hand-to-hand than you. Besides, I have no intention of shooting you, as long as you stay smart."

"Then why's the gun parting my ribs?"

"Wanted to make sure you didn't shoot first. Or raise a ruckus. I got information on Dr. Armatrading. We talk, okay?"

"Okay, if you put that weapon away."

"No, I don't underestimate you, Mr. Zolton."

Still, Ed stepped back, and the gun faded into the shadows. Adam turned to face him. Hard-ass military.

"Where's your partner?" Adam kept his hands loose and in sight.

"He made a phone call he shouldn't have."

Adam remembered the light from a cop car. "Dead?"

Ed nodded. "I was smarter."

"So, be smart and talk."

"I got a code I live by. Protect my people and my country. Always finish the mission. Be true to my word. I play straight and expect that in return. It's not right, someone can do things to you without your say-so."

"You're talking about Ms. Hollister?"

Ed nodded. Apparently he'd done his homework. "She lied to me. I thought I was taking orders from Washington, protecting our freedom. I thought that doc was the enemy, but then I seen how she helped people in that crash."

"So why did you kidnap her?"

"Always complete the mission. I done that—now I'm free to move on."

"Where is she, Ed?"

"I want something first."

Adam clenched his fists. Strangling the man wouldn't help. "Name it."

"I want you to stop Ms. Hollister, and I want you to forget I exist. I disappear. You, the doc, Vitae, I don't touch you and you don't see me again."

"And then?"

"Nothin' you need know about. There's evil out there, and I aim to fight it my way. Do I have your word?"

Adam didn't have to think twice. He shouldn't have trusted Ed with a nickel, but strangely enough, the man seemed to have his own code of honor. "You get me to Grace and you're free. If you betray me—"

"I wouldn't do that, sir." He nodded to the tunnel. "That grill's only for show. You'll have to hunch a bit in the tunnel, but turn left, then left again, and climb the stairs. Dr. Armatrading's at the end of the hall."

"What about security?"

Ed smiled, a little wistful, hitching a knapsack onto his back. The gun disappeared somewhere on his person. "One thing I'll miss about Vitae is the trinkets. Aren't you one of the owners?"

"Yes." Adam wasn't sure where this shift in topic was heading.

"Then this belongs to you." Ed tossed something metallic to Adam.

Adam looked away long enough to snag the object, and when he looked back, Ed had melded back into the night, leaving as silently as he had arrived. Adam didn't bother to call out. Instead, he examined the gold-colored band that hummed with buried circuits. He smiled. More imagination made real. In the game, this scrambled electronic security.

"Drakken Laird storming the fortress. Turn that switch and electronic security can't see you. Meet someone face-to-face, though, you're on our own."

When he turned around, Adam stepped into the tunnel, hoping he'd judged Ed right. The rumble of cars overhead reverberated through the metal tube in waves of sound.

Waves. Energy is fluid.

With abrupt clarity he saw the answer. How they could defeat Regan.

"This is going to hurt," he muttered.

But there was no other way; he'd have to trust utterly in Grace.

As she would in him.

"This is going to hurt," Regan said calmly, finishing her final preparations as she laid the prismatic visor from Kea's lab at Grace's feet. "Put that on. Give in easily, Grace, and I'll make all that pain go away forever."

"Never." Grace straightened and glared at Regan. She'd be damned if she'd let this bitch win.

Regan laughed softly. "You will. By my calculations, this is the night. The hour." She donned her red robe. "Oh, wait, you need something to heal."

With casual ruthlessness, she grasped Grace's hand and snapped the right pinky bone. "You are left-handed, aren't you?"

Grace sucked in air. Mother in heaven, that hurt. Nerves screamed their damage to the brain.

With a swish of her robe hem, Regan took her place at the center of her web. She speared Grace with a vicious stare. "Resist me, and the destruction of your hands will be no illusion. I will shatter each bone, one by one." She grasped the Torch of I'celus at the serpents' eyes, below the wings, then lifted her hands. When the sleeves of her robe fell back, Grace saw the winking of a serpent at her wrists.

The bands amplified her power. That was why Regan didn't need a circle of nine anymore. Once she established the link to Grace, she would take the power Grace commanded, replacing people with her technology.

"I'celus, one seeks to command your power over the thoughts of man, to be that power within." The first words of the complex spell.

Grace's hand throbbed with primitive demand. Stop the pain. Heal the bone, before it became permanently misshapen.

She couldn't be a trauma surgeon if her hands didn't work. Her power responded to her desperate need.

Her skull throbbed under the first recognizable touch of Regan's joining, as the mage followed the familiar path of Grace's healing magick. Grace's vision darkened.

She fought against the invasion and stayed conscious. Everywhere, pain cascaded through her. Not just her hand, but each cell and nerve. Regan's pain united with hers, in nearly unbearable torment.

Heal us, hissed the voice of the Dragon.

Unable to speak, Grace shook her head, fighting back with the words of repulsion she'd studied. She struggled against all her natural instincts to heal.

She clung to a shadow of her protective shield, but she was losing. She dropped to her knees, ripped apart by agony. A faint glow rose from her hands. Regan dug deeper into Grace's mind. Talons lodged in her gut and chest.

"Put on the visor. Lock this meld," shouted Regan. The upheld torch captured the bits of candlelight, the glare from the computers, the winking in the fiber optics. All light streamed into the upheld helix as Regan reached the final stanzas.

Whispers, a million whispers of deeds both bold and evil, crowded out Grace's own thoughts. Horrifying images of gaunt bodies and tortured souls grabbed her with skeletal fingers.

Her protective spell wavered, crumbling under the onslaught.

Heal herself, relieve the pain, and Regan could complete the link. Continue to resist and her mind would be destroyed.

But at least, Regan would fail.

Adam turned off his flashlight in the damp stone corridor, leaving him in unrelieved darkness, and then eased open the door to the ritual room.

An overpowering scent of cinnamon filled the air. He

caught the chanted words, and realized Regan was nearing the end of the spell. Grace still resisted, but he knew she wouldn't be able to withstand the final shattering of her soul. When she gave in, Regan's lock on her mind would be complete.

He would not lose Grace as he had lost Abby, and there was only one way to prevent that.

With blood. He slashed his knife across his hand, reopening the wound he'd made at Raj's. He winced at the sharp stab, slashed the other palm, and then squeezed the wounds to get the blood flowing.

Now, he had to get to Grace. He slid inside the room, keeping to the cold wall. Fortunately, the edges of the room were dark. All the light was absorbed into the torch.

The room was cold, colder than outside, and frost was forming on the walls. Inside the circle that Regan had established, though, both she and Grace were sweating; he could see the ripples of heat coming from them.

Now or never.

He inched his way toward Grace, trying to give Regan no hint of his presence until he reached the light. He had come to the edge of the rainbow circle when Gala jumped out of his pocket and tore around the outer edge of the circle, streaking past Regan in a blur.

Regan's head jerked as she caught the movement from the corner of her eye. She whipped her gaze sideways, to the path of the ferret, and Adam used that moment to lunge forward. He slid into the circle, letting the magick flow across him as smooth as water, and grabbed Grace, laying his palms against her temples, and then her brow and throat, before he heard Regan shout.

"Heal *him!*"

Fire exploded across his gut as her magick-fueled bullet tore his insides. He collapsed to his knees.

Yeah, he was right.

This hurt like bloody hell.

Chapter Twenty-three

"Heal him!"

The cry penetrated through Grace's haze. Adam! Blessed Mother of Mary, he was alive.

She crouched down. No! He'd been gut shot. His eyes glazed with agony, and blood ran through his spread fingers.

"Heal him," repeated Regan.

"Do it," he whispered, his blood-soaked hands touching hers, touching her body, as though he couldn't stop.

Damn him! Coming in all heroic. She'd have sacrificed herself to stop Regan. Instead, she laid her hands on his mangled abdomen.

"Call the magick. Energy is fluid." His voice was raspy. "Trust me. I will always protect you, to my last breath and my last drop of blood."

Her shield hung by a thread, her last defense against madness. If she touched him, the magick would shatter.

Trust him. Heal him. Do it. Adam would never ask her to heal him, if it meant sending her into the abyss of madness. Never. He would have died first, just as she would have.

And then it hit her. On the island, the magick hadn't come because she was away from Adam. The power had come when she'd followed the motion of the waves and the wildness of the night. When she'd followed her heart.

Trust him. With sanity and with life.

Gathering her breath and her love, she picked up the

visor, and the room shattered into streaks of colored lights. She laid her hands upon him and stepped into the inferno.

She looked beyond his eyes and flesh, divining the firing neurons, the pain, and the blood. "Bring to me the power and will to heal and to relieve," she chanted. At the very least, he would come out of this whole.

Power rose up to meet her demand. It spread out through her fingertips, rising through her knees with the strength of earth and water. Magick, hers to command. *Heal him, relieve his pain.* Grace stopped resisting and opened herself to magick, both sweet and invasive.

Regan's relief at she tapped into Grace's healing was a palpable crow of triumph. The gloves on Grace's hands turned warm, glowing with the activation of the bots. Pain free at last, Regan began the final stanzas of the spell.

Out of the corner of her eye, Grace saw Regan smile and point the torch. Two white tendrils from the fiber-optic bands at her wrists spun through the metal helix. They shot from the tip, braiding to a single strand that delicately touched the visor, then separated, each strand sinuously girdling her forehead, branding into her flesh. Wrist to wrist to brow, the lights burned away the barriers and protections of her mind.

Go into eternal sleep now, with these nightmares.

Horrifying images—the transferred manifestations of Regan's pain—took shape in Grace's mind. She stood in a landscape of the dying, of the maimed and tortured. Their screams and pleas blocked out all other sounds. Smells of blood and urine clogged her nose, and the acrid taste of despair coated her tongue. Their pain became hers, their demands for healing indelible and irresistible.

Except, the images couldn't take root. They shifted and morphed, sliding across her mind with no more traction than oil on ice.

Adam! Adam was part of her, now, reflector joined with

mage. His energy flowed through hers like a cool river over burning skin as she healed him.

For her, he fought Regan, but this was a new type of opposition. Not hard like a mirror. He didn't reflect, for that would have shattered both mages. Instead, he bent away the slash of the flame, washed away the power.

Pain might be the great teacher, but blood held the power of cleansing.

In turn, her perceptions deepened. She saw the energies of pain and broken flesh so easily. They writhed across her vision in angry tendrils of orange and chartreuse, burned her nose like ammonia. But she had only to command for new, repairing patterns to appear as she healed Adam.

Regan renewed her attack, harder, more vicious. Fragmented light spread from the torch, web serpents that dug into flesh and mind. Still, Adam absorbed the power, gave with it, swept it off.

Yet, Grace realized, there remained a thin connection between the two mages, the first lock established before Adam joined them. Because of it, Regan remained pain free, unlimited in her quest for power.

Energy is fluid. She recalled Adam's earlier comment. Fluid could flow in any direction.

Grace turned from Adam to Regan, sought out the energy along that single beam.

"This is gonna hurt," she muttered to Adam.

"I know."

She sought deep for the patterns of nerves, the remaining energies of pain. Saw them clearly in her mind. She steadied herself, but the healer in her faltered. Could she do this, when it went against everything she believed?

Bullshit. She caused pain every time she cut open an abscess or started an IV. Until Regan pulled out of her mind, every last bit, she would never be free.

Pain tested the will of the mage; it also set the limits of the spell.

With the speed of a nerve impulse, she cut off her healing. Cut off analgesia. Agony rammed through her. Not just her hands, but every cell and nerve. Regan's pain overcame her, in unbearable torment. Even Adam couldn't withstand the onslaught, but he deflected the pain just enough so she could focus.

So she could feed the pain in Regan. Intensify it.

Regan's face contorted. The mask of sophistication peeled away into raw fury. The torch shifted in her hands. Aimed straight at Adam.

No! Grace slammed the energy into the fiber-optic bands. Amplify.

Regan's hands jerked upward. The torch flew from her fingers and shattered. Power arced from band to band, feeding on agony.

Regan screamed, high-pitched and insane. The bands exploded into blinding rainbow sparks. The thread of connection between her and Grace snapped. Thrown off balance, Grace jerked backward. She heard Adam grunt when she fell on him.

When she could see the room again, she found she was encased once more in phosphorescent-lit darkness. The reek of burned electricity hung in the air.

The torch had disintegrated to shavings. Regan sat on the floor, her face blank, her hands limp at her sides.

Grace clung to Adam, her body shaking. "You're still bleeding," she whispered, her hand resting against his belly.

"Just a flesh wound," he drawled.

Her other hand caressed his cheek, reveling in the five-o'clock shadow, a small proof of life. "I thought you were dead, and then you show up here. Dammit, you knew she would shoot you. What if she'd aimed for your head?"

"If I were dead, you couldn't heal me."

"You were relying on rationality from a crazy woman?" She couldn't keep herself from running her hands over him, assuring herself he was real, not part of some complex illusion. She leaned forward to give him a soft kiss, her insides still quaking. "Don't ever do that to me again."

"Not planning to." He met her halfway in the kiss, his hand cupping her cheek as his fingers threaded through her hair.

His lips were firm, but cool. He'd lost so much blood, yet when she tried to pull back, he wouldn't let her. Their lips and tongues caressed. The rivulet of desire banished the last remnants of horror with sweet passion. They could go no further, not here, but for now, she could savor holding him and hearing his murmured pleasure.

A faint scrape on rock drew them apart. With his gaze still locked on Grace, his hand still resting tenderly along her jaw, he said, "Khalil, what the hell do I have to do to get rid of you?"

Grace twisted to see the mage with his arms crossed, leaning against the doorjamb.

"I am in your debt, Adam Zolton," he said.

"Fine, now how about leaving us alone?"

"The boon of a Weaver is not something to be taken lightly." He surveyed the scene, and then waved his hand. The bonds around Grace's hands came loose, and the manacles at her feet clicked open. "Perhaps I can be of assistance."

Grace eyed the two men. Didn't take woman's intuition to see the antagonism between them. "You two have met?"

"When he tried to drown me." Adam winced as he got to his feet.

She stalked over to Khalil, and then pressed an admonishing finger to his chest. "Don't tell me you still believe Regan's lies."

"I was wrong." He stared at her finger until she lifted it. "In my defense, I sought the killer of the mages and the library Faith had hidden. All paths led to Mr. Zolton."

"As a killer?" she asked softly. "Not if you know Adam."

He lifted one shoulder. "There is still the matter of the library. It should be under the protection of the Custos Magi."

"So you admit they exist?" Adam asked.

"We are rethinking certain of our policies."

"You won't be able to open the library," Grace warned him.

"In time, we will learn."

"So people like Regan can get in?" The bleeding had stopped, but Adam still guarded his abdomen.

"Only I know you have it. Only the top levels of the Magi will know it has been returned."

"Then it's safest where it is."

"And where is that?"

Adam smiled. "With a reflector. If you want something from it, just ask next time. You or Ramses Montgomery, no one else."

For a moment, Grace feared Khalil might react, but the tension in his shoulders lessened. "As you wish, although in time, you could regret that choice, Adam Zolton." His sharp eyes glanced across the room; then he knelt by the unseeing Regan and waved his hand in front of her eyes. She flinched. He looked at Grace. "We have skilled healers who might help her. Unless you think she should be kept in torment. We will abide by your judgment."

Grace bit her lip. Magick had its prices and its consequences, and the mage was responsible for her actions. Much as an unattractive part of her wanted vengeance, to keep Regan in torment as long as she'd kept Abby, the physician in her wouldn't allow that. "Try to help her; I don't have the skills."

"You could learn."

"For Regan? I'm not that magnanimous."

He nodded. "So it shall be. The process will not be swift. We can hope Regan will learn some wisdom in the journey."

"Vitae will put out a press release that she's taken a leave of absence," Adam added.

Khalil took out his cell phone and texted a message. "I will stay here with her until assistance arrives." He hesitated, then said, "Grace, in the past my approach has been clumsy. I've been told I need a more . . . enlightened attitude. But that does not negate the truth of my message. Regan took advantage of you because you were a powerful raw talent. Until you learn to control your power, you are vulnerable. Come to London with me, be one of us. You can find a tutor you connect with; you can continue your medical training if you wish." He glanced at Adam. "A reflector can only hinder you."

She also looked at Adam. "You have an opinion on this?"

"Your decision to make, Grace." His voice was carefully neutral.

"Don't give me that crap. I love you, and you have an opinion about everything."

"You love me?"

"Yeah."

"You want my opinion?" The fierce, caring man she'd come to love broke through. In two strides he was at her side, and he grabbed a fistful of her hair. With an easy tug—she wasn't resisting—he lifted her face to his. Then he bent down and kissed her. Hard, demanding, filling every one of her senses with only Adam. The strength of his shoulders, where she gripped him, the creak of his leather coat, the brush of his industrial-sized, gadget-loaded watch against her neck. Her blood rushed to meet his hard body.

He lifted. "I can't teach you your magick. All I can do is love you."

"I wondered if I would ever hear that from you."

"I've been shouting it for six years. You just weren't listening." His hand traced the curve of her cheek. "You haven't been that forthcoming either."

"Then I'll repeat it. I love you." She gave a small sigh. "I was scared of getting hurt again, but we only grow through pain. Can you accept that I have more power inside me?"

"I don't care if you become a first master or never lift a finger to perform magick. Neither choice will make me stop loving you. Six years ago, our differences would have torn us apart. This time, we're ready."

Khalil's cough drew their attention back. He'd been pointedly staring at the ceiling, but now lowered his gaze to them. "Grace, you have to understand your choice. The truth is, he is a reflector. If you are with him, your magick will always be stunted. Distorted."

Grace took Adam's hand. "You're wrong, Khalil. I've learned more about real magick from Adam than I ever learned from Kea. The Magi have a few things to learn about these ancillary talents."

He inclined his head. "As you wish. Now, my colleagues will be more comfortable with the two of you gone. We shall give proper care to both Regan and Kea."

"He's not dead?" Joy flared inside her.

Khalil shook his head. "But he *was* injured, and he *was* working with Regan."

Grace sighed. "I'd hoped that wasn't true. In the end he did try to do what was right."

"We shall have some questions for him; he will spend some time with us, but we will make sure he receives justice. Is there anything you wish me to tell him?"

"Just . . . tell him good-bye. I shall miss him."

Adam was there as she turned away. He wrapped his arm around her, then called out, "Gala."

The ferret, who'd wisely hidden, scurried out from behind

a computer table and hurried over to Adam. When he picked her up, however, she didn't take her usual spot in his pocket. Instead, after a small pause, she scampered over to Grace's shoulder, then looked at the two of them expectantly.

Grace laughed. "I guess I'm finally accepted."

Her arm around her lover's waist, she walked into the future.

Khalil shook his head as the door shut behind Adam and Grace. He neither understood nor agreed with Grace's choice—true power required dedication. With her attention split by Adam and her medical training, he doubted she would ever become the mage she could be. His friend Ram was similarly challenged. He shrugged. Not his choices to make, but he hoped he never grew so weak.

He cleansed the area, removing as much of the taint of evil as he could, then cast a tight protective circle. He sat cross-legged on the floor, began his meditations, and waited.

His patience was rewarded half an hour later when Kea strode into the room. The other mage drew up, startled.

"You didn't think I would wait for you?" Khalil asked with lifted brow. "After all, you sent me the text message, telling me where Regan was."

"I didn't think I'd be able to get here in time, since I was badly injured."

"Injured? So I thought also, until I remembered your studies had taken you to the fakirs. The ones with the ability to slow the heart and mind in an imitation of death. Also, no matter how besotted you were with a woman, you wouldn't let your guard down enough for her to shoot you. Even one as powerful as Regan."

"You did."

Khalil tilted his head; his failures or motives weren't under discussion.

Kea glanced over at Regan. "I'm amazed Grace had the

strength." He glanced back at Khalil. "Regan set her plans to perfect mind control into motion long before I ever met her. I had nothing to do with the attack on Abigail Zolton. Or the deaths of the mages."

"I never thought you did. And I never suspected Regan because I didn't know she was so gifted. Another secret you kept."

"I was bedazzled," Kea said bitterly. "In love. I admit, a part of me wanted her to succeed. Think of it: all that knowledge." His lips twisted. "An impossible dream."

"The masters will want to question you more thoroughly."

Kea nodded in resignation. But as other mages arrived and assisted with transporting Regan and Kea, Khalil couldn't shake the feeling that Kea was playing a deeper game.

The Dragon was vanquished, yes.

But more than one mage wore the symbol of the mighty beast.

January on the Gulf Coast did not encourage visits to the beach. The wind picked up across the waters, blustering at the shore.

But the air was fresher in winter, without the fish scent, and the beach was emptier. Ram found only Natalie walking along, just out of the reach of the waves. Of course, she was on her phone.

In typical Natalie fashion, she must have thrown on whatever coat was most convenient. That sweatshirt jacket couldn't be warm.

She smiled at him when he joined her, wrapping his arms around her to keep her warm, and kept on with her conversation. "Glad to have you back, boss. See you tomorrow?" She listened a moment, then chuckled. "Grace have anything to do with that hesitation?"

Ram leaned over and nuzzled her neck. She stretched a little, allowing him fuller access. A little purr preceded her answer to

Adam. "Yes, I'm working on the lava creature story. Okay, hope to see you soon."

She snapped her phone shut, then turned to Ram and gave him an enthusiastic I-missed-you kiss.

He took her face between his hands, cupping her cheeks as he bent and returned the favor. When they parted, he smiled. "I missed you, too." He laid an arm around her, snuggling her close, and suddenly the chill vanished.

"Did you learn anything more about Charles's plans?"

"Nothing more than what I told you, but I keep thinking there was more to his request for that photo than sentiment."

He lifted one shoulder. "We'll find out. I'll keep an eye on him, Natalie."

She wrapped her arms around his waist, pressed her hands against his back, keeping him close.

"He told me you're a member of the Custos Magi," she said. "I'm not going to ask if you are. Ever. I love you, but more important, I trust you—your character, your strength. I believe in us, but we don't exist in a vacuum. I have learned things through work that I can't tell you because speaking would break a trust. I'm speculating that's true for you, too. You're involved with something dangerous, but promises don't let you talk about it. The honor, the goodness that compels you to keep that trust, only means that you will be as true to us, to the vows we exchange. Bottom line, I trust you, Ram. Trust in your decency and honor. Mostly, I trust in us and our love."

"But that's not enough for me. Not anymore." He ran a hand down her hair, his heart squeezing tight.

She tilted her head up, a flare of hurt in her eyes.

"I don't want to hold secret such an important piece of who I am, but before now I couldn't break my vow. This trip, I intended to get away entirely . . ."

"I'm glad you didn't."

"How do you know I didn't?"

"Because you're happy and because you're telling me this."

"Look at me, Natalie." When she tilted her head, he kept their gazes locked. "I am a part of the Custos Magi. We aren't perfect; we're only human. But we do good work, necessary work. There is evil out there, and somebody with talent needs to oppose it."

"I've always felt, at heart, you were a guardian."

"You already had this figured out, didn't you?"

"Pretty much."

"I may not always be able to tell you who I'm with or what I do when I'm gone."

"Whatever you can tell me, I'll listen. Although I won't promise not to ask questions—"

He rolled his eyes. "I expect your tombstone will read: 'What am I doing here?'"

After a shared laugh, she sobered. "I just ask two things. You probably see a lot of awful things." She placed a hand above his heart. "If something's eating at you here, talk to me, however you can. I won't shy away from anything you experience or judge anything you do."

He nodded. "And the second thing?"

She drew in a shaky breath. "If something . . . happens to you, one of the Magi will come tell me. Nathaniel's disappearance nearly destroyed me. Waiting and wondering about you *would* destroy me."

Pulling her close, he nodded again. He'd seen what not knowing the fate of her twin had done to her. "I'll make sure they know. Your work can take you to dangerous territory, too." Her hair was silky beneath his fingers as he caressed the back of her neck, and he suddenly found breath hard to come by. "To not be able to hold you like this, to lose you and not know what happened . . . I wouldn't survive that. Will you also promise the same?"

"A mutual promise." She held out her hand. "Shake on it?"

"I had a more lasting covenant in mind." Surprised to find his hand trembling, he reached into his pocket and finally pulled out the ring box. Oblivious to the sharp broken shells and the wet sand, he got down on one knee. Holding her hand, he asked, "Natalie DeSalvo, will you marry me?"

Smiling, she knelt beside him. "In my heart I already have." She sandwiched her hands around the ring box and his hands. "Ramses Montgomery, will you marry me?"

"Yes. Forever."

"Yes. Forever."

"Damn, woman, sex with you keeps getting better and better." Adam stretched facedown on the bed, his body coated with sweat, his arm draped over Grace.

"Mmm," she answered, too breathless to answer.

A breeze came through the open window, stirring the curtains and evaporating the sweat from his skin. New Orleans was having unseasonably warm weather for January, and he'd opened every window in his home before they'd fallen on the bed together.

He leaned over a little and kissed her. "Maybe it's because I keep loving you more." His hand strayed up and down her side, teasing the side of her soft breast. He couldn't seem to get enough of touching her, of reassuring himself that she was here.

Her hand caressed his hair. "Being with you, loving you . . ." Her voice trailed off.

He knew the feeling. Words, pictures, nothing adequately captured this joy. His thumb started to tease her nipple, and—impossibly, he'd have thought a minute ago—he started to harden. Again.

"If you keep that up, we won't get to see your sister until tomorrow."

Adam sighed, knowing he was still avoiding this visit. His sister had been found at Regan's New Orleans cottage. He'd hoped the Dragon's grip had been severed, but his sister's condition hadn't changed. If anything, she'd withdrawn further.

He took his hand away from the satisfying activity of pleasuring Grace and got off the bed. "Let's go."

They dressed quickly, but when Grace went to get her coat, she swore. The coat was on the floor, beside an open book, with Gala sprawled on top of both. The ferret had piled a collection of shredded tissue, binder clips, and pebbles on the coat. "Dammit, Gala."

He laughed. "Good thing you won't need a coat."

Grace started to brush off her coat, then stopped, noticing the open page where Gala had been lying. She read a moment, then gripped his arm. "Adam, we can use this for Abby. I've been reading through the *Vitae Curatio* you brought from the library, but I hadn't seen this spell yet. You can reverse—"

He shook his head, not wanting to believe. "I've tried that before. Abby gets worse."

"Because your talent was fighting Regan's magick. Well, Regan's no longer reinforcing her magick. And you've learned how to mix your energy with the magick of someone you love." She handed him the book. "Look. Read this."

As he read through the ancient ritual, he tried to rein in the racing of renewed hope.

"We can do it." Grace gripped his arm. "You and I together."

When they were ushered into Abby's room, however, they were surprised to see Jonas Washington there, holding Abby's thin hand. Abby lay on the bed, barely breathing.

Jonas turned to them, his face ravaged. "Your mother called me, too, Adam." He drew in a ragged breath. "We're losing her."

Adam could see that. He locked the door, and then knelt

beside the bed, taking Abby's hand in his. "You are not giving up, Abby. Hold on."

"What are you doing?" demanded Jonas, as Grace began chanting to set up her protective circle and cleanse the room.

"I'm going to end this. One way or another," Adam answered.

"No!"

"We're Abby's only chance. You can stay or go, but don't interfere." He looked over at Jonas. "Magick started this; magick must finish it."

"Does she know what she's doing?"

Adam nodded. "She's unique, Jonas. A doctor and a mage."

For a moment, he thought Jonas would argue further, but his friend glanced at Abby, then slowly nodded. "What can I do?"

"Hold her," Grace said. "Keep talking to her, low and soft. Adam and I need to work the ritual. Your voice can give her an anchor." She drew in a breath. "Ready."

Jonas got on the bed and held Abby in his arms. Grace and Adam each took one of her hands.

"This may be difficult for her at first," Adam told Jonas. "I need your promise that you won't interfere. You won't stop us or break the circle."

"I promise."

Using a pocketknife, Adam pricked his finger and squeezed a droplet of blood into the hollow of Abby's throat and at her wrists. Grace circled her hand clockwise, beginning the chant.

Adam tuned out the words, concentrating instead on detecting the energies swirling around him. Something vile hovered inside Abby, reaching deep. It smelled of old blood and rotted straw and curdled on his tongue. Before, when he'd tried to counter it, the magick had turned on Abby. This time, he rode in with Grace's healing touch. Her magick surrounded him as a soothing balm.

He dug deeper, following the line of his blood, calling on his love for his sister to find her stunted well of power. The spell turned inward, driving deep into Abby, and she screamed out, her back arching. But he was with her this time, keeping the magick from going further. The invader fought, filling her with visions of horror and death. Just as he had with Grace, he started peeling back the spell. Grace's chant cooled the fire to ash, sent a balm that dissolved the spell with pure water.

A small chink was torn in the spell and the energies from him and from Grace met, spread, and meshed, filling in gaps until together they were a solid blade, cutting the roots. Adam heard Jonas's voice, wracked with tears but still steady, a thread of sanity that he could see as a beacon weaving through the charm.

And then, abruptly, the spell vanished. Abby screamed again, her body seizing. And then she stilled, silent and unmoving.

Adam came back to himself in time to see Grace whip her stethoscope from her pocket.

"CPR. How do we do CPR?" he demanded, not seeing the rise and fall of Abby's chest any longer.

Grace, listening intently, waved him silent. Then, grinning, she took the stethoscope from her ears.

"She's alive. Heartbeat's strong. Can you detect any remnant of Regan's hold, Adam?"

He shook his head. "We got it."

Would Abby recover, or was the damage permanent? They waited, breath held.

"Abby, please," whispered Jonas, touching the scar at her brow, where Regan's power had fused.

Suddenly, blinding rays of light burst from the scar, and when the brilliance had faded, the scar was gone.

Abby gave a gasp and opened her eyes.

She looked around, confused. "Hullo, Adam." She gaze flicked to Grace. "Who's she?"

"Abby?" Jonas breathed her name.

She turned, and a smile like Adam had never seen on his sister's face—tender and joyous—lit her. "Jonas."

In that moment, he knew his sister was back.

Grace stood with Adam in the utilitarian hall outside Abby's room. They'd given her moments of privacy to dress and pack, although she'd accepted Jonas's help with the latter.

Grace wrapped her arms around Adam's waist. He clung to her, and she felt the dampness of his tears against her hair.

"Thank you," he whispered.

"You did it," she answered. "You never gave up."

"She's still frail."

"And eventually she will remember. She'll need all of your help."

"Jonas wants her to move to Ann Arbor. With Regan gone, he'll need a partner. I'm thinking of taking a more active role in Vitae."

"What about *NONE?*"

"Faxes, phones, trips back. Maybe Natalie would like a share of the paper." He brushed her hair back, kissed her temple. "If Abby comes, my mother will come, too. You've got me, Grace, but now you're getting a whole package deal. Sister, mother, friend."

"I couldn't be happier. Maybe in the summer I'll take you to meet my mother. And grandfather."

"Lord Smithson?"

She nodded. "Just . . . don't mention magick. He's not big on the concept."

"If he roars, I'll be there at your side. Your dragon-slaying knight in tarnished armor."

"No, not the knight," she whispered, standing on tiptoe to kiss him. "I told you I prefer the Chinese version of the myth. The bringer of life-giving rains. The fierce protector. You're my kind of dragon, my love."

INTERACT WITH DORCHESTER ONLINE!

Want to learn more about your favorite books and authors?
Want to talk with other readers that like to read the same books as you?
Want to see up-to-the-minute Dorchester news?

VISIT DORCHESTER AT:
DorchesterPub.com
Twitter.com/DorchesterPub
Facebook.com (Search Pages)

DISCUSS DORCHESTER'S NOVELS AT:
Dorchester Forums at DorchesterPub.com
GoodReads.com
LibraryThing.com
Myspace.com/books
Shelfari.com
WeRead.com